THE ROMANTIC PRINCE "

BY

RAFAEL SABATINI

TOVT BIEN OV RIEN

BOSTON AND NEW YORK

HOUGHTON MIFFLIN COMPANY

The Riverside Press Cambridge

1929

The Riverside Press
CAMBRIDGE · MASSACHUSETTS
PRINTED IN THE U.S.A.

CONTENTS

I. On the Subject of Poets ... 3

II. Severance ... 14

III. The Indiscreet Zealander ... 26

IV. The Surety ... 42

V. The Unfolding of the Scroll ... 53

VI. Johanna ... 62

VII. Friar Stephen ... 76

VIII. The Interruption ... 85

IX. The Return ... 97

X. The Knight of the Tulip ... 107

XI. Betrothal ... 116

XII. The Wife of Philif Danvelt ... 122

XIII. Péronne ... 137

XIV. Checkmate ... 150

XV. The Sedition in Walcheren ... 161

XVI. Danvelt's Arrest ... 172

XVII. The Fool's Philosophy ... 186

XVIII. Rhynsault's Wooing ... 195

XIX. The Fool Advises ... 203

XX. Rhynsault's Buckler ... 219

XXI. Iphigenia ... 227

XXII. The Cheat ... 237

XXIII. Camp and Court ... 244

XXIV. Grand Master of Burgundy ... 257

XXV. The Petitioner ... 263

XXVI.	The Fool's Mission	277
XXVII.	The Memorial	292
XXVIII.	Marriage by Proxy	309
XXIX.	Judgment	325
XXX.	Banishment	338
XXXI.	Realities	347

THE ROMANTIC PRINCE

THE ROMANTIC PRINCE

. .

CHAPTER I

ON THE SUBJECT OF POETS

ANTHONY OF EGMONT contemplated the world with disapproval. He had reached the conclusion that it was no place for a gentleman.

This happened in the year of grace 1467, amid the opulent surroundings of the Burgundian Court, when and where there were abundant grounds for his harsh assumption.

In common with his cousin, friend, and brother-in-arms, Charles of Burgundy, it was Anthony's bad or good fortune — who shall say which? — to have been born in the expiring days of the age of chivalry. Almost from birth he had been imbued with the lofty ideals of that age, and in early years he had taken for a pattern upon which to mould himself that very perfect and peerless knight, the Sieur Jacques de Lalaing, who was almost the last to uphold, in all its romantic effulgence, the chivalrous tradition. And Lalaing, who might have lived for deeds of high endeavour, had been stricken down and slain at the early age of thirty-three at Gaveren, in a battle whose sordid purpose was the imposition of a salt-tax upon the oppressed burghers of Ghent.

As a boy of ten, when newly appointed page to Philip the Good, Anthony had witnessed in the Feast of the Pheasant the last princely endeavour to fan the cooling embers of chivalry into flame and to set on foot a crusade that should rid Christendom of the menace of the encroaching Turk, to whom Constantinople had lately fallen. He had seen that effort, sustained for a full year, languish and finally perish without a single knightly blow being struck, and there, it seemed to him, the spirit of chivalry had finally and utterly expired.

To be sure there were still joustings to be witnessed; but these were no longer of more significance than tennis or hawking or any other of the exercises in which nobility sought amusement. The language of chivalry still continued to be employed; but the meaning of its terms had changed. Great orders of chivalry still existed, of which perhaps the greatest was the Golden Fleece, which the late Duke Philip had founded, and of which Anthony himself wore the coveted collar. But when that same collar was hung about the neck of the twenty days' old Charles, a blow was struck at the very foundations of an institution which demanded that knighthood should be the acquisition of personal merit alone, to be attained only after a long and arduous physical and spiritual novitiate.

Anthony, with a considerable armed following out of Guelders, had been one of the allies who had lately fought on the Burgundian side in the War of the Public Weal, a war undertaken on the knightly grounds of abolishing extortionate taxation and setting free from its intolerable burden the 'poor oppressed people of France.' Because deceived by this pretext, Anthony's disillusion was the greater when the true aims of that war of rapacity became apparent. Burgundy's sole interest in that rebellion of the French vassals against their King was the retention of Picardy and the cities of the Somme, which the crafty Louis was scheming to restore to the Crown of France, to which they rightly belonged.

Anthony had fought at Montlhéry beside his cousin Charles, and he accounted it an engagement reflecting little military and no knightly credit upon either side. At Charles's elbow he had been a witness of the protracted intrigues that followed; of the covetousness, discontent, and treachery among the allies. He had attended the parleys which at last wrung extortionate terms from the rascally little king of France, whom in a world of knaves he had been almost tempted to admire as the most perfect of his kind. He had revolted at the greed of the allies in the division of the spoils, and their complete oblivion in the hour of triumph of the 'poor oppressed people' on whose behalf the war had been undertaken.

Anon he had witnessed the Burgundian ruthlessness at Liège and the drawing up of the Piteous Peace, which had brought that hitherto independent little state virtually within the vast embrace of the Burgundian Duchy. And he had observed the horrors and abominations of the vengeance wreaked upon Dinant for its resistance, so that men said of it, as of old men had said of Carthage, *Cy fust Dinant*. He had returned from that campaign retaining few indeed of those bright illusions which throughout youth he had been amassing. Instead of the imagined high-souled pageantry of war, he had beheld war's stark and piteous realities. The gallant joust he had conceived it had resolved itself into sordid, bestial carnage. And since then, his vision of other things, rendered keener and truer by that one terrible glimpse of truth, he had viewed the court and the great figures that composed it with a new perception of their real quality. Under a noble, glittering exterior which had hitherto deceived him, he now discovered mean faithlessness, vulgar mendacity, and sordid avarice. Yet despite all this, because of something within his own poetic spirit, he still clung to one illusion which lent a glamour to the world about him until the Lady Catharine of Bourbon robbed him of that, and brought him abruptly to the conclusion we have discovered.

Contemporary chroniclers have done rather less than justice to this cultured, sensitive gentleman, anachronistically chivalrous in his Burgundian setting. Mention of him by those writers is so scanty as to be almost contemptuous, and little would be known of him at all but for the comparatively obscure *Chronique Scandaleuse* left by André de La Marche, brother of the more famous chronicler Olivier de La Marche, who was steward of the late Duke's household. Neither the latter nor the equally famous Comines makes

any mention whatever of this Count Anthony, leaving us to
suppose that his younger brother, the infamous Adolph, was
the old Duke Arnold of Guelders's only son.

Better perhaps this silence than the recklessly slanderous
statement, penned, no doubt, out of sycophancy to Charles
of Burgundy, with which Adrian de Budt dismisses the
legitimate heir to the throne of Guelders.

'The extinction of the House of Guelders,' he writes, 'is
no matter for honest men's regret. God will not long suffer
that the welfare of a people should lie in the hands of princes
such as the weak and vacillating Duke Arnold or his wicked
and almost parricidal son Adolph. As for that other son,
known in the old Duke's lifetime as Count Anthony of
Guelders, and since then happily vanished, no man knows
how or whither, this prince combined, with the weakness of
his father and the rascality of his brother, a hypocrisy so
consummate that in early life he deceived the world, and
won the countenance and affection of even such shrewd
judges of men as our good Duke Philip and his noble son,
that thunderbolt of war, that mightiest Prince of the Occi-
dent, Duke Charles. This Lord Anthony simulated a lofty
idealism amounting to little less than saintliness, and for this
was accounted an ornament to that greatest and most
coveted of all orders of chivalry, the Golden Fleece, and was
foremost in the councils of its chapter. Because of his rich
endowment of mind and person, but more particularly because he pretended to observe a chastity such as is prescribed
for, but seldom discovered in our clergy, he endeared himself to Charles of Burgundy, who in these matters practised
an austerity oddly in contrast with the more joyous habits of
his sire. Yet it is an odd irony of Fate's that by the lack of
the very virtue to which he made the greatest pretence was
this false Galahad undone. Inconstancy in an honourable attachment and an adulterous adventure in Zealand were between them the causes of his extinction.'

Never was truth more untruly told.

As to his having vanished, 'no man knows how or

whither,' one man at least there was who knew the full tale of it, and who has left that chronicle from which we may now reconstruct the event.

Already at the time of the War of Public Weal, Charles of Burgundy, who, owing to his father's failing health, had assumed the regency of the vast Burgundian dominions, was concerned with all those measures of statecraft by which a prince consolidates his power. His possessions extending over the two Burgundies, Artois and Flanders, Namur, Brabant, including Mechlin and Antwerp, Limbourg, Holland, Zealand, Hainault, and Luxembourg, rendered him the mightiest and wealthiest prince in Christendom — as the King of France had lately experienced to his bitter cost — one whose ducal coronet was ripe for conversion into a royal crown. Towards this coveted and merited kingship he already steered a course. With the title of King of the Romans, the Emperor should presently crown him to a kingdom mightier than any other in Europe, and to render his position unassailably secure, he was already buttressing it with desirable alliances. By marrying his sister-in-law, Catharine of Bourbon, to his dear friend and brother-in-arms, Count Anthony, he ensured himself the endurance of the alliance already existing between himself and the Duchy of Guelders, to which Anthony was heir.

The beauty of the Lady Catharine had conspired with Burgundian aspirations to melt the Lord Anthony's austerity. It was a beauty that had melted the austerity of many men, and was to melt that of yet more. In the case of Count John of Armagnac, that beauty was hardly required to accomplish so much. For John of Armagnac, as all the world knows, was entirely without austerity of any kind. Greed-begotten disloyalty to his suzerain, Louis XI of France, had driven him into alliance with Burgundy in the War of Public Weal. The alliance had subsequently justified his seeking the relaxations offered by the Burgundian Court at Brussels, and the soft eyes of the Lady Catharine — blue, mysteriously tranquil pools, in which a man might drown his soul —

had been responsible for keeping him there when his welcome, never too cordial, was wearing thin.

Because in all that concerned a lady to whom he was affianced, the romantic, dreamy idealist Anthony was at this stage incapable of thinking evil, it became necessary for the Duke, himself, to draw his attention to what was passing.

Now Charles of Burgundy was never remarkable for any gifts of mincing diplomacy. The downright, uncompromising bluntness which he used in the transaction of private and public affairs was equalled only by that headlong audacity in the field which has made him known to posterity as Charles the Temerarious.

He sought the apartments assigned to his cousin in the palace of Brussels one July evening, and found him, to his exasperation, at his studies in his closet, a small chamber whose walls were hung with tapestries from the looms of Arras. He drove out the single page who was in attendance, and came straight to business.

'By Saint George, if I were betrothed as you are to a lady none too heedful of the honour, I'd at least make my betrothal respected. I would so, by Saint George!'

On the rare occasions when he felt moved to swear, Duke Charles commonly elected to do so by Saint George. This — like the device on his banner — by way of reminding his audience of his English blood. Philip the Good, his father, took pride in being a Valois and French in every nerve of him. But it was one of the idiosyncrasies, almost one of the perversities of this son of Isabella of Portugal, who was of Lancastrian descent, that he must ever be affronting his subjects both French and Flemish by proclaiming himself a foreigner. Sometimes he insisted upon his English extraction. More commonly he boasted himself a Portuguese, which, indeed, his appearance confirmed. Short of stature, broad and powerful of frame, black of hair, and dark of eye, with a big-boned, swarthy countenance prominent of nose and jaw, there was about him nothing of the fair and delicately built Valois. He contrasted oddly, too, with the heir of Guelders, who leaned back now in his tall chair of crimson velvet, faintly startled by his visitor's abruptness. Their mutual affection dispensed with any ceremony between them when in private.

A Flemish wit of singular knowledge for his day, hearing them described on the score of their intimacy as Damon and Pythias, had retorted that they reminded him, rather, of Ormuzd and Ahriman, the powers of light and darkness. If the image is too grossly exaggerated in so far as concerns Duke Charles, it is not without justification in the case of Count Anthony. A creature of light he seemed, indeed; a radiant, joyous personality, with his tawny, golden hair which fell in a wavy mane about the nape of his shapely neck. Serenity sat upon his lofty brow and finely featured, square-chinned face; ardour glowed in his great dark eyes in which at times there was a hint of gold. They were the eyes of a visionary, of a poet, of a man of dreams rather than of action, of one imbued with an energy that was spiritual rather than physical.

In his thirtieth year, and some three years younger than the Duke, there was still an almost stripling grace about his long limbs and slender frame, and this notwithstanding the mantle of dignity and reserve imposed by his lofty station and worn with incomparable ease.

He smiled now in tolerant amusement of the vehemence so habitual to his choleric cousin. He spoke in the even, deliberate tones of a voice that was singularly attractive.

'Who is it that is lacking in respect?'

'Who? The lady herself. Who else?'

Smiling still, Count Anthony sighed. 'Well, well! Shall I blame her for that? It is for me to make myself well-considered. Then, perhaps, she will come to respect that for which I stand to her.'

'It is what I urge!' thundered the other's impatience.

'I am about it now.' Count Anthony took up the quill which, upon his cousin's advent, he had laid down and pointed with it to the sheet of parchment spread before him on the table, a square, solid table tautly covered with crimson velvet which was secured along the edges by ponderous gilt studs.

The Duke saw a deal of writing, most of it erased. This prodigality of ink meant nothing to him, and he said so with his glance. The younger man explained himself. The long, delicate fingers of his left hand touched an open volume beside the sheet.

'I am assisted in my delectable labours by Messer Petrarch.'

'Who's he?' quoth the Lord of Burgundy.

'An Italian poet, lately dead.'

'A poet!' Contempt exploded in the word.

'A greater than either of us, Charles.'

It was by no means the first time that Charles suspected in his cousin a streak of madness.

'A maker of songs!'

'His songs will be remembered when your laws are forgotten — great prince though you be. His name will be cherished when mine and even yours will have perished from the memory of man. His voice will still be heard in the world when your tongue and mine are so much scattered dust.' Count Anthony sighed and smiled. 'Who would be an emperor that might be a poet?'

'I would, for one,' said the Duke of Burgundy.

'Only because you are without perception of what it means to be a poet. A maker of songs, you say. Do you conceive what vision is vouchsafed the man who can make songs, and what else he makes in making them, what spiritual discoveries he reveals to a benighted world, with what effulgence his songs dispel the darkness in which men grope? Could you make this contemptible thing, a song, Charles?'

'Could I?' The Duke shrugged and laughed, between derision and impatience. 'I can make the songs that become my station. I made some at Montlhéry to the music of the cannon.' His smile broadened, displaying the big white teeth of his prominent upper jaw. 'That was music enough for the King of France. It brought Picardy and the cities of the Somme to the Crown of Burgundy. Could your poets have done that?'

'No more than they could have voiced the croak of the carrion crows that followed in your wake.'

But the Duke took no offence at this, perhaps not understanding. His contempt remained unabated and secure.

'I deal in realities, Anthony. Not in dreams.'

'Dreams! You despise dreams and vaunt reality! Will you tell me what reality in all the world was not first a dream? Are not all things of human fashioning the fruit of dreams? Were they not first conceived in the mind before they were given visible, tangible shape? Is not this very world in which we move and live the product of a dream? Where else was it all conceived but in the mind of a Creator?'

The Duke was scowling now. 'You go too fast and too deep. If you are to argue the Creator into a poet, you'd best carry your polemics to the bishops. It need not perturb you if they send you to the fire for heresy, since at the stake you can dream of water to put out the faggots.'

'Charles, I despair of you.'

'As I of you. Though I may despair a little less when you tell me what your Italian poet has to do with Catharine.'

'He lends my poverty a little of his wealth. I borrow from him. Thus:' and taking up the parchment he began to read.

'Cupid's right hand did open my left side . . .'

But he got no farther; for here the Duke, now thoroughly out of patience, interrupted brutally.

'If Cupid's right hand would but open your eyes to what is happening, he'ld find a better employment for your wits than this lovesick caterwauling. The Lady Catharine is a thought too generous of herself. You do not make her sufficiently aware of you. And you give her leisure in which to become excessively aware of other men.'

Count Anthony stared at him, blankly indignant.

'Why, here's lewdness!'

'That is the word, though I hesitated to employ it.'

'I apply it to your mind, Charles.'

'Apply it to Catharine's conduct. It will be more apt.'

Count Anthony came abruptly to his feet, his head thrown back, the colour deepening in his face.

'In God's name, Charles, what are you saying?'

'Am I not plain enough?'

'Too plain, I think. You imply that the Lady Catharine, who is one day to be Duchess of Guelders and the mother of future dukes . . . ' He could not complete the expression of his ugly thought. But the Duke completed it for him.

' . . . Is very much a woman, and the subject of too much gossip. Wait!' He was suddenly of a harsh peremptoriness, and, weary of skirmishing about the subject, drove straight at the heart of it. 'It is being said quite openly that Catharine was the subject of Auxonne's quarrel with d'Épinal; and now there are rumours of bad blood between d'Épinal and Armagnac.'

'Armagnac!' Count Anthony's voice usually so musical was as harsh as the Duke's. 'Armagnac?' he repeated. 'For what is that vile dog in this?'

The Duke shrugged his massive shoulders. 'Catharine has smiled upon him, I suppose. She is prodigal of her smiles. And Armagnac has never been known to resist the allurement of a woman's eyes. The fault, Anthony, is yours.'

'Mine?' Anthony laughed on a note of bitterness. 'My fault that the devil of wantonness is in your sister-in-law?'

'Your fault that, being affianced to her, you sit here with your dreams and leave the reality to others. Will you still prefer the dream? Will you still hug the shadow, while others consume the substance for you?'

Count Anthony stood tense a moment, his thumbs hooked into the belt of red velvet, studded with golden hearts as big as walnuts, that girt his crimson gown about him.

'If you will give me leave, Charles,' he said after a moment, 'I will seek the Lady Catharine at once.'

'I'll do more, Anthony. I will conduct you to her.'

Together they came to the gallery above the great hall,

where a troupe of Flemish players were entertaining the assembled court. The Count, in his eagerness of suppressed anger, went a step ahead of his burly cousin. The latter, keeping close, already began to dread the mischief he might have set afoot. It was characteristic of him to act on the impulse of his mood and to reflect afterwards upon the consequences. Thus was his life made up of such occasions as the present. He mistrusted the purposeful set of Anthony's tall figure and the unusual grimness that had come to invest that fair and gentle countenance. He wanted no open scandals at his court; still less did he want anything in the nature of a breach between two such powerful princes as Anthony of Guelders and John of Armagnac. In any such quarrel, particularly if concerned with his own sister-in-law, he must of necessity intervene, and on whichever side he intervened that intervention must result in setting the other against him and thus in the loss of a valued ally.

CHAPTER II

SEVERANCE

THE antics of the players on the dais at the end of the long hall so fully engaged the attention of the courtly audience that the arrival of the Duke and his cousin went unperceived. It went unperceived also by the Lady Catharine, for all that her attention was nowise bestowed upon the mummers. She occupied a chair by one of the pillars on the right of the hall almost immediately below the staircase by which our gentlemen had been descending, and where, since Count Anthony had perceived her, they now stood arrested midway in their descent, observing.

She was of a fair and exquisite loveliness such as might well have served for a poet's incarnation of his ideal. Tendrils of her golden hair, in violation of fashion's law, escaped about her brow from the dark band at the base of the small pointed hennin with which she was coifed. A more daring violation of that same law was the extent of the *décolletage* of the close-fitting bodice of her gown of green and gold brocade, with its excessive revelation of the ivory perfections of her neck and breasts. Her sleeve, very tight in the arm, grew suddenly to such a fullness at the wrist that a foot and more of it hung below the fine jewelled hand which moved playfully, caressingly, as she spoke or listened, upon the black velvet sleeve of her companion. This was a tall, loose-limbed, youthful fellow, arrogant of bearing, swarthy, black-browed, and handsome in a sinister, unpleasant way. Leaning upon the back of her chair, his cropped head of black hair was bowed as he talked until it almost touched her own; and when she looked up into his face, as she did ever and anon with wanton arts of coyness, their eyes were scarcely a foot apart.

The Duke, for all his usually imperturbable boldness,

glanced with misgiving at his tall companion; nor were his misgivings lessened by the thin, baffling smile that was compressing Count Anthony's lips. He had intended that Count Anthony should observe for himself; but he had hardly expected that there would be quite so much to observe. The moment, he now considered, had been execrably ill-chosen.

Nor were these two upon the stairs the only observers. The dallying pair below were dividing with the players the attention of those more immediately about them. In their neighbourhood the Duchess of Orléans, Count Anthony's kinswoman, sat frowning, as ever and anon she looked sideways at the Lady Catharine; and beside the Duchess, frowning also, and manifestly ill-at-ease, stood the elegant, courtly Saint-Pol, at present in Brussels on a mission from King Louis. Raising his eyes, Saint-Pol perceived those two observing figures on the stairs, one tall and scarlet, the other short and black. He cleared his throat to attract attention and sound the alarm, and scowled warningly upon the pair. But they were deaf and blind to all but each other. The lady's delicate fingers continued their caressing, almost wanton movement upon her companion's arm, whilst Armagnac, bending closer, and greatly daring, shifted his brown hand from the back of her chair and let it rest lightly upon her shoulder at a point where the audacious cut of her bodice left it bare.

Count Anthony resumed his descent of the stairs quite heedless of the Duke's restraining hand.

'Leave this to me,' his highness was muttering, regretting now that he had not taken matters into his own hands from the outset. 'Leave me to deal with Armagnac. He shall go home to-morrow, by Saint George!' And he repeated still more insistently: 'Leave him to me.'

Count Anthony, turning his head to regard him, still with that close-lipped smile upon his fair white face, puzzled him by his answer:

'Why, what is he to me, that I should dispute him with you? Madam Catharine is not yet my wife, for which on my knees I shall render thanks to Our Lady presently.' And he went on.

The comedy on the dais reached its end as the comedy in the hall below took its beginnings. The players had given good entertainment, and, on the closing lines of the epilogue spoken by their leader, applause had greeted them. Flowers, comfits, and money fell in a shower about them from their grateful audience, and then the noisy acclamations sank into the din of talk as the groups in the hall broke up, to re-form elsewhere and break again, and the movement became general.

The summer daylight was fading. Came servants with tapers, ushered by a chamberlain, to light the flambeaux and girandoles, and draw the great curtains, each a masterpiece of Flemish art, vividly illustrating scenes from the *Metamorphoses* of Ovid. Men's thoughts began to turn to supper, but none supposed that it was of supper that the Count of Armagnac whispered just then in the Lady Catharine's ear, invisible under the band of her headdress. Of whatever it may have been, it provoked the lady's laughter, which rose above the general hum like a peal of little silver bells. At least, that is how yesterday Count Anthony would have described it. This evening he discovered no music in it. He found the sound detestable, the frivolous tinkle of a trivial, hollow mind.

Looking up and around at that moment, she beheld him, quietly smiling, at her side, and, beyond him, her brother-in-law, a thundercloud upon his ducal brow. Her laughter snapped in the grip of a sudden and instinctive fear; a fear rather of Count Anthony's vague smile than of the Duke's obvious displeasure.

The Count inclined his bare golden head; he bent a little towards her from his graceful, red-swathed height.

'Of your charity, madam, share with us the pleasantries of my Lord of Armagnac. Let us laugh with you, madam.'

M. de Saint-Pol, the Duchess of Orléans, Madame de Blaumont with the Duke's ten-year-old daughter, little

Mary of Burgundy, and young d'Épinal were the more immediate witnesses of the scene, and their eyes, if we except
the child's, were anxious.

Followed a long and awkward pause, at the end of which
the Lady Catharine withdrew at last her fingers from Armagnac's arm, and he, straightening himself stiffly, shifted
his hand from her shoulder to the back of her chair. Whereupon Count Anthony cried out in a mockery of courteous
chagrin:

'But we discompose you. We intrude. We place a restraint upon you. We disturb fond attitudes. This must not
be. Charles, why did you bring me? We are not wanted
here.'

The unready Duke made a noise in his throat. His scowl
deepened. An exponent ever of the direct attack, he understood nothing of his cousin's enveloping movement. And
meanwhile, as he found no words, his cousin prattled on
quite pleasantly:

'Madam Catharine is reluctant, then, to repeat the pleasantry which moved her laughter. The pleasantry being my
Lord of Armagnac's we can understand her reluctance. His
pleasantries are seldom nice.'

Her ladyship's lovely face, clear-cut in profile as a cameo,
was going red and white by turns; her bosom rose and fell in
its revealing corsage; her eyes were lowered in panic. And
then at last, seeing her tongue-tied who usually was never
short of pertness, the Lord of Armagnac, spurred by the
glances of ever-increasing witnesses, swaggered to her rescue, to save her countenance and his own.

'Do you talk at me, Lord Count?' he challenged.

'At you?' Count Anthony's tone suggested a faint wonder. His dark eyes grew dreamy as they surveyed the
Frenchman. 'I spoke of you, perforce. It was unavoidable.'

Armagnac ignored the subtle innuendo. 'You will be
wise, my lord, to avoid it in the future.'

'Not wise. That is not the word at all. Fastidious. You
are not a pleasant topic, sir.'

There was a movement among the spectators, an audible drawing of breath, and some one laughed outright. It was young d'Épinal, maliciously glad, through the torment of his soul, to see another — and one who had the right to do it — baiting the bully Armagnac. That laugh stirred the fuming Duke into instant action. Almost he shouldered his cousin aside, to take the stage and plant himself squarely before the foolish pair. By his very presence he checked the Count of Armagnac's retort.

'By Saint George, there's been talk enough. Are we playing in a comedy, Anthony?'

'Is tragedy your preference, Charles?'

The Duke disregarded him. He stormed upon that lovely fool, his sister-in-law, who in all her life had never looked lovelier or more foolish.

'You have leave to go, Catharine.' The dismissal was harsh, almost contemptuous. 'Away with you! To your room, madam.'

She rose abruptly, like a puppet whose strings he had rudely jerked.

Finding the Duchess of Orléans at his elbow, he impressed her into service.

'Take the little fool hence, Mary. Go with her.'

He seized the Lady Catharine's arm in his powerful grip, swung her round and flung her into the arms of the Duchess.

'Oh, cruelty!' cried Count Anthony. The Duke stared at him, his countenance almost purple. 'To part them,' the Count explained, and waved a hand from the Lord of Armagnac to the Lady Catharine, who was retreating now in tears. 'They were made for each other, expressly created for mutual joy. Do you not agree with me, M. d'Épinal?'

The young courtier glared at him, understanding nothing of this icy mockery where knighthood, as it seemed to his ingenuous mind, called for fiery indignation.

'If it had been my honour to have been betrothed to that peerless lady, I ... I ...' He faltered, at a loss.

'Well, sir? Well? What would you have done? Instruct me. You perceive my need.'

'I would not laugh.'

'Ah, no! With the breath leaping in flames from your nostrils, like the dragon yonder in the tapestry, you'ld hurl your gauntlet down at the intruder. Indeed, I think I've heard that is your knightly way, even when your engagement does not go the length of a betrothal. You are in the romantic tradition, you suppose.' Count Anthony shook his head in deprecation. 'There is neither romance nor reason in it, unless stags at rutting time are reasonable and romantic.'

D'Épinal stiffened. It grew clear to him that metaphorically Count Anthony was slapping his face for his own adventure with M. d'Auxonne on the Lady Catharine's behalf. And slapping it in such a way that open resentment must render him intolerably foolish. There was a force of truth in what Count Anthony said which stripped of all glamour and laid brutally naked the deed in which the young knight had taken a vainglorious pride.

He stood abashed, without answer, and the Count, with a smile and a nod, turned aside to bend over little Mary of Burgundy whom he found beside him. He talked and laughed with her now as if he had no thought for any in the world but this child who loved him.

Meanwhile the furious Duke had gone off, dragging with him almost forcibly, by the arm, the scarcely less furious Armagnac. He designed to get him beyond the reach of Count Anthony's mordant tongue before irreparable damage should be wrought.

If Charles of Burgundy was no diplomatist, yet a certain rough diplomacy he used on this occasion.

'My lord,' he said, 'it will be better for all concerned, and for the preservation of the peace and amity so vital to us all, that you do not postpone your intended departure from Brussels.'

'Postpone?' quoth Armagnac, who had no thought of going.

'You have prepared, I understand, to leave to-morrow.'

The Frenchman paused at the Burgundian's side. He stared long at his host, cold and haughtily. Then at last, he laughed.

'You give me leave?' he said. 'It is a little . . . abrupt.'

The Duke spread his hands, his face grave. 'In your interests and my own and those of others.'

'And that insolent cousin of yours from Guelders? Does he remain on the field?'

'Here is no field, my lord.' The Duke curbed with difficulty his rising anger. 'Nor have I perceived any insolence. There has been,' he added, warming as he proceeded, 'lack of discretion, which my cousin of Guelders is entitled to resent, and which I shall resent with him if carried further.'

Each stared into the eyes of the other, and the glances of both were hard. Armagnac was the first to bow, as perforce he must when reason prevailed.

Yet, when a few years later war flamed forth again between France and Burgundy, and Count John of Armagnac was found to have sold his sword to King Louis, the cause of this may well have been supplied on that July evening in Brussels.

'Your wishes are my laws, Monseigneur, in this as in all matters.'

The Duke turned away to seek his cousin. But the Count had already departed. Eventually the Duke found him alone in his closet, leaning from the open casement and looking out into the turquoise sky of eventide and the mists that were rising above the great ducal park by which the vision to the north was limited.

It was while dreaming here that Count Anthony of Guelders had reached the clear conclusion that the world — his world, at least — was no place for a gentleman.

The Duke came to fling a vigorous arm about his neck.

'All is most happily concluded,' he announced.

'I perceive the conclusion. Not the happiness.' His tone was wistful and a little weary. It sowed distrust in the ducal mind. Then Count Anthony swung half-round from his contemplation of the eventide. 'What are we, Charles?' he asked. 'Are we real, you and I? Do we live and breathe and act of our own independent wills; or are we but the creatures of a dream — the dream of some vast consciousness other than our own — in which we move, dimly aware of the parts we are set to play, but only in a measure as we play them?'

'God save us!' the Duke ejaculated, accounting himself confronted by stark lunacy.

Count Anthony flung an arm outwards, towards the black mass of the park, the mists, and the sky above in which the stars were palely dawning. 'All that is real! It exists and is at peace. But we, Charles — you and I and Armagnac and the Lady Catharine and this court of yours in which all is greed and lechery — we are not real, for if we were and were masters of our wills we would shape things otherwise. Could Montlhéry have been, and all that went to it, before and after? Could Dinant have been, and the horrors that were wrought there in the name of knighthood? Could any of this be if we were real?'

'Does it profit you to ask if that which is could be?'

'Ah, but is it? Is it?'

'It is. You may take my word for it.'

'Your word, Charles? Your word against my consciousness? You are deceived. Or else it is the life of courts that's false, unreal, rendered so by all the ceremonial in which we trammel it and which creeps into the soul of each composing it; by the illusions of power which are its breath; by the traditions of birth and blood which are the empty bubbles in which it is reflected. Yes, that may be it. We are all actors in this world of courts, Charles; players of parts allotted to us at birth according to the names we bear. Natural we never are. Hence our unreality. And because we are not natural in ourselves, when Nature expresses herself through us despite our panoplies and mummeries, she comes forth travestied and grotesque, stressing our unreality.'

The Duke breathed windily. 'It may all be as you say. But I'll hope it isn't.'

'While you are hoping, I will ascertain, Charles.'

'Let me know the result when you reach it,' the Duke mocked him. 'You read too much and you think too much. You are suffering from indigestion up here.' And he tapped his forehead. Abruptly he changed the subject. 'Armagnac returns to France to-morrow.'

'A pity,' said the Count.

'A pity? What the devil ails you to-night?'

'As I said below, he and your sister-in-law are excellently suited. In your place I'ld have played Providence to force a match between them.'

'God give me patience! Is there no sense in you at all?'

'Indeed, I hope so. Consider: A wife might make of Armagnac a man at least outwardly fit for decent company by rescuing him from the infamy of his incestuous life. Whilst such a husband as Armagnac would curb any wanton disposition in a woman. Thus these two who separately remain worthless might united become worthy. Is there no sense in that?'

The Duke recoiled before him. 'Is there sense,' he thundered, 'in speaking in such terms of the lady you are to marry?'

'Marry?' Count Anthony laughed a little. He shook his golden head. 'That dream at least is over and dispelled. And it leaves no pain, mirabile dictu. But I understand. I was in love with love. The Lady Catharine herself was naught; no more than the armature upon which I modelled the ideal mistress of my dreams. But the armature proving rotten has crumpled within my little edifice, and the form I worshipped being lost I perceive only the clay of which it was fashioned.' He sighed. 'It is but another illusion lost. The last perhaps.'

The Duke was roused to fury. 'Do you live in a romance, Anthony; or in the world?'

'Do I live at all?' quoth the exasperating Anthony.

'You'ld best rouse yourself to realize it. God's death, man, you talk of love like . . . like . . . an Arcadian shepherd. You are a prince; heir to a throne. And whilst princes may love as they please and where they please and when they please, they marry for the welfare of the state.' He swung away from his cousin, across the room and back in long, ponderous strides, talking the while. 'Myself, I was twice married without ever my consent being asked. I was six years of age when I married Catharine of France, to cement the alliance between Charles the Seventh and my father, and I was a widower at thirteen. Yet, though I was twenty when I entered second nuptials, do you suppose I consulted my tastes or personal inclinations on the subject of the bride?'

'Your indifference to women is a byword, Charles.'

The Duke imprecated inarticulately in his impatience. 'What has that to do with it? None could say it of my father, who has left me to provide for some twenty of his bastards. Yet he married as I have married, and as I shall marry again presently: as the State of Burgundy requires.'

'I give thanks to God that I am not Duke of Burgundy.'

'So does Burgundy,' snapped the Duke. 'But you'll be Duke of Guelders one day.'

'Not even that if I may not marry as I choose. I have ideals, Charles.'

'You have insanity.'

'The ideals of one man are the insanities of another.'

Upon this the Duke disdained to argue. He struck directly at the heart of the matter.

'Armagnac is going. Catharine shall hear two words from me on the score of prudence which she'll remember.'

'A prudent conduct to dissemble a wanton heart! Fine linen over a festering sore! Catharine is in soul a wanton, and I desire no wanton for my wife.'

'A wanton!'

'You saw how they played with each other, and that in public. You saw his hand, his foul, lascivious paw, on her bare shoulder. Do you not guess the prurient itch in those vile fingers, soiling her very soul with their touch? And you saw him whisper. Did you mark his eyes when he whispered?'

'Why, here is jealousy — jealousy that will magnify a woman's hair into a rope! Bah!'

But Count Anthony went on relentlessly. 'Am I to marry that, and have perhaps other men hereafter making free with one who, in her wantonness and vanity and greed of admiration, does not know where to place the barriers of reserve? And this to consolidate the alliance between Burgundy and Guelders. Our alliance, Charles, is firm enough without that. So think of it no more.'

'Think of it no more!' The Duke was flung from rage to rage. 'You are publicly betrothed.'

'Let the lady announce that she has changed her mind. Let there be reasons of state why each of us should wed elsewhere.'

The veins of the Duke's brow stood out congested. For a moment he looked as if he would strike his cousin. Then he mastered himself.

'No more of this,' he said coldly, peremptorily, the overlord admonishing his vassal. 'You are angry with her at the moment, and incapable of calm judgment. We'll talk of it again to-morrow.'

'To-morrow!' said Count Anthony in the dreamy accents of one who questions Fate. 'To-morrow?'

'I commend you to consider well your position between this and then.'

On that threat, for it amounted to no less, the Duke was gone. Count Anthony raised his voice to call after him: 'Good-night, Charles!'

But the slamming of the door was his only answer.

Alone, Count Anthony turned to the night again, and questioned the darkling heavens upon reality. It must exist somewhere behind this shadowy phantasmagoria of a court, which obscured it precisely as the mists below obscured the park. Let him seek this reality, and, if found, be lost in it.

He summoned from the anteroom his page, a sleek, well-grown lad of sixteen of the noble Guelders family of Valburg, who was already ripe for promotion to the rank of esquire. He gave him certain orders concerned with the lad's return to Guelders on the morrow, which plunged him into dismay. Then he sent for the master of his household, his intendant, his chamberlain, his secretary, his two esquires, and finally the captain of his guard; and the summer night was far gone before the last of his business with them was transacted.

From his casement he watched the early dawn breaking over the park and giving form to its dark mass; and he pursued his dream of that world of reality, the promised land towards which he was to set his feet.

CHAPTER III

THE INDISCREET ZEALANDER

THE abrupt disappearance of Anthony of Egmont from the Court of Burgundy was something more than a nine days' wonder. It was a source of regret to many, of humiliation to the Lady Catharine of Bourbon, and of fury to the Duke, who accounted himself thereby affronted in his dignity as well as disappointed in his designs. Never a man to brook the disregard of his inflexible will, he at once sent messengers to the provost-marshals of the various provinces composing his State with orders for the arrest of the Count wherever found. M. de Blaumont he despatched to old Duke Arnold's court at Nimeguen, whither he thought it most likely that Count Anthony would have gone, for the purpose of inducing him to return if he were there, or of informing his father of the event if he were not.

But neither M. de Blaumont nor any other of the score or so of messengers sent out by the Duke could come upon the fugitive, and at Nimeguen there was no news of him beyond what was contained in a letter to his father borne by the page Valburg on his return to Guelders. This letter added nothing to what was already known. It announced merely that Count Anthony had left Brussels on a personal quest which he chose to make alone and from which he could not say when he would return.

In the castle at Nimeguen they held a family council on the matter: Duke Arnold, his Duchess Catharine, who was sister to the Duke of Cleves, and their younger son Adolph, a man who, apart from a similar athletic grace, was so different in aspect from Count Anthony that it was difficult to believe them brothers. Where Count Anthony, favouring his father, was fair and frank and gentle, his brother was swarthy, hawk-faced, with a cruel, sneering mouth and mean, close-set eyes.

Sneeringly he solved the riddle. 'A quest, he says. Some such quest as took Lalaing to England. He has always sought to model himself upon Lalaing, or upon what he conceives Lalaing to have been. Knight-errantry will be his quest.'

'But he has gone alone, without page or esquire,' the father reminded him.

'Oh, knight-errantry after his own crack-brained fashion,' was the airy counter. 'Not to break lances in a lady's honour. His endeavour will be done on different grounds.' It was clear that Adolph was nowise concerned by his brother's disappearance. It was also clear that he did not admire his brother. 'God help Guelders when he comes to rule over it.'

'I pray it may be long before that happens,' said the mother gently. 'In the meanwhile he may come by wisdom, Adolph; grow more like you, my child.'

'May God contrive it,' added the Duke in piety, and in affection for this younger son whom both esteemed so fondly. They were to discover their error, like many another deluded parent, later, when they had helped to place it beyond repair.

It may well be that Adolph of Egmont was correct in his sneering surmise, and that knight-errantry after his own fashion engaged Count Anthony on that part of his travels concerning which nothing is to be discovered. He reappears some eight months later in the pages of his chronicler, and Ghent, that prosperous city of weavers, is made the scene of his reappearance. It is possible, indeed probable, that the act in which he emerges out of silence was typical of the matters that engaged him in those months upon which the records are silent. Possibly nothing would be known of this affair — at least nothing remarkable — but for the influence it was to exert upon his whole future career, through which I imagine that La Marche has traced it back.

A young merchant from the town of Middelburg in Walcheren, who was in Ghent for the transaction of affairs, had permitted himself with more daring than wit loudly to animadvert in a public tavern upon the government of the Duke of Burgundy. This rash young man, whose name was Danvelt, was particularly derisive in his allusions to events which had occurred during the Duke's accession-visit to Ghent in the previous June, at the time of the Feast of Saint Liévain. There had been rioting on that occasion in connection with the unpopular tax on all merchandise coming into the city, known as the cueillette; and this rioting had assumed such serious proportions that the Duke, who was inadequately escorted, had stood for a while in gravest peril. From this he had been extricated only by a prudent but inglorious — and, in the case of a man of his proud stomach, almost comic — submission to popular demands.

After his departure, the men of Ghent, cooling from their riotous fever, had leisure to reflect upon what they had done. They considered the intractable pride and unforgiving nature of the prince they had affronted, and dreaded at any moment such a punishment as his father had inflicted upon them at Gaveren for their previous insubordination. It was an affair which they ardently desired should be forgotten, and as a contribution towards that end did their best, themselves, to forget it. They certainly did not wish to be reminded of it in such terms as were now used by this young hot-head out of Walcheren, who alluded to it derisively as 'the joyous entry.'

It was the constant endeavour of the purse-proud, vain, and self-sufficient Mynheer Danvelt to be accounted of consequence in the world, a man whose knowledge of the great was close and intimate; and he conceived, after the fashion of his kind, that the readiest way to his ends lay in the disparagement of his betters. You must make it plain that in some way, however undefined, you are superior to the man upon whom you make it appear that you look down. At least that is the illusion common to the Danvelts of this world. If in addition he imagined — for he was a stupid fellow — that by ridicule of the Duke of Burgundy he would render himself popular in Ghent, he was soon undeceived.

His crude philippics were received at first in a sullen silence of mingled fear and resentment. This he mistook for deference to his opinions. Emboldened by it, he waxed more and more recklessly facetious until suddenly a stalwart weaver, sitting near him, crashed a bludgeon of reproof upon his humour:

'Swallow your tongue, you fool, and give us peace!'

Taken aback by so unexpected an interruption, Danvelt blinked at him, bewildered; then looked to those about him for sympathy and support. Instead, he was met on every side by forbidding glances, whilst the taverner, himself, leaned across the table angrily to admonish him.

'You may hold such fool's talk up in Zealand,' said the fellow, having guessed Danvelt's origin from his speech. 'It's a long way from the Duke's ears. But we don't want it here in Ghent; least of all in my house. So out you go. Out of this!' And he flung an arm backwards, to indicate the door and the evening sunlight on the dusty street.

Danvelt, very red in the face, got to his feet. If he was short, he was sturdy, and with natural truculence he combined incaution.

'I don't know what blew me into your foul kennel,' said he.

'Some wind from hell, belike,' the taverner answered him; and repeated more urgently: 'Begone!'

Without urgency, Danvelt shrugged his broad shoulders in contempt, and made shift to depart.

'Oh, I go. I go. No need to raise your voice.'

He moved on his short thick legs without any undue haste, carrying his head well back, a man whose mental attributes were to be read at a glance in his physical aspect. There was in his prominent, aggressive nose and massive jaw a vigour which his shallow brow announced would ever be ill-directed. Conceit and self-sufficiency were in his rolling gait, which the taverner was not to know habitual to him, but conceived to be assumed for this occasion as an expression of contempt. Exasperated by it, he loosed a vigorous kick at the Zealander behind, by way of accelerating his departure, and by that kick precipitated the trouble which was to go to mould the destiny of Count Anthony and of some others as far removed from Mynheer Danvelt and his hitherto trivial fortunes.

Now, whatever he may have been, this young Zealander was not the man to receive kicks with impunity. He swung about infuriated by a punishment as hurtful to his dignity as to his flesh, and with all his strength, which was that of a young bull, crashed his fist into the round, shining face of the taverner and spread-eagled him across a table.

Riot ensued. Men left their cans to avenge the taverner and at the same time physically express their resentment of this young man's person and conduct. Had that been all, the matter would have ended in his being flung bodily into the street. Unfortunately there were some who took the view that he had been needlessly affronted, and some who in secret, perhaps, had shared his opinion of the Duke of Burgundy. It followed that in an instant two camps were formed within the narrow confines of that tavern. The company may have numbered some thirty men, members of various guilds, besides a few women who shrank in terror against the walls, entrenching themselves behind the long trestle-tables. Stools and drinking-cans and fists were the weapons employed in the writhing clot of fighters which surged hither and thither with Danvelt and the taverner in the heart of it, and which, leaving wreckage behind it, finally burst into the street.

Now it happened that this tavern, appropriately bearing the sign of the Magpie, was situated within a stone's throw of the great market-place and the State House. And it happened further that the Burgomaster's watch was leisurely patrolling the square at this moment. Attracted by the turbulence, it came quickly to the battle-field, some half-dozen strong, and the men, reversing their short halberts, and using the butts as staves, belaboured the heaving mass, breaking a head or two in the process. They might have done no more than add to the turmoil and confusion but that at this moment a gentleman on a big white horse came riding up the street attended by a mounted servant. The gentleman, young and fair and good to look upon, richly dressed and wearing the black liripipe from his round velvet hat swathed under his chin to make that headdress secure, took in the situation at a glance, distinguishing the men of the watch who strove shoulder to shoulder on the far side of these disturbers of the peace. Like a good citizen he accounted it his duty to lend assistance to the servants of the law. He spoke a word to his servant, and thrusting his horse forward, yet restraining it with great skill at the same time, he forced the little crowd to give way on either side of him. Into the gap he urged his steed, his servant following, whilst with the butt of his whip he smote here a head and there a shoulder, commanding them at the same time to desist and stand. It was enough. Finding themselves assailed by horsemen, the rioters imagined that they had to deal with the Burgundian provost, whose hand was a deal heavier than that of the native keepers of the peace. Incontinently they broke and fled, and in a moment all had vanished save the taverner and Mynheer Danvelt. Between the town watch and our opportune horseman stood these two, dishevelled and bleeding.

On the spot, the taverner, whose name was Groothuse, made his raging, vindictive plaint. It was not enough for him to behold Danvelt's torn clothes and battered countenance. He meant to put a rope around his neck for the evening's work, the wreckage of his tavern, the loss of custom, and the physical injuries which he had himself sustained. So he poured out his bitter tale. This foreigner from Walcheren, this treacherous, rebellious Zealander — and all Zealanders, he asserted, were to his knowledge treacherous rogues who would murder their lord the Duke of Burgundy if opportunity offered — this ineffable treason-monger had dared to speak disparagingly of the Duke's Highness in the tavern which Groothuse conducted as became a loyal Ghenter. Because he had ordered him from his house — Master Groothuse said nothing of the kick — this rascally hind had struck him, and then there had been a riot in which he had suffered, as they could see. He wiped the blood from his nose with the back of his hand, and pointed to the tavern. He had suffered not merely in his person. His house was wrecked and his custom gone, as they might behold for themselves; and all this he had suffered because he had sought to defend the honour of Our Lord the Duke, whom God preserve, against this contemptible sedition-scatterer out of Zealand. He repeated some of the things that Danvelt had said of the Duke, as instances of how lost the fellow was to decency and loyalty; things which, to his scandal and that of the watch, appeared to move the mirth of the gentleman on the white horse.

In the end, because the watch knew Master Groothuse for a respectable citizen, they accepted his account of the event, and this the more readily since Mynheer Danvelt made no attempt to contradict him. Because they knew where to find the taverner when they should come to need him for a witness, they left him for the present, and were content to carry off the battered young Zealander as their prisoner, so that he might answer in the Burgomaster's court for having been the cause of this indecorous breach of the peace. The sergeant offered thanks to the gentleman on the horse for his timely help, and desired to know his name and place of abode in case his testimony should also be required by the Burgomaster.

'I am,' he was answered, 'Anthony Egmont, a gentleman on my travels, to be found here at the Toison d'Or for the next few days and very much at your Burgomaster's service.'

He spoke Flemish fluently and choicely, but with a French accent, from which the watchman assumed him to be French, as also from his name, which he pronounced in the

French way. This and the suppression of the particle were sufficient disguise for a name which, after all, was borne by others besides the members of the ruling house of Guelders.

Now it happened that the affair made some noise through the town, and came that same night to the ears of the Sire de Vauclerc, who acted as the Duke's provost in Ghent.

These provostships themselves were rendered necessary by the curious circumstances of Burgundian rule. It is to be remembered that no national unity existed in the States which had gradually come under the Duke of Burgundy's sway; there was not even a bond of federation to connect them. They acknowledged under different titles the authority of a common ruler, because their various lordships happened to be united in one person. Charles, who ruled in Burgundy as Duke, also filled the like office in the dukedoms of Brabant, Limbourg, and Luxembourg, and was in addition Count of Flanders, of Artois, of Hainault, of Holland, of Zealand, and of Namur, and Lord of Friesland and of Mechlin. To each of these States his accession was separate and distinct, and in the capital of each he had exchanged pledges of fidelity with the representatives of the people. Apart, however, from that common sovereignty thus imposed upon them, those various States remained separate and distinct from one another, having no common system of legislation, no court exercising jurisdiction over the whole, no magistrate or civil officer whose warrant ran beyond the limits of his own province. Not even was there any agreement amongst them for the capture and surrender of escaped criminals. So that the hunted assassin or marauder from Brabant was safe once he had slipped over the border into Hainault or Flanders or Artois.

Because Charles of Burgundy was not the man to tolerate such a fruitful source of evil in his dominions, he had placed in each province a representative for juridical purposes in the person of a provost-marshal, invested with the fullest powers to proceed summarily against malefactors by sack and cord at discretion. And because the necessity and desirability of this was recognized by each of the various States concerned, there was no opposition from the native magistrates to a measure which might have been regarded as an encroachment upon their national privileges.

Because of the impression for ready turbulence which the Ghenters had made upon him at the time of his accession as Count of Flanders in the previous year, he had sent them a strong man for their provost-marshal with a stronger backing of Burgundian spears than was usual to a provostship.

A man less stern than the Sire de Vauclerc might have perceived for himself that the Duke's interests would best be served in such an affair as this by disregarding it. Because he lacked this vision, the Sire de Vauclerc conceived that, since it was against the Duke's name that Danvelt had offended, he, as the Duke's officer, was called upon to intervene and to deal with him. And because the unfortunate young merchant, being from Zealand, was regarded as a foreigner in Flanders, the magistracy of Ghent did not consider itself under any obligation to protect him, and certainly did not think it worth risking on his behalf the displeasure of a vengeful Duke who was already displeased with them more than enough for their peace of mind. They had seen at Gaveren, and more recently and more terribly at Liège and Dinant, the manner in which he commonly signified his displeasure.

So when an officer from the Sire de Vauclerc, attended by ten lances, presented himself next morning at the State House and demanded the surrender to the Duke's provost-marshal of the person of Mynheer Danvelt, the Burgomaster made no difficulty about delivering up that unfortunate young man. The officer had precise orders from the provost, whose conception of his duty was to allow no occasion to escape of showing these mutinous Flemings the power of his ducal master and the fate of those who were rash enough to beard it. Therefore, when Mynheer Danvelt came forth from the State House, his legs were in iron gyves and a wooden yoke — a sort of portable pillory — was placed about his neck, as was usual only in the case of the most desperate malefactors.

Thus mercilessly trammelled and otherwise in most pitiful case, his clothes in rags, so that in places the flesh showed, his contused face besmeared with caked blood and with filth from the underground cellar in which he had spent the night, his straw-coloured hair unkempt and matted, the wretched man was paraded round the great market-place for all to see.

He was a spectacle to excite pity, especially considering the fate most probably reserved for him by the provost-marshal.

Among those who compassionated him was that gentleman calling himself Anthony Egmont, who, further, accounted himself in some measure responsible, by the assistance which he had rendered in the fellow's apprehension, for his present miserable plight. From the balcony of his room on the upper floor of the Toison d'Or, our gentleman beheld the little procession of men-at-arms in steel headpieces and glittering corselets with the prisoner shambling painfully in their midst. It was the circular badge on each corselet, enclosing a Saint Andrew's cross, the Burgundian device, which instantly informed Count Anthony of the intervention here of the ducal provost, and so increased his concern and pity on the prisoner's behalf. With sombre eyes he watched the little procession as it passed out of sight along the busy square. Then he returned within to break his fast. But not the dish of succulent stewed eels nor the stoup of dark beer for which Ghent was famed could remove his thoughts from that unfortunate fellow. Pondering the discrepancy between the offence and its probable consequences, he was considering some form of intervention, when he was waited upon by messenger from the provost-marshal with a command that he should attend the trial that morning of Master Danvelt.

This might have its awkwardnesses, but it was not an invitation to be declined. So he presently went forth under that officer's escort into the spring sunshine and the bustling, brick-paved market-place of that important city of a land, which, if not for natural beauty, at least for opulence and for achievement in the arts and crafts, was the rival of Italy.

By way of the Cloth Hall and under the great shadow of the Belfry, which reared its square mass three hundred feet above the ground, he was conducted by the mean alleys which had grown about Saint Pharailde into the open space before the Gravensteen, a massive fortress on the Scheldt defended by a projecting gate-house with octagonal towers above. Over the drawbridge, past the portcullis, guarded by a Burgundian sentry, and across the spacious castle-yard where grooms and soldiers idled, our gentleman was ushered into the keep and up a winding staircase of stone into a hall on the first floor. It was a grey and gloomy place, whose groined vaulting was borne on columns. It was bleak and scantily furnished. There was a long table under the tall trefoil windows at the back, with a chair of state set before it, on the leather back of which the Saint Andrew's cross was stamped in black and purple. There was a bench ranged against the wall near the door, and in mid-apartment stood a three-legged stool, at present occupied by the prisoner under guard of two men-at-arms.

The wooden yoke had been removed from Danvelt's neck, but the gyves were still upon his legs, and he sat there, dull-eyed, huddled together, the incarnation of dejection. The bench in the background was occupied by the taverner Groothuse, battered of countenance and inflamed of eye, his wife, and a couple of his friends who were come to support his testimony with their own. The officer signified to Count Anthony that he might be seated there, too, to await the coming of the provost-marshal. The Count, however, elected to pace the stone floor to and fro, a man clearly without any of the awe of his surroundings by which the other strangers present were so imbued that, when they ventured to speak at all, they did so in whispers. He took their eye as he slowly paced there, tall and elegant in a pourpoint of black velvet that was edged with fur at hem and wrists and caught about his loins in a girdle of hammered gold, from which a heavy gold-hilted dagger hung upon his left hip, behind, and a black leather scrip on his right hip in front. His black velvet hat was again secured upon his head by the long liripipe which was swathed under his chin. This he had retained, as if unconscious that he was expected to remove it. His boots were of the finest leather and with the exaggeratedly long, almost grotesque points which courtly mode prescribed. His gloves were of black velvet with a tiny jewel hanging from each tassel.

He afforded those present an object for admiration and speculation until at last the provost-marshal came to command attention of another sort. In advance of him, an officer in steel and leather, with a little violet tuft of plumes at the back of his peaked headpiece, clanked into the hall by a door at the far end. He was followed by two pikemen, who ranged themselves on either side of that doorway. Next came a clerkly fellow in a rusty gown bearing a wallet of parchments, which he set down on the long table before the chair of state, and a moment later the Sire de Vauclerc himself emerged, a tall, stern-faced gentleman in black with a gold chain upon his breast and a small round hat upon his grizzled head.

Followed by two pages in black and purple, one bearing his sword and the other his purse, he advanced without haste to the great chair. He remained standing a moment after he had reached it, his cold eye raking the thin ranks of those present and coming at last to rest upon the conspicuous figure of Count Anthony. His arched brows met in a sudden frown. His close-set eyes looked down his nose, and his voice rasped harshly in Flemish.

'You know where you stand, sir. You have forgotten to uncover.'

'Pardon,' Count Anthony begged. He unwound the liripipe and, removing his hat, shook out his tawny mane.

The Sire de Vauclerc continued to scowl upon him intrigued now by a resemblance to someone seen elsewhere.

'Who are you?' he asked.

'A simple gentleman on his travels. Arriving yesterday in your city of Ghent, I chanced upon a brawl and lent my aid in suppressing it. Being commanded by you this morning, I am here.'

Thus he avoided mention of his name, and, since it was irrelevant, the Sire de Vauclerc did not insist. He sat down and took up the sheet of parchment proffered him by the clerk.

With the butt of his pike one of the men-at-arms prodded the dazed prisoner from his stool and almost sent him sprawling. He recovered himself, and with a clank of his irons stood hangdog before the Burgundian justiciary.

His business was soon done. The Sire de Vauclerc had a brisk way with him, and it was at once clear that he had prejudged the case from the written statement he held before hearing the depositions. Nevertheless, Groothuse was invited to speak, and he spared no vindictiveness in his recital of the prisoner's verbal offences against the Lord Duke of Burgundy. His bones were sore and his joints stiff this morning from last evening's business, and his condition did not make for kindliness towards the author of these ills.

He was still in full flow of accusation, which he had announced that his wife and good friends there would confirm, when the provost checked him.

'Enough! No need for more unless the prisoner denies. You have heard, Master Danvelt, enough to hang you. How say you? Is it true or false?'

This man, who had strutted it in Middelburg like a cock on a dunghill, was a poor battered fowl indeed this morning in the Gravensteen of Ghent. There was no vestige of a swagger in him now. Humbled before, the mention of hanging reduced him now to panic. He broke into a whimper of excuses. He could not remember clearly what had passed. He had drunk too much Rhenish, and if he had said a tenth of what he was accused of saying it is clear that he could not have been sober.

'So that you do not deny?' said the steely voice of the Sire de Vauclerc. 'No need then to trouble me with further witnesses.'

He passed to judgment, briefly and coldly. The law's delays played no part in the Sire de Vauclerc's discharge of his justiciary's office.

'If my sentence upon you cannot teach you wisdom, it will serve at least to teach wisdom to others, making it clear throughout our Lord Duke's Flemish dominions as elsewhere that his lofty name is to be mentioned only in awe and honour. You would be well served were I to order your bones to be broken on the wheel. But the Duke of Burgundy is a gracious, clement overlord. Therefore you will be hanged . . .'

He paused there, interrupted indeed by Danvelt, who fell on his knees and filled the vaulted hall with his quavering protests and supplications of mercy, until his guards pulled him to his feet again and shook him into silence.

'You will be hanged,' the provost repeated when the interruption had ceased, 'unless it lies in your power to ransom your neck.'

'To ransom it?' the wretched man ejaculated, and his stricken countenance lighted with sudden hope.

'You are from Zealand, are you not?'

'Yes, my lord. My father is one of the wealthiest merchants of Middelburg.' He could not suppress the rash boast, which was never far from his lips.

'You are fortunate in having had an industrious father.' M. de Vauclerc was sardonic. 'Fortunate also in being a subject of so clement a prince as the Duke of Burgundy, whose name, should you be spared, you will hereafter honour.'

'My lord, I shall bless his name all the days of my life.'

'You'll find it cheaper than detraction. As an alternative, then, to the rope, you will pay a fine of a thousand ducats.'

'A thousand ducats! A thou . . .' Danvelt choked in horror at so vast a sum, vast even for the wealthiest merchant in Middelburg. True to his instincts, he offered half, and thereby moved his judge to an explosion of heat not to have been expected from so cold-seeming a man.

'By God! Will you chaffer here? Will you haggle with Justice over the price of your neck? I am reminded that you Flemings part as reluctantly with gold as with blood. Hence most of your insubordination — in defence of your money-bags when a just taxation is imposed. Luckily for you, whilst your blood is useless when shed, your gold is useless until you shed it. Which will you shed now? Resolve yourself.'

'But . . . I have not such a sum at my command. I . . . I . . .' He wrung his hands, he writhed in his distress. Finally: 'Does your lordship give me time in which to find it, to procure it from Zealand?'

'Provided you can find me a burgher of substance here in Ghent to be your surety.'

'I know of none who'll be surety for so much. It is a prince's ransom.'

'It was a prince's character with which you made free. Well, well, among your burgher friends here, are there any two who will halve the surety, or any four who will quarter it?'

Danvelt hung his head and wrung his hands. 'Too little is known of me here in Ghent.'

'And that little not to your advantage, probably. Ah, well! You must resign yourself to hang. You have till evening to make your peace with God.'

'My lord! For pity's sake. I have two hundred ducats at my lodging. Take that in earnest of payment of the whole so soon as I can bring it from Middelburg.'

The provost shrugged his shoulders. 'You weary me with your notions of how justice is dispensed. The two hundred ducats and what else you have are forfeited when you hang. How do I know your father to be what you say? And what do I care? Since you cannot find the sureties, the matter is at an end. Take him away.'

The pikemen's hands closed upon him and he was pulled backwards. He accounted himself lost when he heard another voice ringing melodiously through the hall.

'A moment yet, by your leave, my good Lord Provost.' It was the tawny-headed stranger who spoke. 'I will be this man's surety for the sum.'

CHAPTER IV

THE SURETY

THE provost-marshal looked up in surprise as Count Anthony, easy and self-assured, advanced until only the table was between them.

'You will be his surety? Why? What is he to you?'

'A human being in urgent need of assistance.'

The Sire de Vauclerc stared hard at the speaker, and his thin black brows were raised. It is probable that he had never before met philanthropy.

'What is your name?' he asked.

'You shall read it on the bond, my lord.'

Something in Count Anthony's bearing, something in the calm assurance of his tone, checked the provost-marshal's insistence. Instead he asked him:

'But are you acquainted, then, with the prisoner?'

'I saw him for the first time last evening.'

'Then, sir, why . . . ?'

'One reason, I have given you. If you must have another, shall we say that I gratify a whim?'

'A whim! God's mercy! A whim that may cost you a thousand ducats!'

'Whims are commonly costly.'

'Costly, ay. But . . . . You must be a man of great wealth.'

'I've never ascertained its extent.'

'You'ld better ascertain it now, by Heaven! Ascertain that you can pay a thousand ducats.'

'You'll judge so, I think, when you have my seal.' Calmly the Count helped himself to a quill and dipped it in the inkhorn. Unbidden, as if obeying the unspoken command of this stranger's will, the clerk proffered him a sheet of parchment. Count Anthony bent down and wrote rapidly, sign-

ing with a flourish. He returned the parchment to the clerk.
'Set me the wax,' he commanded.

The fellow glanced at the document, and his countenance
altered to such an extent that the provost-marshal, already
sufficiently impatient, leaned sideways to read what was
written. One glance at this order upon the Intendant of the
Finances of the Duchy of Guelders at Nimeguen, and the
Sieur de Vauclerc understood why the stranger's appearance
had intrigued him. He had seen him at Bruges with the
Duke a year ago. Almost awe-stricken he looked up; then he
came deferentially to his feet.

'You are . . .'

The Count was quick to interrupt him.

'A simple gentleman on my travels, my lord, as I have
said. If you will accept the bond in payment, you may
now set this man at liberty, leaving the debt transferred
from him to me.'

The Sire de Vauclerc bowed without a shadow of hesitation.

'Of course, of course,' and gave the order for the prisoner's
release and dismissal even before Count Anthony had sealed
the bond with the heavy ring which he removed from his
finger for the purpose.

'You have been favoured,' the provost admonished Master Danvelt, 'by a most singular good fortune. Let your
near escape serve you as a lesson for the future.'

It was to Danvelt and to the others present a bewildering
conclusion. Whilst all alike marvelled and speculated upon
the identity of this gentleman who had intervened to such
effective purpose and upon his interest in this trader out of
Zealand, Danvelt himself was so dazed that he scarcely observed the removal of the fetters from his legs, and Groothuse so infuriated that he forgot his awe of the provost-
marshal, and broke into violent protestations, demanding to
know who was to compensate him for all that he had suffered
materially and morally.

He was rebuked by M. de Vauclerc with the assurance

that all that he pretended to have suffered was as nothing to what he should yet suffer if he permitted himself to forget the respect due to the Duke of Burgundy in the person of his representative. Groothuse trembled into silence and mortified dejection. And then, again to the general amazement and particularly Groothuse's own, the stranger raised his voice on the man's behalf.

'After all, my Lord Provost, what this vintner claims is just. He should be indemnified by Mynheer Danvelt.'

The spectators expected the roof to fall. The manner in which this stranger had intervened as surety had been sufficiently presumptuous. But to go the length of instructing the Sire de Vauclerc in the administration of justice was to transcend all bounds. The morning, however, was not yet at the end of its surprises. For the Sire de Vauclerc, usually so dominant, intolerant, and harsh, showed no slightest resentment of this impertinence. He just laughed.

'Let him be indemnified by Master Danvelt, all you please. But I thought you were the prisoner's friend.'

'I am the friend of justice,' he was answered in a tone almost of rebuke; and on that Count Anthony turned to the vintner. 'At what do you set your damage?'

Groothuse gulped, recovered, and blurted abruptly: 'Fifty ducats.'

Again the Sire de Vauclerc laughed, on a jeering note this time. 'You lying dog! You'ld be well paid with ten.'

'Let him have twenty,' said Count Anthony. 'I will add the sum to the bond and so to Master Danvelt's debt to me.'

In this high-handed fashion he disposed, and, having done so, would have taken his leave, but that the provost begged him to remain, and this for a purpose which Count Anthony readily guessed.

When the hall had been cleared, and the two were alone, the Sire de Vauclerc addressed him with a deference which contained a new note of firmness. 'And now, my lord, there is yourself. How am I to proceed without offending you? I have a duty to perform.'

'What duty is that?'

'Orders to detain you, wherever found, and to send you to the Duke's highness under escort have been circulated to all officers throughout the provinces.'

'As a man of law, you know that such orders are illegal. I am neither subject nor vassal of the Duke of Burgundy.'

'Within his dominions, my lord, even those who are not his subjects are amenable to his laws.'

'When they have transgressed them. I have transgressed none.'

The Sire de Vauclerc was uneasy. 'I dare not, my lord, do other than detain you.'

'Force will be necessary, sir,' he was answered, to increase his discomfort.

'I trust not, my lord.'

Count Anthony looked at him in silence for a long moment, studying the gravity of that lean, shaven countenance, and reading there how little the provost relished his task.

'Very well,' he said at last. 'I am lodged, as you know, at the Toison d'Or. You may send your officer to apprehend me there at noon.'

Returning his glance, the provost's cold eyes grew keen as dagger points.

'You will await his coming?'

Count Anthony laughed. 'That is to ask for my parole, and I have already said that I will yield only to force. Regard for your lord the Duke must compel you to exercise it. Regard for me, if I deserve it, may induce you to postpone the step for an hour. The Duke could hardly desire you to be more urgent, or to use unnecessary harshness towards me.'

The Sire de Vauclerc considered. The service of princes is not without perils, as he well knew, and, indeed, as the Count was very subtly reminding him. If he did not arrest Count Anthony, he would have to answer to his stern master for a dereliction of duty. If he did arrest him, he would make an enemy of him, and it could not be good to make an enemy of one who had been, and no doubt would be again when present differences were adjusted, the Duke's closest friend.

Count Anthony, he perceived, was showing him how by the exercise of a little craft both horns of the dilemma might be avoided. He would be failing in his duty if he did as Count Anthony requested, yet he would fail without afterwards seeming to have failed. It would be easy to make it appear that he had used all diligence.

'Indeed, my lord, not only have we no orders to use harshness with you, but we are all commanded to treat you with every consideration. No doubt you will have affairs to settle here in Ghent, and an hour is hardly too much to ask. My officer shall wait on you at noon, my lord. I trust you will be ready for him.'

Gravely Count Anthony bowed to him. 'I shall bear your courtesy in very kindly memory,' said he; and on that they parted with mutual esteem and perfect understanding of what lay immediately ahead.

In the courtyard Count Anthony found himself awaited by Mynheer Danvelt. A little awe-stricken still by his late amazing experiences, the young man announced that he had stayed to thank him and do what else was required in the matter of the enormous sum by which he was indebted. The Count desired to be waited upon by the young man at the Toison d'Or in half an hour precisely, and passed on.

Master Danvelt must have bestirred himself in his anxiety to obey, for within the half-hour not only did he present himself at the Toison d'Or, but he came almost spruce in a new suit of grey cloth, and a bundle of luggage was strapped behind him on the short tubby grey mare he rode. Mynheer Danvelt had had enough of Ghent.

In the inn-yard he found the Count's servant with the Count's horses, and from their saddle-bags it was plain that the Count, too, was on the point of definite departure.

'Which way do you ride?' the Count asked him when,

within doors, the burgher had made known his intentions.

'Back to Middelburg, sir.'

'You'll go by way of Bruges, then, so that we may ride together and there is no need now to delay. The sooner we are out of Ghent, the better.'

'By God, sir, we are of one mind in that.'

They left the city by the Bruges Gate, and rode amain through those flat, low-lying lands from which the ocean is excluded by an embankment, compared more than a century earlier by the Italian Dante with that which separates the desert from the River of Tears. The melancholy of the landscape was mitigated to-day by the spring sunshine irradiating the dusty road between rows of tall burgeoning poplars planted with almost mathematical regularity.

They rode at first in single file, Count Anthony ahead and closely followed by his servant, with the Zealander a little distance in the rear. But some five miles out of the city, when the towering Belfry looked no more than a spear thrusting up into the sky, the Count slackened his hot pace and beckoned the young burgher to his side.

Danvelt went readily enough. Not only was he a man of no reserves, but he was spurred here by a curiosity natural enough on the score of this benefactor who was obviously a person of some consequence. Without even waiting to be addressed, the burgher opened the conversation and this by a question, easily familiar in tone and manner.

'Do you go beyond Bruges, sir?'

For a moment Count Anthony appeared to be studying the contusions on that bold countenance, then answered shortly: 'As far as Flushing.'

He did not consider it necessary to add that from Flushing he hoped to cross to England in his quest of knowledge and reality, and in pursuit of a knight-errantry rather different from that which had taken Lalaing thither years ago.

'To Flushing?' echoed the burgher, and satisfaction was blent with his surprise. 'So far then we shall be companions. That will be very pleasant.'

The Count received the assurance with a smile. 'Pleasant for whom?' quoth he, and by that simple question disconcerted the other's self-complacency.

'For me, of course,' the burgher made haste to explain. 'That is . . . that is, if you will suffer my company.' And then, sensing the aloofness in this gentleman and becoming dimly conscious that he had perhaps used a greater familiarity of tone than was relished, he proceeded to offer some further explanation. 'If I make so bold as to hope so, sir, it is because in Flushing it may be my good fortune to discharge at least some part of this heavy debt between us.'

'Why, as to that ——' Count Anthony was beginning almost disdainfully, and there paused, remembering that to disdain a thousand ducats scarcely sorted with the character of simple gentleman which he had assumed. He changed the intended course of the sentence in completing it. 'As to that, it shall be as you please.'

Danvelt, growing more at ease again, now that he had in a sense explained himself, became at last voluble in expressions of thanks for the great service this gentleman had rendered him.

'I owe you my life and more, sir,' was his peroration, 'and I shall hope for the occasion to prove my gratitude.'

'So shall not I, sir,' he was answered, and again was disconcerted. He found the unexpected quality of his companion's answers a tax on his wits. He was not accustomed to persons who answered unexpectedly. 'Such an occasion,' Count Anthony enlightened him, 'must mean trouble for me, and inconvenience for you.'

'Oh, I see!' The burgher laughed. 'I'ld weigh no inconvenience, sir. I would not, by God.' His tone rang sincere, and the Count liked him a little better for it. Hitherto he had found him singularly unprepossessing, and had written him down as a fellow of little heart and less brain.

And then Danvelt asked the question that had been in his mind since first he had ridden alongside. 'May I know, sir, the name of my protector, my saviour?'

'My name? I am called Anthony Egmont.'

'Egmont? Just that?'

'Just that. Is it not enough?'

'Oh, yes. Oh, yes.' The answer came precipitatedly. The burgher wondered almost had he given offence by his silly question. But he was conscious of a pang of disappointment. In a gentleman with such an air and of such stupendous gestures as that which had saved his neck that morning he had expected something more sonorous, more imposing than a name so plain and simple and unadorned by any title. He spent some seconds in considering the deceptiveness of appearances. He had fancied — and he had been gratified by the fancy — that his protector was some great nobleman. And yet appearances there were that still continued to mystify him; if anything his mystification was deepened by the very simplicity of his companion's quality.

'Forgive me, sir, if . . . if I am indiscreet. Though I think you should consider the question natural enough. What led your worship . . . Why was it that you came to my rescue — to the rescue of a man unknown to you? Or is it, perhaps,' he went on quickly, without waiting for the answer, imagining that he held the explanation, 'is it that you had heard of, that you perhaps know, my father?'

That was it, of course. This Master Egmont must have heard of Frederick Danvelt, the most prosperous merchant in Middelburg, and in befriending the son of so wealthy a man would have had an eye to his own ultimate profit. The friendship of Frederick Danvelt was after all a very valuable possession, and the acquiring of it worth some risk.

Coldly his companion pricked the swelling bubble of that pleasant assumption.

'No,' he said, 'I did not know of the existence of your father.'

'You didn't?' Master Danvelt was plunged once more into the depths of bewilderment. 'Then, why? What reason had you to save me as you did? You had no profit to make, no object to serve?'

'None. I suppose, Master Danvelt, that in the world in which you have had your being, profit is the lodestar of men's actions, and you can conceive of no other. You would find it difficult to believe a man should take personal risks or expose himself to heavy loss on no better grounds than a humane desire to serve a fellow-creature in distress. Probably you would regard such a man as not quite sane.'

That was precisely how Master Danvelt was beginning to regard his companion. He thought he discerned something fantastic in the very way he expressed himself. Nor did anything that subsequently passed between them during their journey to Flushing serve to modify the opinion. So that, instead of coming to know him better as a result of association, Danvelt found that hourly he knew his companion less in a measure as this companion's expressions demolished one theory after another that Danvelt built up concerning him. So widely divergent were their habits of thought and their outlook upon life that it was almost as if they belonged to different races of beings. But that this Master Egmont was a person of some worldly consequence impressed itself more and more deeply upon Danvelt. It was announced in his very bearing, in his air of command, in the calm manner in which he imposed upon others a will which none ever dreamed of disputing; and whilst he used Danvelt with all friendliness, yet Danvelt was ever conscious of a certain condescension, of a gulf between them which not all his natural impudence could successfully bridge. It was a source to him at once of resentment and pride. One attempt which he made to know more of his protector was based upon a shrewd enough inference of his own.

'There is one thing, sir, I cannot understand,' said he.

That was on the following day, when, having lain the night at Bruges, they were pushing on along the yellow dunes towards the estuary of the Scheldt.

'Sir, you are to be envied,' the Count answered him.

'Envied?'

'In that there is one thing only you cannot understand.'

Danvelt perceived the joke, or what he supposed to be the joke, and laughed. 'I mean, sir, of course, one thing concerning yourself.'

'Even there you have the advantage of me. But proceed, sir. Expound this thing.'

'That black-avisaged provost-marshal in Ghent accepted your bond, just your note of hand, as a sufficient surety for the fine. That seems to me very strange; very-significant.'

'I have this in common with you, Master Danvelt — indeed, perhaps I even transcend you a little in it: my father's name, too, is well known and honoured. The Sire de Vauclerc knew that my father, failing myself, would fulfil the obligations of the bond.'

'A wealthy man, indeed, your father, sir. Whence is he?'

'From Nimeguen,' said the Count, who did not think it worth while to prevaricate.

Danvelt nodded. 'Ay, ay. I've heard my father say there are wealthy men in Guelders. But I thought you were French.'

'I have lived a deal in France.' A flight of ducks went overhead, and afforded the Count a pretext for changing the conversation. 'A great fowling country this, I've always heard. There should be good hawking in such open lands. Yet they tell me that Walcheren is chiefly famed for its decoys.'

And Danvelt, as light of mind as he was heavy of body, veered readily to the new topic. 'Faith, yes,' he agreed with his loud and ready laugh. 'The decoy makes a quicker and fuller return than any hawking.'

An hour or so before sunset they came to Breskens, and there hired a great flat-bottomed ferry in which they and their horses were ferried across the Scheldt.

As the vessel drew alongside the quay at Flushing, Count Anthony was inquiring, of one of the watermen who had brought them over, what was the town's best inn, when Master Danvelt interrupted peremptorily:

'No inn for us to-night, sir. We'll lie with my father's

good friend Mynheer Claessens, who'll make you very welcome for my sake, and whose house you'll find a deal more comfortable than any inn. A wealthy man, Mynheer Claessens; prodigiously wealthy; a builder of ships and of all that goes to them; and a man of great weight in the town.'

Count Anthony yielded without further persuasion. The prospect of being received on terms of equality in a burgher household was not without allurement.

Having paid the waterman, they landed, and by the Scheldt Gate in the massive fortifications entered the town and rode the short distance to Mynheer Claessens's handsome house by the Groote.

CHAPTER V

THE UNFOLDING OF THE SCROLL

COUNT ANTHONY'S first glimpse of her burnt into his brain a picture which was to abide there all his days, and which no later impression of her could overlay or dim. Whenever hereafter he should think of her, the mental image his memory evoked was always this.

She stood in the doorway of her father's handsome house to welcome these guests, apprised of their coming by the clatter of halting hooves in the street beyond.

Until her appearance there, Count Anthony had been taking stock of his surroundings: the brick-tiled courtyard about which this red house of goodly proportions formed a quadrangle, the red house itself with its steep roof and unusually ample windows, the shrubs symmetrically shaped and placed at regular intervals in tubs along three sides of that court; the borders of white and yellow tulips; the quails in their osier cage upon the wall, and the tame grey stork, advancing solemnly as a chamberlain or seneschal to meet them.

Then she appeared, and he saw nothing else.

She stood a shade above the middle height, her slender body cased in a gown of blue, high-waisted in the courtly mode, the bodice laced across a white silken undergarment which rose in a broadening wedge from waist to neck. Her head was bare, the plain white wimple flung back upon her shoulders, and the last red rays of the setting sun lighted a golden aureole about the coils of her hair and touched as with an inward effulgence the delicately tinted, delicately featured face.

To Count Anthony it seemed that he looked upon a picture of the Assumption from some cunning Italian hand, and afterwards he was to smile — though very gently — when he remembered how in prey to that momentary but over-mastering illusion, before the holy beauty of that face, he had almost fallen on his knees. Instead, however, he continued mechanically to advance, conscious that her eyes were as steadily upon him as his were steadily upon her — eyes of clearest blue, from which a soul looked out that must be frank and pure and fearless.

He experienced in that moment an inexplicable exaltation. If some verses which he wrote afterwards, and which La Marche has preserved, are to be accepted as truly mirroring his sensations, he was overcome by a sense that this was not a meeting, but a reunion; that his eyes had looked into those eyes before; that somewhere at some dim time he and this girl as yet unnamed to him had been indissolubly united, consecrated each to the other and made one in rapture and in anguish. It was like a memory, dim and elusive as a whiff of perfume borne on the breeze, assailing his conscious senses and in a flash escaping them again before he could identify its source. He was to think of it often hereafter, but never to recapture the experience, pursue it though he might.

And he knew her name, he thought; knew that he knew it. Up through unfathomable depths of memory he felt it rising; but, before it reached the surface of his consciousness, it was shattered by another name spoken aloud in Danvelt's big voice.

'Johanna!'

A shiver of annoyance ran through him. That was not the name his soul had been about to yield — a name that stood, he knew, for purity, for constancy, for courage, for loyalty, because so intimately associated in her person with those things.

And yet it seemed she answered to this name by which his companion hailed her.

'Why, Philip! You are soon returned!' First this expression of surprise, and then a question laden with womanly tenderness. 'But what has happened to you?'

The young burgher laughed off that inquiry as to how he came by bruised nose and swollen mouth and blackened eye, mightily at ease with her, proprietarily almost.

'I've had my adventures, by my faith, and might never have returned but for this good friend Master Egmont here.'

Thus he presented his companion, promoted now to the dignity of his good friend, with a certain hearty patronage which at another time must have made Count Anthony wince. At present, however, seeing nothing but this gentle lady, conscious of no presence but her own, he bowed very low and reverently over the slim white hand she frankly extended to him.

Master Danvelt completed the presentation. 'This is the daughter of Mynheer Claessens. And here is Mynheer Claessens himself.'

'To greet our Philip returning from the wars,' came the jovial voice of the jovial burgher who rolled forward to his daughter's side. A big man this, of a proper portliness, rubicund and kindly of countenance, shrewd and humorous of eye.

He embraced Danvelt as he might have embraced a son, and gave Master Egmont a generous and hearty welcome in words that were presently to be abundantly confirmed in deeds.

Mynheer Claessens kept a good house and a good table; he had a nice taste in wine, of which there was great trade in Walcheren; and he was well attended by devoted servants. Under no better auspices could Count Anthony have sought initiation to the domestic side of burgher life in Zealand.

At supper that night over the succulent ham of a boar from the Ardennes and a brace of ducks from Master Claessens's own decoy, washed down by a mellow Gascony vintage, Count Anthony, whose experiences in the past half-year had not all been pleasant, assured himself that one might live a great deal worse than this and have no ground for complaint.

The talk, of course, was all of Philip Danvelt's travels and adventures, and he supplied most of it himself, readily responding to the spur of an occasional question. It would have wearied Count Anthony into somnolence but for the amusement he found in the note introduced into the narrative by the jactancy inherent in Danvelt. The young burgher made an Odyssey of his journey to Ghent, and presented the tale in such a manner that he was ever the heroic figure in it; and this without departing as outrageously from the truth as he might have done but for the restraining presence of Count Anthony. When finally he came to the part played by the Count at the Gravensteen, the facts constrained him to fall, however reluctantly, into a minor rôle. And the Count, for all his normal calm and detachment, began to grow uncomfortable under the wondering glances of his host and his host's daughter. This wonder turned to stupefaction, at least on the part of Claessens, when the magnitude of the fine was disclosed.

The merchant swore deep in his throat, and asked the question: 'What will your father say to that?'

'What, indeed?' wondered Danvelt with sudden gravity and such a change of countenance that Claessens laughed in good-humoured malice.

'I'ld give a deal to be present when you tell him.'

'So would not I,' grumbled Danvelt. 'Nor shall I; for I mean to tell him of it by letter to-morrow, and await his answer here before I start for home. Before then, too, I hope to pay my debt.'

Claessens was moved to still deeper mirth at the expense of his friend and rival in prosperity, the elder Danvelt. He sobered presently when his mind veered to speculate upon the amazing fact that a stranger of obvious distinction should have come forward as surety for so vast a sum. This, Claessens expressed.

'What, sir,' he asked, 'was your inducement?'

Count Anthony laughed. 'I have been asked the question three times already, and I shall be asked it perhaps three hundred before I die.'

'And the answer is?' Mynheer Claessens insisted.

We know the half-scorn in which twice already Count Anthony had supplied that answer, contemptuous of folk who could not understand the performance of a humane action for its own sake. But it was not the answer that he now supplied. Instead, holding by its stem his silver goblet, his eyes upon the purple mirror of its contents, he replied dreamily:

'Who shall say? Perhaps the future holds the answer to that question.'

They stared at him, and let the subject drop. But that one of them probed his cryptic utterance at least in thought he had cause to suspect next morning.

He had risen betimes from the great bed in the chamber of honour which had been placed at his disposal, and he had gone forth into the stiff formal garden, set like a terrace upon the dunes. Walking there he had found Mistress Johanna, all in grey this morning, from which demure colour she appeared to gather an increased demureness. Her golden head was cased in a wimple kept in place by a hoop of dark blue velvet, plain and severe across the brow. Thus she fronted the breeze — for the morning was fresh with a tang of salt in the air — when Count Anthony came upon her there among the tulips of which already she had half-filled a little basket slung upon her arm.

'You are early astir, mistress,' was his comment when she had given him good-morning and made courteous inquiry touching his repose.

If she stood a little in awe of him, of that indefinable quality, blending radiance and dignity, which he wrapped about him like a cloak and by which he seemed apart and different from any man she had ever known, she betrayed no hint of it in her bearing. Frankly she met the gaze of his dark eyes, and with a composure apparently equal to his own.

'It is our custom here in Walcheren. We are industrious folk. As industrious as we are peaceful.'

'I should be as pained, madam, to restrain your industry'

— and he waved a hand towards the tulips upon which he had found it exercised — 'as to trouble your peace.'

She smiled as she answered him: 'You would not be suffered to do either.'

'Oh, I believe you. You would know how to defend your own.'

'Defend it? Who should trouble to assail it?'

'Why, some reckless wanderer such as I, perhaps.'

'Are you so very reckless?' she mocked him, but without challenge, and suddenly became grave. 'Oh, to be sure you are. Yet hardly to the detriment of others from the instance we have seen.'

'Can you be sure that there was no detriment to any in what I did?'

'In what you did? You saved Philip's life. To whose detriment could that be?'

'Who shall say? Perhaps to Master Philip's. We do not know what the life I saved may hold. Perhaps to that of the wife he is to wed or of the children she is to bear him. Only the future can answer you. Always is it only the future that can supply the answer to the present.'

'That,' she said slowly, 'is how you replied when father asked you what had induced you to go to the rescue of a stranger. What did you mean?'

'No more than I said. A month hence, a year hence, I may know why I did it, or I may die without knowing it. But some day, someone will know, and some day someone will either bless or curse me for the deed.'

'Curse you? For a deed so kindly, so disinterested as to be almost noble? Why?'

'That will be according to its consequences, for which the responsibility will be laid on me. I made myself in this the instrument of Destiny. Ah, mistress, it is a grave thing to take a life — a graver than men realize who do it lightly. It may be even more grave to save a life.'

She shook her head a little and looked out over the dunes to the sparkling sea.

'The more you explain, the less I understand,' she complained and laughed. She was a creature of ready laughter, as of infinite tenderness, inclining to love all things, to see only good, since herself she knew nothing else.

So the Count read her as he watched and paused before replying.

'That is because I have no gift of prophecy.'

'Sir, sir,' she cried in gentle impatience, 'you will speak of the future when I question you on the past. I ask you only why — upon what prompting — you did what you did.'

This time he supplied what she required. 'He was in sore plight when I beheld him. That moved my pity. I considered that his plight might yet be worse, and this so increased my pity that to allay it I went and snatched him from the cord.'

'In short, you obeyed the impulse of a pitiful and noble nature, which is what you are reluctant to confess.'

He made a gesture of denial. 'Ah! You think it answers you. But you are deceived. It supplies no more than half the reason. The other half lies in the womb of Destiny. I know that I was moved to pity. But not why I was so moved.'

'But I have told you why already. Because your nature is noble.'

'Then tell me why with this noble nature of mine I chanced to be so opportunely at hand. Why did I ride into Ghent at that precise hour when they were brawling in the street by which I came, and so rode into the life of Master Danvelt? Was it, perhaps . . .' He broke off. Then, lowering his voice to such a tone of reverence as to rob his words of all offence, he resumed, 'Was it perhaps so that I might ride into yours?'

'Into mine?' Frightened eyes looked into his, then quickly out to sea again. She caught her breath, and, observing the delicate profile of her half-averted face, he saw that it turned deathly white.

He was suddenly aware that he had laid violent, bruising

hands upon this pure, tender soul. Conscience smote him and amazement at himself, at the crude daring of his speech, worthy of some glib court gallant skilled in the paltry arts of dalliance. Yet he knew that the spirit prompting it had been of no such trivial kind; that he had spoken on an impulse from the depths of his being, from some prevision of the future, as instinctive as had been yestereve that uncanny glimpse into some remote and unsuspected past.

He sought to amend, to modify the impression he might have made.

'Am I not here,' he asked, 'as a consequence of my act?' He used a Moslem phrase, odd in her ears and incomprehensible. 'It was written that I should save Danvelt.'

'Written? Written? How? Where was it written?'

'On the scroll of Destiny. What else is written we shall find as it unrolls. We are only at the beginning of that scroll.'

He was relieved to hear her laugh: a silvery laugh, so like the Lady Catharine's, and yet so different. It assured him that she had recovered from the perturbation he had caused.

'You are a master of vagueness, sir,' she protested. 'Once I essayed to read a book that was written as you talk. I understood not a word of it.'

'I'll swear the fault lay in the author as it now lies in me.'

'You swear, then, what you do not believe. The only virtue of that is its courtesy.'

And then came Mynheer Claessens to join them, and bid them in to table, where Danvelt — his contusions changed from blue to yellow — waited with the impatience of the healthy trencherman.

He announced whilst they broke their fast that he had written to his father and would presently be gratified for Mynheer Claessens's opinion on his letter. This moved a caustic humour in the merchant.

'Whatever my opinion, there can be no doubt of your father's, Philip. And it is his that will be interesting.'

Philip grunted, his mouth being too full of salted herring

for a clearer expression of his disgust at his host's deplorable mirth. Thus encouraged, Claessens continued:

'He'll clip your wings, my lad. He'll curb your thirst for travel by steering you firmly into the harbour of wedlock.'

'With all my heart!' cried Danvelt, his mouth being free at last. 'If he'll do that I'll count the thousand ducats well spent.' He laughed noisily, and ogled Mistress Johanna so bold and meaningly that Count Anthony asked himself was a furtherance of their union what Destiny had required of him?

'You spendthrift,' Claessens admonished him. 'Waste finds no favour in Johanna's eyes. She'll need to school you in thrift.'

The lad assumed an air of gallantry. 'She may school me in anything she pleases and just so soon as it is her pleasure to begin.'

Johanna offered no comment. She sat with eyes upon her plate, her countenance so set that nothing was to be read in it unless one looked closer than Count Anthony dared to look just then.

From what he had heard, he drew the conclusion that here a match was already settled. These children of two wealthy burghers were already destined to each other, no doubt with the object of amassing greater wealth by a combination of golden forces. That was the vain purpose of all burgher lives. He was conscious of a little chill at his heart, and suddenly was marvelling at himself. He was a Prince of the House of Guelders, after all, and heir to its throne. Was it possible that, almost without suspecting it, he should have been conceiving hopes where a burgher's daughter was concerned? If it chilled him to discover her fittingly betrothed to one of her own class, the sooner he departed the better for himself and others.

And so he spoke of his voyage to England, and desired to know when Mynheer Claessens could afford him passage.

CHAPTER VI

JOHANNA

'WHAT do you seek in England, Master Egmont?' she had asked him suddenly, and at her question his fingers, which had softly been stroking the lute-strings into sound, fell still.

That was on the afternoon of the following day, a day of wind and rain which kept them within doors. After dining, they had come to this bower of hers above the garden, from whose windows you looked out upon dunes and ramparts and more dunes, and then the sea, now grey and sullen and obscured in misty rain.

It was a pleasant chamber, hung with brightly coloured Flemish tapestries depicting sacred subjects. Here Michael, the celestial knight, with flaming sword, hurled Lucifer and his legions down in ruin. There Gabriel, bearing a lily-wand, descended on a cloud to make the Annunciation, and yonder Raphael stood rending the fish under the wondering gaze of young Tobias. In these archangelic surroundings Count Anthony had found a lute, a pretty thing of mulberry and ebony and ivory, with which he had retired to the ample window-seat.

His music reminded Mynheer Claessens that matters of importance demanded his presence in the counting-house, and sent the over-dined Danvelt into a profound slumber. Remained him for only audience Mistress Johanna, who came to occupy the other angle of the window-seat, and, herself but an indifferent performer, to admire his skill, which indeed was considerable, and to encourage him to continue in its exercise. From strumming little airs of Brabant and Picardy and his native Guelders, he was moved, perhaps by the sympathetic quality of his audience, to essay a little song which he had made. He did scarcely more than speak his lines to a rippling accompaniment of lute-strings.

He ceased, and in thoughtful silence they both sat awhile. The only sounds were the gentle patter of the rain outside and the stertorous breathing of the slumbering Danvelt. The young burgher sprawled uncouthly in his chair, with stumpy, ill-shaped hands locked tight across a paunch too heavy already for so young a man.

The maiden moved and sighed. Deep in her soul something had been quickened by that song, a new conception of life, its evanescence and its glory. Like one entranced, she sat until Count Anthony, perhaps to break the spell that was surcharging him, began softly to play a trivial, tripping dance measure. Then came her question: 'What do you seek in England?'

At the sound of her voice his playing ceased. He rose and went to set down the lute on a side table beside the bowl of white tulips disposed there by Johanna. Returning thence to the window, he stood looking out.

'If this weather holds,' he said casually, 'it will end by making me a burden on your hospitality.'

'Why do you go to England?' she asked him again, and thrilled him now by the direct form of the question.

'To follow in the footsteps of Lalaing.'

'Who was he?' she asked.

'You never heard of Jacques de Lalaing? He was a knight, a very perfect, gentle knight of Duke Philip's court, whose lovely brief life I have had the vainglory to take as a pattern for my own.'

He went on to tell her of Lalaing, of his prowess, his nobility, and his purity of heart. In the telling he spoke intimately of courts and their inhabitants, of a world which to her was almost fabulous, peopled by beings other indeed than herself and those among whom her days were spent.

'Like Lalaing,' he concluded, 'I go to England to make my endeavour, though not quite the endeavour that was his.'

'Are you a knight, then?' she asked him on a note of awe.

Almost he evaded her question.

'Something of a knight, I hope, God helping me. But

more troubadour than knight, and perhaps more fool than either. For who shall say what is wisdom?'

'Do you hope to discover that in England?'

He laughed. 'Faith, no.'

'Why, then, do you go there?'

'To seek reality, to break away from shams that threaten to enmesh me.'

'What is reality?' she asked him.

'A fruit upon the tree of truth.'

'And is that tree so difficult to discover?'

He looked down at her. 'You speak as if you knew its whereabouts.'

'I think I do. I was brought up in the shade of it. I have lived by the mercy of God in its shelter.'

He looked at her so long and intently and in such wistfulness that at last her glance fell in sheer embarrassment.

'Could you lead me to it?' he wondered, but so dreamily that it sounded as if he were thinking aloud and asking the question of himself.

It reached the waking senses of Danvelt, who croaked half-coherently, still slumber-laden: 'Lead you to what?'

The question brought Count Anthony to himself in two senses, and the whole truth lay in his startled ejaculation: 'God forgive me, Master Danvelt! I had forgotten your existence.'

'Forgotten it?' spluttered the burgher, and heaved himself up laughing. 'Continue to forget it and you'll save me a thousand ducats.'

Count Anthony, considering him as he rolled towards them with his swaggering gait, opined in his soul that a million ducats would not be too much to pay for such a privilege. It was a startling thought so self-revelatory that at his prayers that night the Count besought an abatement of the stormy weather to render possible his immediate going. Heaven, however, was deaf to the intercession. The weather grew worse, and for a week the gales persisted in the narrow seas and kept him waiting in that perilous haven. More than once he spoke of setting a term to what amounted to an abuse of hospitality and seeking quarters at the inn. But Mynheer Claessens sturdily opposed him. No hospitality of his, he asserted, could ever be abused by one who had served his young friend Danvelt so nobly, which again but served to remind the Count of the closer kinship with Danvelt which was commonly desired.

Of this desire Claessens was driven in those days to speak to his daughter by an event that fell upon them like a bolt from the blue.

The young burgher's letter to his father had been despatched, and Claessens waited to enjoy the laugh which the sequel should afford. But the sequel when it came may have provoked the laughter of the ironic gods; it provoked not Claessens's.

The elder Danvelt read that ill-scrawled missive from his son, of whose endowments he had never held a high opinion. When he had read, he stood a moment without breathing, his face convulsed. Then his lips began to utter a horrible imprecation that was never finished. He crashed full length upon the floor of his counting-house in a fit of apoplexy, and expired that same evening. Like his son, he was too short in the neck for such shocks as this.

When the news reached Philip Danvelt in Flushing, it sent him off in appalled and contrite haste to Middelburg to perform the last duties by a father whose days he bitterly blamed his own conduct for having shortened.

The event pointed to consequences which Mynheer Claessens mentioned on the morrow to his daughter. He spoke gently, a note of regret in his voice.

'Now that Philip is master of his fortune, I shall be losing you soon, Johanna.'

The roses faded slowly from her cheeks. 'You mean that . . .' She paused. 'I don't know,' she said slowly.

'You don't know?' He smiled a little wistfully. 'But I know; and Philip knows.'

'I don't think I want to leave you, father.'

'You are aware of my need of you, and that is sweet. You were always sweet, Johanna. No man was ever more truly blessed in his child.' He stroked the golden head very tenderly. 'Your mother in heaven will be proud of you, my dear, as I am.' He sighed. 'I shall miss you when you go. But I should be a selfish ingrate to detain you, when your own interest and happiness beckon you away.'

There fell a long silence at the end of which she looked up, and he saw that her eyes were full of trouble. 'May I speak frankly, father?'

'I should not know you if you spoke otherwise.'

'I am not sure that my happiness lies with Philip.'

'Not sure?' Claessens was startled. 'But you are promised to him.'

'I was no party to the promise, father.'

'Nor was Philip. But he's fond of you. Old Danvelt and I knew what was good for both of you. Your fortunes united will make you very rich.'

'Is wealth the only consideration?'

'The chief consideration, as you'll come to discover. And, for the rest, Philip's a good fellow, good-natured, kindly. He'll make you a good husband, never doubt it.'

'Not if I do not love him, father.'

'Love! Love comes with habit, child. Take my word for it.'

She shook her head. 'I must judge for myself in this; judge as my heart bids me.'

Claessens was troubled, and went as near impatience as it lay in his kindly, phlegmatic nature. 'But what ails Philip?'

'Heaven forbid that I should have a fault to find with him.'

'Why, then, all's well. A solid lad. Not perhaps of the grace and airs of such men as Master Egmont, but of a worth that seldom goes with such outward virtues.'

'Master Egmont's virtues are not outward only,' she said, and flushed at her tongue's too-ready betrayal of her mind.

He frowned as he looked at her. 'God save us! This stranger isn't the cause of your looking coldly upon Philip? It isn't that . . .?'

She made haste to interrupt him. 'No, no. It is only that I like and respect Master Egmont. Therefore I will assume nothing unflattering to him. That is all.'

'It seems a deal, child, considering that we know nothing of this man.'

'Oh, something, I think. We know that he is chivalrous and pitiful, and we know that he commands an abundance of this wealth of which you make a virtue. So much is shown by the act that linked him to Philip. We know also that he is courtly, gracious and accomplished. So much our senses tell us.'

'You defend him warmly, child; more warmly than you need, I think. In a few days, when this weather eases, he'll go his ways, and we are not likely ever to see him again.'

She did not answer him in words, but had he looked close he would have discovered more pain in her eyes than he had ever seen there.

He said no more to Johanna just then on the subject of Philip. A wise man this Claessens, in more than the ways of trade. But that evening after supper, sitting alone with his guest, he returned to the subject of his daughter's coming marriage, informing the Count that from childhood she had been promised to Danvelt. And Count Anthony perceived quite clearly the merchant's object in this confidence.

Claessens knew of his guest no more than was to be read in his actions and externals. From these he judged him a man of courts, of noble blood, of a different clay from himself, and he had a strong and well-justified prejudice against unions where such disparity existed. In addition to this, knowledge of the world warned him that, whilst such men as his guest do not marry women of the burgher class, they rarely hesitate to become their lovers, even when they were men of scrupulous honour. He judged this Master Egmont to be something even more. There was a fundamental pitifulness in his nature which would withhold him from doing anything to another's hurt, and there was a lofty dignity which would keep him aloof from banal gallantries. Claessens knew also that his daughter's virtue was a rock. So that between the two he discerned no cause for anxiety; and yet he prayed as fervently as Count Anthony for the fine weather that should permit his guest's departure.

These prayers were answered at last on the morrow. The leaden pall of the heavens broke, the sun shone clear and warm, and the wind died down.

Claessens was able to inform his guest that the sloop which had been waiting to leave port would sail on the next day. Count Anthony thanked Heaven, and was downcast. Thereafter he wandered in the garden with Johanna, a sad garden, damp and battered by the storm.

'You will be glad,' she said, 'to win release at last.'

If the question was in itself a probing one, it was robbed of any such quality by being delivered without suspicion of archness or challenge.

'Release?' echoed Count Anthony. 'I am a boor, indeed, if I have conveyed any sense of impatience at the sojourn here imposed upon me.'

'Ah! But there is your quest.'

'I am not sure that it has not ended already; that I have not found here the only reality worthy a man's seeking.'

She was conscious of quickened heartbeats. Instinctively, in maidenly self-defence, she affected to misunderstand where there was no room for misunderstanding.

'Reality is of many kinds. Here we show you but the somnolent, peaceful sort.'

'Peaceful; not somnolent. Could any show me a better?'

'It depends, sir, upon what you seek; upon the inclinations of your nature.'

'The inclinations of my nature?' There was a rising inflexion in his voice. Then he fetched a sigh. 'Who dares to follow the inclinations of his nature?'

Very gently, as if she read his mind, she answered him.

'All those, I think, who have the courage and the wisdom.'

It startled him to be brought thus face to face with a
truth so simple, plain, and obvious. He looked at her where
she stood beside him, her golden head on a line with his
shoulder, her eyes averted, the colour ebbing and flowing in
her cheeks. For an instant he was assailed by a fierce desire
to take that lovely head in his hands, and to inhale from it
the essences of her being as one inhales the perfume of a
flower. No other man of his station would be so nice in his
handling of this burgher's daughter. Thus a voice within
him whispered insidiously, and at once he knew it for the
voice of the Devil, grown overbold with him in this moment
of his very human weakness. Who harboured a thought de-
filing to the purity and candour of this maid did but defile
himself. If this emotion which she aroused in him was love
— the greatest, perhaps the only, reality of life — then let
him count the world well lost for it. Let him offer himself
here as lover and as husband, and if she took him let him re-
nounce the world to which he belonged and the throne that
ultimately awaited him, and adopt for his own the humbler
world of which she was a part. What was it she had said?
To follow the inclinations of one's nature was for those who
had the courage and the wisdom.

When, at last, having applied the test, he broke the silence, it was to say:

'I am a coward and a fool, Johanna.'

She trembled to hear him speak her name. On his lips it
bore a sound she had never before heard in it, acquired a
beauty unsuspected hitherto.

'In what?' she asked him.

'In that I lack both courage and wisdom according to your
just conception.'

She knew what he meant, knew that the strength to whose
lack he alluded was the strength to climb certain barriers between them, barriers of blood which already she had sensed.
If a cold shadow fell across her soul, if a daring, half-formed

hope withered in her maiden heart, her brave spirit allowed no sign of it to show upon the surface.

Next day he sailed for England, and her world was empty: empty because of the going of a man of whose existence ten days ago she had not been conscious. For comfort she clung to the hope that he would come again, a hope begotten of his last words.

'I leave my horses, by your father's favour. My Schimmel is a gentle palfrey that would bear a child in safety. Use him freely until I come again, and, if I do not come again, retain him for your own as an earnest of the gratitude I bear you.'

'Gratitude?' she echoed, who desired almost anything but that of him. 'For what are you grateful?'

'To you, for more than I could tell,' he said. 'To God, for having known you, Johanna.'

Whilst she stood stricken dumb by that, his lips touched her hand for the first and last time, in all reverence, and he was gone.

She found herself suddenly in tears, and, eluding her father before he should discover it, went to seek consolation in prayer.

Thereafter she took to riding daily as she had never ridden before. Mounted on the big white horse, with her father's servant Jan following on the bay which had belonged to Count Anthony's groom, she made long excursions into the surrounding country, and talked at long length to Schimmel of his master.

A fortnight later, Philip Danvelt returned from Middelburg, and he was not quite the same man who had last gone thither. His accession to a fortune far greater than he had suspected had wrought a change in him. The roll of his gait was increased; on his short neck he carried his head still farther back, so that his nose seemed more aggressive even than heretofore; he was more ponderous of speech and of manner. Although in black, he was dressed with a richness beyond a merchant's station, and he wore his finery none too well. His round hat with the peaked brim carried now a feather brooched into the side of it by a jewel of price, and a jewel of price gleamed upon one of his stumpy fingers. He would have suffered sorely for all this in Mynheer Claessens's esteem had not the kindly man supposed that this fine plumage was assumed for the fascination of Johanna.

He craved news of Egmont, speaking of him boldly as his dear friend, and he desired to know if Claessens had supplied him at parting with any portion of the moneys due.

'He asked for none,' said Claessens. 'He never spoke of it. And when at parting I broached the subject on your behalf, he waved it aside as of no importance.'

'Ay, ay! That's like him,' said Master Philip. 'He treats money as if it were just mud.'

'That is how he thinks of it,' said Johanna.

'He must be either fabulously wealthy or fabulously mad,' said Claessens.

'A little of both,' Master Philip assured them with his loud, fatuous laugh, suddenly checked by Johanna.

'Do you thank God for it, Philip.'

Her championing the absent pleased Master Danvelt none too well. For all that he was made dull by smug complacency, he caught in her voice a note that was hostile to himself. It stirred an uneasiness in him. To allay it, he opened the subject of marriage that night to Claessens.

'It's my belief,' he announced ponderously, 'that a man should settle early.'

'Ay, ay,' said Claessens drily. 'You'll have had enough of travel.'

Philip did not consider the interruption amusing.

'I need a wife, and I've a fine house up there in Middelburg awaiting a mistress. If you're willing, then, good Master Claessens . . .' He spread his hands, deeming it unnecessary to complete the sentence.

Good Master Claessens felt that he was being used with patronage, and was between amusement and resentment.

'It's not my willingness you must ascertain; but Johan-

na's,' was his answer, calculated to give pause to the young
man. It had, however, no such effect.

Philip laughed shortly, a very self-assured master of his
fate.

'Oh, that!' Airily he dismissed the possibility of Johanna's having any but one opinion in the matter. 'I'll speak to
Johanna in the morning.'

The affair thus comfortably dismissed, he passed to other
things: the state of trade in Middelburg; the fortune inherited from his father; the opportunities for increasing it
which his father had neglected; and the gerency of it which
he intended. So that when at last, full of beer and self-
sufficiency, Master Philip retired to bed, it occurred to
Claessens that perhaps Johanna was right in her lack of
eagerness for these nuptials planned so long ago.

In the morning when Philip came late to breakfast, Johanna was away, scouring the country on Count Anthony's
big white palfrey. It astounded Philip that she should do it,
and still more that her father should permit it. He said so,
and enlarged upon his views of a woman's functions in life.
This sort of thing might be well enough for idle wantons
of the court, but was hardly seemly in a sober burgher
woman.

Receiving but indifferent sympathy from the father,
Master Danvelt addressed the daughter in the matter later
in the day. She listened meekly, struggling generously
against the conviction that he was stupid, pompous, and un-
couth, and never so ridiculous as when he regarded his own
opinions as unalterable laws.

'But what harm do I do, Philip?'

He was impatient that she should require the obvious to
be constantly explained.

'No great harm, perhaps. But it's unbecoming in a maid
of your station.'

She considered that Master Egmont had not deemed it
unbecoming, else he would not have left her the palfrey; and
in matters of taste she must account him a sounder arbiter

than Master Philip. At last she said slowly: 'That is a question for my father, Philip.'

'And for your husband,' he snapped.

'When I have one, perhaps.'

'For your future husband, meanwhile.'

'How can I say what my future husband will approve?'

'I am telling you.'

'But you can speak only for yourself, Philip.'

'I am speaking for myself. Am I not to marry you?

'This is very condescending, Philip.'

Missing the irony, he was a little mollified.

'I admonish you for your own good — out of my affection for you.'

'I am grateful. But am I worthy?'

He considered this, and evaded a reply that might go to her head. He liked a woman to be humble.

'My affairs in Middelburg, now that my father has gone and all the burden is on my shoulders, make it difficult for me to come and go. We must cut short our courtship, Johanna. We might be married, I think, before the end of the month.'

She went white. She sat with hands folded in her lap, her downcast eyes considering them.

'It is impossible, Philip,' she quietly answered him.

'How soon, then?' he demanded, and never was lover more peremptory.

She drew a deep breath before replying. 'Philip, my dear, it should be easy for you to find in Middelburg a wife better suited to you than I am.'

This made him impatient. Humility in women is well enough. This, however, was pushing things too far.

'But I love you, Johanna!' he exclaimed in protest.

'I was wondering if you did. I hoped that you did not.'

'You hoped that I did not? When you are to marry me!'

She rose now and confronted him frankly, calm save for a gleam of distress in those clear eyes. 'Philip, dear, I have a friendship for you; even affection. But it is not the kind of affection that should exist between husband and wife if they are to be happy.'

'Why? What do you know of such things?' He was aghast.

'Knowledge has come to me,' she said wistfully.

'Whence?' he demanded.

She paused a moment before replying. 'From myself, of course. Whence else should such knowledge come?'

He laughed through his perturbation. 'But all that will follow. It always does. Trust me, Johanna. I understand these things: life and the rest. I love you, Johanna,' he said again, and now at last became a lover in earnest and began humbly and with some warmth to woo that which unopposed he would phlegmatically have appropriated.

It moved her, distressed her, shook her resolve a little, but did not suffice to beat it down. When she had made this clear, he collapsed in dismayed amazement. 'Then all that our parents planned is to come to naught!'

Gently she stroked his yellow head, as he sat hunched in his chair. 'I am sorry, Philip.'

So pitiful was her nature and so touched was she by his manifest distress that, out of charity, to allay it, had he pressed the matter then, she might have yielded. As it was, she found it in her heart to wish that Master Egmont had never crossed her path to reveal her to herself.

The dejected Philip bore his lament to her father. Gravely Claessens heard him, and thought in his heart that what had happened was very good for Philip's soul and might yet shape him into such a man as Johanna should ultimately be content to marry.

'You've ruffled her, my lad. That's all,' Claessens comforted him. 'You are too downright and blunt. Women need to be coaxed.' Philip snorted impatiently. 'Oh! A good woman's worth coaxing. Take my word for it. I am twice your age. And a maid will often say no to a man at first, and be glad enough to say yes in the end. Johanna is not a girl to be constrained, nor am I the man to constrain her. But I'll advise her — cautiously. I desire to see you joined, and she'll have you in the end. But give her time, and play the lover; pay court to her. Could you be romantic, Philip?'

'What's that?' said Philip.

'I don't know. But Johanna might school you.'

His dejection mitigated by such hope as he could gather from what her father had said, Philip went back to Middelburg, whence came gifts for Johanna, to herald his return a fortnight later. He stayed two days, was discreet, and beyond a tender attentiveness made no advance in the wooing upon which he was now determined.

CHAPTER VII

FRIAR STEPHEN

In the first days of June, Master Danvelt received from his prospective father-in-law a letter in the following terms:

'Dear Philip: Master Egmont has just returned from England, and is lodged here at the Zeelanderhof. If we looked to see him ever again, at least we did not look to see him so soon, and I must suppose the cause of this early return to be that he did not find England to his taste, although I perceive that other reasons may exist. However that may be, his presence affords you the opportunity you desire to discharge your debt to him, and I advise you to take instant advantage of it, in the assurance that our welcome awaits you.'

There was a good deal to be read between the lines of that letter. Claessens stressed the fact that Master Egmont's return so soon had not been expected, hinted that the reason for it was to be sought elsewhere than in the vaguely apparent reasons he mentioned, and almost succeeded in suggesting that the gentleman's presence was not welcome. His urging the immediate discharge of the debt might be suspected to be founded on the fact that once the debt were discharged this guest would have no pretext for lingering.

Master Claessens certainly intended to convey all this and more to Philip; but because at once kindly and shrewd, he could not bring himself to use more precise expressions or to disclose the source of his disquietude. This had begun in the very moment of Master Egmont's arrival. The burgher and his daughter had just dined and they were still at table, when through the open window they heard his voice in the courtyard, addressing first the stork, by its name of Peter, and then Jan who had opened to him. At the sound of that voice, Johanna's breathing had stood suddenly arrested, her face had gone white, and her hand had fled instinctively to repress the tumult of her breast. Then, the shock being spent, the colour came flooding back to her cheeks; she sprang up with parted lips and a joyous sparkle in eyes which of late had been so sad and pensive.

Her watchful father observed these signs. Already in Flanders was a proverb current which much later was thus rendered into French: *Amour qui rougit, fleurette; amour qui palît, drame du cœur*. It occurred to Claessens in that moment; and his heart grew heavy with anxiety for her.

Nevertheless his welcome of the traveller was cordial. Master Egmont was bidden to table, and Jan and Gabriel ordered to supply his wants as generously as larder and cellar would permit.

He was pale and a little careworn; but his dark eyes glowed as they met Johanna's; his lips laughed readily, and soon there was a return of that radiance that men remarked in him.

He had landed, he informed them, an hour ago, and he was lodged at the Zeelanderhof, in the market-place. Father and daughter protested against this in different keys. But the Count was firm. Enough already had he burdened their hospitality. He remained, however, all day with them, entertaining them with descriptions of England and English life, which, after all, was none so different from their own.

That night Johanna came to supper in a gown of sapphire blue, with some simple jewels in her hair and breast, and seemed to her father a being transfigured. Both he and their guest had heard her singing whilst she attired herself with this more than usual care, and there was in this singing a message for each of them. Claessens was reminded by it that he had not heard her voice in song since Master Egmont had left them six weeks before, whilst Count Anthony was startled to hear from her lips the little song he had made and sung to her last April. It thrilled him that she should have borne it in her memory.

There chanced to be a second guest at Master Claessens's

table that night: a Franciscan brother, one of those itinerant friars who wandered through the land supplying the place to be taken in later ages by the news-sheet. Rarely did one of these brethren pass through Flushing without seeking bed and board in the hospitable house of Claessens and in exchange for these comforts retailing to the merchant and his household the current events in the world.

To-night this little brother of Saint Francis had a greater than usual store of gossip for them. Seated there in his coarse grey habit, the cowl of which was thrown back, so that his tonsure, freshly shaven, gleamed within its circlet of greying hair, his twinkling eyes beamed upon the little company from his benign and rubicund countenance. A man of fifty, perhaps, this Brother Stephen, vigorous and still youthful; a man who enjoyed good fare and yet knew how to live hard at need, thanking God for whatever came.

He was last from Bruges, he told them, where the Duke had now established his court; and he began by speaking of the great preparations there for the Duke's wedding to the sister of the King of England, shortly to be celebrated. Very subtly then, by terms in which it would have been difficult afterwards to have incriminated him, he created the impression that this was a union that boded ill for the land. An alliance with England, such as this marriage consolidated, could not be other than an alliance against France, an alliance aiming at the furtherance of the Duke of Burgundy's insatiable ambition. This implied war, and, if the Duke made war with Burgundian lances, he made it none the less with Flemish gold. It would mean a crushing burden of taxation upon the Netherlands already burdened to excess, and this at a time when their normal trade would be dislocated and their normal prosperity stemmed.

Listening to him, Count Anthony recognized him for a Frenchman by his accent, and suddenly asked himself was he one of the agents of the crafty King of France sent thus to sow alarm and discontent through the Duke's dominions and foment among these subject people the spirit of revolt?

Returning, however, to the preparations for the wedding, Friar Stephen told them how the looms were being driven at high speed in the manufacture of tapestries and other fabrics, how painters and artificers of every kind were hard at work upon decorations and embellishments that should be worthy of Burgundian splendour and Burgundian opulence.

He spoke of the bride. Rumour ran that this English-woman, favouring her royal brother, was very beautiful, and he told of jewellers and goldsmiths hard at work upon confections becomingly to deck this royal beauty.

Next he related how the vast tennis-court at Bruges was being fashioned into a banqueting-hall, and the great square into a tilt-yard. He spoke of mummers and minstrels who were pouring into the city of Bruges from every quarter of Europe; of the great displays that were to be made by the foreign trading corporations, especially the Venetians and the Genoese; and of the expected concourse of renowned knights from every quarter of Christendy, who were to display their prowess in the jousts to be held in honour of the event, foremost amongst whom, Brother Stephen knew, would be that famous champion Anthony of Burgundy, the Great Bastard.

He spoke fluently in well-chosen words that painted vivid pictures, yet so craftily that when most he seemed to admire and laud the Duke of Burgundy, the more effectively did he damn him in Flemish eyes. For the ultimate impression he created was one of a monstrous prodigality, of a reckless scattering of gold exacted for these empty splendours from those who had earned it by the sweat of their brows, the skill of their hands, and the laborious cunning of their invention.

And then, because it served his purpose — which to one listener at least grew plainer with every word he uttered — he passed abruptly from Anthony of Burgundy to another Anthony no less famous at the Burgundian Court: Count

Anthony of Guelders. He spoke of him with a sudden over-clouding of his benign countenance. That, he announced, was a knight of a very different order from his Burgundian namesake; a prince of sweet and gentle ways, ever the friend and champion of the afflicted; scholar and poet, soldier and statesman; there was a man of parts, gracious and graceful of person, beloved of all, yet of none so beloved as of the Duke's highness, who, stern, grim, and unyielding as he was to all the world, could be melted and even led by Count Anthony.

'But what's here to sadden you?' wondered Claessens, alluding to the lugubrious tone in which the friar extolled the virtues of this prince of the house of Guelders.

'Alas!' sighed Brother Stephen. 'He is gone, the one good influence in that prodigal court; gone no man knows whither; vanished in a night. He quitted the court when it was at Brussels, close upon a year ago. There have been rumours of him, here and there, but the Duke has failed to trace him, and it is thought that he has gone abroad. It is most sad. The Duke, they say, is more morose and sullen than ever as a result of the affair.'

'Why did he go?' inquired Johanna.

'Ah, that!' The friar raised his eyes and fetched a sigh. 'His highness would have had him marry where he did not love. He was formally betrothed to the Duke's sister-in-law, the Lady Catharine of Bourbon, a very sweet lady; indeed, they say the most beautiful lady at the court. Yet for all her beauty my Lord Anthony would have none of her. He was very difficult, very exacting and fastidious where ladies are concerned, and, though many there are who were known to sigh for him, it is boldly asserted that he was never known to sigh for any. He is of an austerity such as finds no place in courts. The ribald make jests of it; unseemly jests, and suggest for him the cloister. The Duke would have forced him into this marriage. To avoid it and because sickened in other ways — as so austere a man might well be — of courtly life, he disappeared.'

'Why, that says more for him than all your eulogies, good brother,' Johanna commented.

'My eulogies had not been spoken else,' the friar agreed. 'Another in his place would have married the Lady Catharine, and loved when and where he pleased. But Count Anthony has sworn, they say, to marry only where he loves.'

'Which is surely the only marriage in the sight of God,' said Johanna. 'It is love that sanctifies marriage.'

'Nay, nay; sanctification is the work of Holy Mother Church, my child.'

'Can Holy Church sanctify a thing so unholy in itself as a loveless union?'

The friar, no stronger in theology than most minorites, evaded the awkward question.

'Where the Church bestows her blessing all things are possible!'

And then Claessens, well knowing what passed in his daughter's mind, attempted to divert the argument.

'But his flight hardly savours of high courage, such as one would look for in the man you have described.'

Count Anthony, who hitherto had sat a silent listener in the background and a little in shadow, laughed softly. Claessens turned to him.

'You laugh, sir! Why?'

'Because, good Master Claessens, you do not know Duke Charles of Burgundy, his indomitable will and his remorseless powers of persuasion, strengthened by the growing belief that he is divinely inspired.'

'You speak with feeling almost, Master Egmont,' said the burgher.

'Oh! Based on common knowledge,' was the Count's disarming answer.

But it did not disarm the friar. 'Egmont!' he had echoed, when that name was pronounced, and had continued to stare at the elegant figure sitting just beyond the edge of the light. To one who plied his Mercury vocation, this was not a name to pass unquestioned. His perceptions were quickened by it, and almost at a glance he identified that tawny head and lofty brow, those glowing eyes and that sensitive mouth, with the descriptions he had heard of the missing Prince of the House of Guelders. His jaw fell; his eyes dilated.

Count Anthony, realizing that he was discovered, spoke quickly, before the friar could sufficiently recover from his amazement to utter a single word. He, too, could be subtle, as he now showed this subtle friar.

'All things considered, it is little wonder that the disappearance of the Count has been made possible. Who that knew his whereabouts would ever betray him? It were even more wantonly cruel than, for instance, to betray certain indiscretions into which, speaking here in all confidence, you have been lured to-night.'

The friar's jaws came sharply together again. He understood perfectly. What Count Anthony was really saying to him was: 'You keep my secret, and I'll keep yours.' It was not a matter in which he had any choice. The thought of what might happen to him, if he refused this proffered bargain, turned him cold with apprehension. It put an end to his newsmongering for that night, and soon thereafter he begged leave to seek his bed. But the question stirring tumultuously in his brain was: 'What does Count Anthony of Guelders with masked identity seek in this burgher household?'

Knowing his world and its wickedness, he could find but one answer; and it appalled him. Was it possible that, under a cloak of virtue, almost of saintliness, which had earned him the sobriquet of 'Anthony the Chaste,' this elegant, accomplished prince was a libertine and a seducer? Since honest love, aiming at wedlock, was inconceivable between this Prince of Guelders and a burgher's daughter, what else was to be concluded?

Friar Stephen was oppressed. The habit he wore, and to which he was faithful in spite of certain political undertakings, imposed upon him here a clear duty. Yet the con-

viction that, if he now betrayed Count Anthony's identity,
Count Anthony would inevitably betray his activities, and
thus deliver him to the cord, set upon that duty an iron curb.

He bethought him of the Latin tag, *In medio tutissimus
ibi*, and sought the middle course.

When Jan had lighted him to his chamber, and Johanna
had accompanied him thither, doing the honours of her father's house, he detained her a moment, waving Jan away.

'This Messire Egmont, child? Have you known him
long?'

Briefly she told him the extent of their acquaintance and
whence it was sprung.

'What brings him back here?' he asked, holding the candle so that the light fell upon her face. He saw the crimson
flush that overspread it, and deemed his worst fears verified.

She faltered a little in her reply. 'There are certain
moneys due to him.'

'And is that all?'

'What else do you suspect, good brother?'

He set a hand upon her shoulder. His eyes were kindly,
pitiful.

'I bid you beware, child. Beware of him and of yourself.'

'Beware of him? Of him?' She smiled her scorn of the
warning.

'He is a man of courts, of noble blood. He bears it written
plainly upon him. He may be virtuous. I do not know. I
do not say that he is not. God forbid that I should judge a
man without full grounds. But there is little virtue in the
world to which he belongs, especially in dealing with those of
the world which is yours, my child. God and the Virgin
Mother keep you spotless.'

She was crimson again, but not now in confusion, and her
clear, frank eyes were almost hard for once. Without raising
her voice, she gave an edge to her words.

'Such is my nightly prayer,' she informed him. 'Do you
pray God and the Virgin Mother to give you purity of mind
and to save you from the sin of thinking evil.'

On that she departed, leaving the good man uplifted by her rebuke. Clearly no harm had come to her yet. He was in time. But in time for what? Seeking the answer to this question, Brother Stephen fell asleep. He was seeking it still when he awakened next morning, and found it during the brief business of donning his Franciscan garments. He might be risking his neck, but he thought not, for he was subtle and had devised a subtlety; and in any case he was strengthened by the godly assurance that he risked his neck in a good cause.

Towards noon of that same day, at about the same time that Master Claessens's letter was being delivered to Philip Danvelt, Brother Stephen came, dusty and famished, into the grey courtyard of the Gravenhof of Middelburg, the seat of the Ducal Governor of Zealand, and craved audience of that august personage.

CHAPTER VIII

THE INTERRUPTION

A MAN chooses the instruments of his will according to his nature. Duke Charles of Burgundy, being a stern, uncompromising man of the sword, chose stern, uncompromising soldiers for his representatives, and of these — saving perhaps the Alsatian von Hagenbach, whose ruthlessness ultimately helped to encompass the Duke's ruin — none was more stern and uncompromising than the Sire Claude de Rhynsault, the Lorrainer who ruled as the Duke's Governor in Zealand.

He owed the appointment to his conduct at Montlhéry, where by luck or skill he had contrived a movement with the lances under his command which at a critical moment of the day turned the fortunes of the battle in the Duke's favour. He had, too, an ingratiating manner with his superiors, and it is not to be denied that he had given proofs of organizing ability. So the Duke had sent him to Zealand until such time as he should have need of him in the field again; and in Zealand the Sire de Rhynsault had justified his appointment. He had shown himself an able administrator; he maintained an iron grip upon the province, crushing the first sparks of sedition so quickly that no sedition was heard of in his government, and squeezing the taxes so promptly and abundantly out of the Zealanders that the Duke had come to hold him up as a pattern to the governors of his other provinces. For the rest, he was easy of access, of a certain gross superficial affability, and so insatiable an animal where women were concerned that no burgher owning a handsome wife or daughter could ever be entirely at ease.

Such was the man sought by Brother Stephen as the instrument for the preservation of a maiden's virtue. Fortunately, Rhynsault was not to know more than half of what was required of him.

The friar was ushered across a bare stone hall, where men-at-arms lounged in attendance, into a little tapestry-hung closet, lighted by a single narrow window above the court-yard. Here at a table, in a high carved Gothic chair, sat the dread Governor of Zealand, a big man, still young, with a red vulpine face and blue-black jowl, the livid streak of a scar athwart his fleshy nose. Disliking clerics, he scowled now upon his visitor.

'Ha, friar! What news is this you boast will make you welcome?'

On a faldstool at the table's end, nursing one leg across the thigh of the other, sat the Governor's Fool, a wisp of a man with a humped back, in a parti-coloured suit of black and purple; each point of the chaperon carried a tiny silver bell and its hood was crested by a cock's comb. His long, pallid, sallow face was of the delicate and elfin kind so often seen upon such misshapen men, but out of his little close-set eyes, bright and glittering as a rat's, more evil looked upon the world than Brother Stephen had ever seen in human countenance. The friar shuddered as he met the probing stab of those beady eyes. Then he shifted his glance to the Governor and made answer:

'Your excellency will have heard of the disappearance of Count Anthony of Guelders?'

'By the blood of the Pope!' croaked the Governor, 'are you come here to ask foolish questions?'

Brother Stephen was not ruffled. 'That is your excellency's way of answering in the affirmative. Count Anthony was last seen, as the Sire de Vauclerc reported to the Duke's highness, at Ghent in March last, when he went to the assistance of a burgher who had ventured to speak amiss of the Duke. He left Ghent in the company of that burgher, and has not since been heard of.'

'Well? What then?' The Governor was contemptuous of all this.

'The Duke, who has had diligent search made for the Count . . .'

'Ay, ay, I am aware of that. I have certain orders in the matter.'

'. . . would account himself well served by any who should send the Count back to him.'

'Sir, when will you cease to tell me what I know?'

'A little patience, excellency. You may not know that the burgher whom he befriended is a merchant of this city of Middelburg, one Philip Danvelt, at the moment to be found here?'

That moved the Governor. 'Danvelt!' he cried. 'That greasy moneybags?'

'Now, God be praised, I have given your excellency news at last! May I presume to add a word of advice?'

'Are you wanting in respect, sniveller?' The Lorrainer scowled at him, annoyed by his faint note of irony.

The friar was not dismayed. 'It is that you question Danvelt as to what became of his companion.'

'God's light! I'll question him: ay, and wring an answer from him if I have to put a length of whipcord round his temples.'

'Even at this late date he may be able to set you on the track of him; and so, to your increasing honour and profit, you may do good service to the Duke's Highness, whom God preserve. Have I your excellency's leave to go?'

'You're mighty abrupt, Master Franciscan!'

'I would not unnecessarily waste your excellency's time now that I've said all that I came to say.'

'Ay, ay, go your ways,' the Governor dismissed him.

'*Pax vobiscum*,' said the friar, drawing his cowl over his head, and turning to depart.

'*Domine non sum dignus*,' croaked the Fool, to mock him; and Brother Stephen, shuddering at the sound of that voice as he had shuddered under the glance of the Fool's eye, withdrew in haste, yet knowing his work well done.

Within a half-hour an officer from the Governor waited

upon Master Danvelt with a summons from his excellency. Master Danvelt truculently announced that he was about to set out upon a journey, and required to know what the Governor desired of him.

'His excellency will tell you,' said the officer, 'and the more pleasantly, the less you keep him waiting.'

Resentful, and grumbling to support his importance, Danvelt went.

'I am reminded,' the Governor greeted him, 'that in Ghent last April you were in trouble for sedition-mongering.'

'Not that,' said Master Philip. He excused himself without humility, indeed with a certain retention of his erstwhile truculence. 'In my cups I was incautious, and uttered some follies, as men will in their cups. I have paid for that.'

'Oh, you've paid, have you, sirrah merchant? Now give heed to me or you may have to pay again. There was a gentleman advanced you the sum you needed for your fine. You'll remember that?'

'I remember. Yes.' He was merely sullen now.

'Do you recall his name?'

'Of course. It was Egmont. Anthony Egmont.'

'Impudent buffoon! Is that a way for such as you to speak of him?'

'How else should I speak of him?'

'How else? Don't you know who he is?'

'Not if he is anything more than Anthony Egmont. That is all I know of him.'

'Do you know where he is at present?'

'Why, yes: at Flushing, at the Zeelanderhof.'

'Oho!' cried Rhynsault, and 'So! So!' with a raising of brows and a widening of eyes.

Danvelt was dismissed with scant courtesy and in deep resentment of the cavalier treatment received, also in some uneasiness. Returning home, he ordered horses to be saddled, and, accompanied by a groom, set out for Flushing.

Now it happened that Count Anthony and Mistress Johanna were riding by the same road, returning from a little excursion along the dykes. Followed at a respectful distance by Jan and the Count's groom François, they rode with the sparkling sea on their right, whence came a cool breeze to temper the warmth of the June sunshine, and the dunes on their left, with here and there the trees and fields of an occasional polder, like a green oasis in that sandy, silt-born land.

Johanna in a trailing habit of green, her eyes asparkle, her cheeks delicately flushed, with golden tendrils escaping from the band of her horned headdress, was mounted upon Schimmel by the Count's insistence, whilst the Count himself was astride the bay that hitherto had served his groom. The servants followed on hackneys from Mynheer Claessens's stable.

There had been little talk between them, and that little was confined to trivial matters. Then a long silence fell, which Johanna made no attempt to break, happy to be so entirely alone with him. His own happiness was clouded by indecision. Silently he rode, balancing still between the natural inclinations which had brought him back to her so soon, almost despite himself, and the preoccupations of his class, his duty, as he conceived it, to the station into which he had been born. To a man less scrupulous the solution would have been easy. But for Count Anthony the only choice lay between all and nothing. Either he would make her his wife and face the consequences, which might include his being struck out of the succession to the throne of Guelders, or else he would depart again in silence, and this time never to come back.

It was the intolerable quality in the second alternative that drove him still undecided toward the first. Still undecided, he broke at last the silence, hoping to be drifted to a decision by the very turn their speech should take.

'You knew — did you not — that I should return?'

'I hoped it,' she added softly, and only when the words were spoken did she realize, in alarm, their too candid import, and seek to explain them away. 'You see, there was a debt to be repaid you, and there was Schimmel here to be restored.'

But Count Anthony was not to be misled. His heart had leaped at the full admission of that soft 'I hoped it.'

'The debt was naught, and Schimmel my gift to you. You know that it was for neither of these things I came.'

She did not answer. Her eyes were hidden behind veiling lids. Her bosom betrayed a quickened breathing that was not from riding. Indeed, for some time now their horses had fallen to a walking pace. Count Anthony leaned across and placed his gloved right hand on hers, where it rested on the peak of the saddle.

'It was you, Johanna, who compelled my return, shortening my sojourn overseas, filling me with a nostalgy that grew unbearable. You knew it, child.'

She shook her head. 'How could I have such knowledge?'

'How? It is the kind of knowledge that is imparted without words, in the silent language in which soul talks to soul.' He pointed southwestwards across the sea. 'Out there I heard your call. From out there you heard the voice of my deep yearning.'

'Ah, no! Not that!'

'Ah, yes! Just that. But you would not heed it. You fancied it a voice within yourself. You did not know, you would not guess, that time and space do not exist for two souls that are in tune each with the other. And it is my faith that it was always so. Do you recall, Johanna, our first meeting?'

'Do I recall it?' Her tone announced the impossibility of forgetting it. 'I see you now, so clearly, in the courtyard of my father's house. You were all in black, with lynx-fur at the hem and neck and wrists of your tunic, that girdle of hammered gold about your wrist. You looked at me . . .' In sudden shyness she broke off.

Nor did he, lover-like, implore her to continue. He shook his head; and, although his lips were smiling, his eyes were wistful. 'Was that, then, really our first meeting? Did no memory stir in you of something remote, half-lost in the mists of time?'

She turned her head to look at him between tenderness and mystification.

'I do not understand.'

He sighed. 'You'll count me mad, then, if I endeavour to explain. Such things are to be experienced, not related. That first glimpse of you — a vision, it seemed, and all my consciousness was gathered in my eyes, absorbed in them from my other senses — that first glimpse stirred such a memory in me. I could not track it down. A memory, it eluded memory; it seemed to lie outside memory; and yet it bore to me, I thought, the knowledge that you and I were one link in some eternal chain; that each of us was a part of the other, mates predestined by a predestination that is but rarely fulfilled because of other blind, blundering forces that go to shape our lives. If you believe me, you will understand now what it was that moved me to succour Philip Danvelt.'

'Philip!' she echoed, suddenly awake from the dream his words were spinning, and suddenly chilled as if a shadow had fallen upon her.

But he ran on, expounding his romantic view of Fate's way.

'Philip Danvelt himself was naught; just a source of the impulse upon which I was to act, a rung of the ladder by which I was to climb, a sign-post planted by Fate to point me along the road to heaven.'

He ceased and there was silence, for she could make him no answer, knew not what answer to make him. His words were romantically, poetically vague; but it emerged from them clearly that he was wooing her, and, whilst her soul trembled in ecstasy, it trembled too, in an indefinable fear, a fear aroused by the mention of Philip, the thought of Philip and the sudden recollection, thrusting itself unbidden upon her mind, of the words with which Friar Sebastian had last night aroused her indignation. A point was reached at

which the friar's warning was to be submitted to the test
Already her companion had said more than she should suffe
from him unless there was something still to come in justi
fication of it all.

It was not for her, her instincts told her, either to encour
age or discourage him. Hers now the passive part until he
should fully have revealed himself and the true quality o
this love he offered. It was not that she mistrusted him, o
could really believe what the friar had hinted. But she de
sired that of his own free will and without assistance he
should so express himself that no mistrust hereafter coul
be possible, or doubt admissible to poison the happiness
towards which she looked with timid confidence.

Waiting, then, she practised stern repression; nor dared
to look at him, but kept her eyes on the red towers and mas
sive ramparts of the town of Flushing which they were fas
approaching.

And then she became conscious, as did he, of rapidly over
taking hoofbeats behind them. A moment later came a hail
and then two horsemen swept alongside, and the first o
these doffed his bonnet and revealed himself for Master
Danvelt, never more inopportune to her than in this mo
ment.

If resentment to find Johanna again transgressing what he
considered proper in a woman of her station was at all re
sponsible for the cloud upon his brow, it found at the mo
ment no expression.

'God save you, Master Egmont,' was his greeting breath
lessly delivered. 'I have ridden hard to warn you.'

'To warn me?' The Count drew rein, as did the others
now, and they stood, the servants a little in the background
whilst Philip made a full announcement of his morning's in
terview with the Governor of Zealand.

Count Anthony laughed when the tale was told. 'Why
what have I to do with the Governor of Zealand?' he
asked.

'That you should know, sir. Whatever it may be, and

lest it should bode you ill, my duty was to warn you at once in view of what lies between us.'

Laughter was dismissed from his lordship's countenance. 'That, sir, was very worthy, very noble in you.'

'It was no less than I owed.'

'Indeed, a great deal more. You cannot be blind to the risk to yourself had your full suspicions been well founded. If, for instance, the apprehension of my person were intended, and you frustrate it by this warning and so permit me to escape, you cannot be in doubt that you would be called upon to answer, and to answer grievously.'

With Johanna's startled gaze upon him, Danvelt made an answer which suddenly transfigured him in her eyes, endowing him with a nobility hitherto unsuspected.

'Sir, I am well aware of that. But if my life should pay for it, it is no more than the life I owe to you. Moreover, it is through me and the service that you did me that you are tracked.'

'My friend,' said Count Anthony, 'your action more than justifies mine in having served you.' Then he smiled again. 'For the rest, you need have no fear either for me or for yourself. I am no fugitive from justice. There will be messages for me. That is all.'

Danvelt breathed freely again. He was well pleased. He had worn the halo of heroism without any of its inconveniences. And from Johanna, too, there came a gasp of relief and a return of the colour which momentarily terror had driven from her cheeks.

Together now they rode into the town, and parted in the market-place, Count Anthony and his servant going to the Zeelanderhof, whilst Johanna returned home accompanied by Danvelt and followed by Jan.

The Count sat his horse at the inn-door, and watched them out of sight. As they were about to turn the corner, they looked back, first Johanna, then Danvelt. They waved to him, and he doffed his bonnet in reply, little dreaming of the vastly different circumstances in which next her eyes should discover him. Then he fetched a deep sigh, and walked his horse into the inn-yard.

Into that same inn-yard less than an hour later clanked a company of six men-at-arms, from the heads of whose lances fluttered purple bannerols bearing the cross of Saint Andrew. They were led by an officer wearing a white surcoat over his mail and a little scarlet plume in his steel cap. Dismounting he inquired of the landlord for a gentleman calling himself Anthony Egmont.

The landlord, relieved that the business of these Burgundians was not with himself, promptly conducted the officer abovestairs, to the room where Count Anthony sat alone with his perplexities.

So overmastering had been his feelings for Johanna, so passionate his yearnings for her, that hitherto, as he now perceived, he had yielded to them blindly and in utter disregard to every other consideration. Relentlessly they had brought him back from England no sooner was he arrived there, and remorselessly had they closed his senses to all perception of the circumstances in which both of them were placed. It had remained for an act of generosity on the part of Danvelt to check him in his reckless course and bid him consider whither he was heading, bring him to ponder certain contingencies of expediency and of honour. At the risk, perhaps, of his own life, Danvelt had ridden to warn the man who would have stolen Johanna from her burgher-lover. That was how the Count now regarded himself. If hitherto he had discounted without qualms any such aspect of his conduct, it was because Danvelt had appeared to him contemptible and beneath consideration. In this, it was now clear to him that he had been guilty of misjudgment. Then, too, it became necessary to ask himself to what end did he propose to snatch Johanna from another. Was he, a Prince of Guelders, prepared to make this burgher's daughter his Princess? Even if he were, would such a thing be permitted him? And alternatively was he prepared to marry her at the price of renouncing his rights to the throne of Guelders?

Did the clear duty imposed upon him by his birth even permit him to do so much?

These were the questions he was again balancing in his mind to perplex and distract him. Answers he had not found to any when the Governor's officer was admitted to his presence, unless it was a half-answer supplied by his romantic fatalism, that Danvelt's supervention at the very moment when he was about to give his love for Johanna full expression was in itself a sign.

Tormented and despairing, torn between his love for Johanna and his duty to himself, and to her, and even to Danvelt, he almost welcomed the interruption of his distracting thoughts which the officer's advent afforded.

'By your good leave, my lord, I have orders concerning you.' Thus the officer, his manner a careful blend of deference and firmness.

'Concerning me? They are ——?'

'You are to ride with me at once, my lord.'

'I ride with you? Who are you, sirrah?'

'Fritz von Diesenhofen, lieutenant to the Governor of Zealand, to serve you.'

'You seem to know me.'

'I do, my lord.'

'Then what have I to do with your Governor of Zealand?'

'They will tell you that at Bruges, my lord, whither you are to ride with me. Those are my orders. I am to deliver you, together with a letter from the Governor, into the hands of the Duke's highness.'

'You perceive, I trust, that you are being a party to an act of violence which may have grave consequences. I am no subject of the Duke of Burgundy.'

'Maybe not. You must argue it with others. I am a soldier, not a lawyer, my lord. I have my orders.'

Count Anthony rose. 'So be it,' he said. 'Give me leave to write a letter, and I shall be at your disposal.'

But Diesenhofen shook his head. 'Your letter must wait, my lord, until I have made safe delivery of you.'

Count Anthony frowned. 'I am a prisoner, then?'

'You may call it that. Besides, we must set out at once if we are to cross the water before dusk.'

Thus abruptly ended Count Anthony's second visit to Flushing. He departed with Diesenhofen and the six lances, his servant going with him, and, whilst his departure was widely observed, reported, and a source of comment in the town, none supposed him a prisoner, seeing him ride beside the officer unpinioned and sword on thigh.

CHAPTER IX

THE RETURN

BRUGES, which Diesenhofen regarded as their destination, was to prove no more than the first stage of a journey that was to continue for close upon three weeks.

The Duke, who had come thither a fortnight earlier and who had held there his first chapter of the Golden Fleece, had departed suddenly that very day to return to Brussels.

When in pursuit of him they reached Brussels on the evening of the morrow, it was only to discover that he had done no more than spend some few hours in the city, and that he was gone on to Namur.

The place was full of rumours. It was being said that the King of France was arming for the recapture of the cities of the Somme, and that the Duke was taking order to resist this violation of the Treaty of Conflans.

Followed for Count Anthony days of tedious riding, now south, now east, now west, in the erratic wake of the swiftly moving Duke. If the Count was wearied by this and fretted by the necessity for submission to the automaton who held him captive, if inwardly he rebelled against the unlawful compulsion of which he was the victim, he realized the futility of remonstrance.

Each night Diesenhofen locked him into an inn bedroom with a guard outside his door and another beneath his window; and each night of the first week Count Anthony wrote a letter to Johanna, which next morning he destroyed. Such was the bewildered state of his mind where she was concerned, such the persisting and inconclusive conflict between his love on the one hand and what on the other he accounted his duty to himself and to Danvelt, and, consequently, to her, that it was impossible for him to give it an expression at once clear and just.

In the end he wrote no more letters, but spent his nights making sonnets instead, in the Petrarchian manner, sad laments compounded of passion and despair, in the art of which he found some ease from the realities that tormented him.

Finally he abandoned even this vehicle for the relief of his surcharged heart, and before the end of that tedious journey, in which they crossed and recrossed their tracks, he had reasoned himself into a condition of sorrowful resignation. He came to regard the intervention of the Governor of Zealand in his affairs as a wise dispensation of Providence, to rescue him and to rescue Johanna from a situation of hopelessness. They belonged, he and she, to different orders, between which any honourable alliance was impossible, whilst his love for her was too fine and spiritual and holy to admit even the contemplation of an alliance of any other nature. He had lived, he now told himself, in a dream, a poet's dream, all loveliness and hope unrealizable, and for a spell he had imagined that in his dream he had found the realities he sought. Now he was awake again, rudely awakened and being dragged by the heels back to the world and the life to which he really belonged, of which he was a part and in which he had his allotted duties to perform, the life from whose hollowness and apparent unreality he had sought so vainly and futilely to escape. As if a man ever could escape his destiny and the obligations which his place in life imposed upon him at every step from the moment of his birth!

To what, he wondered, was he returning? Would they put it upon him that his honour demanded the fulfilment of his betrothal to the Lady Catharine of Bourbon? Ah, not that! He would not so defile the real love which had come to blossom in his heart, even though Fate denied fruition to it. Though he might never claim Johanna for his own, at least he would remain dedicate to her. He would live and die a celibate in honour of her, consecrated to the thought of her.

It was an uplifting resolve, and it took some of the burden of sorrow from his soul. The sense of sacrifice, the thought of vowing himself to an ideal, abstract love, exalted him. It was in the true romantic spirit.

His sorrow and his fond yearnings partly allayed by this resolve, he came at last upon the Duke at Saint-Quentin. That was on an afternoon in June, two weeks after leaving Flushing and having followed a zigzag course between the pleasant wooded uplands of the east and the dreary flats of the west, which but for the dykes that shut out the sea would have been a morass.

Up through the town to the grim citadel rode Diesenhofen. Arrived there, he left Count Anthony in the guardroom of the barbican, in the care of his men, whilst himself he went forward to seek audience of the Duke. An hour he waited in the spacious antechamber that was variously peopled by courtiers in silk and captains in steel, with here and there the scarlet flame of a prelate's robes, and where the only language heard was French. Booted and dusty as he had ridden in, the Lorrainer attracted some attention. It was assumed his business must be urgent, indeed, that he should come thus into the presence of his prince. By one or two, indeed, he was questioned. But his short answers that he was from Zealand quenched all interest in him in an hour in which all eyes were turned towards France.

At length the curtained Gothic door at the room's end swung open, and, whilst an usher held aside the arras, forth stepped three men, in the tallest, oldest, and most elegant of whom Diesenhofen recognized the Count of Saint-Pol, that Constable of France, who strove to serve two masters. All eyes were turned upon him, and a sensitive witness must have been instantly aware of the general relief when it was observed that he was calm and smiling.

Diesenhofen was still admiring him, when he was roused by the chamberlain's voice.

'His highness commands the officer from the Governor of Zealand.'

Diesenhofen found the Duke alone, leaning against the mullion of the tall Gothic window which stood open to the sunlight. He was frowning thoughtfully, and it was a long moment before he condescended to become conscious of the soldier's presence.

'So,' he said at last, 'you are from Zealand with very urgent tidings. I trust they are not evil; at least not more evil than I am growing accustomed to.'

'I think your highness will account my tidings far from evil.' He bent the knee as he proffered the Governor's letter.

Passing from the window to a table on which a map was spread beside some papers, the Duke broke the seal and unfolded the parchment. As he read, his gloomy countenance lighted. Over the edge of the sheet his dark eyes glowed upon the Lorrainer. 'You have brought his lordship?'

'He waits in the guardroom, highness.'

'The guardroom!' The Duke's frown and the ascending pitch of his voice announced his surprised displeasure.

Stolidly Diesenhofen explained that his orders were explicit, that he took no risks, and that, for the rest, he had used the prisoner with all courtesy and consideration.

He was curtly dismissed to fetch Count Anthony, and Count Anthony, once alone with the Duke, restraining the embrace with which the Duke would have received him, expressed himself freely and with righteous indignation upon this violation of his person and the constraint imposed upon him. At the end of it, he demanded instant liberty to go his ways.

'Liberty you shall have,' said Charles of Burgundy. 'But what are your ways?'

'They are my own. I am not your vassal, Charles, and you have sanctioned a monstrous usurpation of right by might where I am concerned.'

The haughty, tempestuous, and headstrong Duke was patient and meek for once. Affection for his cousin and the perception that this indignation was entirely justified combined now with his own urgent need of every tried friend he could command. So he set himself to use conciliatory arguments, which if none too sound were the best at his disposal.

'There are rights of alliance, Anthony, as well as rights of vassalage.'

'They include no right to subject me to duress.'

'If you were so clear on that, why did you run away?'

'Run away! I departed your court when I grew weary of it. That was all.'

'Without even the courtesy of craving leave of me. Are these the manners of a guest in Guelders?'

'I desired to go in peace. I desired no quarrel with you, Charles.'

'On what grounds did you fear a quarrel?'

'On those of my betrothal to the Lady Catharine.'

'That ground of quarrel, at least, has been removed. The Lady Catharine is no longer available. She has consoled herself with your brother Adolph.'

The Duke's grin was not entirely free from malice. He knew that the statement and its obvious implication would give Count Anthony something to think about. The marriage between Bourbon and Egmont had been projected for the consolidation of the political alliance between Guelders and Burgundy. To give full effect to this, the proper party to the contract on the side of Guelders was the heir to the duchy. That advantage should have been taken of Anthony's absence to substitute his younger brother as the bridegroom was hardly a good omen. It seemed to foreshadow the desire for a wider substitution. Count Anthony was taken aback. Indignation kindled in his long, fair face.

'Was this by your contriving, Charles?'

The heavy countenance sneered at him. 'Oh, I thank you for the thought!'

'But you consented. Your consent was necessary.'

'And still more urgently necessary to marry that baggage Catharine. Adolph happened to be finding favour in her eyes, and I sanctioned what they both desired before the jade could change her mind again, since not even my commands could have constrained the slighted Catharine to await your return or to marry you when it happened. At last perhaps you'll give me reason for the gentle force I've used with you.' He lowered his voice to a grumbling note as he added: 'I had no wish to see your brother Adolph extending his usurpation of your functions.'

Count Anthony shrugged in sheer disgust. There was little love between him and his family, and covetousness ever nauseated him. 'Let him usurp what he pleases, and God give him joy of it!'

The Duke's swarthy face grew stern. He set his arms akimbo. 'Here's frenzy! You'll let your younger brother give rein to unnatural ambition, and ride over you to the throne that should be yours?'

'Is that the aim, then? Will nothing less content him?'

'Must I make Adolph known to you?' wondered the Duke, and he became sententious. 'Like poets, princes are born, not made; born to a sacred trust from on high. Incalculable harm follows upon any disloyalty to that trust. How long do you suppose that Guelders would preserve its independence with Adolph on the throne?'

He spoke in the solemn, impressive manner that is born only of strong convictions. And perhaps no conviction was stronger in Charles of Burgundy — begotten of the adulatory phrases addressed to him from childhood — than that of the divine appointment and divine mission of princes.

Before Count Anthony could answer him, he continued on another note. 'And that is not the only reason why I thank God for your return. I am at the point of distraction, Anthony, and in need, in sorest need, of a trusty friend and more.'

His tone was unusually gentle and wistful, and his expression was entirely stripped of its habitual arrogance. Count Anthony, who loved him, was touched by his manner and melted from any lingering indignation. He has been accounted weak by the undiscerning because he was always weak in his resentments and ever ready to discard them. And now, to complete a reconciliation for which he had shown the need to be on his own side, Charles afforded him a mollifying if not quite accurate explanation.

'My fool of a Governor of Zealand acted too straitly upon orders I issued many months ago at the time of your disappearance. Bear him no ill-will, Anthony. He's a faithful, loyal dog who obeys orders to the letter if without discretion, and apparently he is served by men of the same stamp. I blame not him, but myself, for what has happened to you; and I blame myself sorely. I would not have had you used as you have been used, and yet, by Saint George, I was never more glad to see any living man. Sit you there, my friend, while I recite my woes; and in the end you'll pity me.'

He pushed Count Anthony forcibly into a chair, and thereafter for an hour and more, while soldier, prince, and prelate cooled their heels in the antechamber, he poured into his cousin's sympathetic ears, the tale of his distractions.

'I was angry with you last month,' he began, 'when I held in Bruges my first Chapter of the Knights of the Golden Fleece. You were absent from your place, a thing I do not lightly overlook in any man. Moreover, I needed you then; needed you as I need you now.'

He strode on his short, powerful legs to the window and back, his brows darkened by his thoughts. 'Taking full advantage of the privileges conferred upon them by the rules of the order, the brethren very plainly expressed hostile opinions on my general conduct of affairs.'

Anthony was startled. He knew the existence of the privilege in that exalted knightly brotherhood, but had never dreamed of its being exercised against the sacred person of the Duke himself, the order's natural head, the very fount of honour.

'They censured me with harshness especially to the nobles, alleging that my rigour in punishing faults is out of all proportion to my measures in rewarding virtue and services. They taxed me with parsimony. I hoard the revenues, they say, instead of scattering them in emulation of the princely lavishness of my father.'

'Scattering them on themselves, they meant,' quoth Anthony. 'And you? What did you answer them?'

'What could I answer? I think anger made me dumb. That and the remembrance that who excuses himself accuses himself. Could I condescend to explain myself? I submitted in silence to their reproaches. I needed there an independent advocate to whip them into shame of their own words. That is what you would have done had you been there. That is where you failed me by your absence.'

To this Count Anthony said nothing; but regret cast a little shadow over his countenance. The Duke, pacing ever to and fro, railed on. They were not presumptuous, he declared, beyond the licence granted them by Duke Philip when their exalted order was founded; and yet they were presumptuous in that they pronounced upon insufficient knowledge.

'If I hoard my revenues, I do so against the fearful need that will soon be forced upon me, a need for which all my hoarding is inadequate, as will presently appear. Already last April in the States-General summoned for the purpose by the King of France, it was declared that Normandy must be retained by Louis. That was a fair beginning. To show me whither he was drifting, it was not necessary for him to add, as is reported to me, that the Treaty of Conflans was wrested from him by undue influence. He began to tear it up when the States-General made that declaration touching Normandy. I tell you, Anthony, there is no faith in that shifty, foxy little knave. No treaty will bind him once he thinks it safe to break it. I have word that he is levying troops and organizing forces. He aims, I suppose, at the cities of the Somme. You see what is coming?'

'War, I suppose,' said Count Anthony.

'War,' Charles agreed. He stood erect, his jutting chin held high. 'I welcome it. Since he wants war, he shall have a bellyful from me. I was made for war, I think, and this

time, by Saint George, he shall learn it and remember the
lesson. It is in preparation for war that I have been making
this progress through the frontier provinces, and be sure
I'll prepare thoroughly by the help of God and Saint
George.'

He swung away to the window again. Looking out into
the courtyard, across which the rays of the sun were now
aslant, he laughed grimly, and pointed.

'There go the Constable and de Biche. De Biche, who
was once my father's creature and is now the cat's-paw of
King Louis. Saint-Pol, who, for his own profit, tried to be
the friend of both sides and is faithful to neither, although
to-day he holds the sword of France. They were lately with
me, bearers of lying pacific messages from King Louis, messages calculated to lull my alarm, while he arms to the teeth
against me. He wants time.'

The Duke swung from the window again, and came striding back to the table, his hand on the hilt of his dagger. He
laughed grimly, showing his strong teeth.

'So do I. Therefore, I pretend to believe them. To the
revenues with whose hoarding I am reproached by the
Knights of the Golden Fleece, I shall add levies to be made
upon the Netherlands; gold to be transmuted into steel.
The foxy Louis shall admire my alchemy. In the Rhine
Provinces, throughout the Empire, in the Cantons, in Italy,
wherever men are to be hired, I'll hire them, and I'll put
such an army in the field that my rascally brother-in-law of
France shall pray to patch up the Conflans Treaty again so
that he may shelter himself behind it. I'll give him time, so
that I may have time, myself, for this; for this and my marriage. My marriage! My marriage with the Princess Margaret of York!' He laughed harshly, ruefully.

'Men say,' quoth Count Anthony, by way of felicitation,
'that she is very fair.'

'To the devil with her fairness!' roared the Duke, who had
wrought himself by now into a passion. He crashed his fist
upon the table. 'My God, Anthony, this is no wenching

business. If she were humped like a camel and tusked like a boar, I still must marry her, for the sake of the alliance with England. To this has Louis of France reduced me. Through my mother, who was half-Lancastrian, a quarter of my blood is blood of Lancaster; and I am to mingle this with the blood of York! Yet this, too, must I do to make my dominions safe against King Louis, and to consolidate against him this House of Burgundy, of which I am no more than the life-tenant.' This last he spoke in a tone almost of awe, the man of Destiny alluding to the burden of his mission. Then he flung himself down in his great chair before the table, and looked across it at the grave-faced Count Anthony, who remained silent.

'You perceive my need of you, my urgent need of every friend in camp and council. The lances you may bring me out of Guelders shall be paid handsomely from these hoarded revenues. I'll need every man and every pike that you can muster. But more than those I shall need you, Anthony. You have the calm deliberateness I lack, and I can trust you where I can trust no other of these greedy self-seekers, who will stand by me just so long as they perceive no greater profit to be made elsewhere. Your judgment I trust implicitly. Your advice I know to be honest and sprung from love of me. You'll stay by me now, Anthony?'

He leaned forward, and flung an arm across the table, the powerful short-fingered hand supine and open.

The appeal was not one that Count Anthony could resist. Guelders must stand by Burgundy to the end that Burgundy should stand by Guelders in her need. So much policy demanded. And his personal affection for Charles of Burgundy demanded no less. For this had he returned; for this been dragged from his dreams to face realities, he who had sought realities afar and in vain. So he assured himself. But there was a sense of choking in his throat and a mist before his eyes, and in the heart of it the fair, delicate face of Johanna, sweetly virginal and maddeningly desirable. Then the mist cleared. He fetched a sigh and took the proffered hand.

'Charles, I am yours for your need of me.'

CHAPTER X

THE KNIGHT OF THE TULIP

COUNT ANTHONY welcomed the distraction of the activities now thrust upon him, and sought in them an anodyne for his heartache.

Three days after his interview with Charles of Burgundy, he descended upon his father's court at Nimeguen, to the surprise of all and to the dismay of some. His brother Adolph was absent, with the Burgundian Court at Brussels, in attendance upon Madame Catharine, who was one of the ladies-in-waiting of the Dowager Duchess Isabella. Anthony was thankful for this circumstance, since he found opposition more than enough from the Duke his father.

He submitted patiently to parental upbraidings on the score of his eccentricities and his reckless extravagances during the year of his mysterious absence. His notes of hand for outrageous sums had poured in upon the treasury to the exasperation of the parsimonious Duke, and now he came calmly to demand a matter of twenty thousand gold florins to enable him to raise, mount, equip, and maintain a body of eight thousand lances with which to succour the Duke of Burgundy in his need. If this was the only purpose for which he had returned home, it would have been much better for Guelders if he had remained permanently absent. Guelders, his father informed him, reared no fatted calves for prodigals.

Count Anthony did not argue with his sire. He knew the futility of reasoning with prejudice. Instead, he sought the chancellor of the duchy and arranged with him for the convening of the estates. He appeared before them two days later, and delivered an appeal which La Marche, who has preserved it for us, describes as a model of statesmanly oratory. He pointed out the dangers with which Burgundy

was confronted, and the dangers which would confront
Guelders if Burgundy were defeated. The maintenance of
the independence of Guelders was the first and most sacred
duty of her rulers, and this independence could be ensured
only by stoutly supporting their one great ally and preserv-
ing him in his fullest strength to the end that in turn he
might preserve them.

To the disgust of his father, who regarded it as so much
waste — but dared not say so, lest his words should be reported to the Duke of Burgundy — the money was voted
without demur, to be refunded by a special poll-tax.

After that Count Anthony set about reëstablishing his
household, which he had disbanded at the time of his departure from Brussels. He entrusted the details of raising
and equipping the necessary force to the Sire Bertrand de la
Roche, a gentleman of his confidence and a soldier of experience, and then with a bodyguard of his own, four esquires
and two pages, he left Nimeguen to rejoin the Duke of Burgundy at Bruges, whither he had meanwhile returned.

It was now that he adopted, to the horror of the heralds, a
fresh personal device; on a field gules, two tulips, or and
argent, in saltire — whence he came shortly thereafter to be
known, more or less ironically, as the Knight of the Tulip.

His report of what he had accomplished ensured him a
warm reception from the Duke. To mark his appreciation,
Charles desired of him a service which was in itself an honour: that with the Duke's mother, the Duchess Isabella, and
his young daughter Mary of Burgundy, with Monsieur de
Rumbempré and the Count and Countess of Charny, he
should repair to Sluys as the Duke's representative to receive and welcome his bride, the Lady Margaret of York,
on her arrival there from England. And he sought counsel
of Count Anthony in other matters, as had been his custom
of old, and particularly in the matter of the fresh taxes to be
levied on the Netherlands towards the expenses of the coming war. Count Anthony's advice was sound. Remembering
how himself he had prevailed in Nimeguen, he counselled the

use of similar arguments in Zealand and Friesland. Let it be shown to the estates there how imperative to the maintenance of their privileges was the maintenance of Burgundian power which had ever respected and defended them, and the rest would follow. But the arguments must be presented by the Duke in person. It was the personal appeal that would lead to the ready opening of the burgher coffers.

Persuaded, Charles resolved to act upon this advice, so soon as his marriage and the subsequent festivities should have been accomplished. On the morrow, with an escort of twenty lances, every man in a white surcoat bearing the new tulip device, Count Anthony set out for Sluys as the representative of the Duke of Burgundy.

The Princess Margaret of York arrived with the state and splendour becoming the sister of a king; but it was as moonshine to sunlight compared with the state and splendour of the Burgundian reception awaiting her, a reception which was to mark the wealth and power of a Duke who in both could outrival any living monarch, and to dazzle the world in general and the watchful King of France in particular.

A fleet of sixteen vessels under the command of the Lord Admiral of England was employed to bring the Princess and her escort to the port of Sluys. She was in the immediate care of her royal brother, Lord Scales, and the Bishop of Salisbury, and attended by a troop of knights and gentlemen representing the flower of English nobility of the Yorkist faction and some fourscore ladies of rank, at whose head stood the Duchess of Norfolk, then reputed the most beautiful woman in England.

To receive her on her landing and conduct her to the Castle of Sluys came a noble company in which Count Anthony of Guelders was supported by such illustrious nobles as John of Luxembourg and John of Nassau, the magnificence of whose equipages made her own look provincial and paltry. At her lodging in the castle she was waited upon by the Dowager Duchess and the Lady Mary of Burgundy, by the Count and Countess of Charny, and a constantly flowing train of nobles and dignitaries, until, finally, on the evening of the day after her arrival, came the Duke himself to pay his homage and formally to exchange vows of betrothal. That night from the windows of the Castle of Sluys she saw in the sky to the south the red glow of the huge pyramidal bonfires, each forty feet high, which in honour of her coming were lighted in Bruges.

For a week she remained there very nobly entertained, and then a train of painted and gilded barges luxuriously equipped conveyed this fair, calm English Princess and her suite to Damme, the great fortified port of Bruges in whose basin floated the argosies of all nations, attracted thither by the great commerce which made Bruges, with her population of a quarter of a million souls, the rival of Venice and Genoa. Hither to Damme at five o'clock on the morning of Sunday the third of July came the Duke for the nuptials which were celebrated by the Bishop of Salisbury and the Papal Legate. After the nuptial mass, he rode back with his private escort to the Cour des Princes at Bruges, there to await the state entry of his bride.

She arrived some two hours later at the Gate of Holy Cross, the object and centre of a pageantry the like of which neither her eyes nor those of any of her English followers had ever witnessed or imagined. She came in a horse-litter covered with cloth of gold, the white horses that bore it caparisoned in cloth of gold from which little silver bells were hung, with roses entwined in their flowing white manes. Herself, she was dressed in cloth of silver, a crown of diamonds flashing on her fair head, above which with her own hands she placed the chaplet of roses that was offered to her by a company of nuns at the Gate of Holy Cross. Thence the procession moved towards the heart of that great city of bridges, the Grande Place and the Palace.

At its head went the representatives of the Church, a body of prelates and lesser ecclesiastics, in cope and surplice and stole, with crucifix, reliquaries, and effulgent monstrances. Next came the Collace, the members of the Burgomasters'

Council, in their official robes and chains of office. Followed the members of the ducal household, first the liveries of black and purple, then the higher functionaries in their scarlet pourpoints and long mantles of black velvet. After these came a band of trumpeters, next a troop of archers in gala liveries; then the heralds, poursuivants, and kings-at-arms in their blazoned tabards; and then the representatives of foreign nations, the twenty ambassadors and their households, and the members of each of the seventeen trading companies, amongst whom were, conspicuous for their splendour, the Venetians, the Florentines, and the Easterlings.

Immediately ahead of the bride's litter marched a company of English archers of the bodyguard, whilst on foot, on either side of the litter, walked the thirty Knights of the Golden Fleece in their majestic scarlet robes.

After her rode thirteen of her maids-of-honour on richly caparisoned, snow-white palfreys, and after these came a line of gilded chariots emblazoned with the arms of England and Burgundy, bearing the remainder of her ladies, the beautiful Duchess of Norfolk in the first of these; and, finally, to close that vast procession, an army of knights and gentlemen all gorgeously arrayed, the trappings of their horses glittering with gold and gems and fringed with silver bells.

Thus, in a blaze of July sunshine and under a sky that was like a dome of polished steel, the Princess Margaret of York, now Duchess of Burgundy, rode through the streets of Bruges that were all strewn with flowers and boughs, hung with costliest tapestries from Flemish looms, with silks of Persia and with cloth of gold, and bridged by triumphal arches, from which flights of doves were released as she passed under them.

Progress was slow, not only because of the press of people, but also because of the mysteries, or theatrical representations, with which the bride was entertained on the way, and for each of which a halt was called. They performed for her the story of Adam and Eve, the marriage of Cleopatra and King Alexander, Saint George's defence of a beautiful maiden from a dragon, and the like, to her obvious delight and that of her following.

Well might John Paston, who was in her train, write home to his mother in Cheshire from Bruges on the Friday next after Saint Thomas:

'By my trowthe I herd nevyr of so gret plente as ther is her.

'And as for the Dwyks coort, as of lords and ladys & gentylwomen, knyts, sqwyers and gentylmen I hert never of none lyek to it save King Artourys cort. And by my trowthe I have no wyt nor remembrance to wryte to you half the worchep that is her.'

That, of course, was at the end of a week of daily banqueting and dancing and great passages-at-arms accompanied by almost unimaginable pageantries which were held in the lists erected in the Grande Place.

Meanwhile the bridal procession made its gorgeous, sluggish progress through the city, acclaimed by the thousands who lined the streets, crowded the windows, balconies, and even roofs of the buildings. The bruit of these splendours had attracted folk, not merely from the immediately surrounding country, but some, who could afford the means and leisure for travel, from considerable distances. Amongst these were Mynheer Claessens and his daughter and Philip Danvelt.

Johanna had been dejected and pining ever since the abrupt departure of Anthony Egmont from Flushing. From what Philip had told her and what else she had been able to gather, she chose to conclude that for some reason beyond her knowledge he had been taken a prisoner. It was idle for Philip and her father to point out that the details of his departure did not bear this out. He had ridden sword on thigh with the lances and the officer who had waited upon him at the Zeelanderhof, not as a captive, but as a man escorted. At first, she had accepted this, and had been glad to accept it. But as days passed and grew to weeks without any word from him, she returned to her earlier conviction that he was a prisoner. It was impossible for her to believe that he would neglect to communicate with her if he were free to do so.

Her listlessness in those days became a matter of grave concern to her father. To Danvelt, who was a very frequent visitor now, her condition was less obvious. An intensely self-centred man, he was little observant of others, and interested in them only in so far as they ministered to his own needs. If he observed any change at all in Johanna, he would account it a change for the better, for it accorded with his notions of propriety that women should be self-effacing. He had noted in the past a certain presumption in Johanna, which he accounted the one flaw in her character: there was a disposition on her part to express views upon the serious concerns of life, which he regarded as entirely beyond a woman's province. Her increased demureness, into which he interpreted the outward signs of her sorrow and anxiety, rendered her more desirable in his eyes, and led him in those days to woo her with an insistence which would take no refusal seriously, regarding these refusals as the rather tiresome expressions of an excessive modesty which could bring itself to surrender only after endless onslaughts.

He complained of it to Master Claessens during the last days of June. He represented that the heavy responsibilities devolving upon him by his father's death left him little time for these almost daily excursions into Flushing, and that there was no reason in the world why his nuptials with Johanna should continue to be postponed.

'No reason at all,' Claessens stolidly agreed with him, 'save Johanna's inclinations. It is not a matter in which a maid may with propriety be hurried.'

'Hurried!' echoed Danvelt, and snorted his disgust.

'Be patient, Philip.' Claessens knew well the trouble in his daughter's mind. He put his faith in time to efface the memory of the handsome, courtly Egmont who in an evil hour had darkened his threshold. Whatever the causes that had so abruptly removed him, Claessens was secretly thankful that he had gone. As things stood, the harm done was quite sufficient. 'Johanna is in need of distraction. Life here is dull for a maid.'

'The occupations of a wife will afford her precisely the distraction that she needs,' said Danvelt, pompous as an oracle.

'Maybe,' said Claessens, without conviction. 'Meanwhile there is to be a brave show in Bruges for the Duke's nuptials. Johanna has never been to Bruges, and I have always promised to take her to see the Chapel of the Holy Blood. This might be the occasion for it.'

Danvelt demurred. The town would be full of strangers and the inns overcrowded, their charges outrageously increased. Since he had come into his wealth, Danvelt, who had been prodigal enough before, was grown thrifty to the point of parsimony. Johanna, when the matter was proposed to her, agreed with an interest so indifferent that her father felt a pang of disappointment. But in the end they went, and on the morning of the Princess Margaret's wedding they issued betimes from their lodging at the Orb and Sceptre, and took up a position near the Stadhuis, whence to view the procession.

The dazzling, incredible display aroused Johanna from her brooding. The colour was whipped into her cheeks and a certain old-time sparkle to her eye, so that her father fondly observing these signs felicitated himself upon the step he had taken. But his felicitations were premature.

The body of English archers, stalwart and gay in their feathered hats and their red brigandines quilted and studded, their long bows slung beside them, had just swept by, and now the horse-litter of the smiling young Duchess was coming abreast of them.

Eagerly Johanna craned her neck to obtain a better view of that sweet lady, who sat there enthroned, crowned so appropriately with roses above the sparkling diadem on her brow. And then she was conscious of a tugging at her arm. It was Philip, in a state of boorish excitement.

'Look! Look! Yonder! The first of those!'

He was pointing to the stately line of scarlet-mantled Knights of the Golden Fleece, who walked beside the litter, pointing to the very head of it, to one who in that most honourable company held the most honourable place. Following the indications of his out-flung hand, she beheld, to her inexpressible amazement, Anthony Egmont, her Anthony.

Bewildered, breathless, she continued to stare, to scrutinize. It was he beyond all doubt, just as it was beyond all doubt that he was arrayed in the gorgeous robes of the Toison d'Or, that he wore its insignia about his neck, and its feathered black velvet cap upon his tawny head.

And then she heard her father's voice asking a question of a portly neighbour. He, too, had seen, as his question informed her.

'Who is that, sir, do you know: he at the head of the line of Knights of the Golden Fleece?'

'That, sir?' she heard the questioning answer. 'Whence are you? That is Count Anthony of Egmont, Prince of Guelders, the Duke's cousin and friend, and one of the first gentlemen in Christendy, prince and poet, knight and troubadour; there's none more admired or better loved in all the provinces.' The fellow was garrulous and glad to air his knowledge. He ran on: 'In the passage-at-arms at the Tree of Gold this afternoon, when the Great Bastard holds the lists against all comers, if he meets his match at all, it will be when he meets Count Anthony.'

Claessens's arm was about his daughter's slim waist. She had sunk against him, half-swooning, and he, well knowing what blow had smitten her, set his teeth and prayed God to damn the soul of one of the first gentlemen in Christendy.

CHAPTER XI

BETROTHAL

THE visit of Claessens and his daughter to Bruges ended abruptly, to the infinite chagrin of Master Danvelt. What to the other two had been matter for consternation had been to him a subject for elation. No longer hereafter would he allude vaguely to 'my friend Anthony Egmont, a gentleman of parts.' He could say definitely and without fear of contradiction, 'my good friend, Count Anthony of Egmont, the Prince of Guelders.' He was conscious of an increase in social consequence. For if you cannot be great or distinguished in yourself, the next best thing is to have the acquaintance of those who are great and distinguished. Thus, by reflection, you shine with a little of their glory. To the ignorant and undiscerning the moon is a self-luminous body in the heavens. Nor was the boast one that would strain belief. Under the late Duke Philip, the burghers had been so fostered, encouraged, and treated on equal terms that a great deal of the luxury which marked his own and his son's environment was due to this very cause. Wealthy burghers received at court sought to magnify themselves by an outward display which eclipsed the lustre of the nobles; and the nobles in their turn, not to be outdone by these opulent traders, felt it incumbent upon the dignity of their estate to assume a still greater magnificence. From this competition resulted at the Burgundian Court those splendours which dazzled Europe.

After dinner, father and daughter kept their lodging, on the plea that the heat and glare and noise of the morning had been too much for Johanna, and that she needed rest. Nothing, however, could withhold Master Danvelt from the great joust of the Tree of Gold which was being held in the

Grande Place, and from witnessing there the performance of his friend the Prince of Guelders. He came back in the evening bubbling with the relation of marvels, and particularly with the account of the passage at arms between the Bastard of Burgundy and the Knight of the Tulip, the device, he announced, of his friend Count Anthony. Nor was he discouraged by the listlessness with which his two companions received his tale. There were to be further displays upon the morrow and for a week thereafter, on an ever-increasing scale of sumptuousness. And there was feasting for all. Bonfires were alight and the fountains in the great square were running with wines of Burgundy and the Rhine.

But on the morrow Master Claessens dismayed him with the announcement of their intention to return instantly to Flushing. The state of Johanna's health demanded it. When he could not dissuade them from this, Danvelt at first considered allowing them to depart, himself remaining. Finally he sulkily consented to accompany them, and for the first day of the journey by barge was so resentful of being cheated of his expectations that he scarcely exchanged a word with them.

When, however, they had transshiped at Sluys, he thawed a little. In a measure, as the memories of the glories of the Bruges wedding faded from his mind, this came to be filled instead by consideration of the sweetness, the delicate white beauty of Johanna, now enhanced by the gentle wistfulness in which she was wrapped. As his greenish eyes contemplated her, sitting on the deck of the vessel that bore them across the sunlit sea to Flushing, she seemed to him infinitely desirable, and he grew impatient and a little resentful of the postponements which he had suffered hitherto. Assuredly there must be an end to these.

Of the source of her wistfulness and pallor no suspicion crossed his dullness. Of the shame searing her chaste soul he caught no indication. Even had he known what was passing in her mind, it is to be doubted if he would have understood. For he was gross of fibre without the capacity to perceive that a thought harboured may become as tormenting to a sensitive mind as a shameful deed accomplished.

In Johanna's mind to torture her was the memory of all the thoughts she had entertained on the subject of Anthony, of the words he had spoken, of which those thoughts had been conceived, of his unmistakable wooing of her, and of the shameful purpose which she was now compelled to suppose it to have had. She remembered so vividly the warning of Friar Stephen, and despised herself for her foolish, confident scorn of it.

From the outset she had accounted Anthony Egmont a gentleman of birth; but she had not supposed him of so lofty a station as to preclude in those days his being a suitor for the hand of the daughter of so wealthy a burgher as her father. To discover him on the princely eminence he occupied was to have no illusions left. She felt herself unutterably shamed and insulted by a wooing that had brought her — poor fool — such glowing rapture.

The very reputation for chivalry, in the term's best and fullest sense, which he enjoyed, but made her shame the deeper, her contempt of him and of herself more poignant. She had succumbed so easily to the honeyed phrases of one who was not merely a libertine, but a hypocrite. Where had been her wits, where her feminine intuitions? They had been overwhelmed by her vanity and the lure of her silly senses. Thus Johanna in her bitter introspective self-condemnation. The only thing she did not perceive quite clearly was the motive for his abrupt departure from Flushing, forsaking the enterprise and amusement which she afforded him. That something had happened to render it necessary, however, the circumstances showed. And how lightly he had gone, how lightly abandoned his unholy quest, was more than established by the fact that he had never troubled to send so much as a word of explanation, apology, or excuse to the woman to whom he had been uttering words of love within an hour of his departure.

Into her bitter musings broke the voice of Philip, softly

muted. Unperceived he had crept to the side of the litter in which she reclined in the ship's waist, and now found a seat there on a coil of rope. Her father was on the quarter with the master of the vessel, and most of the men were forward. They were quite alone there in the shade of the bellying mizzen.

'Johanna!' he said softly, 'you are very pensive.'

She turned to look at him. If she considered his florid face and yellow hair, his eyes of greenish brown, his shallow brow and jutting nose and obstinate chin, all that she beheld in him now was honesty and kindliness. She remembered of him only such traits as were in his favour, such things as his readiness to risk his neck in warning Anthony Egmont because of the debt that lay between them. Here was no libertine, no predatory wolf who used gifts of personal beauty, courtly experience, and mental endowments for the furtherance of vile aims; but a man of her own class, a solid burgher, honest, downright, and of decent mind and life. He might be unable to string rhymes, but faith could be attached to what he said; he might lack graces of person, but he was of a solidity upon which a woman could lean with confidence and trust.

He put forth a hand and took one of her own, which she relinquished to him. That hand of his might be squat, and freckled, a short-fingered paw ending in gnawed finger-nails. But it was strong and honest; a hand that would support a woman and protect her; and Johanna in all her life until this hour had never needed protection, and, therefore, as it seemed to her, never valued the features that held the promise of it.

She smiled gently, sadly, into his stupidly masterful countenance.

'Pensive? Yes,' she answered him. 'There is no harm in thinking.'

'No harm; but no profit. No good ever came of it. And of what were you thinking?' His hand stroked hers.

'Of what? Of life.'

'Life's to be lived, not thought about,' said Master Philip. 'To be lived happily.'

'If possible.'

'It must be made possible. I think I can make your life happy, Johanna; I know that you can make mine happy.' There was a note of cajolery in his voice. 'Why do we wait, Johanna? What is there now to wait for? I want you at Middelburg.' He leaned closer. 'I want you so much, Johanna. I may be a clumsy lout in some ways, and I've no experience in dalliance to lend me a lover's arts, but I love you, Johanna. Why will you keep me waiting?'

'I have no experience in dalliance to lend me a lover's arts, but I love you, Johanna.'

The phrase echoed and reëchoed through her mind, touching raw, jangling chords in it.

She had been dazzled by the glitter of those arts of which Philip confessed the lack. It was an easy step in her present state to assume an enduring sincerity of purpose where these arts were lacking. By no apter phrase could Philip Danvelt have served his ends. He set, as it seemed, his own solid worth against the tinsel sparkle of meretricious romanticism. Almost she grew tender towards him, convicted herself of injustice and harshness in past opinions of him, and became dimly aware that only in marriage could she find definite shelter from such experiences as that which she had suffered. The intentions of him who wooed a maid might be in doubt, and by that doubt could a maiden be betrayed; but the intentions of him who wooed a wife were clear from the first word he uttered.

Philip offered her shelter, sustenance, genuine affection, and peaceful security. What more could any marriage offer? What was there in all the world to be preferred to this? And so, in that hour of reactions, she yielded, and thereby placed Philip more deeply in the debt of the Prince of Guelders than he already stood or than he could even guess. Anthony Egmont had not only saved his life, but had won Johanna for him as he could never have won her for himself.

'What is there now to wait for, you ask,' she said, on a note whose bitterness escaped him. 'What, indeed?' And abruptly she added: 'I'll keep you waiting no longer, Philip.'

'Ah!' He sucked in his breath in an amazement which was even greater than his satisfaction. 'When, Johanna? When?'

'When you will, Philip,' she answered quietly.

'At once, then. Let us say in two weeks from now. That will leave time to spare for all that's needed to prepare.'

She felt his breath hot upon her cheek, caught the deep glow in his green-hazel eyes, and something within her shivered, and shivered again when presently he kissed her.

CHAPTER XII

THE WIFE OF PHILIP DANVELT

In August of that same year the Duke of Burgundy mad
his accession progress through the cities of Zealand, Frie
land, and Holland with the twofold aim of receiving homag
after exchanging oaths of fidelity with the representatives o
the people and of levying the large sums of money for whic
the impending war with France created the immediate need

Everywhere, from Middelburg to The Hague, he lavishl
entertained the wealthy burghers and their women-folk an
the civic deputies who came to wait upon him. There wer
banquets and balls and mysteries to which his subjects wer
widely bidden, and he bore himself towards them as gra
ciously as it lay within his stern dour nature. He may, too
have been a little softened by anxiety in those days. New
followed him at every step of the measures being taken b
King Louis, of the invasion of Normandy by the Frenc
troops and of the steady amassing of forces for the overthro
of Burgundy. Meanwhile the Duke's own weapons were be
ing steadily forged for him, and here in the North he wa
providing as quickly as possible the fuel to feed thos
forges. It is doubtful if in those days he had, apart from h
own imperious will, any guide other than Count Anthon
the manner in which he conducted his affairs. The sum
raised in the North, over and above the ordinary tax
ceeded a half-million crowns of fifteen stivers, and so
amount was not lightly to be wrung from Netherlan
The arguments he employed to loosen purse-strin
those urged upon him by Count Anthony. Burgu
represented as the shield and bulwark of Flemish
The evils that might come like a blight out of Ger
France once that bulwark were removed were painted

colours, and thus were the Netherlands persuaded that if their prosperity were to be preserved, if the arts and commerce by which they throve were to remain untrammelled, the strength of Burgundy must be maintained. The wealthy merchants, who would have most to lose by any dislocation of their trade, and the civic deputies, who had in view the welfare of the country as a whole, were readily convinced by such arguments amiably presented at banquets and in the course of gracious receptions in which much honour was done to their wives and daughters. That among lesser folk there would be opposition to the assessments, and that in particular the new imposts upon provisions would press heavily upon poor villagers, were difficulties to be dealt with later when and as they arose.

By the end of August, the progress successfully accomplished, the Duke now homing swiftly made his final halt at Middelburg to persuade from the Zealanders the levy of sixteen thousand crowns which was to be Zealand's contribution to the total.

The town was festively arrayed in preparation for his coming, and in accordance with the orders that had gone ahead of him to his faithful Governor. Triumphal arches, bearing the escutcheons of Burgundy and Zealand, had been erected in the streets. Tapestries and rich carpets decked the windows and balconies and the Burgomaster and his Council met him at the gates with a fulsomely conceived address of welcome. He was acclaimed as he rode through in light armour with his attendant troop of knights and gentlemen, his heralds in coats of blazonry, his bodyguard of cross-bow-men, and his following of heavily armoured men-at-arms. The Sire Claude de Rhynsault had well-engineered show to ensure the satisfaction of his ducal master.

In the Gravenhof the great hall, usually so bare, cold, and forbidding, had been made gay with cloth of gold and some of the richest products of the Arras looms, procured in haste to supply a fittingly splendid Burgundian setting. A dais had been erected at one end of the hall; it was carpeted in red, and under a canopy of cloth of gold was set a gilded chair of state for the Duke's highness.

Enthroned there that afternoon, attended by a dozen of his gentlemen, each vying with the other in magnificence, he accepted the homage of a great gathering assembled there by Rhynsault's invitation and comprising all persons of wealth and prominence, not merely in Middelburg itself, but throughout the Island of Walcheren.

The civic dignitaries and many others whose wealth rendered them of consequence by burgher standards were with their wives personally presented by the stalwart Governor, who stood for the purpose on the first step of the dais on the Duke's left. On the Duke's immediate right, beside his chair, and leaning lightly against its tall back stood Count Anthony of Guelders. He was alone there, and detached from the group of gaily clad nobles clustered behind and to the left of the ducal throne. For all his tall vigour he had an air of listlessness. His long, comely countenance was pale and a little wistful, and there was a dreamy vacancy in his dark eyes as if either he did not see or did not heed the magnificent throng that was parading there.

Over a vest of cloth of gold he wore a pleated pourpoint of purple velvet with long sleeves the points of which reached almost to his knees, and there were tiny jewels in the cords that laced it across his breast. His hose was of violet and he was shod in the long poulaines of black velvet, which in England were by law forbidden to any under the rank of an esquire. The collar of the Golden Fleece was the only ornament he wore.

Standing there, tall and graceful, beside the stocky, seated figure of the young Duke, who was all in black, he took the eye, especially of the women as they came up to be presented. More closely observed by them even than the Duke, he, himself, observed none. There was before his eyes a vision which seldom left it in those days. Memory and longing limned the picture for him: A quadrangular court about which arose a tall red house, a grey stork advancing sedately to meet him; a pair of quail in an osier cage against the wall; a border of tulips, white and yellow, the tulips, argent and or, which he had taken for his device; and then the apparition of a Madonna clad in the blue in which the Italians were wont to paint her, a slim, gracious, golden-headed Madonna with a delicately tinted, delicately featured face, who bade him welcome.

He considered that the bitter fight was over between the love, which had made him for a season forget his birth and blood, and the duty which he accounted owing to his station. He conceived that duty had won the final victory. He should have perceived his error in the persistence of this vision, now before him; in the terrible, aching longing it aroused.

Listless and vacant he leaned there, blind to the glittering throng that moved under his eyes, deaf to the hum of sub-dued voices, to the soft music being played by a troupe of musicians in one of the galleries, and the reiterated plati-tudes which his highness uttered as he extended his hand to be kissed by each kneeling burgher or inclined his head in acknowledgment of the curtsey of each burgher's lady. The old temptation to be a man even at the cost of ceasing to be a prince assailed him again, and with unusual violence. Per-haps it was provoked by his nearness to the ground ever hallowed in his memory by his transient association with her. Five miles away she was, in Flushing. So near, so very near. When these festivities were at an end, should he take horse and ride to visit her, to see her but once again? That was all he asked, all he craved: to see her once again. Strengthened by that sight of her, by word with her, perhaps, he would return to his duty, his yearnings quieted. Thus he deceived himself, not knowing or not choosing to admit that the sight of her would be but fuel to his passion.

And then with startling, appalling suddenness his prayer was granted; granted without any need to go five miles, five paces, or a single inch.

She stood before him.

He stared and stared whilst a man might have told a
Paternoster, not believing his eyes, imagining that he was the
victim of a delusion thrust upon him by the oppression of his
desire.

She was in blue, he noted, that same Madonna colour
which she had worn when first he had beheld her, but this
was of velvet and infinitely richer, as was all her raiment
from the horned headdress, whence a long veil floated behind
to the peaked shoes of cloth of gold that showed beneath
the hem of her gown. She was the same and yet not quite the
same as he had last seen her, three months ago. In the past
her attire, like her speech and manner, had ever been such
as would have become a noble maid in the retirement of her
own home. Now she was arrayed like a lady of the court
both in costliness of material and modishness of design. . .
Yet it was she, and the courtliness of her raiment was after
all no more than was used by the ladies of these opulent
burghers when they came to court, no more than was to be
observed on many another in that considerable assembly.

With conviction that it was really Johanna and that he
was not dreaming, a scarlet flame swept across his face to
leave it paler than it had been, so pale that his great dark
eyes seemed to glow and burn. For a moment breath almost
failed him, his brow was moist, and all the training in deportment and self-command deserted him. He felt foolish
and awkward as any clown, and knew not what to do or how
to bear himself. And then he became suddenly conscious of
another familiar face: a florid countenance with a great nose
and a pair of hazel eyes. It belonged to Philip Danvelt; and
there was the stocky burgher with his head thrown back on
his short thick neck, grinning broadly at him in greeting with
a lift of the hand towards him, to let others see on what terms
of familiarity he stood with this great gentleman who was
the first among the Duke's intimates.

That recalled Count Anthony to himself. He smiled his
acknowledgment of that fulsome greeting, and bowed low
from the waist to Johanna. A moment later and Rhynsault

was presenting her to the Duke. Another moment and she passed on and was merged with Danvelt into the body of the crowd. But the Count's eyes followed her as she moved hither and thither in that shifting throng. Actually he had moved a step to go after her before he remembered that respect for the Duke and his duty kept him rooted where he stood.

Not until some hours later, after the great state banquet which endured almost interminably and when the girandoles were lighted and the dance was in progress, was opportunity afforded him to approach her. It was during the first dance, when the Duke, to set the example, had led forth the wife of van Koeneck, the Burgomaster of Middelburg, and had been followed by all his courtiers and most of the burghers present, that Count Anthony espied her seated alone near one of the tall mullioned windows at the hall's end. He reached her side a moment after courtly elegant Messire de Rubempré of the Duke's following. She was in the act of declining with excuses the courtier's invitation to the dance when suddenly Count Anthony surged beside him. Messire de Rubempré bowed low and retired without observing the deathly pallor overspreading the face which had attracted that fastidious courtier or the tumult of that white bosom which he had so much admired.

With lowered eyes and fingers locked about the handle of her fan of peacock's feathers she sat with the least suggestion of crouching in her attitude while Count Anthony leaned over her.

'Johanna!' he murmured, but received no answer. He read offence in her attitude, in her averted eyes and her obvious agitation. She was in the right to be offended with him, and her sudden discovery of his true identity would hardly mitigate her feelings. But all would be well once he explained, once he told her that this sight of her had scattered his last doubt, his last hesitation; that his dukedom might go hang unless it would accept her for its duchess.

What lady in all the land, in all the world, he asked himself, could rival her for beauty, for dignity, for graciousness, for purity and worth? Hers was a nobility deeper than any nobility of birth and blood. It was a nobility directly bestowed upon her by her Maker, as sometimes happened.

'We must talk, Johanna. I have so much to say to you.'

One upward glance of her eyes she vouchsafed him, to lower them instantly again. But not before he had read scorn and pain in them. Her lips smiled a little in sheer bitterness. Her voice came steady and cold, and her words reached him above the sounds of the music and the shuffle and stamp of the dancers' feet.

'What can a Prince of Guelders have to say to a burgher woman?'

His voice was almost hoarse as he answered her: 'That which will make the burgher woman a princess or else the prince a burgher.'

Again she looked up at him, and if there was still pain in her eyes, and still some scorn, it was now the scorn of unbelief; but more than either was there sheer amazement.

'You go to odd lengths, my lord, in pursuit of your amusements.'

'Amusement! God of my life! Am I amused? Look in my eyes, Johanna. Read my face. Do you see amusement there?'

She marked his pallor, the dark stains under his eyes which added to their feverish lustre, and something indefinable in their glance which allured and terrified and enveloped her will.

'You are mad,' she said faintly, seeking to resist the spell of his gaze. 'Mad.'

'I have been. Mad with yearning ever since that day the Governor's officer carried me away from Flushing. Mad with doubts and distractions and balancings. But the sight of you has made me sane again.'

'The Governor's officer carried you away?' she echoed. It was all that she had heard, and it confirmed her first assumption. 'Against your will, do you mean?'

'A prisoner virtually, by an excess of zeal on the part of the Governor here. He would not allow me to communicate with you, not even a letter could I send until he had made safe delivery of me some weeks later to the Duke. Then . . .'

'Well, sir? Then?' She was almost stern, and seemed oddly composed; no burgher housewife speaking to a prince, but just a woman to a man. And her heart was pounding the while against her corsage.

'Then I wondered if silence were not best.' He hung his head. He spoke almost in shame. 'I wondered if it were not best to leave things where they stood; to vanish without explanation. There was my cursed station, a duty to the Duke which demanded instant labours of me, and a duty to the duchy which I was born one day to rule, as was pointed out to me in the very hour of my deliverance from the Governor's men. I was torn two ways. Between my love of you and all that my birth imposed upon me. I have been so torn ever since that day. But I am so torn no longer. The struggle is at an end. It never could have ended otherwise than this. Sooner or later I must have been as I am now: at your feet, Johanna, a very humble suppliant.'

Something within her seemed to snap. There was in all this a cruel irony he could not guess. Limply she sank back in her chair, and for an instant her head with its stiff head-dress lolled sideways on her shoulder.

'Johanna! You are ill!'

She steadied herself, answering mechanically. 'The heat. It stifles me.'

They were within two paces of a door leading to the open. He proffered his wrist. 'It is but a step to the garden. The air there will revive you. Come.'

Obediently she set her hand upon his wrist, rose and permitted him to conduct her from the hall. They went unheeded by all but one, and this a person of little consequence to either of them: Kuoni von Stocken, the Governor's hump-backed Fool.

In presenting Mistress Johanna that day to the Duke, the

Sire de Rhynsault had remarked her closely, and afterwards had desired his Fool to inform himself concerning her. The Fool, who served his master in many capacities, considered it a part of his task to observe the lady's deportment at this ball, for the sake of the inferences he might draw from it. Therefore he hovered near. Deeply intrigued, he advanced to put himself in the way of those two as they approached the open door. He fell back, however, without uttering the quip he had prepared. The lady's deep pallor, her faltering step, and Count Anthony's grave, preoccupied air, left the Fool stricken with amazement; and profoundly curious, staring after them as they passed out.

They went caring little to what extent they might be observed: he because he did not yet realize the situation in which he stood; she because she realized it but too well.

Beside him she came out upon the long terrace, and by its flight of steps down into the alleys of those spacious gardens, now drenched in the light of the August moon, where cool evening breezes sighed through tall black poplars. Thus leaning upon the arm of this man who to her was the man amongst men, this prince who announced himself ready either to raise her to his throne or else to fling his throne away for love of her, she went and wondered could Fate have found for her a more bitter mockery.

Because she had not trusted to her instincts, she had come to attach faith to the warning of a friar who thought he knew the world because he knew its prurience. In that faith she had dishonoured herself and had dishonoured Anthony. Because of the revulsion and heartbreak that it brought her, she had married Philip Danvelt to provide herself with a shelter under his roof and name from such onslaughts upon her virtue as the one she had so shamefully believed she had escaped. She had married an honest, kindly man whom she did not love, thereby wronging him and wronging herself. And of what a measure was her punishment? It lay not merely in the knowledge that with trust and patience she would have had her heart's desire, but in the realization, which had been with her now for more than half the three weeks that her marriage had already endured, that the man she had married was a man whom she could never love, a man incapable of experiencing love or inspiring it, a man with whom life was to be a dull and dreary servitude bereft of all noble aspirations.

A few days it had taken her to perceive the magnitude of her error, to realize that she would have done infinitely better to have sought in a nunnery the shelter she desired from the world's evil, and bitterly to regret that she had not so sought it.

Honest and kindly Danvelt might be, but only as he understood honesty and kindliness. He proved, upon the more intimate acquaintance of matrimony, gross and boorish, of an almost incredible stupidity and with all the self-assertion and overbearing arrogance towards his inferiors and dependents that is stupidity's commonest expression. He was vain, too, and ostentatious without generosity, and, whilst he could deck his wife richly and parade her on such occasions as the present with all the pride of possession, he had made it plain even in these early days that in his own house he would be not merely master, but tyrant, and that in all things from the slightest to the weightiest his own will must prevail unquestioned, and no opinion must ever be set against his own. He desired in a wife not a companion, but a woman to bear him children and maintain his house, and to discharge both functions precisely in the manner he should decree.

She saw the dreary grey life ahead to which she stood committed, and alongside of it the life that might have been, the life that Anthony was even now offering her, still in blissful ignorance of the insurmountable barrier that already closed the way.

She drew a deep breath of the fragrant air of the summer night, and allowed it to escape again in a long sigh over the grave of withered hopes and forfeited opportunity.

'Take me back,' she said gently; 'I am better now. I should not have come out here.'

'Ah, wait. There is yet so much to say.'

She laughed, but entirely without mirth. 'Neither much nor little, my lord. All is said. All. Words have been spoken that have forged bonds never to be dissolved in life. I am the wife of Philip Danvelt.'

'You are the wife . . . the wife of Philip Danvelt? The wife?' he repeated the words dully, as if seeking to force their meaning upon his reluctant mind.

He clutched her arm, and instantly let it go again. For a long moment there was silence. Then he groaned. 'O God!' And after another pause asked her with forced calm: 'When? When did you become that?'

'Three weeks ago.'

'Three weeks ago? Two months after I had left, believing that . . .' He broke off, and for a spell they stood again in utter silence. Ahead of them at the little avenue's end a fountain plashed in the moonlight, the water quivering like molten silver in the broad stone basin. Behind them the tall windows glowed with golden light. Music and gay voices came wafted out to them. The scent of roses hung heavy about them on the tepid air. It was a moment of mutual anguish neither should ever forget.

Then he spoke quietly, almost coldly in a great dignity. 'It but remains, madam, to crave your pardon for my presumption, for all that I unwarrantably assumed concerning you. And yet . . . and yet . . .' His voice warmed again, and as he ran on the passion mounted and quivered in it, stimulated by the memories he reviewed. 'And yet that presumption was not unwarranted. I displayed it clearly from the very outset; almost from the hour of our meeting I let you behold what that meeting meant to me. You suffered it; you listened to words whose import could leave you in no doubt; you made no attempt to check the course of an adoration that was revealed so plainly. Why? Had you been my Lady Catharine, to whom I once was affianced, or any other lady of a court, I should have held the answer. But you are not as those; or, if you are, then is there no truth in all the world. Oh, and there were other signs. We said things, you and I, for which no words were needed. I spoke of it on that last day you rode with me. Do you remember?'

'Don't!' she begged him, anguish in her voice. 'Of your pity, say no more.'

But he was pitiless. 'I must. I must understand this thing, or I shall never understand anything again. I told you then of the wordless communion of souls that are in tune, and how it was your call that had fetched me out of England, back to your side.'

She answered him now, and answered him by instinct in his own language. 'You heard it then because you listened for it. You might have heard it again at any time from the hour you left me until I saw you in Bruges, walking beside the litter of the new Duchess, a Knight of the Golden Fleece, and was told you were the Prince of Guelders. From that moment I called to you no more because, knowing at last who you were, I knew that you were not for me.'

He put his hand to his brow. 'And you thought . . .' He checked there, horror in his voice.

'You have guessed my thought,' she told him sadly; 'what else was I to think?'

'But did you not reason? Did you not ask yourself why, if I were as vile as that, had I not remained in the endeavour to complete my . . . my conquest?'

'Oh, yes. I asked myself that. I forgot nothing. I found the answer in the assumption that something had happened to remove you suddenly; something beyond your power to resist, perhaps an awakening of conscience in one who was reputed of high knightly worth, devout and pure of life.'

At the end of a little pause in which he stood silent, miserable, dejected, she touched his arm. 'Shall we go in now, my lord? My husband will be wondering at my absence.'

'Your husband!' he cried. 'Danvelt!' He uttered the name contemptuously. There was a dull, unreasoning anger in his soul. That ape to possess this angel out of heaven! This bright, delicate, almost ethereal girl who would have

graced a court, to be subject to that boorish dullard. He
drew her on by the arm, and she suffered it. He possessed
some power over her to which she would never have opposed
resistance. There was a semi-circular seat of stone by the
fountain. To this he led her, and under the suasion of his
will she seated herself, whilst he sank down beside her.

'But to marry!' he protested. 'To marry and so suddenly!
That is what yet I do not understand.'

She answered him too hastily. 'Nor do I, my lord, whilst
there were nunneries in which I could have the shelter I
sought from such perils as the one which I conceived that
you had borne for me.'

'Ah! So! So! It was I, then, who flung you into that . . .
into his arms? I! And already you were repenting. Already
you had realized that this marriage . . .'

She interrupted him. 'My lord! My lord! You must
not!' She attempted to rise. 'Take me back to the hall,' she
implored him. 'There is no more to say between us. Indeed,
already I have said more than I thought or intended. I am a
wedded wife, my lord. I beg that in honour you'll remember
it.'

But his hand upon her arm again kept her seated. She in-
terceded in vain. Anguish and passion set him above all in-
culcated lessons. He found a new philosophy to meet the
case, and voiced it almost fiercely.

'I remember it only in dishonour. For that is what it
spells. You are a wedded wife, you say. What has he wed of
you, this man? Has he wed your love? Has he mated with
your soul? Is he conscious of a soul himself or aware that
there is one in you, the greater part of each of us which is not
to be fettered or constrained? Love, Johanna, is of the soul.
And you do not love this man.'

'You are wrong, my lord. You have no right to say it. I
love him. I am his wife.'

He knew this for the feeble protest of her sense of duty.

'You do not love him, Johanna. Because you love me, and
the love of a woman for a man, true love, is one and indivis-
ible.'

'Ah, let me go. You must not say it!' There was real anguish in her voice, as there was in his, though anguish of another kind when he made answer:

'I must not say it. I must not utter truth. Because of a contract into which your lips have entered, I am to play comedy with you and you with me, and make believe that we are each to each as any other man and woman. That is what you ask me to believe. But truth is truth, and it must prevail above all shams. And love is the greatest truth in all the world; it is the force to which all life is due, and with life all that is best and noblest in the lives of men, a force that nothing mortal can resist, a white-hot flame that devours all make-believe.'

'It cannot devour my marriage,' she answered firmly.

'Can it not? It could if it were strong enough, true enough, if it heeded nothing but itself, as love should.'

She rose at that, shaking off the spell he seemed to weave about her. She stood straight and tense beside him, her chin high. And her voice came firm and challenging.

'Be plain, my lord,' she bade him. 'You spoke of truth just now, and how it must prevail. Let it prevail here, and tell me what are you asking me to do?'

The question stunned him. Before that demand for a practical expression, the hot vapours of passion were dispelled. Reality confronted him and asked a question which must be answered by reality. What was he asking her to do? What, indeed? It was easy to make phrases about her being married but not mated, about the mating of souls to which the mating of bodies was but the outward physical expression, but, meanwhile, she was fast bound by certain legal ties that made her Danvelt's possession, a possession undisputable in honour.

He found the answer at last in his romanticism, in his idealism, and it had this virtue at least, that it was sincere.

'What am I asking? Something so vague, impalpable, and abstract that the world would mock me for desiring it. The love of that part of you which is not given in wedlock to Danvelt, since that is all that now remains unpossessed. Accord me that, hold me in your thought, and I shall not grudge him the husk which he believes to be you. I'll go my ways, nor trouble you again, who have troubled you so much and so clumsily. But I'll go exalted, consecrate to you while I have life, your seal upon me, like the twin tulips which in honour of you I have taken for my device.'

He was startled and thrilled by the fall of a tear upon his outstretched hand. He bore it to his lips. Her answer followed, faltering a little.

'That you may have, because I cannot, if I would, withhold it. You shall be ever in my thoughts. As I conceive that you would have me be, so shall I seek to mould myself. Night and morning you shall have place in my prayers. That is all I have to give you . . .' She paused a moment, then for the first time spoke his name . . . 'Anthony.'

He was on his feet beside her, and his voice sank almost to a whisper.

'I am content. I would not have you other, for you would then be false to my ideal of you. Will you kiss me once, Johanna?'

'My lips are in that part of me which Philip possesses,' she reminded him gently.

He bowed his head in silence, and in silence at last they retraced their steps.

CHAPTER XIII

PÉRONNE

THE Duke of Burgundy made a sudden and hurried departure from the North as a result of the news reaching him of King Louis's movements, and the consequent need for instant measures. With a strong force he crossed the frontier and advanced to the Somme, the cities of which were providing the bone of contention, and he made his headquarters at Péronne, whence he could watch his cousin the enemy.

Now whilst Louis XI would never shirk a fight when no alternative offered, or when the issue was beyond doubt, yet in the astuteness and caution of his nature there was a reluctance to set his fortunes on the hazard of battle if the odds were too closely balanced or if his ends might be attained by any other means. His information now showed him that already the blow which he meditated had been too long delayed. His cousin and brother-in-law Charles was armed to the teeth and backed by a force considerably greater than Louis had supposed it possible for him to bring into the field.

King Louis reconsidered his position. Here guile might serve him better than force. After all, even so rash and choleric a man as Charles of Burgundy will yield something rather than place all upon the hazard of arms, will pay something in order to economize the waste of blood and treasure that war inevitably entails. The case, thought King Louis, was become one for compromise. Although by compromise he might not hope to win all that would accrue to him from a victorious war, yet he might win some part of it — yielded by the other side to avoid the same bloody arbitrament — and let the remainder wait until a more favourable opportunity.

The way to this was rendered easy by the fact that throughout all his preparations for action, he had maintained a superficially friendly correspondence with his 'dear cousin of Burgundy, calculated to veil the circumstance that it was against Burgundy that he was arming, and making it appear that it was the necessity to impose his sovereign will upon his recalcitrant feudatories of Normandy and Brittany which called for the mobilization in which he was engaged. Charles of Burgundy on his side had entered into the spirit of the comedy by pretending that his own preparations were merely for the purpose of keeping his obligations with his allies.

In the parley desired by King Louis, he determined to be his own ambassador, and this despite the alarm and opposition which so rash-seeming a resolve spread among his officers. There was every ground for it. Charles of Burgundy, who appears to have held no man in fear when trial by battle was at issue, undoubtedly feared and mistrusted his cousin of France in an encounter of any other kind. King Louis was a master of arts which remained mysterious to the dull wits of the young Duke of Burgundy. To the mind of Charles his cousin Louis appeared as a guileful human spider spinning webs of intrigue into which the strongest might blunder and find himself entangled. By the employment of these very arts, Louis proposed the meeting in such terms and with such lofty aims in view that it was impossible for Charles, despite all his mistrust of the man, to refuse his wishes. The King would come unarmed — that is to say, attended by no more than a guard of honour — into the Duke's stronghold for the parley, trusting to the Duke's word for his personal safety and leaving it to the Duke himself to supply him with a suitable escort.

In his own hand, Charles wrote him a letter of safe-conduct, wherein he swore and promised by his faith and on his honour that King Louis might come, sojourn, and return in surety.

Content with this, Louis went boldly into the lion's den.

On Sunday the 9th October, the shabby, untidy, mean-looking little king, with his ugly, eager face, rode into Pé-ronne accompanied only by his confessor the Bishop of Av-ranche, the Duke of Bourbon with his brothers the Arch-bishop of Lyons and the Sire de Beaujeu, half a dozen other nobles, and eighty archers of his Scottish Guard. Within a mile of the town he was met by the Duke and a numerous company who had ridden forth to give him welcome with every outward sign of submission and respect due to his royal station.

The present is no history of the long duel between France and Burgundy, or even of this passage in it. But a little must be said to reveal the part — obscured by historians as irrelevant — which La Marche informs us was played by Count Anthony of Guelders to save the honour of the Duke of Burgundy when it stood in direst peril.

In spinning that great web of his for the entanglement of Charles, and in inciting foes against him wherever he saw the opportunity of doing so, Louis had not lost sight of Liège, its grievances for what already it had suffered and its fears for what might yet be to come from the resented pro-tection which Burgundy had imposed upon it. The King's agents had been very active there, representing their royal master as the devoted friend of the Liègeois, sharing their indignation at the unlawful manner in which they had been brought into subjection to Burgundy and determined to assist them in breaking their shackles. Placing their trust in these royal promises the Liègeois had gone about their pre-parations for insurrection at the opportune moment when the Duke of Burgundy should be fully engaged elsewhere. They were strong, resolute, and well-led; and King Louis realized the great value to himself of so formidable an ally in the Duke's rear when he himself should be engaging the Duke's front; whilst they on their side perceived their mo-ment to have arrived when Charles and Louis faced each other on the Somme.

Then came Louis's change of plans and his decision to ne-

gotiate instead of fighting. He despatched a messenger in
haste to Liège on the eve of setting out to parley with the
Duke. But the messenger arrived too late. The Liègeois
were already under arms, and, on the very Sunday that
Louis rode confidingly into the Burgundian quarters, two
thousand of them marched on Tongres to seize the person of
the libertine Prince-Bishop Louis de Bourbon.

Within half-an-hour of his entering Péronne, Louis's confidence in his safe-conduct had been abated by witnessing
the advent there of the Marshal of Burgundy, Thibault de
Neufchâtel. The marshal had arrived that very morning
with the lances raised in Burgundy for the campaign that
was afoot. Having seen to the quartering of these, he made
his way to the castle, accompanied by a body of nobles
whose identity awakened in Louis's breast the very gravest
alarm as he surveyed them from the window of his lodging
opposite the castle gates. They were gentlemen of France,
who had fled beyond the reach of Louis's rancour, and who
in this hour brought their swords to the Duke of Burgundy
that thus they might satisfy the now mutual hatred and
mistrust.

There was Antoine du Lau, the Seneschal of Guienne,
whom the King had imprisoned in the fortress of Usson
whilst an iron cage was building for him, in which, unable
either to stand or lie, and deprived of every ray of light, he
should linger out a tortured remnant of his days. Du Lau
had escaped in time with the connivance of his keepers, who
had paid terribly for his evasion. At Dijon he had found
shelter and service with the Duke of Burgundy.

There was Poncet de la Rivière, who had been removed
from his command in the royal army, after rendering stout
service at Montlhéry. La Rivière had departed France on a
pilgrimage to the Holy Land, from which he had been careful not to return until now, in arms and bearing on his surcoat the cross of Saint Andrew, the badge of Burgundian
service.

Most ominous of all, because of the dreadful precedent

it established against King Louis, there was Philippe de Bresse, with his brothers the Count of Romont and the Bishop of Geneva, all three Princes of Savoy. De Bresse had once gone as a mediator to Louis XI under the guaranty of a safe-conduct from the King, in despite and dishonour of which the King had flung him into the Castle of Loches, and kept him there in a rigorous and long confinement, from which at last he had escaped.

And there were others, a round dozen of them, whom the King recognized as fugitives from his anger and declared enemies of his person.

Never a man of high physical courage, the lean-shanked little king felt himself go cold with fear as he looked down upon the members of that little troop, and as they looked up and met his shifty glance. It never crossed his mind that his presence there at Péronne struck the same fear into them that their arrival begot in him. Apprehensive of some arrangement between France and Burgundy, they hastened to the Duke, Philippe de Bresse at their head, to obtain of him security for their persons.

Knowing nothing of this, already regretting that he had not given heed to those who had stigmatized as rash and hare-brained this visit to Péronne, the King stroked his long pendulous nose and sucked in his shuddering lips. It did not take him long to conclude that if ever he had stood in danger of having his throat cut it was now. No safe-conduct would guard him against the Count de Bresse whose safe-conduct he himself had once violated, or against du Lau and his horror of that iron cage. And if one of these were to pay off that old score, how easy for the Duke of Burgundy to save his honour by asserting that the King had fallen victim to a private vengeance. There might even be a scapegoat. King Louis judged, as we all do, his neighbour by himself. And how convenient for the Duke of Burgundy.

He held a hasty conference with his confessor and with Beaujeu, as a result of which, for his greater safety, and so

that the Duke might be more immediately responsible for
it, he petitioned Charles to remove him from his present
lodging and afford him quarters in the castle itself.

The Duke acceded promptly, having first pointed out
that the Castle of Péronne, being a fortress rather than a
dwelling, afforded no proper housing for a king. The King,
however, less concerned with personal comforts than with
personal safety, removed himself at once, and within the
grim walls of the castle may have felt less apprehensive.
But not for long. On the morrow he had every reason to
suppose that his last hour was at hand. For news of the insurrection and violent action of the Liègeois reached Péronne. King Louis's incitement of them was not to be
doubted. Indeed, there was proof of it. The facts themselves were bad enough. But they were rendered infinitely
worse by the gross tongue of rumour. The story of wholesale
slaughter, brought to the Duke at Péronne by one who
claimed to have been an eye-witness of the events, stated
that the Prince-Bishop, the Papal Legate Onofrio di Santa
Croce, and Charles's Burgundian Lieutenant, the Sire de
Humbercourt, had all been murdered. The same witness
and others who accompanied him swore solemnly that
amongst the leaders of the rebels they had seen certain
agents of the King of France whom they mentioned definitely by name.

Consternation and furious resentment spread within the
castle and town of Péronne. The Duke in his anger swore
that the King of France had come thither to abuse him. It
did not help him that he could not perceive precisely how
the King was to achieve this object. He never could perceive the aims of that sly, subtle monarch.

He ordered the drawbridge to be taken up and the gates
of the town to be closed, and he placed the King — who was
now terrified by a justifiable expectation of the worst —
under a guard of archers, whilst he deliberated upon what
measures should be taken. These deliberations he chose to
make alone with Count Anthony.

In a small, bleak chamber of that cheerless fortress, Charles gave tongue at once to his fury and his fears.

'He has come hither to betray me,' he swore repeatedly, summarizing all that he had said. 'I felt it in my bones when he proposed the meeting. I did all that was possible to oppose it.'

Count Anthony asked a question calculated to summon reason to the Duke's aid.

'If his aim had been betrayal, why should he have come hither to place himself in your power?'

'If? Do you say "If"?' Livid with passion, his strong jaws clenched, the Duke glared at his cousin. 'What else has he done but betray me? You have heard the tale; you have heard how the wires were pulled at Liège by his agents, with the result that an army is on foot there, and these gentlemen of mine have been damnably butchered.'

'He may have done all that, or at least be a party to it all. But how, being here, can he work harm against you now?'

'But if I knew, if I could guess, I should be less uneasy. But there is one way to make sure of him.' And the Duke drew the half of his dagger from its sheath, and shot it home again.

Count Anthony, seated on the deep stone sill of one of the arched windows, cross-legged and nursing his knee in his locked hands, gravely shook his head.

'Not that way, Charles.'

'What better way?'

Count Anthony's answer was indirect. 'His life and person are sacred in your hands. Your honour demands it.'

'My honour? And does not my honour, my very duty, demand that I avenge the butchery of Bourbon of Humbercourt and the Papal Legate? To what end else am I justiciary in these dominions? This knavish king shall be paid in the same murderous coin.'

'But not by you, Charles. There is your safe-conduct to him. Remember the terms of it. You have pledged your faith and your honour for his surety whilst here.'

'Did I foresee this?'

'Unfortunately not. But the pledge is given. No circumstances can relieve you of it. You dare not dishonour it.'

'Dare not! God of my life! Is there anything I do not dare? What man dares, I dare.'

'What gentleman dares,' the Count corrected him. 'And no gentleman dare be false to his pledged word. Would you have it said of you in the world that the Duke of Burgundy lured the King of France to a parley under a safe-conduct, and then murdered him? The deed would be remembered long after the provocation was forgotten, and your name would be execrated for all time.'

In this way, and by opposing a calm firmness to the Duke's heat, he restrained Charles from any immediate measures of reprisal such as he might certainly have taken had he been left to the counsels of his rage.

But on the morrow the battle had to be fought all over again. Early in the morning the Duke summoned a council of his nobles and officers including those who once had been subjects of the King of France, and who because of present rancour were come to offer their swords to Burgundy. That council lasted all day and well into the night, for the arguments were long and fierce. They might have been less protracted but for certain measures taken even in his extremity by the crafty, ever-watchful Louis.

Virtually a prisoner though he might be, yet it was sought to dissemble the fact by permitting certain of his attendants to come and go freely in the performance of their duties by him. Informed through these of what was taking place, alive to his danger, and realizing that perhaps his very life might hang upon the deliberation of the council that was about to sit, he set himself to employ as best he could that most choice of all the weapons in his armoury of guile, and one whose value he had frequently tested: corruption. Using those same few friends as his ambassadors, he made lavish promises here and there until he had committed himself to the extent of some fifteen thousand crowns. If he was mean and parsimonious as a rule, he could also be lavish upon occasion.

Four voices prevailed in that council. First, that which urged that the safe-conduct protected the King and made it impossible to move in any way against his person. Second, that which urged that he be imprisoned and made to answer for the sedition he had stirred up in Liège and the blood that had been shed there as a consequence. Third, that which advised that he be deposed and his brother the Duke of Normandy invited to come and discuss the terms of peace with France. And lastly, the fierce, insistent voice which demanded blood for blood. This was the voice of those who had gone in personal fear of him for years and saw no truce to their fears whilst he continued alive.

It was not easy to silence these last, comparatively few though they might be.

Did one urge the safe-conduct which made such an act of violence unthinkable, there was Philippe de Bresse to remind them, out of the common knowledge and his own particular experience, that a safe-conduct formerly had not made an act of violence unthinkable to Louis himself. Did another urge clemency and the laws of humanity, there was du Lau on his feet to inquire when clemency or laws of humanity had prevailed with a king who put gentlemen to the slow and painful death that came of being cramped in cages.

Count Anthony, seated on the Duke's immediate right, had taken some part in the debate to defend the position that the safe-conduct made action against the King's person impossible. And when Philippe de Bresse appeared to have silenced that argument by putting forward the precedent in such cases which Louis himself had established, Count Anthony's was the only voice that answered him, and in answering him restored at least in part the position which de Bresse had sapped.

'The precedent is less sound than it appears, because there is no true parallel between the situations. The King of France was dealing with a subject who, in his eyes, and in the eyes of the law of France, was guilty of treason and had therefore forfeited all consideration.'

'A safe-conduct is a safe-conduct,' de Bresse had answered him violently. 'You talk like a lawyer, Lord Count, and you quote legal codes. But for gentlemen there is a higher code: the code of chivalry and of honour.'

'I thank you, sir, for the reminder,' said Count Anthony tartly. 'And since you appeal to the code of honour, I shall answer you from that code, which is all against your demands. No offence committed against a man can tarnish his own honour, but only those offences which he, himself, commits against others. We are concerned here, not with the honour of the King of France, which may be tarnished, but with the honour of the Duke of Burgundy, which so far is clear. Do you, sir, do any of you, invite him to stain it by such an act as that for which any court of honour must brand the King of France with infamy? Must I descend to become a rogue so as to punish my neighbour for being one? In honour, sirs, as you well know, it is better to let the offending neighbour go unpunished, at least until such time as he may be punished without dishonour to ourselves.'

'So much seems plain enough,' the Duke grumbled with sour reluctance, and so silenced any further insistence from de Bresse.

'It comes then to this,' sneered du Lau, 'that we are to quit ourselves like gentlemen in dealing with a knave.'

'Each of us quits himself according to his nature,' Count Anthony answered in his passionless voice. 'It is perhaps fortunate for King Louis that he is a knave and that we are gentlemen. But it is fortunate in this instance only.'

At long last, when the day had given place to night, a resolve was reached which appeared to express the desire of the majority: to depose the King and send for the Duke of Normandy. On that resolve, the council at last dissolved, and the Duke summoned his secretaries to prepare the letters he was to send to the King's brother.

News of the decision reached the King in his chamber. It

would have dismayed any other in his place; him it almost elated in that it removed the worst danger he had apprehended, that of having his throat cut. They might depose him all they pleased. As long as he lived and recovered his liberty, they would have to reckon with him in the end. He had, with reason, unbounded faith in his own wits.

But the end was not yet as the council had decreed. Whilst the Duke strode to and fro dictating, and his secretary's quill scratched and spluttered over the parchment, back came Count Anthony, who had departed with the others. The Duke flushed angrily at sight of him, sensing here a fresh opposition to the comparatively mild measure upon which he had determined.

'Charles, dismiss your secretary and hear me. I have something to propose.'

'If it is aught concerning the King of France, you are behind the fair. My messenger is already in the saddle and but awaits this letter.'

'Let him await it a little longer; until you have heard me. What I have to say touches your honour.'

'My honour! Death of God! Who made you guardian of my honour?'

'No one made me the guardian of it. But out of love for you I presume to be its counsellor. Dismiss your secretary. You'll regret it all the days of your life if you refuse to hear me now. For I have found a better way than yours to settle this score with the King.'

The Duke scowled sulkily at his cousin, hesitating.

'Hear me at least,' the Count insisted.

The Duke waved the secretary away.

'Be brief,' he commanded, as the door closed upon the departing scribe. 'Time presses.'

But there was no haste about Count Anthony. He was as deliberate as he was calm.

'First, Charles, you cannot do this thing. Nay, hear me out. If you'll remember what I said to de Bresse, you'll spare me and yourself the tedium of a repetition. Those arguments of honour are unanswerable. The King has your safe-conduct and, in the hour in which it ceases to protect him, in that hour you will have been pulled down to the King's own paltry, knavish level. Men will say of you, as they say already of King Louis, that your honour is a bubble upon which no reliance can be placed, your pledge a mere word as easily given as retracted. You are a great prince, Charles, and you are bound by the obligations of your lofty station.'

'I thank you for the sermon. But it has been preached already, aye, and answered.'

'Has it been truly answered? Is it all false? Are you not a great prince? Is your honour tarnished or tarnishable? Is your word worthless?'

'Devil take you! You know that none of this is so.'

'Then, why make it so? For that is the only lasting thing these letters will achieve. They may bring you a momentary satisfaction . . .'

'They do not,' the Duke interrupted, in exasperation. 'God knows they do not.'

Count Anthony smiled almost compassionately. 'Not even so little as that? Then why persist?'

The Duke pondered him almost sullenly out of weary, blood-injected eyes. 'You hinted an alternative,' he said.

'Why, yes. But first it would have pleased me to turn you from the decision taken; to make you realize its folly. Were I in your place . . .'

'Give thanks to God that you are not.'

'Were I in your place, I would make the King sup on his treachery, make him eat it under the eyes of all the world, so that whatever followed all decent men should point the finger of scorn at him. I would do this after first making terms of peace — the pretended purpose of his visit here. And in the present circumstances, cowed as he is by the fear of his deserts, you may have whatever terms you choose to dictate, short of the crown of France itself.'

'By Saint George!' the Duke's eyes gleamed. 'That had

escaped me, as it seems to have escaped those furious coun-
sellors of mine.'

'You all wandered so far down a bypath that you lost all
memory of the highroad and the journey to be made upon
it.'

The Duke nodded. 'But the other measure: To make the
King eat his treachery, as you say? Be plain on that.'

Count Anthony considered him a moment in silence.
Then he took him familiarly by the arm. 'Come with me to
the King, Charles.'

Angrily the Duke wrenched his arm away. 'Not I, by
Saint George! I will not meet the rogue. I cannot trust myself.'

'Oh, yes, you can. Though you despise the man, you reverence the office. That will suffice. The rest you can leave
to me. Let me be your mouthpiece in the interview, and I
promise you a solution, a triumphant solution, of all your
difficulties.'

'Ah! You promise? But if you do not perform?'

'You need be bound by nothing that I do. Repudiate
me if I seem to fail you.'

The Duke stroked his chin. 'How will you go about it?'

Again the Count took his arm. 'Come with me to the
King, Charles, and you shall see.'

Reluctantly, leaden-footed, the Duke allowed himself to
be conducted.

CHAPTER XIV

CHECKMATE

IN a small stone chamber, vaulted and cheerless, sparsely furnished, the hearth cold and empty and the square window barred like a prison's, sat the King of France, and a less kingly figure you will seek in vain down the galleries of history.

Louis XI was then in his forty-fifth year, and looked older. Of middle height, he was almost delicate of frame with spare limbs and bony hands. He was of a mean and commonplace ugliness of countenance, his nose disproportionately large and pendulous, his lips coarse and sensual. But the craft of the man was advertised in his high cheek-bones, his depth of brow, and his quick eyes, small and bright as a weasel's. He was dressed like a shopkeeper, in cheap garments untidily assumed, and his ill-fitting black hose hung in wrinkles about his lean shanks. For warmth he was wrapped in a coarse grey cloak such as a pilgrim might have worn. The rim of his round hat, which was thrust down over his brows, was adorned with a half-dozen little leaden images of saints.

He was alone with his confessor, the Cardinal Balue, who sat apart, a majestic scarlet figure, deeply immersed in his breviary so as not to disturb his master at his devotions. For the King was praying. Seated at the plain brown table, on which the great silver candle-branch seemed almost out of place, and resting his elbow on the board, the Majesty of France was industriously telling his beads. The hiss of his fervently whispered Aves was the only sound in the stillness of the chamber. There was need for prayer and for fervency. The omens could not have been more terrifying. In the tower to be reached by a door from the adjacent chamber, where the King's bed was made, another King of France,

Charles the Simple, had been held in durance and finally murdered, by another rebellious vassal, the Count of Vermandois. As things had fallen out, it began to appear to the King that there was considerable danger of the coincidence being completed and that Louis the Astute might share the fate of Charles the Simple.

A knock fell upon the door. The King jumped and sucked in his breath. His nerves were in execrable case.

The Cardinal closed his breviary on his forefinger. It was a volume in a rich binding of red velvet encrusted with precious stones. He looked across at the King with solemn inquiry. The King stared back at him a moment, eyes scared in his sallow face, then nodded, and pouched his beads.

The Cardinal rose, and moved with slow majesty, his cloak of scarlet silk trailing along the ground as he crossed to open. He stepped out of the chamber, to return a moment later with the announcement that the Duke himself, accompanied by Count Anthony of Guelders, begged an audience of the King's highness.

The keen, eager eyes of the King flickered at the announcement, and a measure of relieved surprise showed in his face. If Count Anthony of Guelders was in this, his case must be far from hopeless. Count Anthony, that mirror of chivalry and pattern of honour, did not deal in murder or baseness of any kind. He rose, as he desired the Cardinal to admit them.

First came a groom of the chamber bearing a great gilded candle-branch of a dozen candles, whose golden light suffused the bleak room almost with a sense of warmth. When he had gone out again backwards and bent almost double in homage to the Majesty of France, the Duke entered, followed closely by his cousin.

The Count had rightly judged in saying that, whilst the Duke might despise the man, he would reverence the office. In the presence now of the King, Charles of Burgundy, although sullen of face, would have bent his knee in formal homage but that Louis, springing forward, prevented him by seizing his elbows and upholding him. Almost they appeared to embrace as they stood thus for a moment. Then the King spoke in his thin and now rather quavering voice.

'Fair cousin, this is to honour me. And you, my Lord Count, I bid you welcome.' He removed a hand from the Duke's sleeve of rich black velvet, to extend it to Count Anthony, who dutifully kissed it whilst he bent his knee. 'You find me in deep distress,' he ran on, 'at the events which have come to trouble the harmony I had hoped should prevail between us here. It was that hope, that confident hope, which made me anxious to come in person to adjust our differences under the surety of your safe-conduct.'

His keen eyes were on the Duke's heavy, sullen countenance whilst he issued what he considered an urgently necessary reminder.

The Duke began to rumble an answer. 'Monseigneur, but for that safe-conduct . . .'

The King interrupted him, becoming suddenly very royal. 'Will not your highness sit? Thus we shall be more at our ease to talk.' He waved him to a chair by the table. 'And you, Lord Count . . .' He waved again, and the Cardinal, who stood by the third and last chair in that meanly furnished chamber, would have made haste to offer it to Count Anthony but that the latter stayed him in the act.

The King, who retained his hat, resumed the chair from which he had risen; the Duke took another facing the King beyond the board, whilst Count Anthony, a tall, vivid figure in a crimson houppelande that reached to his ankles, stood at the table's head. The Cardinal, in his scarlet robes, glowed and smouldered among the shadows in the background.

Fearing imprudences from the Duke, Count Anthony made haste to assume the spokesmanship.

'Sire, his highness has ventured to intrude upon you in the hope that it may be your good pleasure to fulfil now the purpose of your gracious visit to Péronne.'

His tone and words were of the utmost deference. So much, indeed, that they made the alert King suspicious of their ultimate intention. Why so smooth, he wondered, when he, who knew the Duke's temper, had expected roughness and upbraidings? The only antidote to his quick suspicions lay in the fact that it was Count Anthony of Guelders — whose ways were gentle knightly ways — who spoke now for the Duke. Smoothness in such a man could not be the natural cloak of guile.

He licked his coarse lips, and his quick little eyes flashed from one to the other of them.

'Why, this is good hearing,' said he. 'Excellent hearing. I had feared that the discussions of terms might have been indefinitely postponed by these unfortunate events which . . . which . . .'

Whilst he fumbled for euphemistic expressions, the Duke cut in harshly.

'There was good reason for your fears, monseigneur. These events cry out for satisfaction.'

The King gulped, and his apprehensions mounted again. Things were not, then, to run the unnaturally smooth course which Count Anthony's opening words had seemed to promise.

'These events, my lord,' he ventured, 'believe me, no man could deplore more deeply than I do.'

The Duke laughed. The King jumped visibly at the sound, which was far from pleasant, and he momentarily covered his mouth with a hand which seemed to be all knuckles.

'As God lives,' said the Duke, still with that snarling laugh of his, 'you have good reason to deplore them.'

Count Anthony brought him sharply to the reminder that the matter had been entrusted to his hands. 'By your leave, Charles!' His glance said more than his words, and it was not lost on the watchful monarch. 'The King's reasons may not be as you suppose them.' With the former gracious deference he turned to the King again. 'You perceive, sire, that an obstacle exists to the calm discussion of any terms of peace between France and Burgundy, however deeply de-

sired by both. But if I have brought the Duke here to consider them with you, monseigneur, it is in the very confident
hope that, in spite of the circumstantial reports his highness
has received, you will, yourself, sire, be able to remove the
obstacle.'

The King considered. 'God and Our Lady know I have
the will. As for the ability . . . Will your lordship tell me
the extent of these reports? I know that it is said the Prince-
Bishop has been murdered, and with him the Burgundian
Lieutenant and the Papal Legate. That may be true. It is
not at all surprising. The people of Liège have never shown
any love for Louis of Bourbon. Also it is well known that
they did not willingly submit to the Burgundian yoke which
was imposed upon them. People do not always understand
what may be ultimately for their own good, and the illusion
which they call liberty commonly leads to extravagant ex-
cesses. Knowing the Duke of Burgundy engaged upon my
frontiers, it is not surprising that they should have deemed
the occasion opportune for the revolt they will have been
meditating ever since they were brought into Burgundian
subjection. I conceive and understand my cousin's indignation. I share it even. But for what am I in all this? How is
it reported, how assumed, that I am concerned in events in
distant Liège?'

'It is not assumed,' the Duke rasped. 'There is evidence
of it. We know now of the activity in Liège for months past
of your agents. Officers of your own, soldiers of experience,
such as Frémont de Marle, des Aubus, du Breuil, and Grandmaison were seen to be leading the insurrectionaries.'

'Who says so?' snapped the King.

'My messengers, gentlemen of my own who have ridden
in from Liège. Shall I send for them to tell you, themselves,
sire, what they witnessed?' The Duke half-rose as he spoke.

Count Anthony cut in smoothly. 'But where is the need
for that? The King himself is here, and can speak to it. His
royal word on this or any other subject cannot be held in
doubt.'

Thus smoothly Count Anthony opened for the King as a door of escape the door of falsehood. And the King, for all his astuteness never dreaming whither that door would lead him, bolted through it.

'I thank you, Lord Count,' he said, with a great show of dignity, 'for hesitating to believe that the King of France is a knave. I shall hope to remember it to your advantage, my lord, if ever it should be my good fortune to have occasion to do so. As for these men of mine who are implicated, three of them are men of mine no longer; they ceased to be men of mine in the course of the last half-year. Possibly they saw greater profit to themselves in entering the service of the people of Liège. As for the fourth, Grandmaison, he is to the best of my belief in Paris at this moment. So that in respect of him, at least, your report is inaccurate. If inaccurate in respect of him, why should it be accurate in respect of the others, even if they were men of mine, which I say again they are not.'

'You have not proved it, sire,' said the Duke uncompromisingly.

'Monseigneur!' The King flushed angrily at the implied doubt.

But Charles of Burgundy went relentlessly on to make his point. 'You have not proved that when they ceased to be men of yours as you say, that when they exchanged your service for that of the people of Liège, they did not do so with your approval, by your instructions and for the very purpose which they now have served.'

'Charles, Charles!' Count Anthony admonished him, one hand upheld in warning. 'His highness has indeed proved it by stating the contrary upon his kingly word. Or, if the statement as it stands is insufficient, he will, I am sure, graciously condescend to amplify it.'

'I do,' the King assented quickly. 'When those men quitted my service, I had no knowledge of, or concern in their intentions. I disavow them entirely in whatever they may have done in Liège.'

'You hear, Charles!' cried Count Anthony, in the tone of one who says, 'What did I tell you?'

'I hear,' said the Duke with a sneer.

But the Count had not yet done. He meant to truss the knavish king inextricably in his own falsehoods.

'It only remains, sire, completely to disabuse the mind of his highness by informing him with your own lips of what I am persuaded must be true: that not by the hands of the men named, or by any other hands, or in any way have you had part or share in the insurrection at Liège and the massacre that has taken place there.'

Unhesitatingly the King answered with the full lie required. 'I do so inform him. I am as innocent as he is himself of any part in the business at Liège. I give you my royal word for that, and those who say otherwise are lying enemies of mine who have ends of their own to serve. Is that enough?' His eyes darted from one to the other of them.

Count Anthony fetched a deep sigh. 'More than enough for me, who could never have supposed a king's honour to have permitted such knavery as a breach of the treaties existing between France and Burgundy. But as you say, sire, you have enemies, and they have poured their poison into the ear of your cousin. Look at him, sire. Read the unbelief in his countenance.'

The King looked as he was bidden into that heavy, sneering face, and his soul quaked again within him.

'If, monseigneur, you could afford him evidence of what you say,' the Count suggested.

'Evidence? What evidence have I?' Louis got to his feet, and affected dignity again. 'What better evidence than my kingly word?'

'What better, indeed! And yet you see, monseigneur, what a barrier this thing must present to any discussion of the terms of peace.'

The King saw that, and more. He saw the danger in which his own neck stood, which was more to him at the moment than the danger to the treaty. He began to fear that he had perjured himself in vain. And then the Count came again to his assistance, opening yet another door, but this time one through which he must pass without any eagerness: the door to which the earlier lies of which he had so insidiously been led to avail himself had naturally brought him.

'It occurs to me that you said earlier, sire, that you share the Duke's indignation at the affair of Liège?'

'I did say so,' the King protested eagerly, 'and I say so again. I do share his indignation, and I abhor the action of the Liègeois.'

'Ah!' Count Anthony's face lighted. His next words surprised both the King and the Duke, for it showed them both into what a trap he had manœuvred the crafty Louis.

'I rejoice from my heart to hear you, monseigneur. For of this, at least, you will have no difficulty in giving a proof that will satisfy not only his highness but all the world. And in proving this, you prove the rest. All doubt will be dispelled. Signify this indignation and abhorrence which you feel so deeply by joining hands with the Duke in punishing the insurrection. Bring up a portion of your forces, and with them, in alliance and in company with the Duke, march to the investment of Liège and lend your aid and your countenance in compelling the Liègeois to return to their allegiance to his highness. Consent to that, sire, and you give the lie to all your defamers here. Further, you will have removed the last obstacle to the discussion of the peace between Burgundy and France.'

Livid the King stood and looked at Count Anthony: and if ever hatred looked out of mortal eyes it looked then out of his. He was trapped, caught, tangled in his own falsehood beyond all possibility of extrication. He must do as was required of him or else brand himself a perjured liar. Indeed, if he refused, it would be tantamount now to admitting his guilt in the matter of Liège and justifying any course they chose to take with him, any violence they might offer. If he accepted, if he agreed to move upon Liège in alliance with Charles of Burgundy, and there employ his own hand in striking down those who had trusted to him, those whom his blandishments and promises of support had lured to revolt, his name would stink perhaps for ever in the nostrils of all decent men. Yet there was no choice. It was checkmate. Whether he refused or accepted, he was bankrupted of honour, whilst if he refused he forfeited his life as well.

He bowed his head. He spoke very quietly. 'Yes,' he assented. 'I will do that to prove my good faith.' And he sank limply down into his chair again, nor observed the broad grin upon the Duke's face. 'I will go with you most gladly, my dear cousin.'

The terms of the treaty of peace were soon agreed. The King was in no condition after that for any finesse. Badly defeated upon his own ground of craft, the strength of his mind was temporarily exhausted, and Burgundy obtained from him all the sureties she required to conclude a peace satisfactory to herself. To observe that treaty both parties bound themselves by an oath sworn at the King's suggestion on a piece of the True Cross which he fetched for the purpose from the coffer in his bedchamber.

Not until they were back in the Duke's apartments did a word on the matter pass between the cousins. Then the Duke standing before the Count, with gleaming eyes and a faint flush on his cheek-bones, expressed himself at last.

'God save me from poets when they apply their wits to other things than rhyming!'

'Of what do you complain?' wondered Count Anthony.

'Of nothing, Anthony. The Count of Vermandois went down to infamy for merely murdering Charles the Simple within these walls. King Louis has lost more than life this evening. His honour is tarnished beyond all redemption, whilst mine will shine with greater lustre in that against heavy temptation I have honoured my safe-conduct. I thank you for it. But I would sooner have you for my friend than for my enemy. That is why I say God preserve me from strife with men of romantic minds.'

Next morning the bells rang in Péronne and a *Te Deum* was sung in thanksgiving for the peace now signed between France and Burgundy.

And that was not yet the end. For presently came tidings from Liège to inform the Duke of Burgundy that the first messages had been grossly exaggerated. True, there was insurrection; true, two thousand Liègeois had marched on Tongres to impose their rebellious will upon the Prince-Bishop. But not Louis de Bourbon, or the Burgundian Lieutenant, or the Papal Legate had suffered any hurt whatever.

Charles of Burgundy was aghast at the news and at the thought of how it might have come too late to prevent a step that would have left his honour shattered for all time. It was to Count Anthony that he expressed his deep and abiding gratitude for the greatest service ever rendered him by living man, and he expressed it with a profuseness extremely unusual in so dour a prince.

Count Anthony heard him through with a gentle smile on his countenance which of late had grown so wistful.

'I wonder do you perceive even now on the edge of what a precipice you stood,' he said. 'Who were the bearers of that rumour of wholesale assassination? Your own people. Would it afterwards have been believed that any rumour had existed? Would not the charitable world have assumed that you had manufactured the rumour as a pretext to destroy a king who had placed himself in your power? What of your honour then, Charles?'

Charles gasped and shivered.

Count Anthony continued to smile, a curious, introspective smile from eyes that seemed blind to their immediate physical surroundings.

'Yes,' he said quietly. 'I think I have done well by you, Charles, and well by myself, too.' He was thinking of Johanna, and of how she must commend the manner in which he had saved the honour of the Duke of Burgundy could she have been a witness of it; and it brought him a satisfaction and a sense of peace to reflect that her approval would have been earned. That was now the guide of all his actions.

CHAPTER XV

THE SEDITION IN WALCHEREN

OPPOSITION to the new taxes imposed as a war levy upon the Northern provinces had begun to manifest itself in Walcheren early in October, a bare two months after the Duke's departure thence at the end of his magnificent progress.

There were a few sporadic insurrections here and there which might have led to serious trouble if the Duke had been represented in Zealand by a man less vigorous and resourceful than the Sire Claude de Rhynsault. Vigilant and prompt, the Governor was ever at hand to stamp out the first sparks of revolt before they could spread and unite to form a dangerous conflagration. By fines, pilloryings, and a few hangings, Rhynsault effectively discouraged the rebels, who in the main belonged to the poorer class, against whom the increase in price of the necessities of life operated most oppressively.

When, however, the news of the great insurrection at Liège, spreading like a wave over the land, reached Zealand, and reached it in so exaggerated a form that it was assumed the Duke of Burgundy was likely to be in difficulties, others, who hitherto had looked on in resentment at the tyranny and cruelty of the ducal lieutenant, turned their attention to measures which, if they were not to result in casting off the Burgundian yoke, should at least achieve an easing of its pressure. Among these were some of the wealthier merchants of Middelburg, Flushing, Veere, and Arnemuiden; men of weight and consequence in the guilds, who could sway the opinions of considerable multitudes and could supply the means to arm them. They went to work, not in the clumsy, impetuous fashion of the earlier mutineers, but with thought and plan and secrecy, careful to complete their preparations before they revealed their strength.

The force at the command of the Governor of Zealand was, after all, not very considerable. Its overthrow by a carefully organized attack should be comparatively easy. And once that preliminary victory were achieved, its moral consequence must be a general rising throughout Zealand, which most probably would be followed by a rising throughout the Northern States, Holland, Friesland, and the rest in which the oppression of the new taxes had bred discontent. Once this were accomplished, the Burgundian dominion might be cast off, or else adapted to the needs and conveniences of the burghers.

The ruling spirit of the conspiracy was a knight of Walcheren, a member of a prominent noble Zealand family named van Borselen, and his castle in the neighbourhood of Arnemuiden, where he kept some state and considerable force, was the meeting-place of the chief plotters.

But these comings and goings of burgher traders, however carefully contrived, did not escape the notice of the vigilant Rhynsault. He posed concerning it a question to his Fool, Kuoni von Stocken, who was the only man who possessed his confidence.

'Is van Borselen buying tapestries, or wine or ships, do you suppose? Or is he engaged in bringing wool from England for the Flemish looms?'

The crook-backed Fool looked at his master, his beady eyes steady and expressionless in the yellow, evil mask of his face.

'It's hemp he lacks, I think,' he snapped, and drew a grin to the Governor's florid countenance.

'Faith, he should come to me for that.'

'He should. But since he doesn't, I'ld go to him were I you. You can supply him all the hemp he needs, and perhaps a trifle over.'

On the Fool's advice Rhynsault set out. A fool Kuoni might be, to provoke guffaws from the Burgundian lieutenant who employed him. But through this gross-witted Burgundian lieutenant he enjoyed vicariously power and many other things denied to his mean station and his mean, shrunken frame. Rhynsault might deem himself Governor of Zealand. The truth was that he provided no more than the body of that exalted functionary. That body's soul and brain and ruling spirit were supplied by Kuoni, who was aware of it and secretly exulted behind that expressionless, sickly face and those eyes whose stare, seemingly fixed and unblinking, had the power to make men shudder.

Rhynsault commanded a hundred lances to attend him. The Fool cut the number down by half.

'Fifty will be all you'll need for the business. A hundred would scare him into taking up the drawbridge, and you'ld have a siege on your hands which would land you in difficulties. You are on a tour of inspection, and you crave van Borselen's hospitality for a night. That he may suspect you of seeking nothing further, you will stay first a night at Veere with van Ertvelde, whom no man suspects of anything.'

'By God, that's shrewd!' Rhynsault approved him.

'Shrewd? It's obvious,' sneered the Fool, who, with a soul filled with contempt of all things concrete and abstract, despised nothing in the world so much as his master the Governor of Zealand.

As Kuoni directed, they set out and went about the business. The unsuspecting van Borselen admitted them to his castle with the honours proper to the representative of the Duke of Burgundy. A goodly supper was served to a round dozen neighbouring gentlemen invited for the occasion, and they drank deep as was the custom in the Netherlands. After supper van Borselen desired a song from the Governor's Fool, whose sallies had already helped to keep things lively.

'I'll go fetch my lute,' said the amiable Kuoni, and went out.

He was a long time absent, and the company was growing impatient when at last he returned.

'Now we shall have music,' he informed the gaping company.

He bore a great arch-lute so slung behind him that it almost entirely covered his back, and lent him, when he turned him round, the appearance of a monstrous beetle with a great brown shell walking upright upon two wispy legs, one purple and the other black.

But it was not this that set those Zealanders gaping. In Kuoni's wake came a round dozen Burgundian soldiers in their clanking armour.

'I've brought you cymbals as well as a lute,' the Fool informed them. 'Because I think it's cymbals that you really need. The lute-strings will follow. Or, if not lute-strings, strings better suited to the occasion. And they will supply some of you with dance-music when you come to tread a dainty measure upon the empty air.'

Van Borselen, a big, fair man until now far gone in wine, but suddenly grown sober, fetched out a deep, growling oath, and swung to Rhynsault, who sat quietly smiling at his Fool's terrible humour. 'Is this a masque, a fool's mummery,' quoth he, 'or do you mean me mischief?'

'Neither,' Rhynsault answered him with a laugh. 'We are here to discover what mischief has been meant by you.'

'Are you so?'

In a flash van Borselen was upon the Lorrainer, one hand reaching for his throat, the other grasping a dagger and upraised to strike. But the Governor was a vigorous, agile man of his hands. He caught the Zealander's wrist as the blow descended, and, by a wrenching twist of the arm, sent him sprawling, then sprang clear away before any of the others could leap to attack him in their host's defence.

'Stand where you are!' he thundered at them, 'or, by God, my men shall cut you down.'

Already the injunction was unnecessary. At a word from the quick Fool, the men-at-arms, their heavy swords naked in their hands, had ringed the company about.

The Governor, infuriated by the attack upon him, mouthed and snarled at them, his red face inflamed.

'No need for more to prove your guilt, van Borselen. No

need for more to warrant my hanging you out of hand. But first I'll have something out of you. Make him fast!'

Disarmed, his hands wrenched behind him and his wrists pinioned by a stirrup leather, van Borselen stood, pale and breathing hard, to face the Governor.

Rhynsault advanced upon him slowly, glaring his rage, and struck him violently in the face. 'You'ld draw steel on me, would you, you dog!'

'You are noble,' said van Borselen, contempt in his blue eyes and curling his pale lips.

Rhynsault struck him again. 'You'll sneer in hell when I have done with you.'

'You may be nearer hell than I am,' van Borselen answered him. 'I have sixty tall fellows within these walls, and my gates are closed. You may kill me, but you'll never leave the place alive.'

The Governor's expression changed. Already the dawn of alarm was breaking in his eyes when a cackle of laughter shattered the moment's silence. It came from the Fool.

'Your sixty tall fellows are bestowed, oh, quite snugly, my Lord of Borselen. These Burgundians make good valets. They undressed your fellows of their arms before they were expecting such attentions. I tell you this because I cannot bear to see a man feed his soul upon false hopes.'

The Governor laughed, and ordered the room to be cleared. The guests, all scared, and some of them with good reasons supplied by their consciences, were herded out to be placed under lock and key until next they should be required. Remained in the hall where the candles guttered above the remnants of the feast only van Borselen, the Governor, the Governor's Fool, and two Burgundian soldiers.

Rhynsault pulled a chair to the great fire that blazed on the cowled hearth, and sat down. Beyond the hearth the Fool perched himself cross-legged upon a stool, and nursed his knee, eyes watchful and pallid face inscrutable.

'Now, you Zealander dog,' growled the Governor, 'will you talk, or must we constrain you?'

The Knight of Borselen between his guards stood firm and dignified. The Governor's finger-prints showed red on his pale face.

'That depends upon what you wish me to say.'

'You shall hear.' And Rhynsault told him briefly what he guessed of the treasonable traffic the Zealander had been conducting.

'And the proof?' van Borselen demanded. 'The proof of all this, which is to justify the violence you have shown me?'

'Proof, you fool! That is what I am here for. The proof you shall, yourself, supply.'

Van Borselen laughed. 'Let me understand this thing. Because I keep open house in Arnemuiden, and make welcome here such of my trader countrymen who choose to seek my hospitality, you assume that I am plotting treason. And upon no better grounds you invade my castle, overpower my men, assault my person and my guests, insult me grossly, and threaten me with death? Is that your tale?'

'It is,' said Rhynsault.

Van Borselen laughed again. 'A pleasant tale for the ear of your Duke, I think. I hope you have prepared the answers to the questions he will come to ask you.'

'It is the answers to the questions I am asking you that are your first concern.'

'I have no answers for you. If I am to be questioned, let me be questioned in a properly constituted court and according to the forms of the law.'

'In Walcheren I am the law, and wherever I sit in judgment is a properly constituted court. I administer here the high justice and the low in the name of my master the Duke of Burgundy. You waste my time, man, with your quibbles. Will you answer my questions, or will you not?'

'I will not. I deny your jurisdiction.'

'You'll deny it all you please, but it shall be exercised. Take off his boots.'

'What will you do?' Van Borselen was aghast be it from fear or anger.

'Put you to the question, in a homely fashion and with the means immediately to hand.' And Rhynsault waved eloquently towards the fire.

'You dare not, by God! I am noble, sir!'

'You may be noble. But you'll burn as easily as a churl. Off with those boots of his.'

'You shall answer for this, Rhynsault, as surely as there is a God above us. You have no single scrap of evidence to justify you.'

Said the Fool slyly: 'You were very ready and nimble with a dagger, my lord.'

'By Heaven, yes! Did that look like innocence?'

'Or did conscience prompt you?' wondered the Fool.

Barefoot now, van Borselen was thrust forward by the Burgundians.

'My first question,' said the Governor, 'is: Do you confess that you have trafficked in sedition with sundry of your countrymen?'

Livid but resolute van Borselen answered him. 'You may roast me piecemeal, sir. But not a word shall you have from me.'

'To it!' The Governor began, when Kuoni interposed, uncrossing his legs and leaning forward, his elbows on his bony knees.

'Perhaps if he perceived your justification, excellency, he would be less obstinate.'

'I care nothing for his obstinacy. I have broken the obstinacy of taller men.'

'Ay, ay, but justification is justification; and if it may be had, it were premature to proceed without it.'

The Governor looked at the Fool. The Fool returned the glance with that steady, unblinking stare which seemed at times so full of meaning. With an odd abruptness, Rhynsault obeyed the Fool's suggestion. He ordered the men to take the prisoner out and wait with him.

'What now?' he growled when he was alone with Kuoni.

The Fool rose. 'Without folly to guide you, gossip, you'ld

have run your head into a noose before now. That man is
right when he says that the tale would bear an ugly sound in
the ears of the Duke. Van Borselen is noble, after all, and his
family is powerful. It's courting trouble to treat him as if he
were a greasy merchant.'

'How else are we to reach the truth?'

'Find first some scrap of evidence to justify your measures. He is doing you a service when he urges it.'

'But if there is no evidence, beyond the evidence of our
senses.'

'God save us from the evidence of any man's senses!'

'But there is no other.'

'Where have you sought it?'

'God's death! Where am I to seek it?'

Kuoni raised his eyes to the ceiling, as if inviting the
Heavens beyond to be witness to the impenetrable stupidity
of the man he served. 'Why else are we here?' he asked.
'Why did I perform what I did, and have van Borselen's
men overpowered, if it were not so as to make the whole place
free for our ransacking? Do you dream that men can engage
in treason in a stronghold such as this, and never leave a
scrap of evidence behind them? Search, gossip, search!
Ransack the castle from rampart to dungeon, and see what
you find. Isn't that what we came for?'

'I hadn't thought of it,' the Governor confessed.

'True,' said the Fool. 'I forgot to tell you.'

The search was much more quickly fruitful than they
could have hoped. In the Knight of Borselen's closet they
found papers locked away in a chest, a bundle of letters any
one of which would have served to hang the man who had
sent it as well as van Borselen who had received it, and some
sheets covered with figures, which Rhynsault tossed aside as
of no consequence, but to which the Fool devoted some
study.

It proved the very simplest cypher, a cryptic writing that
would not long have puzzled a child; the numerals stood for
letters and stood for them in the order of the alphabet. The

ool, who had considerable clerkly skill, and, indeed, some
cholarliness, sat late into the night transcribing them.
What at last he bore to his master was a fairly complete ac-
ount of the nature of the plot, the funds subscribed, the
rms to be provided, the number of men to be counted upon
each district, and a list of the ringleaders with whom lay
he responsibility of giving those men the signal when the
moment came.

Rhynsault rubbed his hands in satisfaction. It was very
ell. He had struck in time, and within forty-eight hours
very one of those ringleaders would be laid by the heels.
he conspiracy, thus deprived of guidance, might safely be
ft to perish by itself.

'You've done well, Kuoni,' he commended the Fool.

'It is my habit,' said the Fool.

'Oh, not always.' The tall Governor swung to confront
im, and the Fool liked neither the look in his dark eyes nor
he smile round the corners of his sensuous lips. 'Sometimes
ou are clumsy because you love a jest too well.'

'That's what I'm for, gossip.'

'Ay, ay; in season. Now this evening so that you might
ent your cursed humour, you warned van Borselen too soon
f what was coming to him, with the result that he all but
ad his dagger in my throat.' He took up his whip as he
poke and loosened the thong.

The Fool's weak frame was shaken with sudden fear. His
ountenance lost its habitual impassivity. 'I knew he'ld
ever take you unawares. I thought to amuse you,' he cried
n frantic assurance; then, 'Jesus!' he shrieked as the lash,
ard-driven, cut him about neck and body.

'Oh, it amused me,' Rhynsault assured him. 'But had I
een less prompt with my hands, the laugh might have been
vith Borselen. I meant to lay your bones bare for that fool's
rick of yours. But since you've served me well since in
ther ways, I'll show you mercy, and give you no more than
reminder to let your jests be less dangerous to me in future.'

The reminder took the shape of three more lashes, the last

of which coiled about the Fool's white face, and broke th
skin.

'So!' The Governor flung aside his whip. 'That wil
suffice to-night. Away with you, you whimpering cur.'

The Fool hobbled out without another word. He was ac
customed to be thus punished for his shortcomings. H
sought his bed, and pain and rage kept him awake until i
was time to rise again. Yet next morning, when he came to
break his fast at the Governor's table, he had resumed hi
impassivity, and save for the angry crimson wheal tha
marked the track of his master's whip across his pallid face
save for the dark stains under his eyes which this morning
were deeper and darker than usual, there was no sign abou
him or in his bearing or manner to suggest what he had un
dergone. And his evil, malicious wit flowed freely, especially
later in the morning when the Burgundian lieutenant sat in
judgment upon the Knight of Borselen and four other of
those who had supped with them last night who were im
plicated by the letters found.

There was no defence, only an appeal from Borselen tha
he should be sent for trial to the Duke by virtue of his
knightly rank. That appeal the Governor disregarded. His
secretaries, of whom two accompanied him, drew up the in
dictments and attached to them the justificative documents
to be forwarded to the Duke. The Knight of Borselen and
his four convicted companions in treason were hanged tha
same afternoon on a gallows in the market-place of Arne
muiden. Not even Borselen's request for decapitation in
deference to his rank would the Governor grant him.

The business done, Rhynsault and his lances rode on to
Veere, as the first stage of a progress which had for object to
deal summarily with those whose treason was revealed by
the papers found in Borselen's castle. On the Fool's advice
he proceeded in such a manner that none knew the source of
his information until he was put upon his trial. Thus those
still to be arraigned had no warning save such as their con
sciences might give them.

Some, heeding that warning, made their escape in time. But the majority clung to their counting-houses and to the hope that they had not been incriminated until they found themselves in the hands of Burgundian justice.

It was a fortnight before the Governor came back to Middelburg, a little wearied by his labours, and leaving in his wake a trail of laden gallows to show the way he had gone.

In Middelburg itself half a score of prominent citizens, who suspected nothing, were ripe for judgment. The Governor's secretaries had carefully docketed the letters and prepared a list of their writers.

At the head of that list stood the name of Danvelt, and with Master Philip Danvelt, the Burgundian lieutenant started his Middelburg campaign for the extirpation of treason on the morning after his return.

CHAPTER XVI

DANVELT'S ARREST

PHILIP DANVELT's father had been a man of some taste a[nd] of cultured ideals, at least in physical matters. He had bu[ilt] himself a handsome gabled house on the Lange Delft, n[ot] far from Middelburg's imposing abbey, set in a fair gard[en] and furnished with a sumptuousness, much of which h[ad] been supplied by Italy and the Levant, such as few nob[le] men in those parts could have matched.

In the hall of this house sat Philip and his wife at dinn[er] on that October morning that was big with fate for the[m.] The two wings of a double door of stout oak, strengthen[ed] with bands of iron and iron studs and arched in the Got[hic] manner, opened directly upon the garden. These doors we[re] closed, and a bright fire was blazing on the hearth; but o[ne] of the lattices of the long-leaded window stood open to ad[mit] a little of the pale sunshine, which had broken at last throu[gh] the rain-clouds, whence a deluge had been descending f[or] days upon the town. To the audible dripping from eav[es] and branches was presently added another sound to rea[ch] them through that open lattice: the distant rhythmic tra[mp] of marching men.

They paid no heed to it. Philip was in haste to dine. [He] had word of a cargo of wool which had arrived that morni[ng] from England, and he was impatient to be off to Flushin[g] himself to see it safely landed and to inspect it. His though[ts] upon this, he ate and drank in silence, as indeed was h[is] habit, and not only at table. Sluggish-minded, he was u[n]communicative because he had nothing to communicat[e.] The business of buying and selling made up for him t[he] whole of life. The responsibilities of affairs which had d[e]volved upon him on the death of his father and the taking [of] a wife had sobered him of much of the loud jactancy und[er] which earlier he had cloaked his natural dullness.

Johanna, too, had grown silent lately; wistfully, intro-spectively silent. She was pale; the roses had almost en-tirely faded from her cheeks, and there was a dimming of the erstwhile sparkle of her clear blue eyes. If the change gave her the appearance of an age greater than the three and twenty years which she now counted, yet by etherealizing her beauty it served to heighten it. The graciousness which had ever marked her, deriving as much from graces of the spirit as of the body, was oddly increased by the gentle melancholy which lately had come to settle on her.

To find in one sorrow the only counter-action of another is to subject a human soul to an excessive burden. From the emptiness left in her life by the consciousness of how it might have been filled and fulfilled, she was temporarily rescued by her sorrow in the grave illness and death of her father, an event which had followed a fortnight after the Count's departure from Middelburg.

The attachment between father and daughter had been unusually close. An understanding man, of ready kindliness and broad outlook and a certain persistent youthfulness of nature which kept him in sympathy with the young, Claes-sens had been not only father and mother to her, but also a dearly loved brother and close friend. If he had lived well, yet he had husbanded the resources amassed by his shrewd industry, and his death left her a wealthy woman. If this accession of wealth secretly rejoiced her husband, who saw in the amassing of riches the aim and object of existence, as is natural to men of his outlook and environment, to her it seemed a mockery, an accentuation of her fundamental poverty in those things which glorify our earthly life.

Nor was her soul's emptiness and hunger the sole cause of her repining. A woman devoutly reared and devout and pure by nature could not harbour such longings and regrets without being lashed also by her conscience. She was the wife of Philip Danvelt, and whilst in the worldly sense she was guilty of no shadow of infidelity, yet in the spiritual sense — which in such finely balanced natures counts for as

much or more — she knew that her thoughts were a contin
uous infidelity. She spoke of them to her confessor, di
penance for them, and prayed nightly for strength to driv
them out, whilst at the same time praying — as she ha
promised to pray — for him who was the object of them
Something of herself she had given to Count Anthony tha
night in the garden of the Gravenhof. Nothing that man'
laws could count against her. Yet something that it was n
longer hers to bestow, since all of her had been bestowed i
marriage upon her husband. And however much she migh
realize it and be tormented by this realization, yet she wa
powerless to retract the gift, powerless to withdraw he
thoughts from the romantic prince who had incarnated he
ideals and captured her devotion.

She made what amends she could in an increased diligenc
where the carnal needs of her very carnal husband were cor
cerned. She saw to it that he was well cared-for; submitte
meekly to his unreasonable impatiences; returned never a
answer to grumblings, reproaches, and complaints over triv
ial matters which came with exasperating readiness from hi
natural boorishness. She abandoned all pursuits which i
his narrow view were not proper to a woman of her station
and which he grossly classified as suitable only to bawds c
the court. She gave away or sold her hawks, to the trainin,
of which she had devoted such time and skill, and he
horses, unless ridden by Philip himself or by the servants
were not ridden at all, and rarely used even to bear her in i
litter. A gift of painting which she had, she neglected be
cause Philip accounted it a trivial and unworthy and almos
wanton occupation. In short, so as to compromise with he
conscience, she modelled herself into such a woman a
Philip desired his wife to be, and hoped that by doing so sh
might one day reach the peace that is said to lie in duty ac
complished.

They were waited upon now by her old servant Jan, wh
had come to her when Claessens died, and a youth name
Peter, who had been for some time of Philip's household

Nevertheless, her eyes were watchful ever for her husband's slightest need. And Philip, accepting all as a proper tribute to the master of the house, lacked even the grace to perceive in it a cause for self-congratulation. The memory of his mother, a termagant whose character he had largely inherited, might have served to inform him that all wives were not as Johanna, docile, submissive, and solicitous — to say nothing of being well-dowered — and might have brought him to consider himself unusually blessed and fortunate.

Had you mentioned it to him, he would have answered you: 'Give me a wife who lacks those qualities and observe in how short a time under my tutelage she will acquire them.'

Yet Johanna, because she never provoked unkindliness, and by her docility turned unkindliness aside when it was offered unprovoked, accounted him kindly, knew him for honest and straightforward, and held him in some esteem.

Watching him now as he gobbled greedily, 'You eat too quickly, Philip,' she ventured in her solicitude.

He cleared the platter and reached for his cup of Rhenish before he answered her.

'I have affairs awaiting me.' His tone was gruff. 'It's not for me to sit idle all day like a housewife.' He tossed off the Rhenish, and swung to Jan. 'Is my horse saddled?'

'Waiting for you, master, with Gottfried, who is ready to ride with you.'

'Then . . .' He broke off to listen. 'What's that? They come this way.'

The tramp of marching feet was close at hand; the clank of steel was audible above it and the beat of the hooves of an ambling horse.

Jan stepped to the window, and thrust his head from the open casement.

Beyond the dripping garden, now heavy with dead and sodden leaves, ran a roadway and beyond this, fenced off by a single rail, gleamed the yellow waters of a canal. The pale sunlight flashed on the steel caps and pike-heads of a company of a dozen men-at-arms swinging briskly along, and already abreast with the gate, which was standing open. After them came a big man on a big horse and beside him trotted a little elfin figure all in yellow.

'It's his excellency the Governor,' Jan announced from the window.

'Bah! Devil take him!' growled Master Danvelt, and heaved himself up on his short thick legs.

But Jan's next words gave the merchant pause. 'They are coming here.'

The company was already in the short garden, and on the heels of Jan's announcement came the heavy blow of a pike-butt on the door.

Jan, his face startled, remained standing with his back to the window, which was set in an embrasure, looking at his master, who returned the glance with one of blank, uneasy wonder.

The pike-butt rang again upon the door. Jan moved to open, when Danvelt's upheld hand restrained him.

'Wait. Whatever the Governor seeks here, there is no need for you to meet him, Johanna.'

Danvelt might have, as indeed he had, the utmost trust in Johanna's prudence and modesty; but he was also aware, as was all the world, of Rhynsault's ways, and he would take no risk, however remote, that might lie for him in Johanna's beauty. 'Leave us,' he bade her shortly.

'At once, Philip.' But she delayed a moment to gather up some slight effects, and, in her obedient haste to the door which Peter opened for her, dropped some of them and stooped to recover them. That trivial accident may have been accountable for much that followed.

It was not in Rhynsault's ways to be patient in his dealings with a burgher.

They heard through the open window the sharp bark of an order, unintelligible to them. A moment later the door was smitten by a blow that broke the lock and flung open one of the heavy wings.

Four men, laying their pikes together, and using them as a battering-ram, had hurled themselves against it.

Johanna, stricken and startled by the crash, swung round where she stood to ascertain its cause.

Up the steps came the Sire Claude de Rhynsault, booted and spurred, wrapped in an ample red cloak against the chill damp October air, his head in a black velvet cap the liripipe of which was swathed like a muffler about his neck. After him, birdlike on his thin legs, hopped the Fool; the bells of his yellow chaperon tinkled as he moved; the great arch-lute was slung behind him. After the Fool came a couple of clerkly fellows in plain grey houppelandes, and after these two men-at-arms with broad-bladed halberts, the badge of Burgundy on their soiled white surcoats.

Philip Danvelt scowled as he stared. Easy in his conscience so far as politics were concerned, his natural arrogance asserted itself in the face of the wantonly insulting violence of this entrance. He put back his head on its short bull-neck, and looked along his great nose at the Governor.

'On my life,' he said, 'this is a novel way of knocking at a man's door! What manners be these?'

The Governor, just within the threshold, looked down from his fine height upon Danvelt with the cold contempt of the professional soldier for the burgher. He was, in his way, and despite his scar, rather a handsome man, this Burgundian lieutenant. His florid, shaven countenance was well and strongly featured; his black hair was glossy, his eyes bright and keen and the teeth, displayed now in the smile that drew back his full red lips, were white and sound. He looked what he was, a healthy, vigorous animal, essentially male and essentially carnal.

'When next Burgundy knocks at your door, be more prompt to open,' he said shortly, and came forward, the least touch of swagger in his movements. 'You, I suppose, are Philip Danvelt?'

'I am, and I wait to learn why you break in upon me in

this manner.' He was foolishly pompous considering his
station and that of the man he addressed.

'Whilst I wait for the respect which is due to the representative of your Duke.'

'In your manners, sir, you are more representative of a
robber. Regard me that door.'

'Tush, fool! You shall have something else to think of
presently. You'll think less then of the damage to your
door.'

'Perhaps you'll think more of it, sir, when I call on you to
pay for a new lock.'

Rhynsault was growing weary of this pertness. He lifted
up his voice. 'By the Blood! Will you chop wit with me?
Crow a little less loudly, my burgher cockerel, before we slit
your comb. I like neither your looks nor your ways.'

Scarlet with anger at being thus browbeaten in his own
house, Danvelt still answered boldly. 'My ways, whether
you like them or not, are those that become an honest man
and a loyal citizen who can pay what he owes.'

Rhynsault laughed. 'If you can make good that boast,
I'll buy you a new lock.' Then he spoke over his shoulder to
the two clerks who had followed him into the room, whilst
his halberdiers kept the threshold. 'Set me a chair here.
That one.'

As he turned, he caught sight for the first time of Johanna,
who had shrunk back and was half concealed by a tall clothes
press. She was staring in fascinated horror at the misshapen
Fool, whose eyes, beady and expressionless as a snake's, were
unblinkingly observing her from out of his long pallid face.

Perceiving her, Rhynsault asked himself where he had last
seen her, presently to remember the interest she had aroused
in him at the Gravenhof and the intention then entertained
of seeking her closer acquaintance. The preoccupations of
his office after the Duke's visit had eclipsed the intention.

He unwound the liripipe from about his neck and bared
his head. He might be a despot to the burghers, but he
would never be other than a gallant to their women. And

this woman, as he had already earlier observed, was of a singular and very delicate beauty, from the crown of her golden head, which was uncovered, the hair braided, to the tips of the peaked shoes protruding from her gown of dove-coloured velvet. He observed, too, the pride and dignity with which she carried that head upon the slender white pillar of her neck. She compelled homage, and Rhynsault afforded it. He bowed his sleek black head.

'I implore your pardon, mistress. I had not before observed you. My intrusion here is in the course of the duties of my office. But it would have been less rude had I suspected your presence.'

If his entrance and subsequent conduct had startled her, yet she retained her calm and her dignity. Steadily she met his glance, refusing to perceive the manifest admiration it held.

'I thank you, sir, for the apology. Your business will be with my husband.'

The Fool in the background uttered a laugh that did not move a muscle of his face.

'You do well to remind him. He has a way of forgetting trifles for essentials.'

'Quiet, Fool!' Rhynsault admonished him, and with a 'By your leave, good mistress,' he sat down.

Her husband turned to her. 'You will have household matters to engage you, Johanna.' And then, like the pompous fool he was, permitted himself a sneer at Rhynsault. 'His excellency, no doubt, will give you leave.'

The Governor took the words literally and ignored the sneer in them. 'Nay, nay. Sit, mistress, sit. We should be loath to lose your company.'

Tense and straight, Johanna looked him between the eyes. 'Is this an invitation, excellency; or a command?'

'Why, what odds which?' said the Governor, although a little out of countenance under the steadiness of her regard, the hardness of her tone.

'I desire to know so that I may answer you.'

'Assume it which you please, and answer.'

'Then I will answer both. If it is an invitation, I decline it. If a command, I must ask your authority.'

The Governor sucked in his breath, and awkwardly laughed a little. A man he would have browbeaten. But the dignity of this lady daunted him.

'My authority?' he echoed. 'Am I not the representative of your lord the Duke?'

'You may represent him to his satisfaction in many things; but you will never represent him in constraining a woman against her inclinations.' She dropped him a half-curtsey. 'You will give me leave, excellency.' And she moved to the door. On the threshold she paused. 'You will send me word, Philip, when his excellency has gone.' And on that went out, to the wonder and admiration of all, including her husband, who hardly recognized in that cold firmness the spirit of his softly docile housewife.

The Governor noisily cleared his throat. 'It seems the Duke's warrant doesn't run with any of you,' he grumbled, to save his face. 'Well, well, let's come to business, Master Danvelt.'

'With all my heart,' said the merchant, his weariness of manner a studied insolence.

'You may be less hearty over it by and by. What was it you boasted yourself when I came in? Loyal and honest, was it not?'

'Did I boast myself that? I am entitled to do so.'

'If you were honest you would tell me that you're a liar when you call yourself loyal. Whether you tell me so or not, I know it, which is why I am here, why I enter without cere-mony.'

'Do you say I am not loyal?'

'You heard me, surely.'

'In what have I failed in loyalty? I have taken no part in politics. I know the Duke's rule to be just, and in my heart I believe it to be the best for the Netherlands.'

'Since when have you held these worthy opinions?'

'All my life.'

Rhynsault looked at him frowning. 'God give me patience to sit here while you stand before my face and offend me with such paltry lies.'

'Excellency! Your office gives you no right to insult me.'

'Insult you, fool?' The Governor sank back in his chair, his glance baleful. He lowered his tone. 'I insult you, do I? Carry your mind back to a certain escapade of yours last March in Bruges, when you were laid by the heels and would certainly have been hanged if a noble but ill-advised gentleman, taking pity on your plight, had not stood surety for you in a thousand ducats. What was it brought you into the clutches of the ducal lieutenant there? Was it this fine loyalty to the Duke of Burgundy which you now say has inspired you throughout your life?'

Master Danvelt had grown pale, and his arrogance fled out of him as fear entered in. Was he in these troubled days of seditious movements to be brought to account for that old and now forgotten affair? His body drooped with his spirit. He spoke in a tone so different that his voice seemed that of another man.

'Oh, but that, my lord! A folly committed in the heat of wine, in . . .'

The Governor interrupted him. '*In vino veritas* . . . You know the adage. If not, my Fool will translate it for you. So tell me no more that I insult you when I call you by the names that become you. Your last disloyalty cost you a thousand ducats, and would have cost you your life but for the intervention on your behalf of a potent gentleman who occasionally disturbs the proper course of events for the satisfaction of his own romantic notions. To any but a thick-headed Flemish fool that would have been a sufficient warning.'

'I needed no warning,' Danvelt protested. 'I was not disposed to treason.'

'Then why have you embarked upon it?'

'Embarked upon it? I?' Danvelt was really aghast. '
take oath before . . .'

'Don't perjure yourself in vain, man.'

Mute in his consternation, Danvelt stared blankly at the
Governor. He felt physically sick; the sweat stood in beads
upon his brow. At last, steadying himself upon a conscience
that was untroubled in these matters, he came to the conclusion that here he was the victim of some error which he
could dispel the moment it were disclosed to him. In that
assurance he commanded himself, and cast off his momentary palsy.

'If you would tell me, excellency, precisely of what I am
suspected, and upon what grounds . . .'

'Oh, you shall be told. You shall be told. Not of what
you are suspected, but of what there is clear proof against
you.'

Danvelt actually smiled. 'That I know too well that
there is not, for I have never been a party to any treason.'

'Have you not? Ha! Have you ever heard of one Thomas
Tegel of the Town of Veere?'

'Not until you hanged him a week ago, and then all Zealand heard of him.'

The Fool, who sat at the table, in the place that Johanna
had vacated, his elbows on the board, his chin in his cupped
palms, here interrupted:

'Hanging will often make a man famous that might
otherwise have died unknown. There's hope for you, Master
Danvelt. The hope of fame.' He sighed noisily, and gave
his attention to a dish of comfits.

Rhynsault pursued his questioning. 'And you had never
heard of this Tegel until then?'

'Never to my knowledge.'

The Governor's bold dark eyes considered him intently.
'By the Blood! You're a glib liar.' He turned to one of the
secretaries, who was already fumbling in a leathern wallet.
'Give me that letter marked Danvelt.'

He received and folded it so that only the signature was

visible. 'Come here,' he bade Danvelt, and, when the merchant had obeyed, he thrust the paper under his nose. 'What name do you read there?'

'P. Danvelt.'

'Your own name, eh?'

'Yes . . . It is my name.'

'So! You confess it, then!' Rhynsault rose, handing back the letter to his secretary. 'It is wise of you to spare us further trouble.'

'Confess it?' cried Danvelt between fear and fury. 'Confess what? What have I confessed?'

'Why, that you wrote that letter.'

'Nay, now, nay!' Danvelt protested. His mind was reeling. 'You go too fast. I did not so much as see a letter. All that you showed me was a name.'

'Your name. Your name appended to a letter written to this convicted traitor Tegel, in which you promise him supplies of arms and money to forward the enterprise in hand. A hanging matter, Master Danvelt.'

'For the writer, perhaps, but I am not he.'

Rhynsault showed signs of exasperation. 'Does it not bear your name?'

'My name, yes. But not my signature.'

'Why, what's the difference? Is this a riddle, sir?'

Master Danvelt, exasperated also on his side, answered almost contemptuously: 'A riddle that your Fool — that any fool — can read for you at a glance.'

Kuoni raised his head from the dish of comfits. 'Sir, I read fate; not riddles. I could read yours at this moment with tolerable certainty.'

Meeting his eyes, Danvelt shivered. He turned again to the Governor, and again changed his tone. 'I mean, excellency, that I never wrote that or any other treasonable letter. The signature is not mine, as my signature will show. The name even . . . it is but P. Danvelt.'

'And what should P stand for but Philip?'

'It might stand for Peter or Paul.'

'Or even,' the Fool put in, 'for Priscilla, Petronilla, o
Penelope; or yet for pope or pimp or prude; or again, fo
prudent, pernicious, pestilent, or philosophical. But whe
all is considered, I think it really stands for patibulary. In
deed, patibulary is preëminently prognostic of the fate of thi
Danvelt. Unless . . .'

'Quiet, Fool!' The Governor snapped at him. Then h
waved his pikemen forward. 'Make him fast.'

Distraught, the merchant sprang forward, his hands out
held in supplication.

'Sir, sir, hear me out before offering me a violence th
Duke could never sanction.'

'They all say that,' the Governor sneered.

'This charge is absurd and empty,' Danvelt pursued. '
take God and Our Lady to witness that I have never en
gaged in any treason, never so much as harboured any
thought of treason. I never wrote that letter, whatever i
contains. I swear, I never wrote it.'

'You repeat yourself, and reiteration is proof of nothing.

'A dull, redundant dog,' said the Fool.

'But to assume so much upon so little evidence!' Danvel
protested. 'I am not the only Danvelt in Walcheren; pos
sibly not the only Philip Danvelt. You cannot arrest me o
so slight an assumption.'

Rhynsault looked down his nose at him and smiled. 'An
your antecedents? Do they count for nothing? Your littl
exploit in Bruges?'

'But it is so easy to prove that this letter is not mine
that the writing is not mine. A score of worthy men here i
Middelburg can testify to that.'

'They shall be called to do so. Oh, you shall have a fai
trial, never fear. And if you're as innocent as you protes
you may dispel your alarm. Meanwhile, I cannot leave yo
at large. Fetch him along.' And, turning on his heel, th
Governor strode out.

The pikemen ranged alongside of the merchant, wh
gathered courage from the Governor's last words. He turne

to Jan who had been a stricken witness of these proceedings.

'Jan, you will tell your mistress of this. Bid her not to be uneasy. Reassure her, Jan. You see that it is a mistake. I shall be enlarged again in a day or two when the matter is sifted.'

They marched him out.

CHAPTER XVII

THE FOOL'S PHILOSOPHY

THE Burgundian lieutenant sat over the remains of a generous supper, savouring with his Fool a jug of Rhenish that had been mulled and spiced. They occupied a cosy chamber adjacent to the great draughty hall of the Gravenhof. It was hung with Flemish tapestries, and lighted by a lamp suspended from the groined ceiling. A heaped-up fire of logs blazed and spluttered in the cavernous fireplace.

The fool was busy on a song that should express the whole of his philosophy of life. In these amiable labours he was disturbed by his master.

'I think,' said the Governor, 'that we have now rounded up all the game.'

This in allusion to the five arrests he had that day effected in Middelburg.

'And I think,' he added a moment later, 'that when these Middelburg traitors have been hanged there will be an end of plots against the government of the Duke's highness, and we shall be able to take our ease.'

'Amen!' said the Fool. 'Our ease is what we desire above all else, whether the burghers hang or not.'

'Oh, they will hang,' the Governor assured him.

'All the five of them?' The tone implied a doubt.

'Why not? Whom would you except?'

'Myself, none; for I cannot imagine that any of them will be missed. But there's the evidence. It may give four of them to the hangman. I've a doubt of the fifth.'

'You mean Danvelt? There's his letter.'

'He swears he can prove it isn't his. If he can, he goes back to his beautiful wife. Poor soul! I hope for her sake that he can't.'

The Governor was considering. 'He demands that I send

a courier to his friend, Count Anthony of Guelders. His friend, mark you.'

The Fool laughed. His laughter had the peculiarity of being either seen or heard; but never both at the same time. In this instance the grimace of laughter was on his face, but no sound of it came forth.

'Well, that can't be done at present. The Count is with the army before Liège, and will have enough to engage him. He would resent any such message even on behalf of his friend Danvelt.'

The Governor looked at him. 'What do you conceive to be the link between so oddly assorted a pair?'

The Fool thought that he knew, and said what he thought he knew. But he said nothing of how he came by the knowledge.

'The burgher has a comely — an exceptionally comely wife. Unless it be that, I can't think what it is.'

'You foulness! Is that a thing to say of the austere and chaste Count Anthony?'

'I take no man's reputation on trust,' said the Fool. 'Reputations are notoriously fallacious. How can they be otherwise? To himself a man is what he thinks he is; to others what he appears to be. The real man is known to his Maker alone. Count Anthony is a poet. But then he is also a man. Count Anthony the poet may impose his ideals upon Count Anthony the man. But Count Anthony the man may not always accept them.'

'In this case,' said the Governor, 'the association of these two is older by some months than Danvelt's marriage. It was in March of last year that Count Anthony rescued this man from the consequences of his seditious utterances in Bruges.'

'That would be Count Anthony the poet.'

'But what inducement had he?'

'The fact that he's a poet. It conduces to eccentricity.'

'So I had supposed. But Danvelt suggests a friendship, a bond between himself and the Count.'

'The bond has been formed subsequently and is com
pounded of indebtedness and vainglory on the part of th
burgher. He magnifies himself by boasting of a friendshi
which appears justified by one eccentric act on the part o
Count Anthony. Pay no heed to that, gossip. Besides, wh
should you? Either Danvelt has been playing at treason, o
he hasn't. If he has, you hang him; if he hasn't, you don'
His relations with Count Anthony, even though they wer
brothers, do not affect the issue.'

'You're right, said the Governor, and added: 'He hang
then.'

'You're set on it. Perhaps you're wise, gossip. Hangin
is a good example to others. In this case the evidence, as
stands, will allow you to indulge your fancy either way
You may account it sufficient or insufficient, as you pleas
and none could question your judgment.'

'Who should want to question it?'

'Who, indeed, gossip? Enviable man.'

But they reckoned in their cold-blooded fashion withou
Mistress Johanna, whose arrival at the Gravenhof a servan
came presently to announce.

'At this hour?' The Governor scowled.

'Why should you hesitate?' quoth the Fool. 'The lady i
worth looking at, at any hour, on any pretext. I have rarel
seen so many graces assembled in one woman. Besides, sh
may help you to a decision about her husband's fate. Wit
that off your mind, you'll sleep more peacefully.'

'You mean in the matter of the evidence?'

'What else should I mean, gossip?'

Rhynsault considered, and ordered her to be admitted.

She came, demurely dignified, a long black riding-cloa
over her dove-grey velvet, her head crowned by a tall hen
nin, from which floated a long wispy veil.

The Governor rose to receive her. The Fool, affecting t
ignore her, took up his quill again, bent over his parchmen
and thus, in a sense, effaced himself.

'It is not my custom to receive suitors at so late an hou

madam,' was Rhynsault's greeting, delivered, however, without gruffness. The Fool was right. She was singularly lovely. Even lovelier as he beheld her now in the amber light of his lamp than she had earlier appeared to him.

'I am aware of it, my lord, and grateful for the concession.'

He admired her pride of bearing, the self-command which enabled her almost completely to dissemble an inevitable anxiety. He proffered a chair, which she accepted gratefully.

'A cup of Rhenish?' he invited, adding, as if in justification of this informal hospitality, 'the air is chill.'

'I had to brave it, my lord, in the hope of sparing my husband a night in gaol. No wine, my lord. I would have come earlier, but that I was some time assembling these documents. They should dispel all cause that you may think you have for keeping my husband a prisoner.' She proffered him a little roll of parchments.

Still standing, he took them, frowning thoughtfully. 'What are these?'

'Letters written by my husband. When my servant told me what had occurred, on what grounds he had been arrested, and what the evidence against him, I set out to procure these letters from persons with whom he has corresponded at times when away from Middelburg. I had hoped to be able to come to you earlier. But the search was a difficult one.'

'What have these letters to do with the matter?'

'I have brought them so that you may compare the hands and the signatures. You will see at once that the treasonable letter upon which you arrested him was not written by Philip.'

'How do you know that, mistress? You haven't seen the letter upon which he was arrested.'

'No; but I know that the writing cannot be the same because he never wrote any treasonable letters. He never engaged in any treason.'

'How can you know that?'

'How? He could not possibly have engaged in treason without my knowledge.'

'Why not?' The Governor's eyes were upon her. Indeed, they had never left her since he had received that package from her hands. 'Why not? You'll not persuade me that husbands do nothing that is outside the knowledge of their wives. This Danvelt was frequently from home, for instance, was he not?'

'Sometimes. Affairs took him to Flushing or to Arnemuiden.'

'Arnemuiden! Ay! A hotbed of treason that. How can you speak to the nature of the affairs that took him? Will you pretend that you had his entire confidence?'

She was under no such illusion. Indeed, the self-sufficient burgher sought to magnify himself in her eyes by casting a veil of mystery over his affairs, as though each of them presented a problem soluble only to an initiate.

'Perhaps not,' she admitted. 'But in any case the verification of the handwriting must be one of the first steps towards establishing either his guilt or his innocence.'

'Must it so, mistress?' He smiled down upon her from his fine height. Half-playfully he chid her. 'You are to instruct me, then, in the details of my justiciary's office?'

'Not I, indeed, my lord. I have no such thought. I mention what is but a matter of common knowledge and common-sense.'

'Well, well,' he said. 'The letters shall be kept. I thank you for bringing them to me.'

'As to that, my lord, it is I who shall thank you for making the comparison, and setting my husband at liberty.'

'Let me warn you, mistress, not to place too much reliance upon this comparison. It may be, after all, that you have but added evidence against him.'

She smiled confidently as she shook her head.

'I am quite sure that I have not done that.'

'You love this husband?' he asked her gently.

'He is my husband, sir.' She was suddenly stiff and distant.

'That does not answer my question.'

'There are questions, sir, that are never answered because they should never have been asked.'

'You misunderstand me, madam.' He stooped towards her a little. 'I ask out of concern for you.'

'That same concern should have assumed the answer. If you will make the comparison for which I have brought you the means, I shall be indeed grateful.'

'Oh, the comparison! The comparison!' He was a little impatient. 'It shall be made. Depend upon that. It shall be made in due season.'

'In due season?' For the first time she seemed taken aback, and looked him fully in his handsome, florid face. 'But why not now — at once?'

'There are inconveniences. You will not be importunate, mistress, when I tell you that it would distress me to deny you. This is a matter for my secretaries and for the court when it comes to sit in judgment.'

'But if you can persuade yourself by these that no charge is possible against my husband, what need, then, for judgment? Could you not do it now, at once? So that my husband need not spend a night in gaol? It is to save him this that I have laboured.'

The Governor was properly sympathetic. There were the forms of the law which must be observed. Her husband, having been arrested, could not possibly be enlarged until the forms were satisfied. This could only be through the ordinary channel of the court. He deplored it, he suggested; but he was powerless to alter it.

'Why, only to-day, sir,' she reminded him, 'you boasted in my house that you are, yourself, the law in Walcheren.'

He nodded, smiling gently. 'You are right to say I boasted. I was guilty of overstatement. I am no more than the mouthpiece of the law, the channel through which the law is dispensed. Have patience, madam. Believe me, I would do a deal, a very great deal, to serve you. But be merciful by not asking me to do that which is beyond my power.'

She was distressed. 'When, then? How soon can you give judgment?'

'To save your anxieties, at the earliest moment possible. But bear in mind that your husband is only one of five arrested to-day in Middelburg. The five cases are to be sifted. They overlap and are intertwined with one another. This will take time.'

'But my husband's does not. My husband is not one of these as that comparison of hands will show.'

'I may not take your word for that, madam, much though it would pleasure me to do so. The evidence of a wife! That is no evidence, even if she were qualified to speak. But I'll do what I can to serve you. Be sure of that.' He was considering her ever, and his eyes had lately narrowed a little. 'Come to me again to-morrow, madam. By then I may be able to be more definite. Seek me before I dine.'

In dejection she thanked him and withdrew, lighted by his servant whom he summoned to do the office. When she had gone, he sank into his chair again, and filled himself a cup from the jug. In silence he sat considering the wine before he drank it. In silence he continued after he had drunk.

The Fool, watching him covertly, the least shadow of a mocking smile about his almost lipless mouth, at last broke in upon his brooding.

'Why so thoughtful, gossip? What's to think about? Isn't all plain?'

'Plain?' Rhynsault stared at him across the table with the dull eyes of a suddenly awakened man. 'What is plain?'

'A number of things, concerning both Master Danvelt and Master Danvelt's widow in prospect.' Abruptly he changed the subject. 'Have you ever observed, gossip, that there is no loveliness to compare with loveliness in distress? I marvel that you escaped the appeal of it; that you could still be

arsh with her. But I admire it in you. I admire it and
ommend it. Duty first: that is the motto of the Lord
Claude de Rhynsault. The other things may follow.'

'What other things?'

'The fruits of duty. And that, faith, was a luscious, well-
unned fruit; so white and smooth and warm. Don't tell me
hat you beheld it with indifference. Don't say that you
were not tempted to put forth your hand to pluck it, for I
hall not believe you.'

Rhynsault looked at him again. 'What then?' he said.

'Why, what is temptation for? Certainly not a thing to be
esisted, whatever the priests may say. For what, after all,
s temptation? The hawker of life's most alluring wares.
And what's a priest? A kill-joy. And where are the ad-
antages of being Ducal Governor, Burgundian Lieutenant
n Zealand, Lord of Life and Death, Dispenser of the High
ustice and the Low, if you may not help yourself to be a
urgher's wife now and again?'

'Pish!' said the Governor, and sat on bemused.

The Fool rose and went to fetch his arch-lute from the
ide-table on which it had been placed.

'Here's advice for your case from the new song I've made.'
He thrummed a moment, and then delivered himself in a
oice harsh as a raven's:

> 'Take all things that life can give:
>   Love and wine and laughter.
> Live your fill whiles you may live,
> Scorn the life contemplative
>   Of things that may come after.
>   Ha, ha, ha, ha! Hereafter!'

More would have followed but that Rhynsault silenced
im. 'Cease your hell-cat music!'

The Fool was scandalized. 'Thus you receive philosophy
hat is sound, opportune, and to your needs. I commend
ou to the Saints, and take my leave.'

He went out, his face distorted by his silent laughter.

That there was devilry ahead he knew as surely as he knew Claude de Rhynsault, which was much better than Claude de Rhynsault knew himself. He had done his best to apply a spur to that devilry, out of the sheer malice of his nature and because of the satisfaction which his warped soul found in observing in others the course of passions from whose indulgence he was personally debarred.

From the hall without, the thrumming of his lute and his receding voice reached the brooding Governor.

> 'Flout not Love, for Love will not
>   Suffer it, I warn you.
> Drink you whiles the cup is hot,
> Soon in chilly death you'll rot
>   With only Hell to warm you.
>   Ha, ha, ha, ha! To warm you!'

CHAPTER XVIII

RHYNSAULT'S WOOING

THE hall of the Gravenhof was unusually thronged on the following morning by suitors awaiting audience of the Governor. The arrests of the day before were responsible for this; for in addition to the usual attendance of those who had affairs of one kind and another to transact with the ducal representative, his officers and administrators, there was a number of friends and relatives of the accused, some summoned to render certain testimony, others coming of their own free will to plead and petition. Amongst these, but apart from them, and waiting patiently, sat Mistress Johanna, attended by her servants Jan and Peter and her waiting-woman Grieta. Her outward composure betrayed little of the anxiety and distress within. Apart from the urgings of wifely duty, in the discharge of which she sought to make amends for the lack of those deeper feelings which become a wife as well as for the spiritual infidelity of which her conscience bore the guilt, there was a genuine and natural concern for Philip. In the hour of his distress and danger, she remembered only his good qualities, his directness and honesty, and her own shortcomings, and she was here to strain every nerve in serving and rescuing him.

Above the subdued hum of conversation, a voice broke suddenly, cawing an evil song. The impish Fool surged into the hall by the double doors at the end of it, his lute slung before him, his face inscrutably alight, and sang his way through the crowd of suitors, who fell away before him.

'Out of Love is Loathing born;
  Out of Laughter, Weeping.
Time will wither Beauty's form
Pluck the blossom from the thorn,
  And Death will come a-reaping.
  Ha, ha, ha, ha! A-reaping!'

He reached the Governor's closet and the Burgundian halberdiers who guarded the threshold, and passed in, leaving horror in his wake, especially in the breasts of those concerned for the unfortunate prisoners.

The Governor sat considering a list which had been placed before him by the usher. He looked up scowling at the unceremonious entrance of the licensed Fool.

'You are inopportune,' he greeted him.

'Impossible! Folly is never out of season.'

'Begone! I have affairs.'

'So I perceived as I crossed the antechamber. Let me assist you by indicating the order of them.' At his master's side, he leaned upon the table, and ran a long bony finger down the usher's list until he came to the name of Johanna Danvelt. There the finger paused. 'I should begin there, since this is the only case that offers complexities and may delay you. The others are easily disposed of.'

The Governor and the Fool looked into each other's eyes. Rhynsault yielded to the suggestion, and the usher was instructed.

Johanna came, the usher withdrew, the Kuoni retired into the background to lounge unnoticed on the window-seat, set in a deep embrasure.

She began by thanking his excellency for admitting her so promptly, ahead of others who had waited longer and therefore had perhaps a prior claim.

He was graciousness itself. He assured her that to keep her waiting was a discourtesy of which he could never be guilty, and he pressed her to sit. She had brought him, she announced, yet some further letters, letters written to herself by Philip on the eve of their marriage, so that he might compare the hands.

'So much was hardly necessary. The letters you left with me last night suffice abundantly.'

'You have made the comparison already?' she cried eagerly.

'Nay, nay. That will follow in the proper season.'

'In the proper season?' The implied postponement dismayed her again.

And then came aid from an unexpected quarter. Said the Fool from the background, almost peremptorily: 'What season more proper than the present?'

'Eh?' Frowning, the Governor turned to stare at him.

'Thank you, sir. Thank you!' cried Johanna.

'Nay, mistress; no thanks. I but preach my philosophy of life; which is to seize ever what the season sends.'

If the answer mystified her, it was clear to Rhynsault. He spoke again of his eagerness, his ardent desire to serve her in all things. 'Which is the reason,' he added, 'why I ordered you to be instantly admitted. But despite my good will towards you, I am confronted with difficulties where your husband is concerned, difficulties supplied by his own imprudence. It is not as if this were his first offence. There is that business in Bruges. In the case of a man of such antecedents, my duty to my master the Duke makes necessary the strictest scrutiny. Your husband claims Count Anthony of Guelders for his friend, and desires me to send a letter to him.'

He watched her intently as he spoke. Remembering Kuoni's suggestion last night of the possible link between the burgher and the Count, he desired to test it. Momentarily Johanna's eyes dilated. A sudden dread, a horror swept through her.

The thought of appealing to Count Anthony had already presented itself to her, had been weighed and finally dismissed because of a terrible fear lest, yielding to an overwhelming temptation to remove the obstacle that stood between them, the Count's intervention now might have the result of precipitating her husband's doom. Her confidence in the Count's honour might not really permit her to believe this thing. Yet not even in the last extremity would she dare to put it to the test; and the suggestion now that Philip himself should be the agent of such a thing appalled her.

Yet her bearing revealed nothing of this. Already pale and a little breathless when she had entered, a deepening pallor and an increased breathlessness went unnoticed. Her countenance preserved its calm after that swift momentary flash of fear from her clear eyes. She looked steadily at Rhynsault, and shook her head. She even displayed the ghost of a smile.

'My husband overstates the case when he claims Count Anthony as his friend. Once Count Anthony befriended him, just out of the chivalry and pity of his nature. He had no previous knowledge of him, and has had little since; certainly no knowledge that would enable him to speak to my husband's character and pursuits; nor, can I suppose, sufficient interest to bring him to intervene.'

Rhynsault appeared relieved. 'It is as well,' he said. 'For in any case, Count Anthony is with the Duke's highness in the army investing Liège, and there would be delays and difficulties in reaching him.'

'All to no purpose even then,' she repeated. 'And fortunately not necessary, since you have these letters. If you will compare the signatures . . .'

He unfolded one of the letters, and glanced at it. 'What's this? "My jewel,"' he read.

The Fool in the background laughed. Rhynsault swung upon him in a passion real or simulated. 'Begone!' he roared. 'Out of this! I'll have no ribaldries of yours.'

'Provide your own, then,' said the Fool, as he obeyed, and made for the door of an inner room. 'You'll contrive well enough without me.' He leered, and was gone, with a last look at Johanna that turned her cold.

The smile with which the Governor turned to her again was invested with a fresh meaning for her, now that her senses had been awakened by the Fool. Tall and handsome in his fur-edged purple houppelande, the heavy gold chain of office on his breast, the Lorrainer bowed his sleek black head once more over that love-letter of Philip Danvelt. He had written so few, and so rarely in that tender strain, that

was an irony this one should have survived for its present
urpose.

'"My jewel,"' he read again, and again looked at her
rith his ingratiating smile. 'A jewel, indeed,' he agreed.
Dn my soul too fair a jewel for the wear of any loutish
urgher.'

She commanded herself with difficulty, repressed all show
f the indignation that consumed her, save the scarlet flame
iat swept across her face.

'It . . . it is the signature, my lord, that I desire you to
onsider.'

'Oh, yes, the signature. But there's more than a signa-
ire to be considered, mistress.'

'True. There are dates. They may play an important
art in this.' She half-rose in her dissembled alarm. 'Suffer
ie to call my servant Jan. He knows . . .'

'Let be! Let be!' he interrupted her. 'If you would do
our husband service, we must have a word alone together,
ou and I.' He sank his voice to a gentle, wooing note. He
:t a hand on the back of her chair, and leaned over her as
e spoke.

She used a woman's only buckler in such a case, and af-
cted not to understand.

'You wish to question me?' she assumed, but shrank a
ttle from his closeness.

'Why, what a timid dove it is!' he purred. 'I vow you're
embling, mistress. But why? Surely you are in no fear of
ie. Will you not believe that it is my wish to be your
iend?'

'You . . . you are kind,' she said, conscious of the foolish-
ess of the words.

'Kind?' He laughed. It was, indeed, she thought, a word
or laughter. 'I will be kinder so that you are reasonable.'

'Reasonable?' She was almost palsied by his closeness,
id did not dare to look up. She could feel his breath upon
er neck and cheek.

Only the knowledge of his power and that her husband's

life lay in his hands, and might be blotted out at his pleasure
if he were provoked, prevented her from using the weapon
of righteous anger to break this evil spell he wove about her.

Abruptly he pushed the letters back into her hand. 'Here
take you these.'

'But . . . but you have not compared the writing.'

'Pish! What shall the writing signify to me?' Never a
patient wooer, he drove now straight to his ends. 'Your
husband's life doesn't hang on a row of pothooks. It hangs
on my belief in what you tell me.'

'But there is more than that. There are many who can
testify . . .'

'Perdition take them all! I care nothing for their testimony. Your word is enough for me, and I'll accept your
word that the treasonable letter is not in your husband's
hand.'

'You'll accept my word?' She was between hope and fear.

'Even though I did not believe it.'

Followed a pause in which she could hear the thudding
of her heart. 'If I did that,' he resumed, 'your husband
would be delivered from his peril. And it is a very mortal
peril, I can assure you.'

'But how can that be, since he is innocent?'

Rhynsault straightened himself again, and again laughed.

'Innocent he may be. But I must be persuaded to pronounce him so.'

'What else can you pronounce him when the evidence
is . . .'

'A fig for evidence!' he interrupted her. 'Evidence is for
lawyers and other such carrion birds. Here! Take your
letters, I say.' And again he proffered them.

Mechanically, half-dazed, she put forth her hand to receive them. The next moment it was in his grip. She raised
her glance at last, at this physical contact, and for a long
moment stared into his eyes that smouldered as they now
regarded her.

'What a little hand!' he murmured. 'So white and slim

and frail, yet strong enough to hold the destiny of a man.
Look you, mistress.' He was leaning towards her again, still
clutching that hand which she had not the strength or courage to withdraw. 'I place the life of Philip Danvelt in this
white palm, to do with absolutely as you will. Surely, you
would never have the heart to destroy it?'

In a silence of horror she continued to stare at him until,
swept by a gust of passion, he pulled her roughly from her
chair into his arms at a single wrench.

Now at last active resistance awakened in her. She bat-
tled against the enfolding grip of those sinewy arms. Her
voice rang sharply with authority.

'Let me go! Let me go at once!'

But he tightened his coils until he held her paralyzed. He
spoke quietly into her ear, a murmur which at once wooed
and threatened.

'What? And leave your husband in the hangman's hands?
Be kind, mistress, as you look for kindness in me. One little
word from you, and Philip Danvelt may have his life and go.
One little word.'

With an inarticulate ejaculation of contempt and loathing, she partly writhed out of his grip; enough to liberate her
right arm and hand. In a flash that hand had closed upon
the hilt of the dagger hanging from his belt. Before he could
even guess her intent, the blade was out, the point descending towards his throat. Within an inch of it, he caught her
wrist, and with the same grip so twisted it that her fingers
relaxed their hold and the dagger sped from them to clatter
on the floor.

Enraged, he flung her off, and stood glaring at her, whilst
she braced herself, panting, for whatever brutality might be
to follow. But his anger cooled. It is even possible that her
spirited act, exciting his admiration, rendered her even more
desirable. He smiled at her, none too pleasantly; then
stooped to take up his dagger.

'An ugly claw, mistress, for so fair a hand,' he mocked her.
Then he grew stern. 'Come, now! I've been gentle and

played the gallant long enough. Will you pay for this attempt upon my life, or shall your husband? It is for you to choose.'

And he advanced upon her until her next words checked him.

'You fill me with horror! You unclean beast!'

Some of his many wooings had been repelled in many ways. But never in terms so uncompromising, unflattering and, as he believed, untrue; for he knew that, when all was said, he was a fine figure of a man. The phrase brought him up as if it had been a blow. He went white to his suddenly sneering lips.

'And is it so? Horrifying am I to the dainty fastidiousness of a huckstering burgher's wife? Well, well! We must amend such unnatural feelings.'

With an inarticulate ejaculation, shuddering at the sight of him, she turned abruptly to depart.

But he reached the door ahead of her. With his back to it he finally admonished her.

'Look you, mistress. I am not of those who take, as I might, what is not freely given. That is not my way.'

'Will you let me go?' she demanded firmly, only anger and contempt in her eyes.

'Ay, mistress, since you insist. But you shall come again and soon, or by the eyes of God, I'll stretch the neck of your loutish husband without mercy or scruple.' He held her glance a moment, then turned, flung wide the door, and stood aside to let her pass.

She went out, her head high, without word or glance or even thought for anything but her outraged purity.

CHAPTER XIX

THE FOOL ADVISES

His excellency the Governor of Middelburg dispensed that day a stern and expeditious justice. Long before nightfall the four burghers impeached of seditious activities had been sentenced by him to be hanged. For motives of his own, so as to protract the example which this hanging was to afford, they were to perish at the rate of one a day for the next four days. And he let it be generally known that the fifth traitor, Philip Danvelt, whose trial was postponed for a further investigation of the evidence, would no doubt be sentenced in time to mount the gallows on the fifth day.

'I desire the town to be purged of treason before Sunday,' he had informed the court and the people who thronged it.

But when all had gone, he still sat, alone in that great hall, brooding in the judgment seat! He knew the futility of threatening more than you may perform, and Danvelt's case was exercising him. He had been confident that from one or the other of those arraigned that day, something incriminating Danvelt would have transpired. He had sought to obtain it from each, by threats, cajolery, and trickery. But all his efforts had drawn so blank that he seriously began to ask himself if it might not be that Philip Danvelt was innocent, and that the incriminating letter which he held was from some other Danvelt than this. He came to think that, if this were not indeed the case, Johanna would never have brought him letters so that he might compare the hands. He might have resolved the doubt by making the comparison as she had begged him. He refrained precisely because he feared that the comparison would establish Danvelt's innocence. And he wanted no proofs of that at present.

To his aid in his quandary came that emissary of Satan,

the Fool, entering the great hall abruptly in quest of hi
master.

'Do you sit in judgment upon the ghosts of those you'v
hanged?' the Fool hailed him, alluding to the emptiness c
the place. Atop of his chaperon he had set a cap adorned b
a peacock's feather three feet long. His inevitable lute wa
slung behind him.

He came to perch himself on the edge of the ponderou
table on the judgment dais under the great red canopy tha
bore the arms of Burgundy. Rhynsault took counsel wit
him. The Fool's long face smiled inscrutably as he listened
dangling his skinny legs. His beady eyes were fixed upon th
toes of his long pointed shoes.

He fetched a sigh when he had heard the Governor out.

'Faith, the course of true love never did run smooth.'

'Love!' bellowed the Governor. 'What has love to d
with it?'

'If love had naught to do with it there would be no diff
culty. It's like a cough, gossip. It can't be hid. The othe
difficulty, of course, is that you are a man of your word
Having informed Mistress Danvelt that failing certai
amiabilities her husband will hang . . .'

'What's that? Was your ear to the keyhole, you abortion?'

'My wits are my ears, gossip, and they are ever at th
keyhole of the world. It is thus that I am informed that yo
are perplexed because, if Danvelt were hanged and after
wards proved innocent by this very alert and enterprisin
wife of his, the thing would have its awkwardness. Th
Duke is at times unreasonable. He takes narrow views c
such adventures as the one that is now alluring you.'

The Governor raised his hand and drove a blow at th
Fool. Kuoni ducked to avoid it.

'Hold your hand!' he cried. 'For if you injure my head
you'll injure the only head between us. Listen a moment be
fore you give way to violence. Your course is clear an
simple.' The Governor contained his anger at this. 'All yo
need to do is to establish Danvelt's guilt.'

'But that's the difficulty.'

The Fool shook his head slowly. 'No difficulty at all.
'ou've rack and thumbscrews and all the other implements
)r the extraction of truth. Extract it from Danvelt him-
-lf.'

'But if the truth is that he is innocent?'

'It is yourself is innocent. The truth to be extracted by
ıe rack is of any colour that your needs demand. It is only
matter of turning the screw sufficiently. Come, come!'
'he Fool slid off the table. 'You've ample grounds at law
)r putting him to the question. Put him to it long enough
ıd rigorously enough, and you shall have whatever answer
ou require.'

Rhynsault licked his lips as he considered. Then he
anged the table with his fist.

'I should have thought of it!' he exclaimed and heaved
imself up.

'It needs an acute mind like mine,' said Kuoni. 'If you
ad my wits to your great body, you would be an emperor.'

Rhynsault summoned Diesenhofer, issued his commands,
ıd went presently below to see them executed. The Fool
ent with him, to gratify the feral thirst that was a part of
is warped nature.

Into that vaulted underground chamber with its instru-
ıents of torture they brought the unfortunate Danvelt to
e racked, ostensibly because he was conceived guilty of
:dition, in reality because he was the husband of a beauti-
ıl and chaste woman.

Had he been aware of this, it might have increased his
ourage and his obstinacy, and he might have resisted an
rdeal even sterner than that to which he was subjected. As
was, he acquitted himself well.

Stripped to the waist, they placed him under a giant cob-
eb of grey ropes and pulleys. White and scared, but re-
)lved nevertheless, he answered firmly with a denial when
ıe question was put to him in this position. His wrists
inioned behind him, and the rope attached to them, the

question was repeated, the secretary at his pulpit writing
busily the while. Not only did he persist in denial, but he
protested against the measures being taken with him, urging that there was no evidence to justify it, and that such evidence as was urged could easily be proved no evidence at all

He was a man of strong thews and great physical vigour
and he had the hardy courage usually accompanying these
physical endowments. He persisted with denial through
three hoists, and until with dislocated shoulders he los
consciousness.

They rested him for forty-eight hours, and then stretched
him on the rack. His body, maimed already, turned traito
to his will. Under the exquisite agony his spirit broke. To
win respite, he returned at last the required affirmative to
that reiterated question: 'Do you confess to having written
a letter to the convicted traitor Thomas Tegel, in which you
offered to supply arms and money for the projected rising
against the government of the Duke's highness?'

The secretary took down his answer. He was removed
from the rack, and carried back to his prison. On the mor
row they brought him the confession in a written form tha
he might ratify it, as was by law required. He refused to do
so, and was racked again. This time, he yielded, and when
the confession was again put before him, signed it, and so
signed away his life. Hanging, he thought, and rightly, wa
more easily endured than racking by one in his agonized
bodily condition.

And in those four days, Mistress Johanna, to the Gover
nor's deep surprise and disappointment, had made no sign
Three days longer, Rhynsault waited, then on the seventh
Danvelt was put upon his public trial, confronted with his
confession, which made the calling and examination of wit
nesses supererogatory, and sentenced to death, the sentence
to be carried out upon the following morning.

Rhynsault postponed the signing of the warrant until the
evening, and when he signed it he did so almost as an act o
anger. He had waited confidently, from the moment tha

the news of sentence had gone abroad, for the return of
Mistress Johanna. Indeed, it was to bring her that he had
proceeded to trial and sentence of her husband. He had
confidently hoped, in his limited knowledge and lack of
discernment, that she would seek him in such a spirit that
his signature to the warrant of execution might never be
required. Because her continued absence brought him a
sense of defeat, he signed at last in fury, adding a note that
the sentence be carried out at daybreak. Upon that he went
to supper without appetite.

The Fool, supping with his master, as was the invariable
custom, watched him with those beady eyes and that im-
passive solemn face, whilst inwardly his malicious soul was
shaken with laughter. Here was the great Claude de Rhynsault beaten to his knees after having exhausted in vain all
the brutalities at his command against a poor devil of a
fellow who was probably quite innocent of the crime im-
puted to him. By the lengths to which he had gone, Rhynsault had manœuvred himself into a position in which he
was constrained to sacrifice the fellow's life for nothing. It
was poor comfort to his rage to stretch a neck which he had
meant only to threaten as a coercive measure. The Fool
discovered an engaging irony in the situation, and inwardly
he gloated over the bitterness that he knew to be in Rhynsault's disappointed soul.

He broke at last upon the Governor's sullen musings.

'You are moody, gossip. Shall I sing to you?'

Though the mockery was subtle, a suspicion of it reached
his excellency. He looked sourly and searchingly at the
Fool, and wondered what thoughts stirred behind that bland
countenance and those unblinking eyes.

'I want no songs,' he growled at last.

'Let me weep for you, then.'

Rhynsault made a noise in his throat.

'Not even that?' said the Fool. 'Lackaday! To a crazy
ship all winds are contrary. Yet I could weep an ocean over
the abject folly of you.'

'Folly?' Rhynsault turned bloodshot eyes upon him. H
was clearly dangerous. Yet the Fool had his deep reason
for braving the danger.

'Folly, indeed,' he insisted. 'To have power and to forg
its uses is to be like an ass that carries a load of gold and ye
eats thistles. Shall we change clothes, gossip? You migh
make a poor show in motley. But I in your office woul
know how to use my opportunities. But there! Fortun
gives nuts to those that have no teeth. An old proverb that
and a true one. Lackaday!'

'No more of your chatter,' Rhynsault growled at him, an
reached for his wine-cup. Though he had scarcely touche
food, he had drunk deeply already!

'Chatter? That is what wisdom has become in your ears
You just sit a-dreaming and a-moping and a-sighing, like a
child, for the moon.'

Rhynsault set down the empty cup. The matter that had
so long been simmering in his thoughts suddenly boiled over
'She is obstinate as a mule.'

'Then put a bridle on her,' came the prompt advice.

Through his teeth Rhynsault answered: 'I'm putting a
halter on her husband.'

'And that satisfies you? It brings you what you lack?'

'The fear of it may do so yet.'

'And if it doesn't?'

'Then, let him die and be damned.'

'Which is the damnation of your last hope. Lend an ear to
sound sense, gossip. Hope is a good breakfast, but a bad
supper; and once you've hanged him, you'll have supped on
your hopes. You will have consumed your most persuasive
argument; which is his life. I can't rate the prescription
highly. But, to be sure, when love is the disease any doctor
is an ass.'

Dully Rhynsault looked at him. 'You talk and talk,' he
complained sourly. 'Sometimes I wonder what purpose
you serve.'

'And sometimes you discover it to your own advantage.'

The Fool leaned forward. 'What need to have ordered his hanging for the morning? That is the haste of vindictiveness, and vindictiveness is always stupid. You fail, and I deplore to see you fail, particularly when, guided by my wits, you might so easily succeed.'

'Succeed?' The bloodshot eyes grew more inflamed. In that hour there was hardly a price that Rhynsault would not have paid for success. His desires had been so kindled by thwarting that they were burning up his reason. 'Show me the way to that, and I'll overlook your insolence.'

'Now here's a rich reward! No matter! I give it not for guerdon, but from the generosity of my nature. In your place I would have postponed sentence and very graciously sent word to Mistress Johanna that she is permitted to come and visit her unfortunate husband. You've left him in pitiful case, a man burnt to the socket. His condition must awaken her compassion, and compassion is a very melting emotion. It could do no harm, and might accomplish . . . anything.' He paused, and considered the Governor, who sat in sullen silence, his chin upon his breast. 'That is what I should have advised had you consulted me. Unfortunately you did not, and now it is too late.'

Rhynsault reared his head at that. 'Too late?' he echoed.

As if to answer him, a servant entered. Mistress Johanna Danvelt was below, and begged the Governor to grant her audience.

'Mistress Johanna!' The Governor heaved himself up. His face lighted with an evil satisfaction. He looked across at the Fool and laughed. 'Too late, eh?' he mocked him. Then to the servant: 'Bring her up. Nay, wait.' He grew suddenly cunning. He would stretch her will upon the rack of suspense until it snapped under the strain. 'Say to her that I am immersed in affairs; but that if she will wait a while I will endeavour to spare her a moment. More is impossible. Let her wait in the hall.'

The lackey withdrew to bear the message. Rhynsault poured himself more wine, and laughed again, deep in his

throat. 'Too late, eh?' he mocked the Fool. 'Too late, is it
you well of wisdom?'

His satisfaction awoke the malice of Kuoni. He would
give it pause. He would plant an uneasy thought and perhaps something more in the dull brain of the Burgundian
lieutenant. For like a skilled chessplayer, Kuoni perceived
by several moves what might ultimately follow his present
suggestion.

'Laugh your fill, gossip. But too late it is. The warrant is
signed. The hanging as good as performed.'

'He's not hanged yet.'

'No. But the fact is published that he confessed his guilt
upon the rack. The court has sentenced him to death. It
could do no less. As a consequence, you have signed the
warrant. You could do no less. What, then, have you to
offer?'

'His reprieve, you numbskull.'

The Fool grinned his pity. 'You'ld reprieve a man who
has confessed to supplying the rebels with arms and money,
and upon whom you have passed sentence? A nice tale that
for the ears of the Duke of Burgundy.'

Rhynsault looked at him with eyes of wonder and wrath,
touched by a certain uneasiness.

'Was it not yourself advised me to wring the confession
out of him by these means?'

'But not to publish it. Not to make it the ground upon
which to sentence him in open court. There your own vindictiveness, your own fidelity to your rashly plighted word,
is alone to blame.'

Rhynsault drank again. Thereafter: 'Bah!' he said.
'What's a burgher more or less that the Duke should trouble
about him whatever I decide?'

'Yet in your shoes I should walk warily.'

'Caution is not my habit.'

'Alas, no! Yet Caution, gossip, makes an excellent body-
servant.' He rose. 'I'll be going. You can supply enough
folly of your own in what's to do.'

Rhynsault gave him leave by a nod. At the door, Kuoni paused.

'A last word of advice,' said he. 'A philosophical fragment for your study: Take all you may, give nothing more than you must. Weigh that well. It is pregnant with the wisdom of the ages. And let the lady wait yet awhile. Suitors cool with waiting. She may heed a word from me in passing, and that, too, may help! A happy night to you, gossip.'

He went out, closing the door after him. With his shoulders to it, he looked down the long hall, now full of shadows, and to the island of light by the table in the middle of it, where Johanna sat. Behind her stood her two servants, Jan, old and lean and tough, and Peter, stalwart, young, and vigorous.

She sat with her fur-edged cloak wrapped tightly about her to repress her shivering which sprang not only from the chill of the place. She was tormented at once by apprehension for her husband and memories associated with this very hall in which to-night she waited, a stricken suppliant. Those memories of another night, in this place, three months ago, came crowding thick upon her, to be transmuted by her too sensitive conscience into a cause from which the present dread effect was sprung. It was in this very hall, to-night so chill and dank and gloomy, but then a scene of brilliance, the like of which she had never formerly beheld, that she had last seen Count Anthony. Vividly the eyes of her mind beheld him again, first on the dais, leaning familiarly upon the back of the Duke's chair of state, later bowing before her and addressing her, inviting her to go forth by those doors, now closed and barred, into the fragrant gardens beyond, which now were desolate in the grip of an early winter, akin to the desolation and winter in her heart.

This, perhaps, was her punishment, for having undutifully listened to a lover's words, and thus, having been unfaithful to her marriage vows. Her presence here again was the only amend she could make. She would brave the insults of Rhynsault's gross, carnal wooing, that she might stay his murderous hand by pleading and perhaps even by threatening. Her duty to her husband demanded no less of her. It must in any case have demanded it. It demanded it all the more because of her earlier departure from that duty.

The Fool, considering her from the shadows about the Governor's threshold, was oddly enough assailed by memories akin to her own. He, too, remembered that tepid August night when they had been so gay and festive at the Gravenhof, and the particular attention paid this lovely woman by the austere Count Anthony of Guelders, who had conducted her forth and sought privacy with her in the scented gloom of the garden. The Fool speculated again, as he had speculated already, upon the link between that brilliant prince and this simple burgher's daughter and burgher's wife. He had planted a suggestion in the mind of the Governor to the end that the Governor might ensnare the truth from her; this because the Fool saw a certain use to be made of the knowledge. But Rhynsault was a clumsy numbskull who had not known how to act upon the suggestion.

The Fool's arachnidial mind was busy about the spinning of a tentative web of evil. His crooked soul glowed with satisfaction at his skill and the end which he foresaw.

He moved down the hall on his spidery legs, and came into the island of light about the table. He bowed his grotesque dwarfish figure before Mistress Danvelt, who stiffened as she might have done at the approach of a snake.

His voice cooed softly. 'His excellency will not long keep your loveliness waiting.'

She stared at him without answering.

'If meanwhile there is aught you lack...' His gesture implied that she had but to command. 'His excellency would have you at your ease.'

Still there was no answer from her beyond that dread fascinated stare of her blue eyes. A little in the background her servants looked on, and their glances, particularly Jan's, were lowering. But Kuoni paid little heed to them. His attention was upon Johanna.

'Come, mistress,' he urged. 'Take heart. Here you have nothing to fear.' He approached her by another step, and stood now very close to her, his head, although she was sitting and he standing, scarcely above the level of her own. 'You are come, as I conceive, in the hope of averting the doom pronounced to-day upon your husband.' He paused a moment, to add rapidly: 'Why should you merely hope for that which it is within your power to govern?'

That stirred her to speech at last. 'Do you mock me?' she asked him witheringly.

'Mock!' He raised hands and eyes. 'Heaven be my witness, I would be your friend and help you in your need.'

It was incredible that any good should come out of this creature whose exudations of evil were instinctively apprehended. Yet in her desperate case, clutching at straws, she troubled to question his assertion.

'You help me? You? The Governor's man?'

He answered her with a truth that went deeper than she or any could have guessed.

'I am no man's man, if, indeed, I am a man at all. Whatever I am, mistress, I have the wit to belong to myself.'

'And you would help me?' She looked deep into those inscrutable beady eyes. 'Why?'

'Why? As I do all things. For the interest I derive from it; the interest and the diversion. Look at me well. I am as hideous almost, mistress, as you are beautiful. But to compensate me for my lack of comeliness, I am master of the rarer gifts of wisdom and knowledge. Yet did I use those gifts no better than you use your beauty, I must have starved long since, or have perished even more miserably.' He paused, and for once a faint expression crept into the mask of his face, an expression of contempt. 'You move through life a pious, plangent thing of snivelling intercession. You know no way to your ends but prayer. You pray to man for the things that you would have, and, when man fails you, you pray to God, who fails you likewise. O mistress, were I a woman and had I your beauty, I'ld so transmute that beauty into power that the world should be my footstool.'

She put forth a hand in a gesture at once of dismissal and appeal. 'Please leave me. You . . . you bewilder me.'

'To be sure,' said he, more briskly. 'Wisdom is ever bewildering. I'll be plainer. You wish to save your husband from the hangman?'

'You know that that is why I am here. I have come to plead . . .'

Harshly, almost fiercely he interrupted her. 'To plead! Of course, to plead! That is your way, as I have said. To plead! To plead where you should command.'

'Command? I?'

He leaned towards her, setting his elbow on the arm of her chair, and crossing his legs, so that he looked more grotesque and distorted than Nature had fashioned him. As he spoke, rapidly now, he used his hands freely in gesture, hands of long fingers and big knuckles, disproportionately large.

'Listen, mistress. For a week Philip Danvelt's life has hung in the balance. In that week what have you done? To be sure, you have worn your lovely eyes red with weeping, and your shapely knees red with praying to an unresponsive Heaven. But what practical thing have you done to effect the rescue of your husband?'

Whilst marvelling with herself that she should trouble to answer this mocking thing of evil, yet she answered him out of a desperate hope that from all his evil some little good might yet come to her if unawares.

'What could I do?'

'You could not bring yourself to pay the price that Rhynsault asks, because my lord is a gross fellow, artlessly clumsy in his wooing as in all else, a heavy-handed lout who crushes the delicate fruit he touches.' He paused, and his face was turned fully to hers, his unblinking eyes looked into her own. 'But was there none other to whom you might have turned in all that wasted week?'

She had shrunk back from him a little during his speech, as far, indeed, as the confines of her chair permitted. 'I know of none,' she said, still clinging to the hope that he was about to point the way.

'Think now! Think!' he urged her, watching her keenly the while. 'What of one, handsome and radiant as a prince of faerie, a noble and puissant gentleman, a mirror of chivalry, self-appointed protector of the oppressed? One who once served your husband in his extremity?'

'Count Anthony!' she murmured.

The Fool chuckled, and straightened himself from his fantastic attitude. 'Behold how quickly he leaps to your mind, mistress!'

She stared at him, a deathly pallor in her face, yet something of indignation in her eyes. He laughed outright.

'Not so austere, this Count Anthony of Guelders, as repute pretends! Not above treading a garden path on a summer's night with the lovely lady of a Flemish burgher. My Lord Rhynsault had best go warily with his exalted Chastity for a rival.'

She sat appalled. So that indiscretion of hers was not buried as she supposed in her own heart. This evil creature had seen enough to infer more. And as with him, so, no doubt, with others. How much had they seen, indeed, and how much in their vileness did they surmise? Indignation surged up in her, but it was indignation on the Count's behalf.

'You dare to insult one who is as pure and noble as you are abominable and evil!'

'But what self-betraying heat on the pretty gentleman's behalf!' he mocked her. 'O Piety, thy name is slyness!'

A hand fell on his shoulder, and held him in a crushing grip. Jan's voice growled in his ear. 'Venomous toad! I'll crush the poison out of you once and for all time.'

Johanna was on her feet. 'Let him go, Jan! Let him go!'

The command, sternly delivered, was, however, scarcely necessary. The Fool had twisted himself out of that grasp, and spun nimbly round to face the groom, a snarl on his pale lips, the livid gleam of steel in his right hand.

'It were wiser,' he said viciously. 'There's a nasty sting about me that makes me dangerous to handle.'

'By Heaven!' said Jan. 'I'll take my chance of that.'

And, ignoring both the command and the threats, he was advancing again upon the Fool, when down the hall rang a brisk metallic voice to check him.

'Of what will you take your chance, sirrah?'

Rhynsault came slowly into view from the shadows about the doorway of his closet. He continued to speak as he advanced.

'Well? Of what do you take your chance? Let me tell you. You take your chance of a whipping when you raise your voice in here, you dog.'

He was level now with the grinning Fool. 'Were you baiting him, Kuoni?' he asked, and took the Fool by the ear.

'Baiting him!' said the Fool. 'God give me patience with you, gossip! Since when have you known me whet my wit on lumps of Flemish earth?'

But the Governor, retaining that grip of his ear, lugged him forward almost to the feet of Johanna.

'I trust, mistress, that this malapert Fool of mine has not been giving you annoyance.'

'Oh, that . . . that is no matter, sir.' She was suddenly breathless.

'You are too clement. Whatever befall your husband, there is no charge against you, and I will have none offend you.' He let the Fool go, nevertheless. 'I had hoped, mistress, that you would have come before. Before we were constrained by duty to come to extremes where your husband is concerned. Still, better late than never, as the proverb runs.' He raised his voice to call. 'Who waits?'

An officer clanked in by the great doors which stood open at the hall's end.

'To command, excellency.'

The Governor waved a hand towards Johanna's servants. 'Conduct these knaves below, and let them wait there.'

Johanna interposed. 'By your excellency's leave, I should prefer them to remain.'

He seemed surprised. 'Mistress, I have that to say to you . . . touching your husband . . . which is not for the ears of lackeys.'

'Your excellency can have nothing to say to me that may not be said before them.'

He admired her spirit; a spirit worth the conquering, he thought, whose conquest might afterwards be dwelt upon with pride. Gravely he shook his head.

'It is not my way, mistress, to open my mind before grooms. They go hence alone, or they go hence with you, at your pleasure; but they go hence at once.'

There was a pause in which she fought down her loathing and her dread, a battle of which the only sign was the twisting and untwisting of her hands. At last she yielded.

'Very well,' she said, as calmly as she might. 'Go wait below for me, Jan.'

But Jan, that old and faithful servant, pervaded on her behalf with that loathing and that dread to an extent scarcely less than her own, ventured to advise her. To him Philip's life was as nothing compared with the least hurt to her.

'Come away, mistress,' he muttered urgently. 'Come away home with us.'

She was cold and stern with him. 'Go, Jan!' she said shortly.

The servant seemed to shrink together a little. He made a mute gesture of despair, half-raising his hands, and then letting them fall heavily to his sides. He shrugged despondently, turned on his heel, and with Peter stalked down the long hall under the officer's escort.

Rhynsault turned to the Fool. 'Well? Why do you wait? You are not wanted here.'

The Fool grinned. 'Am I not? As usual, gossip, you are

wrong. You never needed me more urgently or the thing
could tell you.'

'It will keep till morning.'

'So it will. But by morning it will be too late.'

'So much the better, then. Begone!'

'You're wasting breath. I've no mind to linger, or to talk
I only mention that there is a thing I could tell if I were so
inclined, which . . .'

'Begone!' the Governor roared at him.

'I am gone,' he was answered in a laugh. 'Ever have I
been your friend, and it were unkind now to let a thought o
the morrow mar the sweetness of your night.'

He skipped out. From beyond the door they heard his
voice receding in the distance, singing:

> 'Flout not Love, for Love will not
>   Suffer it, I warn you.
> Love is soon by Love begot;
> Life is cold where Love is not;
>   So take you Love to warm you.
>   Ha, ha, ha, ha! To warm you!'

CHAPTER XX

RHYNSAULT'S BUCKLER

WITHIN his snug closet, whither he conducted her, the Governor considerately desired Mistress Danvelt to sit, and would have relieved her of her fur-edged cloak but that she clung to the garment, urging that her business was but brief and would not consume much of his time. Abruptly she came to it. They had brought her word of the sentence passed that day upon her husband.

He sighed. 'Your concern comes a little late, mistress.' He stood quite close to her, half-sitting upon, half-leaning against the heavy table. He looked down upon her with eyes that glowed out of a face which he schooled into lines of kindliness. 'You know that it is for to-morrow morning.'

No need to ask him what. His meaning was plain enough. Panic fluttered her.

'Yes. That is what they told me. But you dare not! You dare not!'

He pondered her for a long moment. Then he spread his hands, his whole attitude expressive of dismay.

'Your distress moves me profoundly,' he said slowly. 'I did not think that it could mean so much to you.'

'You did not think . . .?' She was between surprise and indignation.

'What cause did you give me to think it? I placed Danvelt's life in your hands. Did I not offer to set him free at a little word from you? Before the trial, it would have been so easy. Now!' He hunched his shoulders, paused, and then resumed: 'And you have had a whole week in which to speak that word. Since you haven't chosen to speak it, what was I to suppose? Why, that, like so many wives, you would count yourself well rid of an importunate husband.'

She looked up into that handsomely florid countenance.

'This is noble,' she said. 'It is generous to mock an un
fortunate woman in the hour of her affliction.'

'I do not mock,' he assured her in words which his very
glance belied. 'If it is not as I have supposed, why did you
not come before?'

She answered him firmly, for all her mental anguish. 'Be
cause, knowing him innocent, I did not believe it possible
you could find him guilty. I waited confidently for his trial
for I believed that in the Duke's judgment seat you dealt in
justice; that you would not dare to deal in anything else.'

'You were right. I have dealt in nothing else.'

'Close upon twenty witnesses waited to testify. They
were brought here in answer to my appeal and you were in
formed of it. They could have spoken to my husband'
character and pursuits. They could have proved beyond
question that he did not write the letter upon which you
arraigned him. Yet those witnesses were denied a hearing.

'To have heard them would but have wasted time. The
evidence of your husband's guilt was complete!'

Her eyes burned in her white face. 'Complete? Why
what a poor pretence is that? Will you maintain it before
the face of the Duke your master, as you may yet have to
do?'

He frowned, but his full lips still smiled. 'You threaten
mistress?'

'What else do you expect of me? I threaten that which
shall not hesitate to fulfil. Am I to be mocked with your
pretence of justice. Is the Duke to be mocked by your de
filement of his justice? I am a poor, weak woman, you sup
pose, capable only of pleading. Well, I may go plead else
where, and you know the tale I shall have to tell: you know
the motive I shall have to disclose; the real motive which
urges you along this path of infamy. Didn't you make it
clear to me a week ago in this room, when you refused to
consider any evidence, when you . . .'

'When I placed your husband's life in your hands, to do
with as you wished,' he interrupted, unmoved by her

threats. 'It is you, not I, who send him to the hangman in the morning.'

It was a moment before she could answer him, stricken dumb by her indignation and her crushing sense of impotence. When at last she found her tongue again, it was to pour words of bitter scorn upon him.

'You are a great soldier! A captain of renown! The Duke of Burgundy's trusted representative! Holder of the sacred office of justiciary! And yet you can stoop from your high place to such ignoble depths, accounting no means too base to win to your evil ends!' Her voice swelled up in scorn. 'I imagined you a high-handed, masterful villain. But you are not even that. You are just a paltry rascal on the level of the thief, the forger, the utterer of base coin. You misuse your office to entangle my husband in a net of lies, and you shut out the evidence that would have torn that net to shreds. But I warn you! I warn you solemnly, my Lord Rhynsault, that, if you persist in this infamy, the Duke your master shall be fully informed and you shall be brought to account to him.'

She had risen, leaving her fur-edged cloak of blue velvet on the chair, and stood before him, a slim, white-clad figure with flaming eyes and heaving breast.

He considered appraisingly the white delicate beauty of her, and marvelled at the restraint he imposed upon himself. For never had she seemed to him more desirable than now in this white heat of righteous anger. But he had a part to play, a check to administer, which he thought should bring her to her knees, whence it should be his glory to uplift her.

'The Saints give me patience with you, mistress!' he exclaimed. 'If it was lies entangled Philip Danvelt, the lies were his own.'

'His own? His own?'

'His own. He confessed his treason; and he set his signature to the confession, which was written down in a measure as he uttered it.'

This was a blow between the eyes to her. Her anger was shouldered out by dismay and growing terror.

'Confessed?' she echoed, gasping, faltering. 'He confessed, you say? What did he confess?'

'That he had written the letter upon which I impeached him; that he had supplied arms and money to equip the rebels.'

'But that is not true!' she wailed. 'It's not true! How, then, could he confess it?'

'He should know the truth of it better than you, mistress.' Rhynsault now affected a tone of regret. 'All that you can say is that he never took you into his confidence in the matter. It is not likely that he would have done so. Shrewd men do not tell secrets to their women-folk, especially secrets that will put a rope about their necks.'

'But I was not alone in my belief, in my knowledge,' she answered, battling desperately against the odds that were suddenly heaped against her. 'The letter was not in his hand. Twenty of the witnesses could have sworn to that. If he confessed . . .' She broke off. Suddenly she saw the explanation, and cried out in horror: 'You tortured him!'

Rhynsault shrugged and pursed his lips. 'He was put to the question. It is the usual practice. On the rack, he confessed, as commonly happens when a man is guilty. What, then, is to tell the Duke my master? That I hanged a man who avowed himself a rebel?' He laughed softly. 'You see. Good mistress, you threaten me with thunderbolts of lath.'

Thus the foundation of menace upon which she had built so confidently gave way under her feet. She half-turned from him, with a little moan of pain, and swayed as she stood there. He had beaten her down, indeed. Not even vengeance remained, so that it was idle to threaten him with it in the hope of averting her unfortunate husband's doom. And the horrible thought arose slowly in her mind, further to torture her agonized spirit, that it was she had been the innocent means of bringing this doom upon poor Philip.

She reeled to the chair, and sank limply into it, her limbs momentarily bereft of strength.

'O God, pity him!' she cried. 'You wrenched him limb from limb, until, in his agony and to obtain respite from your cruelty, he confessed a falsehood that has given you power over his life. And this because ... because ... O God!' She sank her face into her hands, her body convulsively shaken.

Still half-sitting on the table's edge, he watched her with those smouldering eyes, the ghost of a smile about his lips. Then he reached forth, and set a hand upon her shoulder. He spoke very softly, in a tone of gentle remonstrance.

'It was in your power to save him,' he reminded her; and added, after a moment's pause: 'For that matter, it still is. Even now, even at this eleventh hour, you can have his life if you will. The hand that signed the death-warrant can sign the reprieve. If you have come to speak the little word I begged of you, you have not come in vain.'

She lowered her hands from her face, and turned to look up at him again, loathing and defiance in her glance. 'I have not,' she told him fiercely.

'Not? Why else, then, have you come?'

She relapsed into the weakness from which she had momentarily arisen.

'Is there no pity in you?' she cried. 'Is there no fear either of man or God in your dark soul? What do you look to gain by sending my husband to his death? Nothing, nothing, nothing! What shall it profit you to leave me widowed? What satisfaction shall you have from that? Is that a man's worthy vengeance upon a woman whose only offence against him is her virtue? You do not fear the justice of your Duke, you say. My husband's confession is your buckler. But have you no fear of the justice of God? What shield will avail you against that when your hour comes? Will you imperil your immortal soul for this empty satisfaction you are contemplating?'

Rhynsault moved from the edge of the table, swung round to confront her, squarely planted upon his feet.

'Look you, madam, I have listened long enough. If you are come to deafen me with words, to weary me with a sermon upon heaven and hell, you distress yourself in vain. Heaven and hell have nothing to do with us at present. We are upon earth, we two, and alive. Talk to me of this, and I will listen. For the rest, I do not want your husband's life. It is the law that claims it.'

'You are the law in Middelburg.'

'Its minister only. If I were to check it now, and set your husband free, I should be false to my duty as the Duke's lieutenant here. Yet, for your sake, I would do even that.' He paused a moment to add: 'But I have my price. And you know it, mistress.'

With hands clenched between her knees and lowered eyes and in a half-strangled voice she answered him. 'Yes, I know it. And I know that, if I paid that price, my husband would curse and abominate the life I had so purchased for him.'

'Are you so sure?' said Rhynsault softly, and with that provoked a revival of her earlier indignation.

'Sure? Am I sure?' She looked up at him in scornful wonder. 'I am sure that my husband is a good, honest man, reverencing purity.'

'Yet life is very sweet,' the Governor reminded her.

'Honour is sweeter to honourable men.'

Rhynsault leaned down a little from his fine height. He spoke persuasively. 'What need he know, since you are so tender of his feelings? A thing done in secret is as a thing not done at all.'

That brought her to her feet in a noble rage. 'You pitiful knave! You infamous villain!'

He flushed, but kept his temper. 'If I am that, it is love has made me so.'

'Love?' She flung the word at him in deepest scorn.

'Ay, love,' he insisted. 'Love such as you have never known.'

'And never shall, please God,' she answered him.

For a long moment he stood meeting the defiance of her glance, pondering the lissom grace of her figure so stiffly erect, the proud poise of her golden head, the distracting, maddening beauty of her delicate face. The wolf was aroused in him, yet dominated by the perception that to prevail he must here play the fox. He commanded himself, clenching his hands until the nails bit into his palms. He smiled a little, very wistfully, and fetched a sigh that was pure artifice.

'So! You are resolved, then, to let him die?'

'I have prayed to our Father in Heaven to purge the evil from your heart, to let the light of grace fall upon your soul before it is too late, before . . .'

He broke in. 'You pray for a miracle which your own will can accomplish.' His self-control was slipping from him. Whipped on by the scorpion-whips of his desire, he advanced upon her with open arms. 'Johanna!' he cried, and there was a hoarse note of pleading in his voice.

She recoiled before him. 'Don't touch me! Don't dare to touch me with your evil hands!'

He checked. He was white to the lips, and the sweat stood in beads upon his brow, just below the line of his sleek black hair. The purity and saintliness of her opposed to him a resistance almost physical, a resistance which he could not beat down by brutish force. He spoke through his teeth.

'You ask for mercy with the voice of cruelty. Can you hope that your prayer will be heard?' Abruptly he gave up the contest, a man defeated. He strode to the door, flung it wide, and called the officer of the guard by name.

'Cassaignac!'

A voice answered from the distance. Approaching steps rang hollow in the vast hall outside. Turning where he stood, Rhynsault spoke to her in dismissal, harshly.

'You had best return home, madam. Here is no more to do.'

Confronting this finality, her panic momentarily returned. 'Ah, no, no! Wait! Wait!'

His white face sneered at her. 'Wait!' he echoed. 'I have waited already a week. I am a man of short moods, madam. Yet I have stood here with a patience that I hardly recognize for my own, whilst you have heaped insults upon me, and threatened me with vengeances temporal and spiritual — what am I to wait for now? Another sermon?'

The officer surged on the threshold. With a shrug Rhynsault turned away from her.

'Cassaignac, you may reconduct this lady.'

She staggered where she stood, one hand clutching her heart. Then, controlling herself, realizing indeed that all was lost, that she had suffered insult in vain, that further intercession or delay were worse than idle, she gathered up her long cloak of blue velvet from the chair, and drew it about her shoulders.

Leaden-footed she moved towards the door and the waiting officer. Midway she halted.

'You'll give me leave to see my husband before . . . before he suffers?'

Out of the malice of his rage a denial leapt to his lips, to be thrust down again by the memory of something the Fool had said, a piece of advice which he had forgotten until this moment, of which it had been necessary that she should remind him. His eyes kindled again.

'Why should I deny you that? But time grows short. If you would see him, you had best see him now. At once.'

Without awaiting her reply, he ordered Cassaignac to bring Danvelt from his prison and allow him to have speech alone with his wife in the hall. Then he held the door for her whilst she passed out to await the coming of her husband.

CHAPTER XXI

IPHIGENIA

IF her little time of waiting was an agony, the first sight of him when at last they brought him to her was even worse. He was scarcely recognizable for the man he had been a week ago. The healthy fullness of his cheeks was gone; the great bony structures of his face stood gauntly forth from the stretched yellow skin, and his eyes, which seemed to have receded in their sockets, burned feverishly; even his incipient paunch had shrunk completely. He no longer walked with that slight, swaggering roll and the forward thrust of his chin, but moved slowly and stiffly, bending forward like an old man. He wore no pourpoint, and over a shirt that was soiled and stained with sweat and blood they had thrown a cloak. His yellow hair was tousled and dishevelled.

That first sight of him wrought in her such an uprush of pity and womanly tenderness that she ran to meet him, to enfold him in her arms. But he almost shrieked in her embrace, whereupon her arms were instantly relaxed and melted from him. She fell back in dismay.

'You . . . you hurt me!' he gasped, and added the explanation: 'I have been racked until I am one living ache.' He looked at her fearfully with those burning eyes about which the shadows were so heavy. 'What are you doing here, Johanna? Here in hell?'

She could do no more than murmur his name, her soul flooded by compassion and distress. Very gently she conducted him to a leather chair set by the table in that little island of light. Cassaignac and the men who had brought him went out, and the two were alone in that vast place of gloom and chilliness.

He mumbled explanations to her. 'I stood as much as flesh and bone could bear. Then, when I could endure no more, when I was stark mad with pain . . . I threw away my life to buy a moment's ease. I said what they wanted me to say. I would have said anything, anything that was required of me. I confessed that I had written that letter to that man . . . What is his name? I have forgotten it. No matter.'

She was kneeling beside him, an arm very gently set about his shoulders.

'And so you put it into that villain's power to murder you with safety to himself.'

He started violently and looked round, an abject creature, utterly broken in spirit by the breaking of his body. 'Sh!' he hissed in craven alarm. 'Take care! For pity's sake!'

'Care of what? Dear Heaven, what have I to care for, to hope for, or to fear? And as for you, my poor Philip? What more can they do to you?'

He shuddered, and his head hung limply on his breast. 'They have told you, then?' he whispered.

'The Governor sent me word. That is why I am here. I came to plead with him.'

'Plead?' His lips writhed. He kept his voice low, but the bitterness of it came clearly enough. 'As well might some poor damned soul plead with the Devil for release from hell, as man or woman plead for pity with my Lord Rhynsault.'

He looked at her, and from his self-pity he gathered now a tenderness which had never been part of his normal self. 'My little wife! We were so happy and at peace with all the world! So happy, my Johanna!'

It was like a sword of reproach to her, this insistence upon their happiness, when in her heart she knew that her sole happiness had been in her illicit dreams.

'A week ago,' he babbled on in his weak, plaintive voice, 'we hadn't a single care to trouble the sweetness of our lives. To-morrow . . .!' He broke off, shuddering violently again. Then, through his teeth in his impotent rage, he cried: 'Is there no God, that a devil such as that should walk the earth, wrecking men's lives?'

'Hush, dearest! There is a God. Place your trust in Him. He will sustain you, Philip, and He will avenge you. Oh, be sure that He will avenge this wickedness.'

Almost he sneered. 'Will that give me back my life? Will it . . .'

In anguished thought for his soul, she checked him. 'Don't, Philip! Don't, my dear. God's ways are mysterious ways to us. Trust in Him now. He will not forsake you.'

He was silent awhile, bowed and limp. 'I am so broken and distraught,' he complained weakly, tears in his voice. 'When I look back on all that was; on the perfection of our happiness, so wantonly destroyed, I . . . I am driven mad.'

Her sudden weeping recalled him in some measure to himself. He put forth a feeble hand to touch her cheek.

'Nay, now, Johanna! Nay, now! Don't weep! Don't! Help me . . . help me to be strong. I need strength, God knows.'

She controlled herself. 'There is strength in prayer. Shall we pray together, Philip?'

'Ay, together,' he agreed. 'For the last time together. For the last time!' And then panic took him and convulsed him. 'To-morrow!' His voice was hoarse with horror. He broke forth into frenzied protests, in dreadful, unreasoning, impotent revolt against the doom that was overtaking him. 'Oh, why should I die? Why must I die?' He rocked now in a mental anguish that extinguished bodily pain. 'Is there no power to save me, no power to help? Is there no escape from this horror?' His terrified gaze was upon her, appealing to her. 'Am I to be butchered like a sheep because a self-sufficient fool of a Governor has blundered? Is there no help for me?'

'Only in prayer, Philip, dear,' she answered him, distraught by his agony, holding herself in hand by a supreme effort because of his great need for strength in her.

He was petulant almost. 'How can I pray? How can you ask me to pray? Why did you come, Johanna? You should not have come. I was man enough until I saw you. Your coming has . . . has made a child of me.'

'How could I not come?' She spoke in tones calculated to soothe his unreason. 'How could I refrain from attempting to move that dreadful man? I warned him that God's vengeance will overtake him. But such as he are dead of soul. He only mocked my warnings.'

'Yet he allowed you to see me. That at least was considerate in him.'

'Oh, yes; he is considerate; considerate to himself,' she answered with incautious bitterness, 'thinking to further his evil hopes.'

'Hopes?' He stared at her. 'What hopes?'

'That . . . that is no matter.'

But he was not to be put off. There was something here he did not understand; something that she withheld. Her tone had betrayed it; her tone and that word 'hopes,' with its suggestion of infinite possibilities.

'What hopes had he? Tell me. You must tell me.'

Kneeling beside him, she sank back until she was sitting on her heels. Her hands folded in her lap, and her eyes lowered, she answered him, speaking very quietly, almost emotionlessly.

'You do not dream, Philip, out of what vileness is woven the net in which you are taken. It is a net, Philip, in which you are not so much the victim as the lure.'

'The lure? What do you mean? What lure?'

She lowered her voice until it was hardly more than a whisper, so that he had to strain to catch her words. 'He offered me your . . . life . . . at a price.'

Danvelt gasped. He could hardly believe his ears. Hope was suddenly reborn in him. It throbbed through his being, shortening his breath, deepening if possible the pallor of his ghastly cheeks. 'What . . . what do you mean?' His voice quavered. 'Do you mean that he offered to sell you my life? Why, then, in that case . . .'

At once she perceived the mischief of hope she had

wrought but to add to his mental torment. A sob convulsed her, a sob of pity for him.

'Ah, but the price, my dear!' she cried, assuming that from her very tone he must guess the truth.

But his wits, never penetrating, were now as blunt as lead. 'Price?' he echoed, his voice going suddenly shrill. 'What price could be too high to pay for life?' Excitement grew in him. 'Does that covetous captain want all our wealth? Then yield it to him. Yield all so that I may live. You'ld suffer poverty with me so that . . .'

She interrupted him, her hands now clutching the arms of his chair, her tear-stained face upturned to his. 'Can you dream I should have hesitated had it been but that? Oh, don't you understand? The price he proposed to me was to be paid by me. By me.'

He stared at her, and slowly understanding pierced those heavy wits of his. The light of hope perished in his eyes, like a candle that is blown out. He covered his face with his emaciated hands.

'The dog!' she heard him mutter. 'The foul Burgundian dog!'

There was a spell of silence, at the end of which she spoke very softly and gently. 'You see, my dear. You could never have forgiven it, or . . . or done other than loathe me if I had paid such a price as that for your life.'

To which his only answer was to echo that last word: 'Life!' Uncovering his face, he stared straight before him with unseeing eyes. Presently he asked a question: 'And you? What . . . what did you answer him?'

'As you would have me answer.'

Slowly he nodded. 'You refused.'

'I told him that, if I paid that price, I must be as detestable afterwards in your eyes as in my own; that you would curse the life I had so bought for you.'

He made no answer. He continued to sit there staring straight before him into vacancy, into realms visible only to the eyes of his spirit.

'That is the truth, Philip, dear,' she said presently, irked by his silence.

Still he neither moved nor answered.

'Isn't it?' she asked him, more sharply.

He answered woodenly: 'Is it? Perhaps . . . perhaps it is.'

'Perhaps!' It was a cry that reëchoed through that vaulted place.

It startled him. He stirred, looked at her and away again. Then he pressed his hands convulsively to his brow. He spoke in a voice of dull passion. 'Oh, I don't know! I don't know! My brains are as broken as my body.'

This she understood, she thought. She was conscious of a little pang that even in his condition such things should need to be made clear. She attempted to do so, by little more than a reiteration of what already she had said; but this time she put it almost questioningly.

'Yet, my dear, if I had done this thing, you would have cursed me afterwards for my unfaith.'

'Would I?' he asked. He was staring into vacancy again, away from her. 'How could I? How could I have cursed you? The thing if done . . . would have been done . . . for my sake. An act of . . . of sacrifice . . .'

'A sacrifice of infamy, of shame,' she urged.

'Yet I should have lived.' He spoke like a man in a dream.

She wrestled with his weakness. 'To abominate your life; to loathe me once I were defiled.'

'Defiled? Ah, no! How could you be . . .' Then at last, the man in him asserted himself. 'Yes, yes!' he cried. 'You are right! You are right! It is unthinkable! Better a thousand times that I should hang!' And then, as if the very utterance of the word brought back the horror of its meaning to drown all else, he repeated it in shuddering awe: 'Hang!'

It bore a message to her, a clear, unmistakable message, a prayer from this husband against whom she had offended, in

the first place by taking him to husband whilst withholding
a wife's love, in the second by having bestowed that love
elsewhere and avowed it since her marriage.

She came slowly to her feet, a tumult of thought distracting her, deepest affliction in her face. Yet she spoke quietly,
in a measured voice of enforced calm.

'There is nothing, Philip, that I would not do to serve
you; no sacrifice I would not now make for you, save one.
And even this one I would make at your own bidding; but
only at your bidding; so that afterwards you should have no
right to spurn or reproach me, since the act would then be
more yours than mine.'

'Bid you?' he cried. 'I bid you commit this infamy
against yourself? This horror?' He paused, wrestling with
temptation, and when at last he completed his answer, it
was but to give reasons why he could not complete it as she
asked. 'How can I bid you? It would shame my manhood.'

'Why, then . . . You see, Philip?'

'See? What do I see?' The conflict within him between
his self-respect and his fear, between his manhood and his
will to live, came forth in a torrent of petulance. 'O God!
Don't ask me such questions! Don't tempt me with them!
It is to agonize a man in my extremity. God knows I love
my life. It is as sweet to me as the thought of death is horrible and repellent. Perhaps . . . perhaps this horror distorts
my judgment, for to me it seems, it seems . . .' He hesitated, still in prey to that conflict, then abruptly added: 'It
seems that a defilement is the lesser evil.' Then, in a voice
of despair again: 'O God! I do not know; I should not be
asked. A defilement may be cleansed away. A life that is
put out can never be rekindled.'

She looked at him, and her eyes were as dead eyes in a
face of stone. Cold and hard as stone came her voice: 'Then
bid me to do it, Philip. I am your dutiful wife in all things.
I swore obedience to you at the altar. That vow, at least,
I have kept. I will obey you now if you command me.'

He struggled up in a state of revulsion. Perhaps her tone

had brought him a measure of self-contempt. 'No, no!' he cried. 'Never! I will never command you to that. I neither beg nor bid it, Johanna. Do you understand? I forbid it! I forbid it! Do you hear, Johanna?'

'I hear you, Philip,' she answered very steadily.

The door at the end of the hall was opened, and Cassaignac came in to announce that it was time for Master Danvelt to return to his cell.

He shuddered at that summons and clung a moment to Johanna, who stood silent and rigid.

'Pray for me, Johanna, if . . . if we do not meet again. God keep you, wife. God keep you!'

'God help you, Philip,' she answered him.

He broke away abruptly. There was about him an attempted resumption of dignity, a pale ghost of his old swagger. 'I am ready, sir,' he informed the officer, and so dragged himself painfully down the hall.

She had a last glimpse of his white, piteous face before he vanished and the doors closed again. Then she loosed the hold she had kept upon her spirit and sank into the chair which he had just vacated. Her lips were mumbling: 'A defilement may be cleansed away; a life that is put out can never be rekindled.'

His command upon her had been clear enough. Only shame had made him retract some part of it ere he went forth. But his command remained, and she was an obedient wife. Obedience, indeed, was the only part of the marriage vow in which she had kept faith. Had Philip married another, this danger would never have encompassed him. It was she who had brought this doom upon him. It was because she had appeared desirable in the eyes of Claude de Rhynsault that her husband's life was being employed to coerce her, and would be vindictively destroyed if the coercion failed. In marrying him she had cheated him. She was very conscious of that now. It lay in her power to make some measure of amends by purchasing for him the life he desired so passionately, the life which he valued far above her honour. If she could not give him spiritual fidelity, at least she could in this give him obedience, and in such a measure as to compensate for all that she had withheld. Against her there was the outrage to herself. But of what account was she? For whom should she keep herself pure and undefiled? Not for Philip, who opined that a defilement might be cleansed. And not for Anthony of Guelders, who was as far as the stars beyond her reach.

And then the Devil was at her elbow whispering. Let the justice of Burgundy here take its course; let Philip hang; and perhaps Anthony would not then be so far, so hopelessly removed.

Horror of herself shook her at that, as no horror of defilement could have shaken her. The temptation which might have turned her from paying so terrible a price served by its reactions but to goad her on.

She fell, shuddering upon her knees, crossed herself, and turned, as all her life she had turned in difficulty, to the Mother of Chastity for guidance.

'Sweet Mother in Heaven,' was the burden of her prayer, 'turn not thy face away from me, but regard only the motive and not the act.'

Whilst she knelt there, softly the door of Rhynsault's closet opened. From the threshold, unobserved and unheard, he stood regarding her for some moments. Then he advanced towards her, his feet rustling through the rushes with which the stone floor was spread.

The sound disturbed her. She cut short her intercessions, crossed herself, and rose to face him, oddly calm.

He halted before her, a smile in his baleful eyes. 'Well, mistress? Are you still of the same mind?'

Regarding him steadily, inscrutable of face and voice, she asked him:

'You offered me my husband's life, did you not?'

His eyes narrowed mistrustfully. 'I did,' he said slowly, 'and I do again. For the last time. I will sign the order for his gaol-delivery, so that you speak the necessary word.'

Hotly and fiercely came her answer: 'Sign it, then. Sign it now. And I will speak that word.'

For a moment his incredulous glance devoured her. Then abruptly, with an inarticulate sound arising deep from his throat, he took her in his arms. With rough, almost brutal hands, he tore the tall-crowned hennin from her golden head, the lace from the neck of her white undervest, then stooped to kiss her eyes, her lips, her throat, like a vampire slaking its dreadful thirst.

CHAPTER XXII

THE CHEAT

In the wintry light of early morning a woman issued from the apartments of the Governor of Middelburg, and stumbled, groping and uncertain, down the grey hall of the Gravenhof, where the shadows still lay deep and objects were as yet but ill defined. Her hair was dishevelled, a rich cloak of blue velvet edged with lynx fur, flung carelessly about her white-clad, lissom body, trailed after her, sweeping the stale rushes on the floor. The hand that held it about her clutched a paper.

By the table she halted, and stooped over something lying there at her feet. It was the hennin, swathed in its veil, which last night had been brutally torn from her head. As if it reminded her of a yesterday which, gone for ever, had in its going altered all her life and all her world, a sob broke from her. Then she commanded herself. To sustain her in her affliction of shame, to temper the self-loathing in which she now held herself, she clung to the thought that what she had endured was a sacrifice made in the interest of another. This brought her, perhaps, some feeble ray of that ecstatic inspiration which is known to martyrs.

She picked up the tall headdress and set it on the table, whilst swiftly and mechanically, depending upon her sense of touch alone, she restored some order to her hair. Then she put on the hennin, adjusted the cloak more carefully about her shoulders, and resumed her way down the hall to the double doors that opened upon the stairhead.

Beyond these she found two halberdiers on guard, who, upon beholding her issuing thence, stared as if she were a ghost.

She asked for the captain of the guard, in a voice whose normal tones amazed her.

The men's glances questioned each other; then one of them, leaning his pike against the wall, departed to summon the captain. He returned almost at once accompanied by Diesenhofen.

The red-headed Lorrainer grinned at her with horrible understanding.

'You are early astir, madam,' said he, and she knew that he mocked her, as hereafter all the world might mock her.

With fingers that shook a little she unfolded her paper, and proffered it.

'This is an order for my husband's immediate gaol-delivery.'

'His gaol-delivery?' Diesenhofen's grin was effaced: his eyes grew round. Then he studied the paper. 'It is correct enough,' said he, and handed it back to her.

Mechanically she took it, and thrust it for safety into her bosom.

'You will conduct me to him at once,' she said.

'It will be more convenient, mistress, that I bring him here to you.'

'But at once,' she insisted.

'Oh, at once,' he assured her. 'Meanwhile you had best wait within. I will find you a chair . . .'

'I will find one for myself. Go, go. Do not keep me waiting longer than you must.'

He went, and she reëntered the hall, paced back to the table, and sat down heavily. There, her thoughts a swirling maelstrom around which swept her husband, Count Anthony, and von Rhynsault, each holding her attention in turn, she waited for a full half-hour, thankful at least to be left to wait alone.

At last she heard the doors open behind her, and, springing up between dread and eagerness, expecting to behold her husband, was confronted instead with the pale, scared faces of her servants Jan and Peter. Jan uttered an inarticulate cry and hastened forward. His lean old face as grey almost as the hair that hung about it, with deep shadows about eyes that were bleared by sleeplessness, he stood before her fiercely anxious.

'Mistress, mistress! What has happened? We have waited all night.'

'Happened?' she echoed. She uttered a short, joyless, dreadful laugh. 'A soul has been down to hell, to purchase a man's life. That is what has happened. Your master is free. When the captain brings him, we will go home.' And she repeated the word curiously: 'Home!'

'Captain Diesenhofen is coming up now. He sent us on ahead of him.' Thus Jan, talking as men will when they feel it desperately incumbent to talk. But his eyes were upon her, and it was to be read in them that his thoughts knew little of his tongue. Suddenly he covered his face with his hands, and broke into sobs.

'Jan!' she commanded him. 'Jan! Will you drive me to kill myself?'

'Mistress!' He fell on his knees before her, caught her hand, and bore it to his lips. 'Mistress!' he cried again. It was all that he could say, but his broken-hearted tone said all the rest.

Heavy steps sounded beyond the doors, which the servants had left open. Diesenhofen entered, followed by two men who bore a stretcher, on which lay supine under a cloak the figure of a man. Within six paces of the door they set it down at the officer's command. Johanna stared, not understanding.

'But . . . my husband? Where is my husband?'

Diesenhofen waved away the bearers before answering her. 'He is here, mistress.'

'Here?' Wild-eyed she looked at the stretcher. 'Merciful God! Have you been torturing him again?' This she conceived to be the explanation. The light, after all, was dim in that place. They had so broken him that he could not walk. 'Philip!' she called, and swept quickly towards him. 'Philip!'

As she reached the stretcher, a wild fear gripped her

heart. A moment she hesitated, then snatched away the
covering cloak. One glance, and soundlessly, her nether lip
in her teeth, she recoiled, staring a fearful question at the
stolid captain. He answered it.

'He was hanged at daybreak, mistress, in execution of the
sentence passed upon him yesterday in the Governor's
court.'

She swayed there a moment, then staggered forward, and
went down on her knees beside the body of her husband.
And her first thought in that dreadful moment was that at
least he would never know, and so never come to spurn her
as unclean and defiled by the sacrifice made to save his life.
Other thoughts followed, terrible, searing thoughts, in which
grief and shame and rage were indissolubly commingled.

Thus Rhynsault found her when presently he emerged
from his closet, and checked, frowning, to discover this
scene in a place which he had imagined empty by now. He
would have withdrawn again, assailed by a certain sheepishness, but that he found her servants' eyes upon him.
With his thumbs in the belt of his long scarlet gown, he advanced softly, and softly addressed himself to Jan.

'Best take her home,' he said.

But though he spoke softly, the sibilant voice pierced her
absorption, and brought her to her feet, almost at a bound.
She wheeled to face him, erect, stiff, oddly majestic. The
only colour in her white face was supplied by the trickle of
blood from the lip through which she had bitten. Her eyes
blazed.

'You have cheated me!' she said deliberately.

He almost cowered before her anger, conscious of its
righteousness and of the vileness which, in his view, sheer
necessity had put it upon him to perform.

'Best go home, mistress,' was all that he could mutter
sullenly.

'You promised me his life, so that I bought it at your
price. I have paid your infamous price, God knows! And
you cheat me with this. Wantonly have you cheated me.'

'Nay, nay. Not wantonly.' That at least he could truthfully urge. 'What I promised I intended to fulfil. I did, as God's my witness.'

'God is your witness,' she assured him, her tone minatory. 'God is, indeed, your witness. Beware of that, at least. Witness of the deed of shame between us. Witness of a vile bargain, vilely broken by a lying, treacherous devil!'

That shook him out of his sheepishness, awoke the bully in him, brought the blood to his face and anger to his brow.

'By the Blood!' he swore. 'You'd better have a care, madam!'

'A care of what?' Defiantly she threw back her head. Defiantly she gave him back look for look. 'Do you dream that after what I have endured there is anything on earth can daunt or frighten me? You have killed my soul, Rhynsault, to every human feeling but one.'

'Words!' he growled. 'You are distraught! Let me remember it, and use patience with you.'

'The world shall know how you have cheated me.'

At that he shrugged and sneered. 'You mean that you'll proclaim your harlotry? Pray do so, if you think it will profit you. But meanwhile, get you gone from here while my patience lasts. Away! Away!'

'Ay, we'll go,' she said wearily, and commanded her servants to take up the bier.

They passed out ahead of her with their burden. In the doorway, as she was following them, she paused again, and turned. Out of a white face that was expressionless her flaming eyes considered him.

'Remember, Rhynsault, your own words — that God is your witness. He comes with leaden feet, but strikes with iron hands. Remember that, too, as I remember it to strengthen me. You walk proudly in your brutal arrogance. But lord of life and death though you may be in Walcheren to-day, you shall yet be brought so low that you shall come to envy this poor clay that was Philip Danvelt, come to wish that it was yourself had been hanged in his stead this morning.'

'You ranting beldame!' he roared in fury, 'Diesenhofen! To the door with them!'

She went out, Diesenhofen following.

Rhynsault, still trembling with anger, an anger aroused not only by her words, but by a deep, inescapable sense of discomfiture, stood there awhile in thought, then ill-humouredly resumed his way to breakfast.

He was a cheat, as she had so insistently dubbed him; and it was a vile thing that he had done in having broken his part of the bargain made. There was no escaping that accusation of his conscience. It was an accommodating conscience as a rule, not easily disturbed by any of its master's actions. He might have debauched the wife of every burgher in Middelburg without ever a remonstrance from that conscience of his. But this thing that he had done entailed sin against the code by which he lived. He was a knight, and a knight's plighted word or uttered promise was a sacred bond that could not be dishonoured without loss of self-esteem.

He cursed the necessity under which he had been on this occasion to depart from his pledged word. But the necessity was present and very real. Kuoni had pointed it out to him. He could not, without danger to himself, and without the risk of being called unanswerably to account for it, reprieve a man who had been sentenced to death upon his own confession of having conspired against the government of the Duke.

It was only now, as he sat brooding without appetite at table, that he perceived that there were other ways in which the difficulty might have been overcome. A new trial might have been ordered, the witnesses examined, the handwritings compared, and thus a plausible reason reached for reversing the earlier judgment. The Fool had led him astray in this; had driven him to act with a rashness culpably stupid, which laid him open to be truthfully dubbed a cheat. And all for what? For the possession of a stone. He shivered with rage, disgusted and disgruntled. If he had cheated, why so had she. She had seemed so maddeningly delectable and desirable, and in possession had proved a statue, cold and inanimate as marble.

From beyond the doors came the thrumming of a lute and the voice of Kuoni singing:

> 'Out of Love is Loathing born,
>   Out of Laughter weeping.
> Time will wither Beauty's form,
> Pluck the blossom from the thorn,
>   And Death will come a-reaping.
>   Ha, ha, ha, ha! A-reaping!'

The door opened, and the Fool appeared upon the threshold, his lute slung before him. With mockery on his lips and in his little round eyes, he surveyed his master. It was as if he knew what was passing in that troubled mind, and took satisfaction in it.

'Good morrow, gossip!' was his greeting in a voice of sly malice.

For answer, Rhynsault picked up a flagon from the table, and hurled it at him. It caught the Fool squarely on the brow, and stretched him senseless on the floor, whilst about his head a puddle formed of blood and wine.

CHAPTER XXIII

CAMP AND COURT

IT was on the night of Friday, the 28th October, that Johanna Danvelt paid her fateful visit to Claude de Rhynsault at the Gravenhof.

On that same night the army of the Duke of Burgundy, on the heights of the amphitheatre of hills about the city of Liège, lay under arms prepared for the final assault, which was to be delivered at dawn upon the stricken, exhausted, and despairing city. With this formidable and pitiless Burgundian host was Count Anthony, who had brought to it — and this to his present deep shame and mortification — his levy of eight thousand men of Guelders.

He occupied a room in the house in which the Duke himself had found quarters. He had gone early to bed in view of the work to be done to-morrow, work in which he must perform his part, however deeply and rightly he may have loathed it. From his slumbers he was awakened abruptly in the neighbourhood of midnight, and sat up on his soldier's couch with Johanna's voice ringing in his ears. The voice had reached him when in that condition between sleeping and waking which is the dream-stage of the senses, but so clearly and distinctly that, as it brought him fully awake into that sitting posture, he believed her to be present in his room. Indeed, the sense of her presence was so strongly impressed upon him now, as he sat there startled and listening, that at length he called out:

'Who's there?'

He was answered out of the darkness by the voice of an equerry named de Steeg, who occupied a couch in his room.

'My lord?'

Count Anthony collected his wits and rose. He was half-dressed in preparation for the morrow, since they were to march at daybreak. He ordered his equerry to kindle a light, and not until this was done and the emptiness of the room revealed was the illusion of Johanna's physical presence finally dispelled. Then, desiring de Steeg to lie down again, Count Anthony remained awhile sitting on the edge of his bed, evoking again and pondering the accents of the discarnate voice that had aroused him.

It had called his name thrice, and it had been so laden with appeal, and with despair, that the memory of it now drove into his soul the conviction that she was in distress or danger, and for a moment in that conviction he was frenzied by the thought of the distance separating them. Then the impression faded. The calm sway of fully awakened intelligence supervened. He had dreamt; that was all. Often voices are heard so in dreams. What harm should come to her? She was secure and sheltered, the honoured wife of a prosperous burgher.

Thus he reasoned away his uneasiness. But the sense of it lingered even when reason had dismissed it, a sense of distress, oppression, and wretchedness, which, however, he assigned to other causes.

He was so wide awake that to woo sleep again was out of all question. He rose, and, bidding de Steeg to take no thought for him, drew on his boots and his pourpoint and took up his hat and a heavy cloak. Wrapped tight in this, for the night was bitterly cold, he went forth into the village street, where the mud churned up by men and horses during the day was now freezing into solid ridges underfoot.

Long he paced there under the stars, reviewing and reviling the course of events since that evening when he had left Flushing under Captain von Diesenhofen's escort.

From Péronne he had accompanied the Duke to Liège with this great army at their heels, brought thither for the purpose of inflicting a terrible and merciless vengeance upon that little independent state which had dared withstand Burgundian encroachments upon its liberties. The Duke had sworn that he would deal with Liège as he had dealt with Dinant, which was much as the Romans had dealt with Carthage.

This ruthless abuse of strength had outraged Count Anthony's sense of chivalry. It was not for this that he had brought his men of Guelders into the ducal army. He had joined hands with Charles to withstand a menace of war from the King of France, not to aid in the butchery of a population of artisans who had improvised themselves into soldiers because their homes were threatened. And butchery, a massacre, was Burgundy's present object, deliberate and avowed. Liège was to serve as an example.

The Papal Legate had come in tears to intercede with Charles to spare the lives at least of those unfortunate people. Even their own Prince-Bishop, the profligate Louis of Bourbon, on whose worthless behalf this war had first been waged, had implored for his subjects the lenience of the Duke. But Charles had met their prayers with scorn. Liège, he declared, should be demolished and its people stamped out of existence like vermin, under the heels of his troops.

Amongst those present when the Duke thus opened his mind to the Papal Legate was one who more than any other man in Christendom should have raised his voice to plead the cause of the people of Liège, the man chiefly responsible for the rash act that was bringing this doom upon them. That man was the King of France. In vain Count Anthony looked to him for a protest or a prayer. He sat there wrapped in his fur pelisse, his thin legs crossed, listening to intercessions and to their rejection with the same propitiatory smile about his tight-lipped mouth. He wore his infamy without shame in those days, as lightly and carelessly as he wore the badge of Burgundy among the leaden saints in his hat. Having chosen this road out of the perils that had encompassed him at Péronne, he had resolved, it would seem, upon treading it with tripping feet and a debonair manner.

At the height of the discussion, the Duke, with a certain contemptuous defiance in his manner, had turned to the King to ask him what course he considered should be taken with this city of Liège. King Louis had uncrossed his legs, and leaned forward to deliver himself.

He chose to express himself in a parable, delivered with that same ingratiating smile.

'Once upon a time,' said he, 'my father had a high tree near his house; the crows that built their nests in its branches disturbed his slumbers. He caused the nests to be removed; but the crows built again, and yet again after the nests had been removed a second time. At last, he had the tree cut down at the roots; and after that he slept in peace.'

'You hear, gentlemen,' the Duke had said, sweeping his eyes over the assembly, a sneering smile alike for that royal answer and for the profound silence in which it was received, even by those who had been loudest in advocating extermination.

And then cutting sharply into that silence came Count Anthony's voice.

'We hear. But some of us do not believe our ears, or at least, do not believe that a king has spoken. For since there is neither statecraft nor chivalry in the counsel, it is unworthy of a prince.'

If prudently he left the indictment there, when he might have added so much more, it was that he desired to bring no avoidable bitterness to the discussion.

There was a general gasp, a rustling movement among the members of that assembly, who may have numbered a round dozen, and then an ominous stillness, all eyes upon the affronted King.

But he who has drunk vinegar need not make a wry face over green wine. The smile never left King Louis's lips, though it may have acquired a slightly sub-acid twist. With characteristic slyness he turned to the Duke.

'Fair cousin (beau cousin),' said he, 'this touches you as closely as it touches me.'

The Duke's colour rose a little and he scowled. Nevertheless, he brushed the matter aside as an irrelevancy. 'From what touches me I know how to guard myself,' he

answered proudly, and the glance he directed upon Count
Anthony was baleful. 'As for the statecraft of the course,
that is debatable ground. Chivalry is not in question in
dealing with such a rabble.'

'Let us then debate the statecraft,' was Count Anthony's
reply. Thereupon he marshalled his arguments calmly, and
even boldly, considering the general hostility in which he
knew that he was heard, a hostility rooted in sycophancy to
the Duke. From this he could not even exclude his own
brother, Adolph of Guelders, who was present; Adolph,
who meanwhile had married the Lady Catharine of Bourbon, and who, on the score both of the closer kinship thus
established with the Duke of Burgundy and of the office
of Marshal of Guelders which he held, had insisted upon
leading the Guelderland troops which Count Anthony had
laboured to levy.

Count Anthony's present argument was that a wise prince
would not stamp out a populous, industrious, and wealthy
city which with its dependencies might yet be brought
within the ambit of his dominions to enrich him. At another
time Liège might proudly and defiantly have clung to her
independence. But now her pride was broken, her defiance
stilled. She would submit if submission were proposed to
her, and submit with a gratitude which should assure her
future loyalty.

But the obstinate Charles of Burgundy, having already
determined upon his vindictive, remorseless course, was but
confirmed in it by this opposition.

'We desire no such pestilent subjects,' was his angry reply. And save for the Legate, who was dejected and silent
because he realized the futility of speech, and the Prince-
Bishop, who, after all, was concerned for his own property
and the source of his chief revenues, every voice approved
the Duke.

Thereupon Count Anthony significantly took his leave,
implying that he could have no further part in such a business.

But he resumed the discussion anon in private with his cousin and persisted in his advocacy of clemency until the Duke gave way to anger, and, thereby acting as steel upon flint, provoked anger in the Count. High words passed between them, and the Duke ordered the Count out of his presence. The Count, greatly daring, refused to go.

'Not thus, Charles,' he had answered, 'I will not go from you in anger. First I will remind you that I am here to serve you. You may have brought me back from my retirement by force. But I remained out of love for you, in your need of me, when you knew not upon whom you could depend in view of the French menace. You have no lack of friends now that you are on top and master of the situation. But then, when the self-seekers who fawn upon you to-day were waiting upon events, there was not one of them whom you could trust. Therefore, I stayed, that you might have one loyal heart beside you. Never yet have I failed you, Charles. At Montlhéry I saved your life; at Péronne I saved your honour. Suffer me to remind you of these proofs of my devotion, so that you may believe that only devotion inspires me now.'

The Duke was mollified. Like most men of ungovernable temper, he was as easily turned from wrath as to it.

'I do believe it,' he growled.

'Then believe me when I tell you that this thing you contemplate is an outrage upon chivalry which, if you persist in it, will tarnish your bright escutcheon for all time.'

'That is a point upon which we do not agree.'

'Very well. But let me remind you that the lances I brought from Guelders to reënforce your army were brought to defend you from the threatened onslaught of the King of France. They are not to be used in a massacre of helpless citizens.'

The Duke was scowling again. 'You mean that you will refuse to lead them into Liège?'

'Holding the views I hold, can I do less?'

'The question is, can you do so much?' The Duke laughed

unpleasantly, revealing his strong white teeth. 'You forge
your brother Adolph. He is Marshal of Guelders, and h
leads your men. And he'll lead them to hell at my biddin
and to win my favour, especially if he suspects it will anno
you.'

And Count Anthony, realizing the truth of this and th
defeat and humiliation that must await him in insistence
had gone forth dejected. He would have quitted the Duke'
camp but for the hope gleaming faintly amid despair tha
opportunity might yet be offered him of doing something i
the dear cause of chivalry.

All this he passed in bitter review as he paced there unde
the stars of that chill night, on the heights above the fertil
valley of the Meuse, so soon to be a scene of desolation. H
thought of the Duke, passionate and obstinate, of the King
treacherous and sly, and of all those opportunists who fol
lowed them, each intent in his acquisitiveness to turn to hi
own profit, in despite of honour, these failings of thos
princes.

More than ever was Count Anthony persuaded that th
world in which he had his being was no world for a gentle
man. Bitterly now did he repent him of his return to it
What havoc had he not thereby wrought in his own life an
in a life infinitely dearer to him than his own! What a foo
— ignoble, paltry, and contemptible — had he not been t
have weighed birth and blood — phantasmal attributes — an
princely duty even, against natural instinct! What, afte
all, was this princely duty? There was his brother Adolph
ready, indeed eager in his insatiable ambition, to grasp th
reins of government; daily betraying his resentment of hi
brother's seniority, missing no opportunity — as witnes
his marriage with the Lady Catharine — to strengthen hi
own position against possible eventualities. Brotherly lov
should have existed between Adolph and himself. But am
bition in Adolph made brotherly love impossible, as al
natural ties, it seemed, were impossible to princes. After all
was not Adolph better fitted than himself to be a ruler i

such a world as this? It had no surprises for Adolph; he perceived in its pompous surface mockeries and underground intrigues nothing that was not as it should be; it was a world which Adolph understood, of which he was a part, equipped with a stomach which could digest with ease the things that nauseated Anthony. Such a man would make the better prince, no doubt, because untrammelled by any of those ideals that made men regard Anthony as a romantic dreamer.

If he had bethought him of this, if only he had reasoned thus in time! Now it was too late. The chance of better things, the chance of a life of realities nearer to his ideals, had slipped past him whilst he was fettered by preconceptions. He might now rule his duchy when he came to the throne, since there was no longer any better thing to be done, and live out his years in empty pomp and lonely state in Nimeguen.

He was aroused from his thought by a steadily increasing rustle in the stillness of the night.

He had come some way beyond the end of the village street and past the last of its mean houses, and he stood now on a hillside road in open country. The sound came from below, and listening attentively he presently identified it. It was the laboured breathing of men, of a multitude by its volume, scaling otherwise stealthily the steep hillside.

It needed but a moment's reflection to realize its meaning. What other could it be than a surprise attack by night? And a surprise attack it was. For those whose stealthy advance Count Anthony overheard were the six hundred men of Franchimont on a forlorn hope to save Liège at the eleventh hour by the assassination of Charles of Burgundy and Louis of France. They were guided in their desperate attempt by the very men who owned the houses in which the princes lodged.

Count Anthony turned at once, the soldier's instinct driving him, and ran back to rouse the sleeping camp and call out the archers of the guard.

Of the skirmish in the glare of hastily kindled torches and
blazing tar-barrels amid the farmhouses and cottages, be
tween the desperate men of Franchimont on the one side and
the Burgundian soldiery and Scottish archers of the King of
France on the other, you may read elsewhere in detail. For
the men of Franchimont, hemmed about and overwhelmed
by numbers, it only remained to sell their forfeited lives as
dearly as possible.

Detected in time, their attempt to avert the doom of
Liège failed. It proved the last spark of resistance from that
expiring city. In the morning when the army marched to
the onslaught, the King of France riding in the press, and
shouting 'Bourgogne!' with the loudest, it met with no
opposition from a city whose walls had formerly been razed
to the ground and whose spirit was finally crushed.

As to what followed, there is no more terrible page in the
terrible history of sacked cities, abandoned deliberately to
the lawless greed and lust of a brutal soldiery.

To each division of the army a district of the city was as
signed, and within that district all was to be theirs without
restriction. Rapacity, cruelty, and lust were thus let loose
upon Liège by ducal licence. Nothing was spared. The very
churches were sacked, and those who had sought sanctuary
in them butchered without regard to age or condition. The
very convents were forced, the very nuns taken in prey by the
Burgundian soldiery.

The order of the day was to despoil and to exterminate, to
strip naked of wealth and of life this proud city of which the
Duke did not intend that one stone should remain upon
another.

And whilst spoliation, rape, and carnage engaged the
soldiery, the King of France sat dining at his ease in the
Bishop's palace and complimenting his fair cousin upon
this victory which rendered him the most fortunate prince
alive.

Some of the inhabitants of Liège had fled upon the approach of the ducal army; others belatedly had recourse to

flight when they perceived the incredible ruthlessness of the conquerors. They were perhaps less fortunate than those who fell under the Burgundian steel, who were hanged or drowned by the exterminators. They survived that dreadful day only to wander homeless, fugitive, and hunted — for armed bands were sent out to hunt them — through the hills, through the rigours of a weather as inclement as the Duke of Burgundy. Many perished of starvation, as many later of exposure to the cold during a winter so bitter that the wine for the soldiery scouring the countryside for fugitives was served out in solidly frozen pieces cut with hatchets from the casks.

For a week the sack of Liège endured. Then, the part of the soldiers being fully accomplished, they were replaced by an army of labourers from Luxembourg, who, under the direction of Burgundian officers, were to destroy the city by fire and then level the ruins with the ground.

For seven weeks after the Duke's departure, Liège continued to burn, until only the churches and the houses of churchmen remained standing in the charred desert that once had been so fair and populous and prosperous a city. And whilst their homes were burning, those who had fled from them were being hunted down. Upon them and others in the Ardennes the work of carnage and destruction went on. There was that district of Franchimont which had yielded those temerarious six hundred, and there were other districts which had proved troublesome in the past, to be schooled in what was due to the Duke of Burgundy. Thus, leaving a blackened train of ruins in his wake, and accounting the work either accomplished or to be accomplished in his absence, the Duke went home at last to Brussels to spend Christmas with his duchess, and to deal with the heavy arrears of business connected with his Flemish states which had accumulated during his campaigning absence.

He returned with his credit in the eyes of the world enormously enhanced, his position as one of the first, wealthiest, and most powerful princes in Europe fully consolidated.

He had brought the King of France to his knees, used him like a vassal, and heaped upon him an amount of ignominy that was limited only by his imperious will. Upon a small but powerful principality that had dared to presume with him he had wreaked a terrible vengeance, to advertise his might and serve as a warning, not only to the various states making up his great dominions, but to others beyond their confines. He was, although he knew it not — and considered his present position but a stepping-stone to greater heights and greater achievements, among which were to be included a kingly crown — at the very zenith of his career, dazzling the world by his noontide lustre, courted, honoured, and feared by the nations of the earth, receiving at home in the magnificent splendour with which he surrounded himself the intoxicating incense of adulation.

But one there was who had refused to join in that chorus of praise and reverence, one who remained absent from the court, and whose absence left a conspicuous gap which vexed and fretted him, seeming to mark a lack of completeness in his triumph. Companion of his boyhood, sharer of his adolescent adventures and enterprises, often his guide and counsellor in them, and beside him in every crisis since his accession, the deliberate absence of Count Anthony of Guelders in such an hour as this filled him with chagrin. This presently grew into resentment of the disapprobation which he knew it to signify, and there was at least as much haughty annoyance at Count Anthony's absence as desire for his presence in the message which he despatched to him at Nimeguen in the early days of January of that year 1469.

It took the form of a summons to attend a meeting of the Chapter of the Golden Fleece. It was, as Charles well knew, a summons which Count Anthony could not in honour disregard. In reality he desired that his cousin should be present for another function, one which should show that absurdly romantic idealist that the deeds which had provoked his censure were the objects of very different sentiments among the great princes of Europe.

Reluctantly Count Anthony came, as he was in duty bound by his knightly obligations. The alternative, to resign his membership of the Order of the Golden Fleece, were too gross an affront to offer, being in a prince tantamount to a declaration of war.

The Duke's affection for him, underlying all resentments, dissipated the anger from the ducal mind when the Count presented himself. And the cordial, loving welcome he received made Count Anthony almost ashamed of his sulking at Nimeguen.

He made philosophy to meet the case and to justify himself for accepting the situation as he found it, and condoning of what was done. The Duke, after all, acted according to his lights, and how is any man to be blamed for that? He acted not only according to his own lights, but according to those of other reigning princes of his time, and was not conscious that he did any wrong or in any way exceeded the rights or violated the obligations imposed upon him by his princely rank. The argument may have been unsound, but so is argument always when either hate or affection tempers judgment.

To confirm him, Count Anthony was present, a prominent member of that brilliant gathering assembled in the great hall of the palace at Brussels on Sunday, the 15th January, when the representatives of the city of Ghent came to make submission and sue for pardon for past events in the city on the occasion of the Duke's accession. With the example of Liège before their eyes, they realized the stern necessity for the measure.

The hall was hung with tapestries figuring the achievements of Alexander and Hannibal, selected as suggestively appropriate to the occasion. On a dais that was carpeted with cloth of gold sat the Duke, magnificently robed. He was supported by the Prince-Bishop of Liège, the Prince of Savoy, the Duke of Somerset, the Knights of the Golden Fleece and the ambassadors of France, England, Russia, Prussia, Austria, Bohemia, Naples, Milan, Venice, and other of the world's great states. Outside in the snow which lay thick in the courtyard humbly waited a crowd of men of Ghent, all of them men of consequence and wealth — the best that Ghent could send to represent her — the members of the municipality and the deans of the fifty-two guilds. For half an hour and more they stood there in the cold like mendicants, and when at last admitted came humbly as mendicants to sue pardon, profess submission utter and absolute to the Duke's will, and to implore him to take the city of Ghent under his exalted protection. To this Charles consented only after administering a harsh and stern rebuke upon past conduct, and publicly and formally destroying the royal charter, known as the Great Privilege of Ghent, whereby a King of France a hundred and fifty years ago had conferred upon the Ghenters the right of electing their own magistrates.

CHAPTER XXIV

GRAND MASTER OF BURGUNDY

AFTER the Chapter of the Golden Fleece had met, and Count Anthony had heard in that assembly, by now famous for the frankness of its criticisms even of the conduct of princes, only encomiums upon the Duke's prowess, statecraft, and foresight, he begged leave of Charles to return to Nimeguen.

'Here's a very sudden fondness for the place,' Charles had sneered in quick resentment of this haste of Anthony's to withdraw again.

The Duke sat over the fire in his closet, spreading his hands to the blaze, for it was a raw January morning, and all the town lay under a crust of frozen snow, glittering in a pale sunshine that was barren of heat. Anthony, beyond the hearth, was leaning on the overmantel. He fetched a sigh.

'The longer I live,' said he, 'the more persuaded I become that I am not fitted for the world. My views do not seem in tune with the views of my fellow-creatures. It is a depressing persuasion, which at Nimeguen I can escape by shutting myself up in the fair library my grandfather assembled. There I can commune with minds which I can understand.'

'You should marry and get children.'

'I don't think that I ever shall.'

The Duke grunted. 'In that case, and being otherwise as unhealthy-minded as you say, why not seek the retirement of a monastery?' His highness was sarcastic.

'I've thought of it,' said Count Anthony simply, whereupon the Duke lost patience with him, and read him a considerable homily. He spent too much time in dreaming and too little in doing; he was eccentric and fantastic in his notions; he practised an unnatural austerity; he was too much of a critic of other men's performances, whilst himself performing nothing. That was his trouble. What he needed was occupation. It was a need the Duke could supply. He pointed to a writing-table piled with documents, letters, petitions, charters, all manner of legal parchments awaiting consideration which his secretaries had sorted out and placed there for his study and pronouncement. And these were only some of the arrears which his absence from court had accumulated. Let Anthony lend him his assistance, as he had done of old. He would find time hang less heavily on his hands, and he would be afforded more profitable occupation than brooding over the imperfections of a world which he had had no hand in creating, or stringing rhymes out of strands of moonshine.

And there were other matters besides claiming attention. There had been trouble in Zealand during his absence. Fortunately he was well represented there by the Lorrainer Claude de Rhynsault, the most capable and resolute of all his lieutenants. The vigilance of this ducal lieutenant had detected the first signs of the revolt, and he had rounded up the leaders and dealt with them out of hand, thus crushing the beast of sedition before it had even ventured to rear its head. That sedition was something for which indirectly he had to thank the King of France. The rising at Liège had confirmed a suspicion in Zealand that the Duke of Burgundy was about to meet defeat if not annihilation on the French frontier. The Duke laughed. Well, well! He had shown them the kind of man he was, and the example he had made of Liège should put sedition to sleep for years in Zealand and elsewhere. Meanwhile Rhynsault had done well. By his prompt and effective action he had saved the necessity for sterner measures which by their dislocation of trade must have had a disconcertingly inconvenient effect upon the revenues derived from Zealand. Rhynsault deserved well of him, and should be rewarded. It should not be said of the Duke of Burgundy that he could be prodigal only in punishing. He would promote Rhynsault to the vacant governorship of Ghent. He required a strong man there, and Rhynsault was of all his ducal lieutenants the strongest, the very man for the office. Also there was a vacancy in the Chapter of the Golden Fleece, and it might be well to bestow it upon Rhynsault.

'That,' demurred Count Anthony, 'is a very high honour even for so great a service.'

'I am aware of it,' the Duke answered. 'Hence a certain hesitation. But it would not only be a fitting reward to one who has served me with exceptional ability always, but an encouragement to other ducal lieutenants to watch over my interests with the same zeal.'

It was one of the matters for consideration and discussion upon which he would welcome the Count's opinions. Then there were his audiences of justice, so long suspended of necessity that the list of petitioners who desired to sue directly to him had grown to enormous length.

These audiences of justice were banquets to his vanity. Three days a week it had been his custom to sit in open court all the morning to hear all claims and grievances in person, and to deliver judgment like another Solomon. Few duties of his princely office were dearer to him than this which he had imposed upon himself. He derived from it an incense such as no courtly adulation could supply; for this wielding power at first hand over the lives and destinies of men gave him a sense of being elevated almost to the rank of a divinity. Therefore, although it imported that he should resume that progress through the Northern provinces which necessities imposed upon him by the King of France had interrupted, yet he would postpone for two or three weeks that resumption in order to enable him to deal in person with some of the older petitions awaiting his attention.

The sum total of all this was that, whilst on the one hand it was of the first importance that he should visit those Northern provinces in which the accession oaths had not yet been exchanged between himself and the representatives of the people, on the other it was of almost equal importance that he should remain at home to deal with the arrears of affairs which his campaigning absence had accumulated.

And since it is not given to any man, not even to so exalted
and quasi-divine a prince as the Duke of Burgundy and Brabant, to be in two places at one and the same time, it became
clear that he must find a deputy to act for him at home,
whilst abroad he went to give and receive those oaths which
could not be pledged by proxy. In this deputy certain rare
qualities were essential. He must be of a rank as nearly
equal as possible to the Duke's own, to ensure him the reverence which an office rarely commands unless the holder himself commands it; he must be of exceptional ability in affairs,
so that the Duke's interests should be properly safeguarded;
and — most rare of all qualifications — he must be of
proven fidelity to the Duke and entirely trustworthy, above
all venal temptations.

'That,' the Duke concluded, 'is the man I need to be my
Grand Master of Burgundy and my Vicegerent here during
my absence in the North. You will agree that he is not
readily found. Indeed, having carefully considered, I know
of but one man who could fill that office for me in such a
manner that I should be able to sleep in peace whilst on my
travels. That man, Anthony, is yourself.'

The Count was almost startled. 'But the responsibilities
of such a charge are . . .'

Peremptorily the Duke cut him short. 'Are such as you
could bear with ease and dignity.' He rose. 'It is an honour
which you cannot refuse without affronting me. Just as you
are the man I need for the office, so is the office the thing
you need to give you back your manhood which you are in
danger of losing in a mist of dreams.' He set his strong, firm
hand upon the Count's shoulder, and looked up into that
solemn, comely face, with an expression in his dark eyes
which was at once imperious and entreating.

If the responsibilities and dangers of such an office daunted
the Count, and were more than he cared to shoulder in the
listlessness which had latterly descended upon him, on the
other hand, he was not merely honoured by this proof of
trust in his ability and integrity, but also deeply touched by

an affection in the Duke which could so fully survive their
late disagreements. He perceived that refusal was impossible; that, as the Duke said, it could not be made without
affront.

He bowed his head, and smiled a little. 'Since you desire
it, Charles, and if you are sure that none could serve you
better . . .'

'Are not you?' the Duke asked him sharply.

The smile on the Count's features broadened. 'I think I
am,' said he.

And so that very day the parchments were drawn up,
signed, and sealed appointing Count Anthony of Egmont,
Prince of Guelders, Lord of Valburg, and Knight of the
Most Noble and Exalted Order of the Golden Fleece, to be
Grand Master of Burgundy, Ducal Lieutenant in Chief and
Ducal Vicegerent throughout the Dominions of the Duke of
Burgundy and Brabant, whereof public proclamation was
duly made.

If a certain reluctance had signalized Count Anthony's
acceptance of the office, none was perceptible in the manner
in which he threw himself into its duties once he had accepted it. It was a full month before the Duke quitted
Brussels for that necessary Northern visit. But not until
then did Count Anthony wait to take up the onerous burden
he had agreed to bear. At first in concert with the Duke, but
gradually more and more independently in the Duke's name,
he set about dealing with those weighty affairs which already
had been awaiting attention overlong. There were affairs of
England, affairs of the Empire, affairs of France, of Venice,
Milan, and a dozen lesser states. And he went about them
in a manner of so much graciousness, shrewdness, and tact
that everywhere he smoothed away difficulties and strengthened ties. Details of his administration are to be found in
La Marche by the curious in these matters, and it is possible
to agree with La Marche that had Count Anthony of Guelders remained in his office and retained his influence over the
Duke, the latter would have fulfilled his highest aspirations

and raised Burgundy to the first power in Europe instead of plunging by his uncontrolled rashness to disaster.

That, however, is another story.

Amongst the domestic affairs transacted in those days, and in which Count Anthony bore a part, the only one that concerns us is that of the promotion of the Sire Claude de Rhynsault. It was decided to give him the important governorship of Ghent, and if it was not yet decided to hang about his neck the collar of the Golden Fleece, neither was it decided not to do so. Decision was postponed because this was a matter in which the Duke and his newly appointed Grand Master could not see eye to eye. Count Anthony took the view that Rhynsault's birth and antecedents were not of such a quality as to entitle him to a place in the Chapter of that exalted order until he added to them as a qualification some achievement of more than ordinary worth which in itself should lend his name the lustre which origin failed to supply. The Duke, on the other hand, chose to account the man's long and tried fidelity and the skill with which he had handled the affairs of Zealand and stifled there all danger of a revolt, at a time when a revolt might have had the most serious inflammatory qualities upon other neighbouring states, as sufficient grounds for bestowing upon him the highest honour in his gift.

To this disagreement between the cousins was due the postponement in submitting Rhynsault's name to the Chapter for election to the vacant place. Meanwhile, however, the Governor of Zealand was summoned to Brussels by a very friendly letter from the Duke, which intimated to him that the object of this summons was to promote him as a mark of the Duke's appreciation of his services and worth.

CHAPTER XXV

THE PETITIONER

AT the audiences of justice held by the Duke in the great hall of the palace of Brussels during those four weeks that he spent there, a lady attracted the general notice by the beauty of a countenance on which dignity, candour, purity, and sorrow were blended into an arresting whole. It was not a countenance which man or woman would pass without a second glance. She was a little above middle height, of slender, graceful shape, and bore herself with that gentle dignity which commands the respect of all whilst offending none. She was richly dressed in black from the veil on her steeple headdress to the toes of her peaked shoes, and she was invariably attended by two grooms and a waiting-woman, which proclaimed her a person of consequence.

Her daily presence provoked inquiries touching her identity, and these elicited that she was from Zealand, the daughter of a wealthy merchant of Flushing and the widow of another wealthy merchant of Middelburg, one Philip Danvelt, who had suffered there some three months ago for sedition. This, if it lessened the desire to make her acquaintance, quickened the curiosity as to the purpose of her presence in such a place. What justice could be sought or hoped for from the Duke, by the widow of a convicted and executed traitor?

It was observed, or else rumoured, that she courted the ushers in vain to obtain her a hearing from the Duke. Having failed with these, and, as time was slipping away and the last audience before the Duke's departure fast approaching, she transferred her attentions to the captain of the archers of the guard, who was invariably in attendance upon the Duke on these occasions.

Because the captain of the archers, the Sire de Chavaigny,

was young and because she was very beautiful, she found at
his hands a consideration deeper than that which she had
received from the ushers. He at least manifested concern
and an ardent desire to serve her. But at the same time he
was reluctantly compelled to confess his powerlessness. The
lists were so full that there was little hope that the Duke
would be able to hear half the plaints that sought his personal ear. The Sire de Chavaigny would add the lady's
name to these lists, but that was not to promise her an
audience. Each petitioner must take his turn, and it was far
beyond all possibility that her turn would be reached during
the present session. Either she must postpone her plaint
until the Duke's return from the North, or else present her
case in the ordinary courts of justice.

'When will the Duke return?' she asked. Wrapt in that
unfaltering dignity, she betrayed no impatience, no fretful-
ness. There was something about her of the calm purpose-
fulness of Fate itself.

The Sire de Chavaigny hunched his shoulder. 'Who can
say, madam? Perhaps in a few months. He will not remain
absent longer than he must.'

'A few months!' A little wistful smile broke over the
placid pallor of her face to invest it with a sweetness which
the Sire de Chavaigny found devastating. 'Already I have
waited three months with terrible patience, Sir Captain,
waited for the Duke's return from the wars, counting upon
being heard by him the moment he returned.'

'Three months!' he echoed. 'And you present yourself
only now? That is the error you have made. You should
have come at once and set down your name, the moment
your grievance arose. Then you would have been heard at
the first opportunity.'

She perceived now her error. She should not have awaited
word of the Duke's return from his campaign before setting
out to seek him. She should have come to Brussels at once
and sought guidance of those who were acquainted with the
ways of courts, instead of sitting idly in Flushing, brooding

over her wrongs and sustaining her life and her broken spirit upon the thought of justice to be obtained upon the evildoer.

She had gone to Flushing, back to the house that had been her father's, the house where the stork still strutted in the courtyard and the quail fluttered in their cage upon the red wall above the tulip beds. She had gone thither because Middelburg had become unbearable. There were its associations of evil, there was the presence of Claude de Rhynsault, and, worse than either, there were the evil tongues of the women, which had been busy with her name, and had woven about it a tale of infamy. No sacrificial victim was she in this tale, but a willing adulteress so shameless and insensible that she had been in the arms of her lover at the very time that, by his orders, her husband was being hanged.

That story had its source in the guards whom Johanna had surprised by issuing from Rhynsault's quarters soon after daybreak on the morning of Philip's hanging. They retailed the thing in the wine-shops and taverns as a most excellent jest. It spread until in its course it reached the ears of the burgher ladies of Middelburg. Some of these, to their honour, rejected it as an infamous invention. But many there were who welcomed it and helped on its propagation. A woman may not possess the beauty and endowments of Johanna Danvelt without arousing the malice of the spiteful of her sex. Then, too, there had been an aloofness about Johanna, which may have sprung from the fundamental unhappiness of her life since she had come to Middelburg. This had been interpreted as empty pride by many of those who had vainly sought her intimacy. And some there were who not too unwillingly had been through the hands of that very carnal governor, to whom the thought was very welcome that the austere, aloof, and apparently pious Johanna Danvelt, who had ever been regarded as a model of circumspection, should, in fact, be no better than themselves.

Amongst them the ladies of these various classes built up the story of her adultery, until it was widely if not commonly accepted that she had long been in secret the Governor's paramour, and that, if he did not show mercy to her husband, it was precisely because the man's removal would render her easier of access. It did not matter that the subsequent events gave the lie to this detail. It did not matter that on three occasions, when Rhynsault presented himself at her door, he was denied admission, by uncompromising and even minatory messages unfalteringly delivered to him by the faithful Jan. Rhynsault on each occasion had ridden away laughing at the threats. But it was significant that he had ridden away, instead of forcing his way into the house and into Johanna's presence, as was to be expected in a man of his temperament and manner. Yet the current tale almost implied that on each occasion he had entered and been welcome.

Soon Johanna became aware of the havoc gossip was making of her character. The bold, unfeeling stare of the women when she went abroad to take the air or on her daily visit to church, their nudges and sneering whisperings, the absence, not merely of any of the expressions of sympathy which her widowhood should have inspired, but of greetings of any kind, soon began to make her aware of how she was regarded. And then one evening Jan came home with a swollen eye and a bleeding nose. He had fought a man who had called his mistress a vile name. In answer to her inquiries touching his condition, he told her the plain truth; told her of the infamous things that were being said of her in Middelburg; told her in a foaming passion, out of his love and reverence for her, to the end that she might take some action to still these lying tongues.

This full knowledge of calumnies already suspected did not touch her. To one who has been in hell, what can purgatory matter? The only thing that touched her was the evidence of Jan's devotion. She smiled calmly upon his fury.

'What action can I take, Jan? As well might I seek to stem a river with these two hands.'

But action of another kind at least she did take. She dis-

mantled the house in Middelburg, left the affairs of her late
husband's trading-house in the hands of a steward, a man
who had grown old in the service of Danvelt's father, and
withdrew to Flushing to the home of her maidenhood, to the
house in which Count Anthony had wooed her in days that
now seemed to belong to the experiences of a former lifetime.

There she waited, with a patience that would have been
impossible had it not been rooted in what was now the
single purpose of her existence, for word of the Duke's return from the wars. She had placed agents in Brussels, and
relays of horses were posted from there to Sluys, and maintained at her expense, so that instant word of the event
might be brought to her. Meanwhile, she maintained herself in readiness for departure, and daily went over the memorial she had so carefully prepared. Rhynsault considered
himself safely shielded from all consequences by the confession he had wrung from Danvelt under torture. Let her
but gain the ear of the Duke and it might be that Rhynsault
should come to realize his confidence misplaced. And to
gain the ear of the Duke she was prepared to spend every
ducat of her considerable fortune; for by her double inherit-
ance from her father and her husband she was to-day the
wealthiest woman in Zealand. Her father's death had not
closed his shipbuilding yards. Philip Danvelt was not the
man to permit his wife to cut off so rich a source of revenue.
He had placed those yards under the care of a man of his
own, and they continued to flourish. Now that Philip was
gone, it was to the widow that Plancenoir, the man appointed, came regularly to render an account of his steward-
ship. Calmly, quietly, as she did all things, she received
him, considered his accounts, listened to his suggestions,
and discussed with him whatever it was necessary to discuss.

But under that calm of hers she bore a sad and stricken
heart. The house itself with its associations contributed to
her sadness. Yet sooner than be deprived now of those associations she would have borne twice her burden of sorrow.
There were rooms and articles of furniture that were inti-

mately connected with her kindly, generous father. And there were all the things that brought back so vividly the memory of Count Anthony. Scarcely a room was without something to remind her of him. If she sat at table, she saw him sitting at the end of it, where he had sat on the night Friar Stephen had visited them. If she entered her bower abovestairs, she beheld him lounging on the window-seat, the lute in his lap, the sunshine behind him setting an aureole about his tawny head. If she walked in the garden above the dunes, he was there stepping beside her, telling her again of his journey to England, until she could hear the deep, level tones of his dear voice speaking in that fluent Flemish of his which gathered refinement and distinction from its French accent.

He haunted her in those winter days of waiting, and almost was she sadly content to abide there with her ghost.

And then at last, after close upon three months, at a time when the snow lay thick upon the land and the ice was everywhere, came one evening news that the Duke was returned to Brussels. She took ship at once with her servants despite the inclemency of the weather, and, landing at Sluys, travelled thence by swift stages to the ducal court. She used her wealth to procure her not only speed, but a certain state. Since her haste would not brook that she should wait to join some party of merchants or the like travelling to Brussels under escort so as to ensure them safety from any of the predatory bands that roamed the land, she had an escort of her own of twenty tall fellows well-horsed and equipped, men of trust, the half of whom were derived from her ship-yard at Flushing.

Thus she came on New Year's Day to Brussels, and was lodged with her escort at the Lion of Brabant, near Saint Gudule. But it was not until a fortnight later that the audiences of justice were renewed, and not until then that she made the discovery that long lists of those who desired to petition the Duke in person were already drawn up, and that she must await her turn. Not until another fortnight had slipped away did she make the further discovery that the Duke's sojourn in Brussels was soon to end, and that it was impossible that the existing lists should be exhausted before his departure. Then, at last, a feverish anxiety began to burn within her, however cold an exterior she might continue to present. It was then that she attempted to enlist the sympathy of ushers, to waste gold on bribes which were accepted greedily enough and knavishly enough by men who knew that it was beyond their power to earn them. Thus, at last, we find her making her appeal to the Sire de Chavaigny.

'Can you not help me, sir,' she begged him, 'to repair my fault in this matter?'

'Help you to an audience, do you mean?' the young captain asked her, much as he might have asked did she mean him to help her to heaven.

'That is what I mean,' she said.

The Sire de Chavaigny pondered her with his clear young eyes for a long, thoughtful moment, then he fetched a half-sigh.

'Madam, there is nothing I would not do to serve you,' he said gently, wistfully almost.

She looked up sharply, a little frown between her brows. Since the bitter lesson learned at the hands of Rhynsault, she — who formerly had used all men with a trusting frankness — had grown mistrustful of all, quick to look for insult.

'Why do you say that to me, sir?'

'*Pardi*, because it is true. If you ask me why it is true, faith, that is more than I can answer. I only know that to behold you and to be aware of your need is to desire to satisfy it.'

He spoke with a blunt candour, free from any hint of gallantry such as she had apprehended, and in his eyes and countenance there was only deference. It moved her oddly, thawed a little of the ice that in these past months had settled about her heart. Her eyes were moist as she thanked him and implored him to yield to his kindly concern and discover some way to assist her, whose need was very urgent.

'It is what I am considering, madam. There is one possible channel through which an audience might be procured for you.'

'Ah, yes?' She was suddenly all eagerness.

'But I warn you that it is not probable. In the dispensation of his justice the Duke desires, and logically, that the forms themselves shall be most just. He may consider that to give a preference to a late-comer is in itself an injustice to others. Still, we can but try. Have you a memorial of your plaint?'

He need scarcely have asked, for the sheaf of parchments, folded, tied with silk, and sealed, bulked in her left hand. She held it up.

'Will you intrust it to me, madam? There is one who might prevail upon the Duke to read it, that is my Lord Almoner, the Cardinal of Ghent, who is confessor to his highness.'

'If he will read it first, himself, he will find it his Christian duty so to prevail,' she answered, her hopes now high.

But the Sire de Chavaigny smiled a little crookedly. He knew his world better than did Mistress Johanna; knew that a prelate's notion of his Christian duty was not always what one would suppose from his profession.

'I will do my utmost to induce him,' he promised, but without confidence. 'It happens that he is my uncle, so that at least I have access to him. What I can do to serve you shall be done, madam. Depend upon me.'

She thanked him warmly, enjoined upon him great care of her memorial, and, leaving it in his hands, turned to depart, and found herself face to face with Kuoni von Stocken.

Three days ago he had arrived in Brussels in the train of the Sire Claude de Rhynsault, who had come in answer to that summons from the Duke. And Rhynsault having little need of him here at court, the Fool prowled whither he listed. Thus he had wandered into these halls of justice, thinking that here he might find entertainment and matter upon which to furbish up his wit, which had grown stale in the flat lands of Walcheren.

When first he had espied Mistress Danvelt among the waiting clients, he had known that the entertainment would be certain. He could have no doubt of the objects of her presence in this place. Her pleadings should be amusing, all things considered; most amusing if they should happen to prevail.

He had watched her as she approached the young captain of the guard. His eyes keener and his wits more alert than the Sire de Chavaigny's, he had not overlooked the package in her hand nor made two guesses as to its nature. Seeing her so long in talk with the officer, he became intrigued, and so detached himself from the fringe of the waiting throng, and wandered as if idly towards those two, moving with a noiseless step and ears alert.

She needed to look at him for a long moment before she could be sure that he was not an apparition. He wore a scarlet hood and chaperon that entirely cased his head and ended in long points which reached down almost to his girdle. Below that, his pourpoint and hose were all black, as was the little round hat he wore atop of his hood. This he doffed to her, and bent his humped back until he was almost double.

'God save you, Mistress Danvelt,' he greeted her.

She did not answer him. The pallor of her face had deepened, and her breath was quickened. There was fear in her glance and some horror too. Abruptly, ignoring his salutation, she passed out to the vestibule where her servants waited.

The Fool followed her out of sight with his beady eyes. Then he donned his hat again, setting it at a rakish cock and solemnly considered the young captain, who stood a little bemused.

'A lovely woman, sir,' said he dryly.

'Lovely as a saint from heaven.'

The Fool raised his eyebrows. 'When did you last see a saint from heaven?' quoth he. Then, while the captain sought an answer, he relieved him of the need. 'Oh, to be sure! Your uncle is the Cardinal of Ghent. That gives you an insight into celestial matters. Well, well, my nephew of a cardinal, if you have your uncle's word for it that they're like that in heaven, we had better see to it that we get there.'

'You are ribald,' the captain reproved him, frowning.

'That's my trade. I should not be a Fool else. But under my ribaldry there's a heart, just as my crooked body holds a soul, although you might never suspect it from the aspect of me.' He sidled nearer. 'That sweet lady, now, moves my compassion. She has been deeply wronged.'

'Wronged!' The captain was outraged at the thought. 'She has been wronged?'

'When you are a woman and as beautiful as a saint from heaven, it's very difficult not to be.'

The captain gripped him by the shoulder. 'What do you know of her wrongs? Can you speak to them?'

'I could, nephew of a cardinal. Should your saintly uncle desire to hear me in private, I might have a useful word to say.'

He disengaged his shoulder from that heavy hand, and was gone. He chuckled as he went, in anticipation of unexpectedly rich entertainment ahead. After that he grew very thoughtful on a conjecture which he desired to test. The opportunity came that evening, after supper.

The Duke sat at cards with his brother the Bastard, the Duke of Somerset, the Cardinal of Ghent, and the Sire de Rhynsault, who was being shown so much favour and so greatly pampered these days that it was going to his head. He permitted himself odd familiarities, which if slight were yet beyond the usual in a court in which the most rigid etiquette was observed. Thus, he now ventured to propose that his Fool should sing, to amuse the ladies. The young Duchess saved his face by applauding the proposal, and the Fool obeyed quite readily. Whether he knew no better, or whether he was moved by the perversity of his crooked nature, he chose to sing the song that he had made last autumn in Middelburg, one stanza of which had already earned him a broken head. Or yet it may be that he perceived the opening such a song might make for him with one whom he desired to sound, one who was himself a poet, and a member of the Fool's present courtly audience.

The song was not well received.

'A vile, loathly ditty,' the Duchess Margaret pronounced it, in English, to the Duke, who spoke the language as fluently and easily as became a man who boasted of his Lancastrian blood.

The Duke agreed with her, and turned to Rhynsault to convey to him her opinion and his own. Rhynsault flushed under the half-reproof, the first check to his popularity since his advent there. His baleful eye sought the unhealthy countenance of Kuoni, whose very impassivity was an added provocation.

'It's a perversely ribald hound,' he said by way of apology. 'I should have mistrusted him. But he shall be schooled in better manners before the ladies.'

'Nay, nay,' the Duchess intervened. 'He but exercises the license of his kind. And perhaps he will yet make amends.' She was moved to pity for that deformed and weakly creature and desired him no such harm as the Sire de Rhynsault's tone appeared to promise.

The Fool bowed low. 'For your highness, and at your bidding then.' And he sang a wistful little lament of a maid for her lover slain in the wars, as fragrant, delicate, and tender as the earlier song had been repellent. It brought tears to the eyes of more than one lady, and applause to the lips of them all as his lute-strings quivered into silence.

Anon, as he was seated alone by the fire, Count Anthony came wandering over to him.

'You have a great gift of rhythm, Sir Fool,' the Count commended him, and added the reproof: 'Why, then, make a harlot of your muse?'

'Is sincerity harlotry, Grand Master?' quoth the Fool.

'Sincerity? You were sincere in that vile hedonism?'

The Fool shrugged. 'I base my philosophy on life as I find it.'

'Which in itself is false. For philosophy deals with life as it should be.'

'Unless the should be may be, and is, then is it not philosophy, but moonshine.' He spoke mournfully. Count Anthony, scenting suffering, was moved to compassion.

'Has life used you ill?'

'From the hour of my birth, Grand Master. Look at me. But I take not myself for model. I am the exception among men, a *lusus naturae*. Because of this, because I may not take my part in the great play, I have been the more attentive an onlooker. And I have seen little to make me love my kind. Greed, lust, cruelty. These are the compounds of the soul of Man, of Man who claims to have been created in the image of a god. But . . .' He broke off, and leapt to his feet as if suddenly remembering the rank of the Prince who addressed him. He laughed, for once both visibly and audibly. 'This is to be a traitor to my trade.'

'I prefer you so,' said the Count solemnly, 'though you are, I think, too sweepingly bitter. All men are not so fashioned.

'True. Some oysters contain pearls. But you'll not argue from this that it is in the nature of the oyster to grow pearls. And when it happens that a man or woman is not of the more common make, does the world reward or reverence them for being different? Let me illustrate the point, Grand Master. In Middelburg there lately lived a lady of the burgher class, the young wife of a merchant who was involved in plots against the Duke's government, and who, confessing his crime, was duly hanged. Now this lady appeared to be of a pure and saintly life, pious, charitable, and good to all. Offences in themselves in the eyes of many of her sisters. To these she added the still greater offence of a beauty of body to match her beauty of soul. Yet, after her husband was hanged, the tale crept forth that she was the Governor's leman, and that she had been with her paramour at the very hour at which her husband met his death. What is one to think of life and of humanity in the face of such a story? Here was a woman who used all the Christian virtues as a cloak for sin. Can one accept evidence of virtue after that?' He paused and sighed. Then ended: 'The indignation so rose against her that she was forced to quit Middelburg and retire to Flushing, where she had lived as a maid, to the house of her father, since deceased.'

Count Anthony was staring at him with a singular look in his dark eyes, a look that almost made the Fool afraid. It was clear that his mind was not at all upon the application of the story, but upon the later details of the identity of its central figure.

'What was her name?' he asked in a voice out of which all the usual melody had departed.

'The name of her husband was Danvelt.'

The next moment his throat was between the Count's two hands, and the Count's voice was rasping in his ear: 'You lying dog!'

Only for a second did Kuoni think that his last hour was come. In the next heartbeat he was released, flung off, and so swift had the whole action been that none at the other end of the room observed its real nature or supposed that Count Anthony did more than amuse himself with Rhynsault's Fool.

And meanwhile the Fool was gasping: 'You misapprehend me grievously, Grand Master. The lie is not mine, if lie it be. I but retail a story current, to show the infamy of human nature. For, if the tale be not true, then there is the infamy of those that spread it. I know not, in faith, which it were better to believe.'

But laughter shook his soul the while, for the Count had given him a full answer to the question that all day had been bubbling in his mind.

'You say "if it is true." Is there the possibility . . .? Bah!

Do not answer, for I have not asked that question, or if I had, I know the answer to it.'

'Almost,' said the Fool, 'one might suppose your lordship to have acquaintance of the lady.'

His lordship did not answer him on that. 'And Danvelt is dead, you say?'

'As dead as a man may be who was hanged for half-anhour.'

'Dead!' he repeated, as if to himself, and his eyes, wide-open, were staring into the heart of the fire. Then, abruptly, he swung on his heel, quitted the Fool, and, like a sleepwalker, went down the long room and so passed out.

CHAPTER XXVI

THE FOOL'S MISSION

BETIMES next morning the Fool presented himself at the Lion of Brabant to wait upon Mistress Johanna. He limped, and his back was sore, where last night Rhynsault had whipped him until he bled, for jeopardizing his popularity by that unseemly song. But the Fool took little thought or care for these things this morning. He had a spiritual unguent for his bodily wounds and the promise of sweet entertainment soon to come. These human puppets should dance to his wire-pulling; the very souls of them should leap to his touch. He might be humped like a flea, grotesque of face and skeletal of limb, but it was in the mind that real power abode, and his mind was as much above that of his fellow-creatures as theirs were above the minds of apes. Thus Master Kuoni looked upon himself in exultant introspection, worshipping his own genius and contemptuous of the stupidity of those upon whom he was to exercise it. Among these he numbered — and this with the greatest of all relish — that bully braggart numbskull the Sire de Rhynsault, whom Kuoni's own wits had steered into the ducal esteem in which he was at present basking. And all that he had ever had for his pains had been kicks and cuffs and whippings — oh, yes, and a flagon at his head one morning last October which had all but extinguished him. He could chuckle now over the memory of that flagon and the horrible exasperation which had prompted Rhynsault to hurl it. Just as he chuckled, too, over the thought of Rhynsault strutting it in his pride, puffed out like a peacock by the favour of the Duke. Well, well, there were obstacles in every man's path, and only a fool would walk with his nose in the air. King Louis had a saying, the Fool remembered, that when Pride rides before, Misfortune follows fast behind. A shrewd rogue that King Louis; a man entirely after the subtle Kuoni's own heart.

Although but three days in Brussels, his figure was known already. One of the advantages of his grotesque shape was that men remarked him and remembered him. The land-lord of the Lion of Brabant had seen him in the street in at-tendance upon the puissant Sire Claude de Rhynsault, who was high in favour with the Duke and to be made, men said, Governor of Ghent. Therefore he was respectfully received. As Kuoni was wont to say, whilst he was a Fool among lords, among fools he was a lord. And he had a manner too, and a certain haughty air which he could assume, despite his stunted shape, set a gulf between himself and com-mon citizens such as only the most audacious would pre-sume to bridge.

He was invited to wait in the common room. And there before the blazing logs he loosed his heavy cloak, contemp-tuously indifferent to the other occupants of the room, not even deigning to remove the round black hat which he wore over his scarlet hood.

Whilst he was thawing his chilled limbs came Jan, as Mistress Johanna's representative, to inquire his business, and this none too respectfully, for Jan had memories which did not make him love the Fool. Indeed, few things would have delighted him more in life than to have stretched the Fool's neck like a capon's.

The Fool looked him over with that beady, magnetic eye of his, of which many had experienced the subduing effect.

'My business, sirrah, is to serve your mistress,' he an-swered shortly.

'Ah!' said Jan, and stroked his shaven chin reflectively. 'And exactly how do you propose to serve her?'

'That I shall do myself the honour of telling her in per-son, if she will condescend to see me. If not . . .' He paused, and hunched his shoulders. 'If not it will be her loss. Bear her that message, sirrah, and bring me the answer sharply. I am no suppliant, and I am pressed for time.' But as Jan turned to depart upon the errand, the Fool deemed it well to add: 'Tell her touching a certain memorial of hers that I may be able to indicate a channel by which it should reach the proper hands. That is all. Make haste.'

It followed that he was presently invited to ascend to a long low-ceilinged chamber on the first floor, where presently Mistress Johanna came to him.

He pondered her with the eye of an expert in things of beauty. How delicately white she looked and how graceful in that sheathing gown of black with its long tight sleeves which descended to the knuckles of her fine hands. Her suffering seemed to have refined her, fine though she had been before, to have bestowed upon her a certain grave dignity, almost a majesty.

She advanced calmly towards the Fool, who had now uncovered and uncloaked, and stood forth in his scarlet hood and chaperon above his suit of black.

'Sir, though I can scarcely believe the message you have sent me by my servant, I have consented to see you. I beg that you will state your purpose.'

'Incredible though it may seem to you?'

'I have come to learn that the incredible is not always the impossible.'

His appraising, probing eyes were boldly upon her. 'And that, I should opine, madam, is the least of your discoveries.' He did not wait for her to question him upon his meaning, but went on, himself, to explain it. 'I detect a new note in your voice, a new strength in your carriage. Knowledge has aged your soul, and shrunk this little world to its proper mean proportions in your eyes, so that it no longer terrifies you, eh? And you are adding to your knowledge fast. You are here in Brussels to ask for a justiciary, and they offer you an almoner. It is most apt. For, being interpreted, it means that here, at the fount of justice and the source of honour — barren, poetical phrases these — justice, when dispensed at all, is dispensed by way of alms: disdainfully, grudgingly, stingily.'

'I see that you are informed of the steps I have taken. No doubt their object will be clear to you.'

'Quite clear, of course. But do not be afraid, madam.'

'Afraid!' She laughed, a little frosty laugh that was like a tinkle of silver bells. 'Of what should I be afraid? There is nothing in the world with power to hurt me now.'

He shook his hooded head. 'Nay, lady, nay! You have travelled far; but not yet quite so far as that. I doubt, indeed, if you would have the strength for such a journey. You do not know the peculiar asperities of the road to the grim kingdom of Insensibility. I do.'

That awoke in her another feeling besides her growing mistrust. The Fool had opened his mind to her for one moment, allowed her a glimpse into his soul, and in that swift, fleeting glimpse she had seemed to perceive that under the warped evil of his surface there was a suffering man; almost had she perceived — for his tone as well as his word had been full of self-revelation — that suffering and injustice had made him what he was, and that by cruelties endured had cruelty been fostered in him. In short, that he paid the world back in the only coin he earned.

It disposed her — as understanding ever will — to judge him more leniently, even to believe that he made kin with those who suffered.

He broke the long moment's silence. 'Will you give me leave to sit, madam? I am a little weak this morning.'

'Why, surely,' she said, observing the abnormal pallor of that ever bloodless face and the dark stains that ringed his eyes. And as with a word of thanks he moved to a chair, 'You are lame!' she cried. 'Have you hurt your leg?'

'The lameness is not from my leg, but from the end of my back. It is naught. I was paid my wages last night. When that happens, I often go lame for a few days.'

'Your wages?' she echoed, not understanding.

'A Fool's wages, of course,' said he with a wry smile. 'I bear a load of them on my back at present. They do not greatly incommode me until I come to take off my shirt. Oh, I was well paid last night. But not quite so richly as one morning last October in Middelburg with which you were concerned. On that occasion I was almost paid in full.' He thrust back the close-fitting hood from his brow to reveal a great livid scar at the root of his hair which was already very grey.

He saw the bewilderment in her eyes. And added sufficient to explain it, but no more. It was never his way — not, indeed, the way of his kind — to deal explicitly.

'It's a sweet, generous master, the Sire de Rhynsault,' he said, in bitter mockery.

'I see.' It seemed to her that she understood a great deal; in fact, she understood precisely what he intended that she should understand. If she inferred for herself that he was there to offer an offensive alliance against one whom he had cause to hate, the thing would seem infinitely more credible to her than if he were to protest it. She drew nearer, and came to stand by the table at which he had seated himself. She faced him across it leaning towards him.

'Do you tell me, sir, that you took that wound . . . that you suffered on my behalf at Middelburg?'

'In a sense,' said he. 'But I brought it on myself. That morning after you had gone, I mocked him. I did it to sting and goad him. I accounted him contemptible and vile. I have always accounted him contemptible and vile, which is why I have served him.'

'Why you have served him?' This at least was incredible. But he had an explanation for it.

'Because it amused me to push him into vileness and to see how far he would go, once in it. You stare at me as if I were not real. But what else was there for me in life? I am no Rhynsault. What I lack in physical lusts I make up in mental ones; where he amuses himself with bodies, I amuse myself with souls. I am frank with you, madam.'

'God knows you are,' said she, appalled, and shivered.

'Oh, compassionate me a little.'

'I do. From my soul.'

'Then I proceed. I have feasted upon the spectacle of Rhynsault's grossness, his ineptitude, his maladroitness,

and his egregious vanity, so much that it has been worth
while to endure his occasional brutalities; worth while because the knowledge was always within me that in the end,
when I grew weary of his apish capers, when they ceased to
amuse me, I could tumble him back onto the dunghill
whence he originally arose.'

Her eyes flickered at that. She began to see more clearly
the purpose of this candid, merciless self-revelation of a
crooked soul.

'Chance gave him the deputy-governorship of Friesland;
that was close upon three years ago, when as Comte de
Charolais our present Duke was virtually regent of the Burgundian dominions. He owed the office to the fact that he
was a good soldier. So much must be admitted for him.
And Duke Charles, himself a soldier first and last, loves a
good man-at-arms above all other men, and commits the
error of conceiving that a good fighter is necessarily a good
administrator. It's a mistake he makes in his own person.
But no matter. I was at Rhynsault's elbow then. I steered
him through the difficulties of an office for which he was
utterly unqualified. I had learning, knowledge of men and
of the world, and wits. These I lent to Rhynsault. He quitted himself so well that, when the governorship of Zealand
fell vacant, he was appointed to it. There he has done better
still. I have helped him to the very summit of a perilously
high ladder, of which he could never have climbed the half
without my aid. And now upon his giddy eminence, swollen
with pride in achievements which are not his own, a daw
into whose tail I've stuck a handful of peacock's feathers,
petted by the Duke, the envy of men, the admiration of the
ladies, about to be made Governor of Ghent and perhaps
even decked with the collar of the Golden Fleece, now is the
moment to kick away the ladder and stand by to watch the
egregious fall of him. I am by trade a maker of jests,
madam. And this is my masterpiece.'

'A masterpiece of evil,' said she.

'Evil? What is evil? But let that rest. It is too big a

question. Whatever it may be, can it be evil to feed such an
evil fool until he bursts? Is it not, rather, good, inasmuch
as it supplies a warning to others of his foul kind?'

'Why do you tell me all this?'

'Why? The unneccessary question! Because your aims
and mine are one to-day. By helping you to yours, I achieve
my own. You have suffered a wrong which should not go
unpunished. I require an unguent for my bleeding back and
for the memory of many other bleedings of this same crooked
back.'

'It is not so crooked as your soul,' she told him sadly, for
in spite of all he aroused in her a certain pity. 'Had it been
sympathy for my wrongs that moved you, I had gladly
hailed your help, sir. As it is . . .' She spread her hands, and
shook her head again quite eloquently.

He blinked at her owlishly. Where, he wondered, had he
blundered? He had told her more or less the truth because
he was too shrewd to suppose she would have believed him
had he come to her with any pretence of altruistic sympathy. She was in desperate need of help to ends which must
be dearer to her than life, if he judged her at all correctly.
Why, then, so squeamish? He thought he perceived the
light, and betrayed it in his next words.

'Well, well, madam, you may be less scornful of my help
when you find his excellency the Lord Almoner indisposed
to trouble himself with your memorial.'

'You speak as if you knew that he would.'

'I do, madam.'

'How can you know that?'

'How? I have a gift of knowledge, amounting at times to
prescience. Let me lift the veil. At worst, my Lord Almoner
will be peevish, and your memorial will be returned to you
unread, the seals unbroken. That is what most probably
will happen. At best, he may be in a benevolent mood, and
he will condescend to lay it aside that he may slumber over
it after dinner. So that the argosy of your destinies, if it
floats at all, may be said to float upon the juices of a capon
or the rosy contents of a flagon.'

'Go your ways, you mocker,' she scorned him. 'His excellency the Cardinal . . .'

He interrupted her. 'Is a thought too excellent to trouble himself about such little things. Excellency breeds corpulency and corpulency breeds somnolency, and somnolency breeds . . . pshaw!' He waved a bony hand in contemptuous dismissal of the Cardinal. 'I am a mocker, yes. It is my trade to mock. And shall I tell you the whole secret of this trade?' He got to his feet, and tapped the table with a long, lean forefinger as he answered his own question. 'It is to pluck the fair veil of illusion from the nasty face of truth.'

'And is the face of truth, then, always nasty?'

'I've always found it so.'

'God help you, sir!'

'I thank you for the prayer. I am dismissed, I think?'

She confirmed him in the suspicion with amiabilities. If he would dine below at her charges ere he went, or if he would drink a cup of spiced wine against the cold, or accept a purse to repay him for his trouble, these things were at his command. But the Fool declined them all. He would not linger where he was not a welcome guest. He took his leave.

But at the door he paused, and turned.

'Your trust, I know, madam, is in your Cardinal. I hope it may not prove misplaced. But should this purple ambassador to the Court of Heaven by whom you set such store prove indisposed to meddle in so earthly a matter as a woman's wrongs, pray bear in mind that you have a ready helper in the Fool. A message to me at the palace will bring me straight to you. No written message will be needed. It might not be safe. A blank sheet folded and bearing a plain seal is all that you need send, and not by Jan or any servant who was with you in Middelburg. Nor let the messenger seek the quarters of the Sire de Rhynsault. Let him hand the paper to the first archer in the guard-house and bid him convey it at once to the Fool of the Sire de Rhynsault. God save you, madam.'

He departed by no means ill pleased. In his shrewdness he had not allowed so much as a hint to escape him of the channel by which he proposed to guide her memorial to the Duke. For if she refused to avail herself of that, all hope was at an end. And she might well refuse so long as there was any other hope to which she might cling. Let the failure of that hope, now centred in the Lord Almoner, reduce her to despair, and then would be his opportunity to make these puppets play the comedy his fertile wicked brain had authored.

Nor did the sequel disappoint him. Betimes next morning, which was Sunday, a lackey brought him a letter under a plain seal which had been left for him with an archer of the guard. He opened it to find the paper blank. A little later, whilst the court was at Mass, from which he made some excuse for remaining absent, he slipped out and, close-wrapped against the biting north wind, made his way through streets that were carpeted with frozen snow to the Lion of Brabant.

This time he was admitted to Johanna's presence without preambles. She awaited him, a little impatient, a little fretful even, in that low-ceilinged room abovestairs, where the gloom of the grey morning was relieved by the leaping flames of the generous fire on the cowled hearth. Spiced wine was steaming in a jug upon the table, and beside it a package, which he guessed to be her memorial, its seals, he observed, unbroken.

Here then cheek-by-jowl he beheld at once his welcome and the cause of it.

She rose from the armchair by the fire, in which she had been sitting, and in rising broke from the chrysalis of her fur-lined cloak and stood forth slim and shapely in her sheathing gown of black, her golden head uncovered.

'You are good to come so promptly.'

He answered with a Latin tag.

'*Bis dat qui cito dat.*' He advanced to the fire, like a moth to the flame, for being a thin-blooded creature he felt the cold intensely. He unwrapped himself from his voluminous cloak, let it slip from him, drew up a three-legged stool, and sat down almost within the hearth. She poured him a cup of the hot wine and brought it to him. He rose to receive it, thanked her, pledged her, and drank a deep draught of it, then resumed his seat, and spread his bony hands to the blaze.

'So, so! That warms,' said he. 'It is not good to be cold. It numbs the wits together with the limbs, and I shall need my wits this morning if I am to serve you, mistress.' He looked at her, and his thin lips, which, like his nose, were still blue, smiled rallyingly. 'So your memorial has come back unread from his purple portliness.'

'You saw it on the table,' said she.

'Ay; but knew before I saw it. For otherwise you would not have sent for me. Why so reluctant, madam, to accept the help of one who desires to serve you?'

'That is not what I understood from you yesterday. You desire to serve yourself. I am but the means to your ends.'

'As I am the means to yours, madam. So let us cry quits on that.'

She sighed deeply. 'I must, since I can command no other,' she told him frankly. And straightly asked him: 'What means have you to bring my memorial to the Duke's highness?'

He shifted on his stool; he laughed a little, the laughter of full self-confidence.

'At least in my hands that memorial will not depend upon the dull humour of a fat-bellied prelate. Let me borrow for it Cupid's wings, and I'll warrant such flight for it that before nightfall it will have come to rest in the Duke's lap. Having sent forth the raven in vain, now try the dove, Madam Noah.'

She leaned forward, her elbows on her knees, her face eager, but a little frown of perplexity between her fine brows. 'I don't understand.'

'If you did you would not need my help. Shall I be plain?'

'In Heaven's name!'

Yet he seemed to hesitate, to avoid directness. It was as if, so as not to shock her sensibilities, he must gradually disclose, and, in disclosing, educate her to the task ahead.

'Your error lay in seeking no better interest here at court than that of this poor captain of the guard. He was well-intentioned towards you, of course. Your beauty made him that. But so it would have made others; others whose interest is of greater weight. Madam, you do not yet know the value to you of your beauty, the power that lies in it.'

She flushed under that steady, expressionless glance of his, which watched her with so disconcerting an intentness. 'I have no wish to know it,' she told him sternly. 'I remember that once before you sought to arouse that knowledge in me, under a pretence of serving me. Do you play the same tune now, Master Fool?'

He avoided the question; answered instead the statement. 'Ay, but then you dealt with a base trickster, a foul cheat. How was I to know that . . .'

'Leave that,' she bade him sharply. 'Come to the present matter. Be short and plain.' She was peremptory. 'In one word: Whom have you in mind to act as my agent with the Duke?'

'In five words, madam — the Grand Master of Burgundy.'

To her this was but a title. She knew nothing of its recent bestowal.

'What influence have you with him?'

'I? None.' And then, very slyly, an unmistakable significance in his glance, he added: 'But you might have; nay, you would have if I know anything.'

There was a long and uncomfortable spell of silence in which she looked at him with eyes that at first were aflame with anger, and then of a steely coldness. At last, with a little smile of scorn, she answered him.

'So this is all your vaunted help? A piece of foul advice,

which, had I been the woman to do as you propose, I should not have required. Where were your wits there, Master Fool, that you did not think of that?' She rose. 'There is no more to say between us, I think, save to thank you for your wasted pains. I must seek other means. Heaven will reveal the way to me; for there is justice in heaven.'

'Ay — in heaven,' he agreed. 'But we're upon earth, where justice is for sale.' He got up at last and stood before her, and his voice quivered with impatience, almost with anger. 'God's light, madam! Will you hesitate to buy vengeance upon the guilty at the price you vainly paid to save the innocent?'

She continued to ponder him with that cold, steely glance, a certain tightening about the corners of her lips.

'It was not necessary to put it quite so plainly. I had understood you already. Tell me, Master Fool, have you never in all your life met with anything pure, disinterested, chaste, or noble, that you must proceed as if all souls were vile?'

'Ah! Bah!' he snorted, and stooped for his cloak, which lay upon the ground where he had let it fall. He snatched it up viciously, as if to vent upon the garment the impatience and ill-humour by which he was assailed. 'Purity! Chastity! Nobility! Words! Superstitions! Chimeræ!' He barked them out, the pitch of his voice steadily rising. 'What is this chastity by which you set such store? A denial of Nature, an illusion with which blind, groping fools torment themselves.'

'Blasphemer!' she answered him. 'You speak of things you do not understand.'

'Do I?' He leered at her. 'Then why do those who seek to practise chastity find it necessary to flee the world? Why do they entrench themselves behind convent walls, and there, with hair-shirt, flagellation, and lean diet, make their arid stand against Nature's angry onslaughts? You will allow an illusion such as that to lead you into neglecting the clear duty of avenging the murder of your husband and the base cheat that was practised on yourself? If you did not allow it to . . .'

'Give me peace!' she interrupted in a voice of pain. 'I will hear no more. I beg that you will leave me.'

He made shift to do so, but without the intention. He had yet another card to play. He shrugged, like a man resigned, adjusted his cloak, and flung one wing of it over his left shoulder to swathe him. Then he took up his hat. He bowed in silence, and moved to the door. Midway thither he checked. He turned, and looked at her across the wintry gloom of the chamber, and the dark furnishings on which the firelight flickered. He sighed, and his long, sallow face was sorrowful.

'Oh, bethink you, madam! Forsake these hollow shams on which you build in vain; these empty bubbles blown by make-believe. Deal in realities. Use the irresistible weapons of your beauty.'

She was silent, her shoulders turned to him, facing the fire, one lightly shod foot upon an andiron, one hand upon the chimney cowl. He took one returning step towards her, leaned forward, and his voice was eagerly persuasive. 'Come, madam, give me a token to Count Anthony, and leave the rest to me.'

She span round to face him, white to the lips, her eyes dilating.

'Whom do you name?' she cried, her voice strained and harsh.

He feigned surprise at so much emotion. 'Count Anthony of Guelders.'

'What has he to do in this?'

'He might have everything to do if you would but follow my advice.'

'Your advice?' Horror pervaded her soul, such horror and such dread as she had never known in all her trials. Controlling herself, she asked him: 'Why do you name him now? Why did you not name him before?'

'I did. From the outset. He is the Grand Master of Burgundy, newly appointed. He is second in power only to the Duke, and what he wills the Duke is easily persuaded to perform. Give me a token that will bring him to you, so that you may make your prayer to him, and I'll warrant . . .'

'Never! Never! Never!' Her vehemence startled him, and dashed his rising hopes. She advanced upon him, a wild creature now, frantic with fear and shame and horror. 'Never, do you hear me, Master Fool? He is . . .'

She broke off. Even in her agitation she perceived how unnecessary it was to give the Fool her confidence, to tell him that Count Anthony of Guelders was the one man in the world to whom she could not appeal, the one man whom she could never bear to see again, the one man whom she could wish should never know her shame and her defilement. She desired if possible to continue to live in his memory as he had known her in Walcheren. If that were not possible, if knowledge of the events must come to him, at least let him never again behold her, let her hide herself from him, the only man who had power to revive her shame so that it must scorch her up and shrivel her to ashes.

But of this she said nothing to the Fool. Something of it he guessed, however, from the abrupt manner in which her self-control had slipped from her, from the terror that had glittered in her eyes.

She controlled herself now, to be seared by a new thought. It was to Count Anthony of all living men that this creature proposed that she should sell herself for justice. But swift on the heels of that sudden anger with the Fool came pity. How little he knew his world, after all, this apostle of evil, to judge Count Anthony a man to be so bought!

'Go, sir,' she dismissed him. 'There is no more to be said between us.'

He departed, vexed and crestfallen. Things were not to run the course he had planned for them. Here were destinies which he had thought to shape with his thumbs as a potter shapes his pots. But unexpected elements had been present in the clay, elements unusual in the clay of humanity as Kuoni knew it. All was not done yet. By no means. But the consummation towards which he aimed, so far as the Sire de Rhynsault was concerned, would not be quite so poetically humorous as he had intended.

CHAPTER XXVII

THE MEMORIAL

THE FOOL retraced his steps, ruminating as he went. Having failed with Mistress Johanna, it now remained to succeed less picturesquely with Count Anthony. The manner of this required consideration. But no consideration was allowed him. His hand was forced by the events.

Within a bow-shot of the palace, he met a company of riders; twenty lances, coming two by two, and after these a string of laden pack-horses, each led by a mounted groom. The men-at-arms wore on their surcoats the device of Guelders, and at their head rode Count Anthony himself. It required no two glances to inform the Fool that Count Anthony was going a journey. Almost at the risk of being trampled under the hooves of the horses, which were moving briskly, the Fool flung himself forward.

'Grand Master! Grand Master!'

Count Anthony drew rein. 'What now, Fool?' His countenance was very stern under its plumeless black velvet hat.

'Whither away, Grand Master?'

'Does it concern you, Fool?' Yet he added: 'I ride to Zealand.'

The Fool's pulses quickened. Despite the cold he broke into a perspiration at the thought of how nearly he had been too late. 'Then it does concern me,' said he. 'And if it concerns the affair of which I spoke to your lordship last night, turn back, Grand Master. For what you would do in Zealand may better be done here.'

'What do you mean? Explain yourself, man. Be brief and plain.'

He could not be plain without betraying an excessive knowledge; and when one cannot be plain it is impossible to be brief.

'If you desire to sift that matter, the chief witnesses are here in Brussels. I have just discovered it. The lady herself arrived here some days since, and has vainly been seeking an audience of the Duke in this very business. Considering your . . . interest last night, I was on my way to tell you now.'

Obviously Count Anthony was startled and deeply moved. 'Come with me,' he bade the Fool, and gave the order to go about.

In his closet, presently, booted, armed, and cloaked as he was, the Count flung himself into a chair. He was breathing hard. 'Now, sir, your tale.'

'It is already more than half-told.'

He lied of necessity to complete it. He had been to Mass that morning at Saint Gudule's and to his surprise had seen there the lady of whom last night he had spoken to the Count, the lovely widow of the merchant Danvelt, rendered if possible more lovely still by sorrow. From her servants he discovered that she was come to Brussels with a considerable train, which included many necessary witnesses, her object being to lay a plaint before the Duke's highness. So far her endeavours had met with no success, and, in view of the Duke's departure in a week's time for Friesland, it was feared that weary months of waiting lay ahead of her, by which she was profoundly downcast.

Count Anthony heard him out in silence, and continued sternly to consider him when his tale was done.

'What is the nature of her plaint?' he asked. 'Does she seek justice upon her calumniators?'

The Fool hesitated. 'My lord, I was not told what is in the memorial.'

The Count's sternness deepened. 'What else should it contain, Fool?'

'If you desire to know, Grand Master, were not the knowledge best sought in the memorial itself?'

'Or directly at the hands of Mistress Johanna?'

'With submission, Grand Master, first in the memorial.'

Count Anthony leaned forward, an elbow on his knee. 'What do you know, yourself, of this business, Fool? You were with Rhynsault at the time.'

It was an awkward question. The Fool could but evade it. 'Will you question a witness before the plaintiff has been heard, Grand Master? First the memorial, then ask me such questions as it may suggest, and to the best of my knowledge and ability I will answer you.'

He beheld hesitancy in that stern face. Then, suddenly, resolve. The Count stood up, thrusting back his chair. 'Where do you say Mistress Johanna is lodged?'

The Fool raised his hands in entreaty. 'My lord, you would commit an imprudence in seeking her, an imprudence which may defeat all. I gleaned certain things from her people,' he added hurriedly, to explain the depth of his knowledge. 'I am your loyal servant, Grand Master, and the servant of Mistress Johanna. Be advised by me to begin with the memorial.'

'But unless I seek her, how else is it to be obtained?'

'Never that way. I have cause to know. But I think I could obtain it for you within the hour, if you give me leave to go about it in my own fashion.'

'In God's name, do.'

The Fool summoned a servant, and sent him to fetch the Sire de Chavaigny.

'What has he to do with it?' quoth Count Anthony.

'You shall learn, Grand Master. I am using some of the knowledge gleaned this morning from her people. Suffer me to take certain liberties with your name when the captain comes.'

The Sire de Chavaigny clanked in, and bowed profoundly to the Count. It was the Fool, however, who addressed him.

'Ha, nephew of a cardinal, you sought, I think, to obtain your uncle's interest in a memorial left in your hands by Mistress Johanna Danvelt. You think that unfortunately you failed, and so you have returned her parchments to her. But the fact is you have not failed. His excellency your uncle has reconsidered the matter, and will be glad now to study this memorial. At least that is the message which my lord the Grand Master desires you to convey in person at once to Mistress Johanna, adding nothing to it, and subtracting nothing from it. But above all adding nothing to it: no word of this, you understand, or of any person's interest in the matter other than his greatness the Lord Almoner.'

The captain looked at Count Anthony with eyes that plainly asked a question.

'Do as he says,' the Count bade him.

Thus the memorial, so gladly surrendered by Johanna in the belief that Heaven had lent an ear at last to her intercessions, came during that same afternoon into the hands of the only man on earth from whose eyes she would have withheld it.

The reading of it almost stunned Count Anthony. When his senses had recovered, horror, anguish, rage, indeed, all the bitter emotions of which the human heart is capable, surged up in him. That Johanna, that chaste Madonna-like maid of whom his first impression had been one to fill him with reverence, that pure and austere wife so firmly entrenched within wifely continence, should have been thus defiled, subjected to this shameful martyrdom, was almost too horrible to be sanely considered by him. And Rhynsault? Such was his fury at the part this man had played that had he yielded to it he would have sought the fellow out and stabbed him without warning. It was perhaps the vindictive thought that a speedy death were too light a payment for such a debt that restrained and calmed him, and brought him back to a second, closer, and more detailed reading of that dreadfully circumstantial document.

It occupied ten sheets, closely written in her own hand, so fine and beautiful that it might have been learnt in Italy. Though it was his first sight of her writing, he had no doubt that it was hers. It had the grace and delicacy and compact beauty that was in herself and consequently, he reasoned,

must be in all things that issued from her. Appended to it
was the copy of a brief document, an order for the gaol-
delivery of Philip Danvelt, which announced that its original was in her keeping. After this came another half-dozen
sheets, each being the deposition of a witness, in every case
a man of consequence in Middelburg, attesting the loyal
character of the deceased, and the fact that they had attended at his trial for the purpose of offering evidence upon
the document on which his indictment had been based,
but that their evidence had been excluded. Each declared
himself in Brussels with Mistress Johanna, in readiness to
come forward and make oath before the Duke of the truth of
what he had written and to submit himself to be examined
upon it.

Count Anthony set down the memorial on the table before him, and covered his face with his hands to shut out the
horrible picture which the fundamental fact of that indictment evoked before his eyes. Thereafter, with elbows on the
table and his head in his hands, the fingers buried in his
tawny mane, he sat long immovable, pondering all, and
above all pondering his own part in this. For that he had a
part, he saw quite clearly, and it was a part that in his eyes
made him almost the chief culprit in this crime.

He began by cursing the day when he had gone to the
rescue of that oaf Danvelt; cursed the hour in which he had
delivered him from the hands of the ducal lieutenant at
Bruges. Better, indeed, to have left the fellow to hang than
that he should have lived to bring this unutterable thing
upon Johanna. But if he had done that, he would never
have known Johanna. What then? Better a thousand times
that he should never have known her; better for both of
them. What but misery and unhappiness had he brought
her between his romantic love and his prosaical indecision?
If she had never known him, her soul would never have been
numbed by his desertion of her after he had awakened it to
the awareness of life and love; and that numbness it was,
that ensuing hopelessness, with its listlessness and indiffer-

ence, which had made it possible for Danvelt to marry her and to bring this martyrdom upon her. It was his conduct, his actions from first to last, which had made this horror possible. For what he had done let him pay now, God helping him, by every exertion in his power, at need by every drop of blood in his body.

The resolve was quickly taken; but action upon it was postponed until the morrow. That day he could not trust himself. He was all tremors and frenzies, assailed by successive impulses: the impulse to run to Johanna; the impulse to seek the Duke and storm out his accusations against Rhynsault; the impulse to seek Rhynsault himself, and strangle him. All these he had to meet and curb. It was necessary, he understood, to wait until he should be calm enough to bring cold reason to his measures. For he realized here the need for care and prudence. Rhynsault at the moment was the spoilt darling of the Duke; and, whilst Charles might not be disposed to overlook so grave an offence as this, he would not be likely, considering his present attitude towards his Flemish subjects and after the things he had sanctioned at Liège, to visit it with any punishment that could satisfy Count Anthony unless he were very skilfully handled and approached.

Early next morning, by when he was again master of himself, Count Anthony waited upon the Duke, even as the Duke was about to set out for the audience of justice.

'You may, if so it please you,' said he, 'begin here and now your justiciary work by glancing at this memorial. The affair is, as it seems to me, of unusual gravity, not only in itself, but in consequence of the persons it concerns. Otherwise I should not intrude at such an hour.'

They were in the Duke's closet. The captain of his archers, two pages, and two secretaries were in attendance and about to accompany him to the hall. In the corridor outside two files of archers of the guard awaited him.

His highness demurred. He was opposed to petitions and memorials reaching him through any but the ordinary channels. It meant, he complained, giving a preference over the petitioners already on the lists. Finally, however, he allowed himself to be persuaded, and sat down again to read the parchments which his cousin thrust upon him.

As he read, his brow grew black; as he read on, it grew blacker; then, before he had reached the end, his face was lighted by sudden understanding. He tossed the memorial down, unfinished, and uttered an impatient laugh:

'Ah, bah! This is just a tirade of vindictiveness from one of these sly, hard headed burgher women because Rhynsault showed her traitor husband a proper lack of mercy.'

'Yet that he hanged her husband is but half this woman's plaint,' said Count Anthony quietly, 'and as it seems to me the lesser half.'

'Oh, as for the rest . . .' the Duke shrugged. 'It is natural she should say the worst that occurs to her so as to blacken his character. What witnesses could there ever be to disprove an accusation of that character?'

Count Anthony was a little appalled, a little mystified even. Charles was not usually quite so stupid. But he preserved his patience, well aware that without it he would accomplish nothing.

'It may not require disproving. Confronted with the accusation, Rhynsault may admit the truth of it. He is, after all, of knightly rank, and owes something to his spurs.'

'Would you have me question him?' The Duke showed irritability. 'Question him upon this trumpery indictment?'

'I should presume to advise it. The charge, after all, has its grave side. If you will read to the end, you will see that this lady has brought witnesses who swear that they could have given precious evidence, which was excluded from the trial.'

'That must have been because Rhynsault was convinced without it.'

Count Anthony shook his head. 'It can never be good

law to exclude evidence of any kind; and he is no good law-
giver who excludes it.'

'And there you are wrong, Anthony. All that may be excluded which being superfluous serves only to waste valuable time. And you are wasting mine,' he ended, irritably,
growing impatient under contradiction.

'I'll waste less of it, if you will suffer me to call the Sire de
Rhynsault before you.'

'Call Rhynsault? To answer to this rubbish?'

'Are you afraid to call him, Charles?'

'Afraid! Af . . . By Saint George!' He flushed to the
temples. 'Is that a thing to say to me?'

Count Anthony perceived that it was, indeed, a thing to
say to him, understood correctly now the source of his irritability. The Duke did not desire to look into this affair
lest decency should compel to take action upon it. Such
action might result in his losing or having to curtail the services of an instrument so valuable to him as he accounted
this Sire de Rhynsault. Rather than this, he would prefer to
close his eyes to an offence against one of these burgher subjects who at present were filling him with resentment and
contempt.

The Duke scowled at his Grand Master for a long, silent
moment. Then, under the compulsion of the doubt cast
upon him, he swung peevishly to the waiting captain.

'Chavaigny, bid the Sire de Rhynsault to wait upon us
here at once.'

Chavaigny went out, and the Duke continued to scowl at
his cousin, who had the power to shame him into doing
things he did not wish to do. 'After all, what's to come of
it?' he demanded. 'What, after all, if true? A soldier is not
an anchorite. If I were to dismiss every man of mine who
has made free with a burgher woman, I should have no army
left. I am not the keeper of their souls, nor I shall be damned
for their lechery.'

The more he grew heated, the more cold grew Anthony.
'You can hardly have read the memorial attentively,

Charles. The charge is of a complex nature. You may have missed some of the points.'

'Nay, I missed none of them. But it's not to be believed that all are true. I never yet knew a memorial to hold nothing but the truth.'

Little more was said until Rhynsault was ushered in. He came, jauntily, elastic of step, head erect, a smile upon his full red lips, a picture of vigorous, self-confident manhood.

'My homage to your highness.' He bowed to the Duke. 'Your servant, my Lord Grand Master.' He bowed to the Count.

Charles cleared his throat. He found himself taken unawares, for in his sullenness he had not rehearsed where he should begin. Finally he picked up the memorial, to verify the name it contained, and blundered boldly into the heart of the matter.

'Whilst at Middelburg, in October last, sir, you hanged a man named Danvelt.'

Rhynsault stiffened, taken entirely by surprise.

'Danvelt? Yes . . . That is true, highness.'

Count Anthony cut in quickly. 'You have been hurrying, sir,' he said.

'Hurrying?' Rhynsault looked at him, not understanding.

'You are a little out of breath,' the Count suavely explained, and so increased Rhynsault's uneasiness. But he attempted to carry it off.

'Ah, yes . . . naturally . . . in my eagerness to obey the summons of his highness . . .'

'Of course, of course,' purred the Count.

The Duke tapped the table with his forefinger. 'Tcha! Tcha! What's that to the point? This man Danvelt was charged with treason, with supplying arms and money to the rebel movement. What was the evidence?'

'Chiefly a letter from the man himself found among the effects of another convicted traitor.'

The Duke nodded. 'I am really reluctant to trouble you,

my good Rhynsault. But you should know that I have received a plaint against your administration of justice in this case.'

'A plaint?' Rhynsault appeared to be surprised. Then he quietly smiled. The Duke's manner had entirely restored his ease. 'There are always those who complain when a man is hanged.'

'My own view,' the Duke agreed. 'Let me ask you to furnish me with answers which will justify me in dismissing this petition. Since it has been preferred, I must afford an answer to it. First, then, there is a deposition here from a burgomaster of Middelburg, who saw the letter at the trial — or so he states — and is ready to make oath that neither the hand nor the signature was that of the accused.' The Duke paused for a reply.

'Then why did he not state it at the trial?' Rhynsault demanded.

The Duke referred to the memorial. 'He writes here that he did, but that his statement was peremptorily brushed aside.'

'That hardly sounds the truth. Your highness will consider that I conducted many similar trials in those days, and that it is impossible for me to speak with certainty to the details of any one of them. But if this burgomaster made any such statement at the time, it is impossible that I should have shut out such evidence. Quite impossible.'

'So I should judge,' the Duke agreed with him, and would have passed on, accounting the question answered, but that Count Anthony, leaning on the table's edge at the apex of a triangle, whose other two angles were occupied by Rhynsault and the Duke, interposed.

'Danvelt, after all, is not an uncommon name in Zealand, and the initial " P " of the signature need not necessarily have stood even for Philip. Was any comparison made between documents known to be in the writing of the accused and the writing of his letter?'

'It was not necessary,' said Rhynsault with assurance.

'How, not necessary?'

Rhynsault almost chuckled as he returned the pregnant answer: 'The man confessed his guilt.'

'Confessed?' cried the Duke.

'Confessed, your highness,' Rhynsault repeated firmly. 'I hold his signed confession and can produce it.'

The Duke laughed outright. He was immensely relieved. 'There!' he exclaimed in triumph over his cousin. 'That pricks your bubble.'

But Count Anthony's obstinacy, as the Duke accounted it, would not yet permit him to agree.

'Is the confession which you hold written in the man's own hand?'

'No, my lord. It was taken down by one of my clerks in a measure as he uttered it.'

'Ah! I see. You put him to the question?'

'Of course, my lord.'

'And racked him until he confessed whatsoever you required.'

Rhynsault showed himself scandalized by such an implication. There was, however, no need for him to defend himself. The Duke took up the office of advocate on his behalf.

'Nay, now, nay!' His tone was between tolerance and indignation. 'That is unfair, cousin. This good Rhynsault was within his rights. Fully within them. Surely there is no more to be said. And I keep the audience waiting.' He pushed back his chair, preparatory to rising. But he was checked in the act by the Count's persistent return to the attack.

'Was the confession ratified?'

'It was, my lord.'

'Did you compare the signature of that with the signature on the letter that incriminated him?'

Rhynsault shrugged. Sure now of the Duke's support, he permitted himself a certain easy insolence of tone. 'Who would trouble to compare the illegible scrawl of a man who had been racked with something that he had written when in full vigour? Had his signature not been attested on the confession by my clerks, none could say whose signature it was.'

The Duke stood up, at the end of his patience. 'You see, Anthony? My Lord Rhynsault answers too straightly and clearly to leave any doubts. To persist is to affront him, and it is not my way to affront those who serve me well.'

Rhynsault bowed himself double before the Duke's approving smile.

'You have leave to go,' the Duke graciously dismissed him.

But Count Anthony had not yet done. Greatly daring he interposed again.

'One question more, Charles! One question in your interest.'

The Duke made a gesture of impatience, and but for Rhynsault's excessive audacity that question would never have been asked, or, at least, not then.

'Oh, a dozen questions if you please, Lord Count.'

'I may take advantage of your generosity, then, to ask you two. First, sir: Were you fully satisfied in your conscience of the guilt of this man whom you sentenced to be hanged?'

Rhynsault became immensely dignified. 'The question in itself is almost an insult,' he answered. 'I answer it, nevertheless. I was.'

'You were. And now, sir, the second question.' And Count Anthony leaned forward, and spoke deliberately. 'Why, then, did you reprieve him?'

'Reprieve him? I?' Rhynsault laughed outright. 'But the man was hanged.'

'Oh, yes. The circumstances of that are set forth in the memorial. But it still remains that you granted a reprieve, which by accident or by design of yours — I say not which — was presented too late to be effective.'

'That,' said Rhynsault deliberately, 'is a lie.'

'A copy of the terms of the reprieve is attached to the memorial,' said Count Anthony.

'If twenty copies are attached, I still say it is a lie. Why, what's a copy? Really, my lord! These be very slender grounds upon which to doubt a man of such tried fidelity as mine.'

'And so say I,' the Duke agreed with him heartily.

'If you pledge your knightly word that no reprieve was granted . . .' Count Anthony was saying, when Rhynsault so far forgot himself as to interrupt him.

'I do so pledge it!' he cried defiantly. 'My knightly word.'

'Will you pledge it also in the matter of the wrong you are here accused of having done the widow?'

'I wronged the widow? I?'

Count Anthony was more precise. 'It is writ there,' he ended. 'A woman, unless she be an abandoned one, will not so freely set down the story of her shame. Do you pledge your knightly word that this, too, is false?'

Rhynsault hesitated. Here he perceived quite clearly that he was upon dangerous ground. He lacked the wits of Kuoni to point the way for him. Finally he took what he deemed the safest course.

'So,' he said. 'Now I understand. The memorial is drawn up by this vindictive woman.' He shrugged, and of intent permitted himself to look a little shamefaced. 'Nay, there I confess my wrong. But what would your highness?' He appealed him to the Duke. 'I yielded to a very ordinary temptation. The lady was beautiful, alluring, and not unwilling, and . . .'

'Not unwilling! You infamous base liar!'

His head thrown back, his eyes ablaze, the invective had burst from Count Anthony's lips before he could reflect.

It startled both Rhynsault and the Duke by its terrible vehemence. Rhynsault sucked in his breath. Squarely, defiantly he looked Count Anthony between the eyes.

'Do you make yourself this woman's champion, my lord?'

And now it was the Duke who gasped, thinking that he perceived the drift of Rhynsault's course, and yet unable to believe what he perceived. In no court of Europe was the etiquette more rigid than at the court of Burgundy, where all public functions took on the semblance almost of religious rites, where precedence was observed with an iron rigidity. Rhynsault, because of valuable services, had been accorded certain liberties, but there was a point at which the Duke's dignity demanded that a line should be drawn. Was Rhynsault about to trespass beyond that line?

Meanwhile the Count had answered firmly. 'I do. What, then, sir?'

And then the outrageous thing the Duke suspected happened. With a coarse laugh, Rhynsault plucked a glove from his belt. 'That simplifies the issue, my lord,' said he. 'If I am to be put upon my trial for my commerce with this lady, let it be trial by battle, which I make so bold as to claim with you as is my knightly right.' And he flung the glove down at Count Anthony's feet.

The Duke was speechless. That any man should so far forget the respect due to his person as to offer a challenge in his presence, and on a matter in which all questions asked might be assumed from the questioner to be asked upon ducal authority, was beyond belief. And there was aggravation of the offence in the disparity of rank between one who was, after all, an upstart soldier of fortune, and the other, to whom he presumed to toss his glove, the prince of a reigning house and the peer as well as blood-cousin of the Duke himself.

But no word that he might have found could have been one half so scathing and searing to the Lorrainer's pride as those which were spoken by the Count.

'Captain,' he said to Chavaigny, who looked on round-eyed, 'the Sire de Rhynsault has dropped his glove; by accident, I think. Be so good as to restore it to him.'

Chavaigny stooped to obey the order, whilst Rhynsault, scarlet with fury, lost all self-control.

'By the Blood!' he was roaring. 'I might have known . . .'

And then the Duke found his voice suddenly, and used it to roar louder than Rhynsault. 'Silence, buffoon! Will you raise your voice in my presence? Will you utter threats and vaunts and challenges before my face? Who are you, in God's name? What are you, and what am I? Do you know, sirrah knight?'

Before that instance of the fury of which Charles of Burgundy was capable, the Sire de Rhynsault's soul quailed within him; the bully effaced himself, his wrath extinguished like a candle that is blown out. In a moment he was all humility.

'Highness!' His voice shook. 'I admit my fault. Humbly I crave your highness's pardon. Humbly!' But he went on to explain himself. 'It heated me to be given the lie.'

'Heated you, did it? If you were given the lie, sir, it was the Grand Master speaking with my voice who gave it you. To raise your voice to my Grand Master, acting in the discharge of the functions of his office, is to raise your voice to me. And that, by Saint George, I suffer from no man; not from a sovereign prince, much less an upstart mercenary who is what he is by my favour alone.'

Thus the storm crackled about the Lorrainer's head. By his presumption he had damaged himself more deeply — if only temporarily, for the Duke's rages were as brief as they were terrible — than by a dozen admissions of such matters as the memorial contained. As eager in his wrath to see Rhynsault's crest reduced as he had hitherto been anxious to spare him these vexations, the Duke turned to the Count.

'Continue your questions, Grand Master, and let him beware how he answers.'

'I have no more questions, highness. The Sire de Rhynsault has admitted that he did this wrong. What he would have added in extenuation, if true, which it is not, can be no extenuation. Judgment now is for your highness. It is for you to say whether you are content that such things shall be done, which, being done by men who hold office as your lieutenants and representatives, may almost be regarded as having been done by your own self.'

If it was disingenuous and craftily calculated to keep the Duke's anger directed along its present course, it was at least justified by all the facts. Dispassionately Count Anthony summed up the matter, so dispassionately that none could have guessed the extent to which his passions were concerned.

'However satisfied the Governor of Middelburg may have been in his conscience, as he says, that this Danvelt was guilty, it was an injudiciousness to exclude the evidence of those who would have testified to the handwriting. The natural impression would be that he desired to hear nothing that would tell in the prisoner's favour; that, in fact, he had ends of his own to serve by presuming the prisoner's guilt. When you consider the burgomaster's solemn attestation that the incriminating letter which he saw was not in the handwriting of Philip Danvelt, this impression receives an unpleasant confirmation. Justice unjustly administered, or even carelessly administered, is a fomenter of discontent, and rightly so, especially among a subject people. And your highness is well acquainted with the evils arising out of that.'

'I am so, by Saint George!' the Duke agreed. In the hostility which Rhynsault had drawn upon himself, the Duke was easily swayed by arguments which otherwise he might have brushed aside.

Count Anthony continued.

'When all this is considered, it seems impossible not to attach belief to the story of this lady's wrongs, which, moreover, I repeat, the Sire de Rhynsault admits, even if his admission may not go the length of the lady's own statement.' He paused. 'It is for your highness to pronounce,' he said.

Malevolently the ducal eye was pondering the crestfallen Governor of Middelburg.

'It is something,' he sneered at him, 'that you do not fling your other glove, or raise your voice again to bellow here of your knightly rank. As for that knightly rank of yours, which you derive from me, I tell you plainly that, unless you make reparation to this woman you confess to having wronged, your spurs shall be hacked off.'

Rhynsault's face turned grey. 'Reparation!' he faltered. 'Reparation, highness?'

'That is what I said. Reparation. Or else you lose your spurs and all further office in my service.' It was necessary, the Duke thought, other things apart, that this upstart, who presumed so readily, should realize that the hand that had made him could break him just as easily.

'What . . . what reparation does your highness suggest?' quoth the humbled bully.

'Nay, I'll make you no suggestions. Not I. It is for you to ply your wits, man.'

'What reparation can he make for such a wrong as that?' put in Count Anthony, betraying in his tone at least a little of the impatience that consumed him.

Rhynsault was almost in despair. 'I am eager to obey your highness,' he protested. 'That has ever been my endeavour.'

'Leave the past, my friend. Come to the future. You shall have until to-night to think about it. I'll waste no more time on you now. The audience waits. You have leave to go. But let me hear from you again before I sup.'

He waved him away. Rhynsault stumbled out, unuttered curses in his heart.

CHAPTER XXVIII

MARRIAGE BY PROXY

IT was, of course, the Fool, that unfailing mentor, who showed Rhynsault how to swim these difficult waters by which he was in danger of being submerged. Into the Fool's ear the browbeaten yet raging Rhynsault poured the tale of the events in the ducal closet.

'I warned you of the dangers of that reprieve,' Kuoni reminded him. 'See now in what peril you would be standing if Danvelt had not been hanged.'

'Fool, if he had not been hanged, there would be no peril at all, for there would have been no memorial.'

'Would there not? If you believe that you'ld believe anything.'

'I'll have no pertness,' Rhynsault warned him. 'I'm in no mood for it. The peril as it stands is grave enough.'

'This? Pooh!' The Fool was disdainful. 'To what does it amount? The loss of your spurs. You can grow another pair in time. But you could never have grown another head.'

'Leave that, and come to what's to be considered. What reparation can I offer that will quiet the Duke's humour?'

'The natural reparation: that which is accounted the reparation proper in such cases. You made the lady a widow. Make her a wife again, and the harm will be undone.'

'Do you mock me? Can I bring her husband back to life?'

'It isn't necessary to go to so much trouble, gossip. Provide her with another one.'

'Where shall I find him?' cried the exasperated Rhynsault.

The Fool looked at him, grinning silently awhile. Then he sighed and shook his head.

'Lord! How your wits need stirring! You'll have to execute yourself, of course.'

'Marry her, myself?' Rhynsault was round-eyed at that.

'What else? Isn't that the proper and complete reparation? The form of it in such cases that all the world approves? And, on my soul, you are to be felicitated. She's well favoured and said to be rich. The Duke must perforce approve such reparation as that. Behold your difficulties all solved for you, gossip. Am I not your good angel?'

'But . . .' Rhynsault broke off and fell to pondering; he grinned, his eyes twinkled; then his face lengthened again. 'There's one thing you've forgot.'

'Not I,' the Fool assured him with a deadly grimness that escaped him. 'I never forget anything.'

'What if she refuses to marry me, as well she may?'

'That is her affair and responsibility. Yours ends with the offer of reparation. If she declines it, shall the Duke blame you for that?'

'By Heaven, I believe you are right.'

'By Heaven, I agree with you.'

Rhynsault chuckled. He rubbed his hands. He laughed outright at the humour of the whole thing. And, oddly enough, so did the Duke when Rhynsault put the proposal to him that evening. His ducal rage had passed like a summer storm. He had been well pleased with his administration of justice in the course of the morning. This mellowed him. When Rhynsault came, humbly seeking audience in compliance with the order earlier received, the Duke was disposed to be lenient. Rhynsault had probably learnt his lesson in circumspection, and so that he could offer some reasonable amends which would absolve the Duke in the matter of the judgment passed and his word pledged, all would be well, and he need not lose a valuable servant and a very desirable governor for that stiff-necked city of Ghent.

But Count Anthony, who was present, did not laugh at all. He could not believe the proposal.

'You will marry her, do you say?' he asked incredulously.

'It's a great deal,' said Rhynsault, entirely mistaking the incredulity, 'and it's the best that I can offer. I offer it ungrudgingly. It is a proper reparation; indeed, the very fullest reparation for such wrong as I may have done her in a soldier's way.'

'In a soldier's way!' echoed Count Anthony, who with difficulty repressed the impulse to strike that impudent Lorrainer. He looked at the Duke for the answer, and the Duke returned his glance, the laugh still lingering on his countenance.

'It is, as he says, the best that he can offer, and it would generally be considered a reparation in full. We must be satisfied; and, indeed, I think it should content the lady.'

'Content her?' Count Anthony was white. His eyes glowed as if he had the fever. 'You dream that she will consent to this?'

'Why not? If she would consent to be his mistress, will she not consent to be his wife?'

Count Anthony was in despair. He perceived clearly enough that the Duke's rage, being spent, was considering only the value to himself of this Lorrainer, and out of that consideration desired to be rid of the whole affair. In this mood, the Count perceived, no justice was to be obtained. The Duke cared nothing for this woman's wrongs; cared nothing that among the traitors hanged in Walcheren one might have been innocent. All his earlier noble-seeming rage had been concerned with nothing but a breach of etiquette. A burgher more or less was of little account to the Duke, and not for a moment to be set in the balance against so valuable a servant as this upstart mercenary.

Suddenly, however, Count Anthony saw something else: saw what Kuoni had seen when out of his cruel humour he had sent Rhynsault upon this fool's errand of reparation by marriage. He saw where the Duke was in a cleft stick by virtue of the ducal word he had pledged that morning in his anger — that reparation should be made. If Johanna refused, as refuse she would, outraged by the very proposal, then the reparation that Rhynsault offered could not be made effective. He said so, and the Duke answered him with the false argument with which Kuoni had fooled his master.

'If she refuses, the matter is at an end.'

'Not so,' Count Anthony ventured to retort. 'You pledged your word that she should have reparation. In justice it follows that it must be such reparation as she will accept.'

The Duke was annoyed because he perceived the soundness of the argument and at the same time perceived that she might have unanswerable reasons for refusing reparation in this form.

'Will you tell me what is your interest in this woman, that you insist on pressing the matter to extremes?'

And Rhynsault's eyes echoed the Duke's question if his lips were prudently silent.

'This,' said Count Anthony, less than truthfully, and with his hand he struck the memorial which lay upon the table.

The Duke shrugged impatiently.

'I am concerned for your honour, Charles,' the Count continued. 'I will not have it dragged with impunity through kennels by any lieutenant of yours.'

'Of course, of course!' The Duke's peevishness increased. Then he took his resolve. 'Look now: for the moment we have gone far enough. It is not necessary to waste time in pursuing the matter further upon pure assumption. Adequate reparation is offered — adequate in my eyes, as it must be in the eyes of all the world, however the woman may regard it. I will indite my judgment thus. It shall be attached to the memorial, and so returned to her. If she accounts it inadequate, or unsuitable, let her name her alternative, and we will consider further. Meanwhile, I should advise her to be satisfied. Rhynsault, at least, has done his part.'

'But if . . .' the Count was beginning, when the Duke peremptorily cut him short.

'Enough! I'll waste no more time on this trumpery affair, which has become swollen out of all proportion to its significance. I have a mass of business claiming my attention, and but five days left in which to deal with it.' He called one of his secretaries. 'Set down my judgment.'

Count Anthony went out defeated, but not despairing. When Johanna's refusal came the matter must be reopened. Then would be his opportunity. Meanwhile, he burned with shame for her that such a proposal should be laid before her.

A ducal equerry attended by two lances drew up that evening at the Lion of Brabant, and dismounting came to deliver to Mistress Johanna in person her memorial, now bearing the ducal seal on the silk that bound it, informing her that the Duke's judgment was attached.

Trembling with eagerness, she broke the seal. The Sire de Chavaigny had been as good as his word; the Lord Almoner had been kindly disposed; justice was awarded her at last. Then she read the judgment and was on fire from head to foot.

'I asked for justice, and I am offered a lewd insult.'

'Madam!' The equerry was scandalized. 'That is not the way to speak of a judgment of his highness.'

'Convey my words to him,' she answered in a royal rage. 'Let him call me to account for them. Or let him punish me for my temerity if he chooses. I think I should prefer that to his favour, if this be the expression of it.'

'That, madam, is not a message of which I can be the bearer.'

'It is the message that I bid you bear; that I beg you to bear; every word of it. Or shall I set it down in writing?'

'If you insist that it should reach the Duke. But let me beg you to reflect, madam . . .'

'It needs no reflection. I have known too much shame and sorrow ever to know fear. I had looked to the Duke of Burgundy to lighten my burden, not shamefully to increase it.'

She found pen and ink and in the space below the Duke's seal and signature she quickly wrote her defiant repudiation of his judgment; this in no neat Italian hand like that of the memorial, but in a crabbed scrawl, the best her shaking fingers could accomplish.

When the Duke came to read it, his face turned purple. He sent for Count Anthony.

'This woman whom you choose to protect is insolent!' He tossed her writing to his cousin.

Count Anthony read and nodded. 'This is not insolence. It is righteous anger at a judgment which is accurately described for what it is — a lewd insult.'

It was rash of him. But his seething anger committed him to it. He was to regret it a moment later when he witnessed its effect, an effect which he should have foreseen.

'A lewd insult, is it?' Fiercely the Duke smote the table with his powerful fist. 'Call it what you will, it stands.'

'How can it, if she declines to be a party to it?'

'That is her affair.' And, fuming, he sent for Rhynsault.

'You mean that if she refuses this, she shall have nothing. What, then, becomes of your pledged word that she should receive reparation for what yourself you pronounced her wrong?'

'I have offered her, as from Rhynsault, reparation that I considered adequate. If she refuses it, is my pledge broken? You rant. I might offer her my ducal crown and my dominions in reparation, and she might refuse that. Should I then be forsworn?'

'What she wants . . .'

'I know what she wants,' the Duke snapped at him. 'The vindictive vixen wants Rhynsault's head. Well, it happens that I want it, myself; and I can't spare it her.'

Rhynsault came in, and was shown what she had written.

'My Grand Master argues,' said the Duke, still snorting in anger, 'that her refusal checkmates you along this line. What do you say to that, Rhynsault?'

Rhynsault mistook, as well he might, the source of the Duke's wrath. From what had been said earlier, he had feared this difficulty and its consequences to himself; also he had been successfully considering how to meet it should it indeed arise.

'It is no reason, highness, why I should not discharge the reparation I suggested and your highness imposed.'

'How can you, if she refuses to be a party to it?' quoth the Duke in the very words which he had lately had from Anthony.

'I could marry her by proxy.'

'By proxy?' The Duke was surprised and showed it, indeed, almost bewildered.

'If I did that,' said Rhynsault submissively, 'I should discharge my part of the obligation, and your judgment, Lord Duke, would be given effect.'

It took the Duke a moment to appreciate the situation. Slowly he stroked his shaven chin, sitting forward in his chair, one elbow on the table. Slowly his dark eyes kindled, and a smile curled the full lips of his prognathous mouth. That would be a keen retort upon the insufferable insolence of this Flemish beldame. At the same time it relieved him of his pledge, and made an end of this pestilent matter which already had engaged too much of his attention required by weightier affairs.

'Do so,' he said. 'Any serving-wench will serve your turn. Let it be done at once.'

'Charles!' Count Anthony was appalled.

'It is finished,' said the Duke peremptorily. He rose. His hand waved Rhynsault away, and Rhynsault bowing took his leave, to set about finding that serving-wench without delay.

'But have you considered that you go beyond your rights, beyond your powers?'

'Beyond my rights?' It was news to the Duke of Burgundy that any limits could be set upon his rights.

'You place this unfortunate and suffering woman under the authority and at the mercy of this man. You prescribe a compulsory marriage. It is a thing illegal.'

'Not if I have pronounced it. I am the law.'

His jaw was set, his eyes hard as they looked into his cousin's, and Anthony, knowing his obstinacy, knew that it would be worse than vain to seek to move him now.

He said no more. He had need to be alone, to think, to devise some means of saving Johanna from all the horror which this forced marriage must imply. If all else failed, he must give Rhynsault the trial by battle which once the Lorrainer had had the temerity to claim. But not only was it repugnant to him to meet on equal terms so base a creature as Rhynsault; there was the danger that he might be slain in the encounter. It was not the peril to life that daunted him. He would cast away his life, his rank, his very honour, to serve Johanna in an extremity to which he himself had so largely had a hand in bringing her. But if he were slain, she would be utterly at the mercy of Rhynsault, and of a Rhynsault immeasurably strengthened in his position towards her by a husband's rights. It was unthinkable, an intolerable thought. There was no issue that way.

He considered seeking Johanna, and taking counsel with her. But he was restrained by instinctive knowledge of her aversion to receiving him, by the conviction that it would give her pain to discover that it was he and not the Lord Almoner who had borne her memorial to the Duke, and that his endeavours on her behalf had brought upon her a horror almost as great as any that she had already undergone.

In the end he sat down to torment his soul once again by the perusal of that terrible memorial. Thereafter he was lost in thought for a time. At last, after some hesitation, he sent a page in quest of the Sire de Chavaigny.

The captain came at once, leaving his supper in his solicitude to wait upon the Grand Master.

'May I depend upon your silence, Messire de Chavaigny?' the Count asked him.

The captain gave the required protestation.

'Because this is a matter in which my name must not appear.' And he proceeded to it. 'You interested yourself, I understand, in Mistress Johanna Danvelt to the extent of seeking your uncle the Almoner's interest in her memorial. She has reason to believe that this interest brought the memorial to the Duke's hands. Considering the result to her, your credit may not stand as high as it might. Still of your good intentions she may be persuaded; and, so, disposed to trust you yet again. Represent yourself as still acting on your uncle's behalf and endeavour to obtain from Mistress Johanna the original of this document.' He showed the captain the copy of the reprieve which was attached to the memorial. 'She may be reluctant to part with it. But do your best to induce her, by assuring her — mark this well — that your uncle, chagrined at the deplorable miscarriage of his hopes on her behalf, desires to make yet an attempt to obtain a modification of the judgment his highness has pronounced.'

Her reluctance proved less than Count Anthony had feared. Word had been sent her of the final decision taken, and that, despite her refusal to marry Rhynsault, the marriage was nevertheless to take place, by proxy. With her indignation at this mockery had come utter despair. She had waited in vain through all these weary months, comforted herself in vain with the thought of a just vengeance. There was, as the Fool had told her, no justice on this earth save such as could be purchased. Oh, the Fool knew his world, was justified of his cynicism and of the evil tools with which he worked and which he sought to thrust on others. But not on that account could she be guided by his advice even to the extent of seeking the intervention of Count Anthony in her affairs.

Nothing now remained for her but departure. She would return to Flushing, realize so much of her property as she could, and remove herself beyond the dominions of the Duke of Burgundy; she would go to France, perhaps, anywhere where she would be secure at least from the further persecutions which she rightly apprehended from Rhynsault's brutality, now that it was about to be legalized by the Duke's judgment and sanctified by Holy Church.

Thus it happened that the Sire de Chavaigny found her in the act of packing.

His errand gave her pause. Was there yet a hope? Was Heaven, through the instrumentality of my Lord Cardinal, to assist her, after all? The reprieve, that original document to which she had clung so tenaciously as the culminating piece of evidence against Rhynsault, was readily surrendered. It was her last stake. If it were lost now, no matter, since all else was lost.

Bidding her be yet of good heart, the young captain went his ways.

Count Anthony thanked him with a warmth which in Chavaigny's opinion far exceeded the trivial service he had rendered, pledged him to secrecy again, and so dismissed him.

Nevertheless, two days later, on the Wednesday of that week so very fateful to several of the actors in this tragi-comedy, the Sire de Rhynsault led to the altar in Saint Gudule's a waiting-maid of the Duchess Margaret's, who stood proxy for Johanna, the widow of Philip Danvelt, whom the Sire Claude de Rhynsault, Governor and Ducal Lieutenant of Middelburg, took to wife in compliance with a ducal mandate.

The Fool, who was present, was bewildered. Somewhere the machinery which he had set in motion had become jammed. This great blundering numbskull of a Rhynsault was breaking easily through all the snares Kuoni had so cunningly laid.

Mistress Johanna, who was informed of it, took fright, and again prepared to go. But again the captain of archers came to wait upon her with another message from the Lord Almoner, to the effect that all was not yet done.

That night Rhynsault made merry in his apartments, celebrating, with some improvised guests and some of the lesser nobles of the court, his brideless nuptials and his safe deliverance from what might have proved a nasty snare. He was elated above all because assured by an approving

clap upon the shoulder from the Duke when he returned from
church that his highness bore him no resentment and had
not in any way diminished his intentions concerning him.
Marrying might have few attractions for a man of the Lorrainer's mettle. But if a man must be forced into it, he could
have little grounds for complaint when he found himself the
husband of the wealthiest woman in Zealand and probably
the most beautiful. Having married her, it remained for
him to woo her. He would prove no laggard there, and he
would stand no nonsense.

Nevertheless, a laggard he did prove perforce for three
days more. The best part of two of these days was taken up
with labours connected with the governorship of Ghent, to
which, to his immense satisfaction, he was now definitely
appointed under the Duke's seal. There were voluminous
instructions to be received. And the ducal secretaries for
two whole days addled his brains with the contents of a
mountain of parchments. The governorship of Ghent, he
realized, was a very different affair from that of Friesland or
even Zealand.

There were legal questions, financial questions, commer-
cial questions, municipal questions, even ambassadorial
questions, and many others in which it imported that the
Governor should be instructed.

On Friday there was a banquet given by the Duke on the
eve of his departure, to which Rhynsault was bidden, and in
which he cut a figure of some importance. And then at last,
on Saturday morning early, the Duke took his departure for
the North, leaving Count Anthony as Grand Master of
Burgundy to act as his deputy in all matters until his return.

Having witnessed the pomp and circumstance of that departure and of the Duke's attendant train which was almost
of the proportions of an army, Rhynsault went to complete
his own preparations for quitting Brussels, intending that
very day to set out for Ghent, and there relieve the Deputy-
Governor, who was meanwhile discharging the duties of the
office.

These preparations were to include his wife, of course. And so at about noon, which would be some four hours after the Duke had left, Rhynsault, with a couple of attendants and followed by a horse-litter intended for the conveyance of the lady, presented himself at the Lion of Brabant, and in his big voice loudly demanded to be conducted to the Lady Johanna de Rhynsault. Before the obsequious and intimidated host would conduct him, it was necessary for him to add that he meant the lady who lately had been known as Johanna Danvelt.

His descent upon her was as the fall of a thunderbolt from a clear sky.

She was seated at her window in that long, low-ceilinged chamber, wondering what hope could be left now that the Duke was gone, yet desperately clinging to such hope as she could find in the last message borne to her by the Sire de Chavaigny and the fact that since then there had been no word from the Lord Almoner.

She heard without heeding the heavy ascending tread upon the stairs and the clank of a scabbard against the rails. Without knock, or by-your-leave, her door was flung open.

She turned sharply in her surprise, and there upon the threshold she beheld the Sire de Rhynsault, a magnificent figure filling the narrow doorway, his tall, vigorous body decked in scarlet, a heavy chain of gold upon his breast. His sleek black head was slightly inclined, his full lips smiled upon her not without a hint of derision, and there was an odious terrifying gleam in his bold blue eyes.

'Madam wife,' said he, and bowed a little. Then he entered, and closed the door upon the startled face of the landlord, who had followed him.

In retrospect to her afterwards that entrance was like an evil dream, and, whilst the horror it had inspired in her remained vivid, the details of it were obscured as by a mist. Frozen in that horror she remained seated, staring at him, her face piteously white.

'Well, madam,' said he. 'Have you no greeting for me?'

He advanced upon her. To her startled eyes his proportions seemed to increase as he advanced. He was like a mountain, a scarlet, fiery mountain toppling irresistibly over to crush out her life under its vast bulk.

To shake off that nightmare spell was an effort demanding every ounce of her strength. She sprang up at last, and back from him until she stood with her shoulders squarely to the window-panes.

His great hands took her by those shoulders, and drew her relentlessly to him, a leer on his big handsome face. He kissed her, and she suffered it, paralyzed by terror. Through her mind reverberated as if on the note of some great bell the word 'Betrayed!' She had been cheated again, either by the smooth-spoken Sire de Chavaigny, or else by the Lord Almoner himself. Their interest, their assurances had been a lure to hold her there at this monster's disposal, when but for her trust in those betrayers she would have found safety in flight whilst yet there was time.

He held her at arm's length, and considered her critically, his head on one side.

'You lack responsiveness, madam wife. But that will follow. At least it will follow if you value your ease and my good will. If not . . . But let that be at present.' He took his hands from her shoulders. 'I have a litter awaiting you below. If you will come with me now, your servants may follow with your packages.'

Before her eyes the scarlet bulk of him shrank and swelled alternately. She was on the point of swooning. Yet such was her spirit that it conquered at least the weakness of her body. She found her voice.

'I will not come with you.'

'Not come with me?' He laughed. 'You are my wife. I wedded you on Wednesday, though you lacked the grace yourself to be present. But my wife you are, and you shall practise wifely obedience. So come, madam. We ride to Ghent, where you are to fill the proud place of Governor's lady.'

'I will not come with you. I am not your wife. This is a mockery. A woman may not be wed against her will.'

'The facts contradict you, sweetheart. Married you are, and, if you've not had the will to it hitherto, you'll be wise to find it for the future.' There was a minatory note tempering the laughter in his voice.

'I will not,' she reiterated. She was almost frenzied. Bitterly now she regretted the qualms which had prevented her from sending an appeal to Count Anthony. Better he should know her shame, bitter though that thought of his knowledge must be to her, than that she should thus lie now at Rhynsault's mercy.

'Come, come,' he growled. 'No tantrums. I'm a man of short moods. You'll need to remember it if you would live at peace with me. We ride to Ghent, mistress. Come!'

He caught her by the wrist, and half-turning attempted to drag her after him. But she resisted with all her strength. He let her go again. He was angry now. He planted his feet squarely, set his arms akimbo, and thus confronted her.

'Pay heed, Johanna!' he admonished her. 'I have married you by no desire of my own in the first instance. A memorial which you sent the Duke, and upon the matter of which you and I may yet come to have a word or two, placed me under the necessity of this. But having married you, I mean you well so that you prove submissive. If you do not so prove of your own inclination, you shall come to prove it by other means. There is no sense in struggling against bonds from which you can gain no deliverance. If you do not like your nuptial fetters, you have only yourself to blame for them. You have brought this upon yourself, my girl. You should have held your peace, and left the past behind you. Enough said! We will go now or else . . . never mind that. I am not one to threaten. I perform without warning, as you'll discover. So come, I say, and I say it for the last time.'

She stood leaning against the table, looking at him, but making no movement to obey, and answering no word.

Steps sounded upon the stairs, and again the clank of a scabbard against the rails.

He jerked a thumb backward over his shoulder in the direction of the door. 'You hear? Those are my knaves. They'll carry you to your litter, however you may kick and scream, and you'll find them rough tirewomen. Better come of your own accord.'

The door behind him opened. He wheeled impatiently at that, speaking as he turned.

'Who bade you . . .' he checked. He was looking at the Sire de Chavaigny. Behind the captain on the landing, Rhynsault caught a gleam of steel from the headpieces of three or four archers. 'What the devil do you want here?' he asked, his anger blended with astonishment. He was to be more astonished still.

'I am seeking your excellency.'

'Seeking me? For what purpose?'

'To arrest you, sir.'

It was a moment before his excellency found his voice. 'To arrest me? To arrest me?' This was utterly incredible. 'Are you mad?'

'My orders are quite clear. Your sword, sir!' And the captain held out his gloved hand to receive it.

'But I am even now about to ride on the Duke's business to Ghent, of which I am Governor. This is some error.'

'If it is, the error is not mine, my lord.' And again he said: 'Your sword!'

But he would not yet surrender it, could not yet believe that he was not dreaming.

'But in God's name, with what am I charged?'

'With high treason, excellency.'

'High . . .' He choked. Then he recovered, and drew himself up stiffly. 'Upon whose orders do you act?'

'Orders of the Grand Master of Burgundy. Come, sir, you must not keep us waiting. Your sword, if you please, and let us go.'

Behind Rhynsault a woman's laugh was heard. To Johanna, rendered faintly hysterical for the relief of this eleventh-hour intervention, it seemed that the scene which lately had been played between Rhynsault and herself was being repeated; but now Rhynsault was in the rôle he had forced on her. Just as reluctant was he to obey this invitation to depart as she had been when he had similarly pressed her.

He turned upon her in a fury. 'It amuses you, you . . .?' he rasped at her.

'Come, sir, come!' Chavaigny was peremptory. 'Else my knaves must handle you.'

'Even that!' she said, white to the lips, her eyes glowing like live coals. 'Even that! Now will you believe in God, Sire de Rhynsault?'

He stayed to sneer at her. 'Laugh your fill, madam wife. You shall have more to laugh at when I've squelched this trumpery charge under my heel. The Duke shall make this Grand Master of his sorry for himself before all's done.'

Out of patience, Chavaigny stood aside and signalled to his men. They tramped in, laid hands upon the Sire de Rhynsault, and thrust him violently out, raging and blaspheming obscenely at this fresh indignity.

CHAPTER XXIX

JUDGMENT

THE Grand Master of Burgundy was well aware of the dangerous game to which he set his hand the moment the Duke's back was turned. And so was M. de Chavaigny when the Grand Master sent for him to be his instrument.

'You will take what men you need, sir,' Count Anthony had instructed him, 'and you will at once proceed to the quarters of the Sire de Rhynsault, or wherever else he is to be found, and place him under arrest. The charge against him, should he require to know it, will be high treason.'

The Sire de Chavaigny looked grave. The Grand Master proceeded.

'You will see to it that from the moment he is in your hands he is allowed to communicate with no one, and, above all, to send no messages. I ask your strictest adherence to these instructions.'

The Sire de Chavaigny bowed stiffly.

'Will your lordship set them down for me in your own hand?'

A smile lighted Count Anthony's pale face, which in this last week had grown haggard. 'I see that you understand,' he said. And added: 'It is done already. I commit no one to responsibility for actions that are mine.' He took up a paper from his table, and handed it to the captain. The captain scanned it, bowed, and withdrew to go upon that startling errand.

Rhynsault stormed and blustered from the moment of his arrest until he found himself back in the main room of his quarters at the palace, where he was informed that he would for the present be confined. He demanded to send messages. He was denied. He announced that his messages were for the Duke, that a courier must be sent after him at once, and

he dared any man to risk the consequences of the Duke's
subsequent anger were this refused him. But Chavaigny,
secure and immune from any consequences by virtue of the
clear written orders under which he acted, left the Governor
of Ghent to rage impotently alone, deprived of all personal
attendants, and under a strong guard.

Over Sunday he continued there, visited only by those
who brought him food and drink, and even these were not
his ordinary attendants, but archers who were appointed to
the service, and who never came singly, and were never
twice the same, so that Rhynsault could not address himself to corrupting or bribing them.

On Monday morning at the early hour of eight, it was
announced to him by the Sire de Chavaigny that his judges
waited. Cowed now, and even a little scared, chiefly because he could not see clearly the line by which it was sought
to establish this preposterous charge of high treason, he
suffered himself to be conducted.

The trial was to be held in the great hall of the palace,
where the Duke himself dispensed justice, and a bruit of
what was to take place there that morning having already
gone abroad despite the Sire de Chavaigny's precautions,
there was already a goodly attendance when the great ducal
lieutenant, who had been cutting so brave a figure during
the last few days in Brussels, who was pointed out as a man
whom the Duke honoured, was brought by his guards
within the barrier.

Thither, too, in response to a summons brought her by a
poursuivant, came Mistress Johanna, attended by her servants and followed by that train of friendly witnesses from
Middelburg supported by her here in Brussels at her own
charges.

She came in awe; almost with reluctance. There was an
ordeal ahead of her far sterner than any for which she had
been prepared, in that she must now meet the eyes of Count
Anthony with the knowledge that he was informed of all the
grounds of her bitter, shameful plaint. The Fool had visited

her last night, and had resolved for her any perplexities which the sudden turn of events might hold for her.

'It looks,' he had said, 'as if I might be out of employment soon. I am to suffer this because I am an altruist. What you would not do for yourself, Mistress Johanna, it was necessary that I should do for you. Your Lord Almoner throughout has been as somnolently indifferent as I predicted. I practised a deception on you, madam. Your friend at court has been my Lord Anthony of Guelders from the moment that I brought the matter to his notice. I have a notion that he, too, may be out of employment soon. You shall presently behold in him, as in me, the reward of virtue. Since we are altruists both, and poets both with a full sense of the poetic, Count Anthony and I might get on very well together. If he should need a Fool, I shall certainly need a master. As a reward, when they present you with Rhynsault's head upon a charger, perhaps you will use your good offices with the Count on my behalf.'

If she began by being vexed with him for the part he had played, he soon dissolved that vexation in the reminder that but for that same duplicity of his she would by now be on her way to Ghent as the Governor's lady.

She came, then, fully informed of the steps by which the present situation had been reached. The poursuivant who conducted her led her with her attendants and her witnesses within the barriers, and found a seat for her on the benches ranged there. On the topmost of these benches, which ascended in three tiers at right angles with the dais, the Fool had perched himself, an expectant spectator.

The judges, four of them, were already in their places, two on each side of the dais. At a table below and a little to one side sat four clerkly fellows preparing their quills. A pikeman, in corselet and headpiece, his halbert ordered, stood at each of the four corners of the enclosure. Others were ranged at intervals down the two sides of the hall to keep order among the people.

Came a flourish of trumpets such as usually announced

the advent of the Duke, and all heads were bared in the great hall. Johanna's eyes were raised to the doorway immediately facing her whence the four tabarded trumpeters had issued and on either side of which they had ranged themselves to deliver their fanfare.

Through this doorway came first the Sire de Chavaigny, closely followed by four archers of the guard; after these came a herald bearing the sword of state, and then in a robe of cloth of gold, such as the Duke wore on these occasions, a flat bonnet of scarlet velvet on his head, pale and stern, the Grand Master of Burgundy emerged. His eyes, meeting Johanna's as he entered, lighted suddenly, and as suddenly were veiled. Calmly and slowly he passed to his high seat on the dais, two archers following to range themselves behind him, immediately under the great escutcheon bearing the Burgundian arms.

He looked at Chavaigny, who stood waiting before him at the foot of the dais. His voice, that clear, melodious voice the memory of which had ever haunted Johanna's ears, rang through the silent hall.

'Bring in the Sire Claude de Rhynsault, Ducal Lieutenant and Governor of Ghent.' Thus he gave the prisoner in full the new title which had been to him so great a source of pride.

They brought him in, still wearing the magnificent scarlet suit in which he had been arrested, but with his bearing shorn of much of its habitual magnificence. He had neglected to shave that morning, which increased the haggard look of a man who for two nights had known little sleep; this as a result of rage rather than of fear.

'Read him the indictment,' the Grand Master commanded.

A clerk rose at the table, and in a nasal, whining voice discharged that duty. It was not quite what the Sire de Rhynsault had expected, and there was a quality in it which shook the assurance which hitherto had fully sustained him, awoke the alarm from which hitherto he had been immune.

There was no question, as he had so confidently supposed, of rejudging the case of Philip Danvelt by establishing Danvelt's innocence, impeaching his judge for careless administration of justice, and for excluding evidence which, fully as available then as now, should certainly have been admitted. The indictment was framed upon quite other lines. Danvelt's guilt was assumed, accepted on the man's own confession without any question as to how it might have been extorted. Indeed, the assumption of his guilt was actually made the corner-stone of the present charge. The Sire de Rhynsault's offence was made to lie in the fact that he had subverted to his own ends the Duke's justice, by reprieving a man whose guilt of treason he accounted fully established by the evidence upon which he had sentenced him to death, since otherwise it was inconceivable that he could so have sentenced him. To this was added the comparatively minor charge of his having neglected to proceed as by law required to the confiscation of the property of a man convicted of treason and by that neglect having defrauded the Duke's revenues.

As the clerk finished the reading and was resuming his seat, Rhynsault bounded up and bellowed out his answer, so that he could be heard to the hall's end.

'This is a judged affair,' he protested angrily, froth upon his lips. 'It is judged and closed and finished by the Duke's highness in person. And I challenge your authority to re-open it. You are abusing your office, sir, in the Duke's absence. I answered all points which the Duke saw proper to raise upon this matter, and answered them to his full satisfaction, as you well know, sir.'

Very calmly the Grand Master answered him: 'My Lord of Rhynsault, it was not yet my intention to come to that, although come to it in the end I must. But if you rest your defence upon it, I am content to proceed along the line you are opening.'

'I do rest my defence upon it. His highness has pronounced in this matter, and it is closed.'

'A matter that is closed by a false statement may be reopened at any time when the truth becomes apparent. The Duke's highness, as you correctly state, closed this matter upon receiving your clear denial that you had granted this reprieve, a denial backed by your knightly word. You will remember that.'

'I do remember it. I am relieved that your lordship does the same. I ask myself, this being so, why you presume to molest me in this manner and to drag me here to be questioned again.'

'It is because, sir, since you uttered that denial to the Duke, certain further knowledge has reached me which makes it clear that by that denial you abused the Duke's confidence and his trust in the knightly word which you had pledged. It is upon this further knowledge that the present indictment has been drawn. In this I proceed as I must suppose the Duke himself would proceed had he remained to learn what I have learnt.'

'Had he remained, you would never have dared . . .'

'Shall we keep to the indictment?' He was of a most exquisite courtesy in meeting the deliberate rudeness of the accused. 'Do you maintain here the defence you made before the Duke? Do you persist in the denial that you granted this reprieve to a convicted traitor?'

'I answer now as I answered then: the man was hanged. That is answer enough. How could he have been hanged if I reprieved him? The charge is ludicrous. The facts destroy it. You speak of abuse of the Duke's trust. I would beg you, Grand Master, and you, sirs' — he swept the judges with his fierce eyes — 'to beware how far you abuse that same trust, yourselves.'

'I will answer your question, sir,' the Grand Master replied, ignoring all else that Rhynsault had said. 'How this man came to be hanged notwithstanding the reprieve is a matter not to be cleared up without seeking more evidence than we possess at present. But,' he continued, impressively and surprisingly at least in the ears of Rhynsault, 'that matter is not of great importance; indeed, hardly relevant. The existence of the reprieve is a full proof of the intention; and in matters connected with treason, as I need not explain to you, who are yourself a justiciary, the intent is as punishable as the act itself.'

Rhynsault was utterly contemptuous, in his confidence that all this was mere bluster, based upon a faith attached to the copy of the reprieve which formed part of the memorial.

'The existence of the reprieve might do that,' said he, a thought too rashly in his arrogance. 'But where is this reprieve?'

The answer took his breath away. 'I have it here.' And the Grand Master displayed a sheet of parchment, which his hand had held from the moment he had entered the hall. He turned to the judges. 'You had best examine it for yourselves, sirs.'

Whilst it was being passed round and scanned, there was a murmur of excitement in the hall. These proceedings grew interesting as a puppet show.

Rhynsault's face changed colour. Stupidly he had never supposed that the original had survived. He had imagined it handed to Diesenhofen by Mistress Johanna on that fatal October morning, and he had been careless — culpably, stupidly careless, as he now perceived — in not making sure of it afterwards. Then he took heart again. He was starting at shadows. This was no such ponderous matter, after all.

He stood up. 'May I see this document which I am said to have signed?'

'Not merely signed, sir; the whole of it is written in your hand. Let him see it for himself, M. de Chavaigny.'

The captain brought it to him, and held it under his eyes. This was the document, indeed. He took the only possible line. 'That is not my hand!' he blustered. 'An impudent forgery vindictively prepared to . . .'

'Messire de Rhynsault!' So impressive was the Grand Master's voice and raised hand that the Lorrainer fell silent to listen. 'Is it worth your while to perjure yourself further?

There will be men in plenty in Middelburg who know your hand. There are two within this hall at this instant, who can swear to it: your Fool and the Burgomaster of Middelburg. In addition, I could bring an officer of your own to swear not only that this reprieve is in your hand, but the very circumstances in which it was presented to him, which will hardly leave a doubt as to how it came to be issued by you. Is it worth while? Shall I call these present witnesses? If you persist in denial, I must. But let me remind you that the only consequence will be to bring you into increased contempt.'

Rhynsault did not need the reminder. He perceived it clearly enough. Perceived that he was snared. His Fool he could not trust; there was no knowing which way that ape might jump. The nature of the Burgomaster's testimony was certain, and the truth would easily be wrung out of Diesenhofen. But in what, after all, was he snared? Why, in a cobweb that a gesture of his could destroy. He made that gesture without further thought. The Grand Master who pursued him so relentlessly might desire to convict him upon these trumpery grounds. But it was beyond his power to do so without the agreement of the judges, and not by such paltry means as those at his command could he ever sway them to move against a man whom all the world knew to be honoured by the Duke.

'Bah!' he cried. 'I will not waste your time. It is possible that I wrote this thing. I had forgotten it — an easy matter considering the pressure of ducal business in those days when I worked unremittingly to stamp out treason in the province entrusted to me. His highness is well aware of my labours. It is because of them that he has graciously promoted me to the governorship of Ghent. Will you, sirs, venture to punish me for deeds which his highness rewards?'

'This, sir, is not one of those deeds, as you well know.'

'But can you suppose that this one trivial affair is to be set by his highness against all the other deeds of mine which have so stoutly served him?' He was contemptuous.

'To suppose otherwise would be treason in itself, since it
would assume that his highness dispenses justice not according to the laws of which he is the custodian, but according to
his own caprice.'

'I said not that!' cried Rhynsault. He was alarmed to see
how his words were being twisted, and this so as to impress
the judges who were sagely nodding their approval of the
Grand Master's construction.

'Not consciously,' Count Anthony agreed. 'But it is the
meaning of your words when they are properly interpreted.
Let us, however, keep to the facts, and leave argument until
afterwards. I understand you, then, to acknowledge this reprieve to be in your own hand.'

Rhynsault shrugged. 'I have already answered you on
that.' And he added insolently: 'You may make the most
of it.'

The Grand Master eased at last the stiffness of his pose,
and sat back, lounging a little in his great gilded chair of
state. He seemed to imply by this that the work was done,
the matter at an end. The Fool, watching him intently with
his beady eyes, missing no word that he uttered, and fully
aware of the tripping cords which each of his utterances had
supplied for Rhynsault, admired the only wits he had ever
seen at work which could compare with his own. Johanna,
stealing glances now and again at Count Anthony, marvelled
at his impassivity and the silky suavity of his voice, and
knew that here an avenger had arisen for her wrongs whom
nothing could resist.

He addressed the judges. 'Sirs, the Sire de Rhynsault is
to be commended, at least, in that he has not put it upon us
to protract this trial beyond what is strictly necessary. You
have heard his admission that he uttered this reprieve upon
a man whom he had convicted of high treason, and in view
of his admission, it is for you, who are men of law, to say
whether the indictment charging the Sire de Rhynsault
with high treason has been justified. I will limit myself
with indicating the point of law upon which the indictment

has been based. It runs, I think — if I am wrong, sirs, it is for you to set me right — it runs that he who comforts, shelters, nourishes, aids, or sustains, however lightly, a man convicted by a competent tribunal of the odious crime of high treason, is himself guilty of that odious crime, and is to be accounted the accomplice of the man convicted and to suffer in the same degree.' He paused, and looked to right and left of him. 'Is that interpretation of the law correct?'

'It is, Grand Master,' each answered him in turn.

'It would appear, then, to be beyond dispute that a man who misuses the powers of his gubernatorial office to grant a reprieve to a convicted traitor must be held to have given aid to that traitor in the highest possible degree, and therefore to have rendered himself the man's accomplice and thus, himself, become guilty of high treason. I say only that it would appear so, because after all it is for you, who are to speak to the law, to say whether in effect it is so or not. That is what I now invite you to consider.'

Their consideration was a brief one, their answer unanimously that the law of the matter was clear, and the Grand Master's application of it to the particular case under consideration unanswerable.

The Sire de Rhynsault's face became the colour of lead, and the sweat stood in beads upon his brow, for all that it was chill within that hall.

'In that case, we need not concern ourselves about the lesser matter of the guilty neglect to confiscate the property of the convicted traitor. That is an omission which his successor in the governorship of Zealand may amend. Your decision, then, upon the question of law, amounts to a finding that the prisoner is guilty of the high treason with which the indictment charges him?'

He put it interrogatively, and the senior of the four judges rose in his place to answer him.

'That, Grand Master, is indubitably our finding. But we would urge on the prisoner's behalf that which he, himself, has not forgotten to urge: that against this misdemeanour, of which he is guilty, should be weighed the zealous services which he rendered the Duke's highness during his governorship of Zealand.'

Rhynsault took heart again at that. These judges, after all, were not quite so rash and reckless as the Grand Master. He leaned forward in his consuming and fearful anxiety.

Very quietly came from Count Anthony the question: 'Have you ever, in all your vast juridical experience, sir, known services of whatever magnitude to be permitted to weigh against the heinous sin of treason?'

'I confess, Grand Master, that I have not.'

'What reason, then, can you have for urging the services admittedly rendered by the Sire de Rhynsault?'

'Not a reason so much as the recollection of the high esteem in which the Sire de Rhynsault is held by the Duke's highness. Remembering this, we do, whilst delivering judgment upon the particular action submitted to us, respectfully but earnestly enjoin your lordship that this judgment of ours be laid before the Duke himself so that his highness may pronounce upon it.'

Count Anthony smiled upon the venerable senior judge. 'Your respect and your earnestness are not lost upon me, worthy sir. But in this injunction you transcend, I think, the functions of your office. It is for you to speak to the law, and to this you have spoken with your accustomed wisdom. To the rest it is for me to speak, and I do so with a full sense of my responsibility as the Duke's Vicegerent.'

He paused, but already the Sire de Rhynsault perceived the doom descending upon him, and was too appalled to speak, too appalled even to curse himself for the readiness with which he had acknowledged that reprieve. He should have denied, and denied, and so made delays. Then he found the beautiful sombre eyes of his judge directed fully upon him. But he saw no beauty in them. He saw only remorselessness, belying the gentle tones of the voice that reached him in that hushed and breathless place.

'Claude de Rhynsault,' the voice said, addressing him now

as felons are addressed without the courtesy of any title, 'you have heard the finding of the judges, which convicts you of the high treason for which you have been indicted. To what they have uttered it is not my wish to add more than your case makes strictly necessary. High treason is not an offence that has ever been regarded at any time or in any country with any leniency, for of all offences it is the most dangerous to the state and the most contagious. Therefore, and as you, yourself, no doubt felt when you passed sentence of death upon Philip Danvelt, it is the duty of those who sit in the seat of justice to extirpate it effectively wherever met. To an offence already in itself the greatest, you have added in this case a singular and unusual heinousness, not to be condoned by God or man.' He said this slowly, incisively, so that its inner meaning — not apparent to the general public — should cut deeply into the understanding of Rhynsault. 'You have abused the powers with which the Duke's highness invested you, and defiled the sacred trust imposed upon you by your office. In short, you have made a harlot of the Duke's justice, to serve aims and purposes of your own.' He paused for a full moment to let that phrase sink home. Then he continued: 'What those aims and purposes may have been, we do not now inquire, since the knowledge could not possibly extenuate your offence, and its further aggravation is not necessary to the ends of justice. But in your heart you will know them, Rhynsault, and whatever they may have been, I can but urge you now to seek the clemency of God, for the clemency of man is by the law denied you.'

He reached for the hour-glass, standing on the pulpit by his side, the upper bulb of which was empty.

'To seek that divine clemency, you shall have one hour. When these sands are run, the sentence which I am now to pass upon you shall be executed. You are to be taken to the great square, and there in public your spurs shall be struck off and you shall be degraded from your knightly rank, and after that your head shall be severed from your body.'

An audible shiver ran through the hushed press in that great hall, as if a gust of wind had stirred through it. The Grand Master reversed the hour-glass and set it down upon the little table. Then he stood up to depart, and all who were seated rose. At last the awed silence was broken by the voice of Rhynsault, hoarse, and clamant, the man himself restrained by the guards who clung to his arms and held him back from hurling himself forward in his frenzy. His voice rose almost to a scream. He threatened them with the vengeance of the Duke if they dared to execute that sentence; he demanded the right to appeal to the Duke in person.

The Grand Master, already moving on his stately way from the dais, paused, and raised his hand for silence. Rhynsault checked, that he might listen, wildly hoping that his threats might have intimidated that rash justiciary.

'The sentence I have passed upon you,' he said, 'has been passed with the Duke's voice. For here I speak for the Duke as you spoke for him in Middelburg when you passed sentence there.'

More than his words, the look in his eyes bore Rhynsault the assurance that it was no earthly judgment, but the judgment of God which had overtaken him.

CHAPTER XXX

BANISHMENT

RHYNSAULT was gone, dragged out by the men-at-arms. The Grand Master had departed with his judges and attendants. The hall was emptying, and still Johanna sat, a woman entranced, her hands folded, her eyes almost vacant. Her servants and her friendly witnesses waited aloof.

Over the benches behind her the Fool climbed down from the high place whence he had viewed the show. His voice came sibilantly into her ear to rouse her.

'Not Solomon in all his glory was more beautiful, more poetical, or more just than the Grand Master of Burgundy. To be sentenced to death by such a man was more than my Lord Rhynsault deserved, and certainly more than he had the wit to appreciate.'

She looked round upon the hunchback, like one who awakens. 'Do you mock even now?'

'I do not mock, madam. I exult. I glory and delight in the splendour of the Grand Master. Compared with him, I am but a common trickster. He fooled them all to his own ends, Rhynsault, the judges, and the law itself, and he may even fool the Duke when the Duke comes to ask him to render an account of this day's work. Oh, it was all magnificently done, and all in your honour, madam. You may take pride in the thought.'

'Pride!' said she.

'Satisfaction at least, then.'

'Satisfaction? What satisfaction is there in vengeance? It is Dead-Sea fruit. It crumbles to ashes when it is grasped. It cannot restore; it cannot repair.'

'Lord! And this after all you laboured to obtain it! You are hard to please, madam.'

Considering him, she shook her head, and he saw that

there were tears in her eyes. She drew a purse, a heavy, well-filled purse, from the scrip at her girdle, and proffered it. 'You have served me well, after your own fashion. God alone knows why, considering what you are or what you pretend to be.'

He recoiled, a stricken look leaping to his unhealthy face. He had served her well! He! It came to him now that he was the author of all her woes, all done in wantonness from sheer love of evil. For the first time in all his life he was ashamed of his own vileness, and knew not why, knew not what withered chord of righteousness had suddenly been touched to life within his soul by her. But her gold he would not take, not though the imminent loss of his master must cast him adrift upon the world.

The habits of a lifetime supplied him with an explanation.

'I take no payment for my work beyond the payment I have had already in laughter over the pricking of that fool's bubble who was to be Governor of Ghent. Give your gold to the poor. I am rich, for I lack nothing. God save you, madam! I must hurry if I would secure a good place to see the fall of an empty head.'

And with a bow which his shape alone rendered fantastic, he was gone.

She followed soon. From the window of her room in the Lion of Brabant she saw the great crowd come flocking down the street, as she sat there a little later. They were returning, she knew, from the show provided by the execution of Rhynsault, and it occurred to her that for the second time in her young life she was a widow, she who had never really been a wife.

A little later still, a tall, cloaked figure came striding down the street and across the threshold of the inn. Presently a knock fell upon her door, and when it opened in answer to her bidding, the tall figure stood there under the lintel, the cloak now loosened, the head bare. She fell to trembling violently, as with a half-stifled cry she rose from her window-seat.

Count Anthony advanced. Her eyes devoured his face, noted its haggard look, and the lines that had crept into its young comeliness since last she had beheld it at close quarters on that August night in the garden of the Gravenhof, when she defeated temptation in a battle which he had scarcely suspected.

He stood before her, smiling gravely, sadly. It seemed impossible to her that he should know all and still stand thus before her, still smile thus upon her. Then he spoke, and his voice was low-pitched and gentle as a lover's voice.

'Are you content, Johanna?'

'Content?' she echoed, and she answered him as she had already answered the almost identical question from the Fool.

'Indeed,' he agreed with her, 'we are not gods, and therefore we have our limitations. But within those limitations that man has paid in full. He went out to die with the iron of retribution deep in his soul. I drove it home from the judgment seat before I let him go. He understood me.'

'As I did,' said she. 'But what then? He is dead, and I am living. Am I the cleaner by his death? Not all his blood could wash out one spot of my defilement.'

'Defilement?' quoth he, and frowned.

'What else? What else do you account it?'

It was a long moment before he answered her, and in that moment they looked deep each into the eyes of the other. His answer when it came rang out. 'A sacrament that has left you holier than you were. Defilement, do you say? As well might we suppose the martyrs of our faith to be damned for suicide, because they welcomed a death it was within their power to avert.'

Such thoughts had she used to restore her self-respect and imagined them just sophistries. It was an ecstasy to hear him utter them, and so know that they must be true.

'Purity,' he added, 'is of the soul; and over your white soul, Johanna, Rhynsault possessed no empire.'

'Yet the world . . .' she was beginning.

'Ah, leave the world,' he bade her, and took her hand. 'Or face it under the shelter of my name.'

'Your name?'

'I am asking you to be my countess, Johanna. It is more than I ever hoped would be permitted me by Fate. I will make amends to you, my dear, for all the suffering I have brought upon you.'

'You have brought upon me? You?'

He explained himself, and tortured her with the explanation, with a joy so exquisite as to be near to pain, and the pain so tempered with pride in his words as to be akin to joy.

'Your hesitancy, being what you are,' she told him, 'was uttered by the voice of prudence. If you would listen to it now, you would not offer me what you have offered. O Anthony, I love you. That I need not deny to-day. But because I love you, we must go our ways, my dear. Let it comfort you, and banish the thought that you are to blame for any unhappiness of mine, to know that this answer I should have made you in Flushing, in my father's house when I was still a maid, if in asking me you had told me who you were.'

She set a hand upon his shoulder, turned her face upwards, and frankly met the sombre gaze of his dark eyes now full of pain. 'I shall thank God every night of my life that you have sought me, Anthony; for in the pride you have brought me, you have restored to me all that I had lost.'

He strove to move her from this by every argument a lover knows. But she remained unshaken.

'You are a great prince, and I am the daughter of a merchant and the widow of another merchant. We are not matched as the world judges.'

'The world! The world!' he cried impatiently. 'What have we to do with the world?'

'Merely to live in it,' said she.

'You and I are outside all of that, predestined mates, as once before I protested to you that my instincts told me, some inner voice whose truth is beyond doubting.'

'Will you convince your father, the Duke of Guelders, of that? Or your lady mother? Or your kin? Or the people over whom you are one day to rule and who would then have me for their duchess? Don't you see how impossible it is, my dear?'

He saw, but cared not. They should accept what he desired. And so he argued long, but all in vain, and at last upon the rock of that resolve the argosy of his rich hopes was shattered.

He bowed to her will when that befell. 'I will not press you further now. But I am as certain that the destiny which has made clear at last the path will not suffer us to end our lives apart.' Abruptly he asked her: 'Whither do you go, Johanna?'

She told him that she would be returning to her father's house in Flushing, to continue the supervision of the ship-building yards which she had inherited. 'As for the heritage from Philip, I was glad to hear you pronounce to-day that it shall go from me.'

'It was an inevitable part of the line I took,' he said. 'When I did so, I had hoped so confidently to make you the reparation in which you deny me.'

'Do not give yourself concern. I have enough without that, and I have no real right to it.'

She suffered him to kiss her at parting. It was their first kiss, and her own firm resolve that it should be their last.

Next morning early she departed from Brussels, her mission there so singularly accomplished. If she bore sorrow and longings with her, yet she bore more peace than she had ever hoped to know again.

Behind her, however, she left little peace in the heart of Anthony. And to his unrest on her behalf was presently to be added unrest on quite other grounds. For at noon that day, to the amazement of all, the Duke attended by a small company of men-at-arms rode into Brussels and straight to the palace. In spite of all precautions, the news of Rhynsault's arrest had gone after his highness, reached him as he was about to embark at Sluys, and brought him back in a towering rage.

It was fortunate, thought the Grand Master, when he beheld the furious Duke come striding into his closet, that he had caused execution to follow so swiftly upon the heels of sentence.

'You know why I am here!' the Duke blazed at him.

Count Anthony had risen. He strove successfully for calm to meet this onslaught. 'An event of yesterday has probably been misrepresented to you.'

'Misrepresented? Yes, if you mean that it is untrue that Rhynsault has been tried and executed for the affair of Middelburg. God of my life! You have dared to abuse my trust! Dared to trump up this business and to reverse the judgment which I myself already had pronounced! That is to push temerity singularly far. It is something for which you may have to meet a heavy reckoning.'

'You have, indeed, been misinformed,' said the Count. 'It will save time if you read the judgment, which was set down in detail by the clerks. There you will find that the matter upon which I judged him was not at all the matter upon which you acquitted him. He was indicted for high treason. But read the judgment for yourself.' And he proffered it.

Before so much apparent calm, arguing an easy conscience, the Duke's wrath took pause. Swiftly he read the document thrust upon him. But not to the end. Two thirds of the way through, he flung it down.

'Trickery!' he roared. 'Sheer trickery!'

'You cannot have observed that the judgment was pronounced not by me, but by your own judges. After that I had no alternative but to sentence him to death.'

'You coerced them into it. You duped them! But, by God, you do not dupe me! You knew that I valued this man, that he had served me well, and that I needed him in Ghent. And you have deprived me of him to satisfy an obstinacy of your own. Of what did you accuse him? Of subverting my justice to serve his own ends, was it not? That shall be your own indictment.' And he swung in his passion upon a cowering page of the Count's. 'Summon me the guard, boy.'

'The guard!' said Count Anthony. 'Charles, you cannot arrest me. I am a Prince of Guelders.'

'If you were the Pope of Rome and, having accepted the office of Grand Master here, had so misused it, I should arrest you and bring you to account.'

'You will regret this when you are calm.'

'As you will regret having taken off Rhynsault's head. God of my life! The audacity of you!' He advanced upon him in his fury, and suddenly putting forth his hand seized the emblem of the Golden Fleece that hung upon Count Anthony's neck. With a wrench he snapped the chain that carried it, and so tore it from him. 'You wear that no longer, sir. If I am Duke of Burgundy, a hempen collar shall take its place.'

Count Anthony stiffened. 'You dishonoured that collar, Charles, when you thought to hang it about the filthy neck of your knave Rhynsault. My only regret at being deprived of it concerns the way in which you have taken it.'

This had the effect of further infuriating that man of violent passions. He raised his hand. Count Anthony did not flinch. His eyes were steadily upon the Duke, and the voice was steady in which he admonished him.

'Nay! If you strike me, Charles, I shall be constrained to dispel your growing illusions that you are divine.'

The Duke's hand fell to his side. The guard came in at that moment.

Count Anthony's arrest made some stir. His brother Adolph posted off to Nimeguen with the news, and from the old Duke of Guelders came strong representations to the Duke of Burgundy, which the Duke of Burgundy entirely disregarded.

The trial followed ten days later, presided over by the Duke in person, and was attended by as much of Brussels as could pack itself into the great hall of the palace, where it was publicly held. Count Anthony had demanded trial by the Chapter of the Golden Fleece, as was his right. The Duke had trampled upon that right, as he was prepared at all times to trample upon every right that stood in the way to his self-willed ends.

But he was to make the discovery that there were certain things upon which he could not trample. One of these things was the law, however much he might boast that the law was embodied in himself. After all, he sat with judges, the same judges who had sat with Count Anthony; and scowl upon them, browbeat them though he might, he could not move them from the interpretation which they chose to put upon the law, which was the interpretation that Count Anthony, ably arguing, compelled them to put upon it.

'I take my stand with confidence,' he had said in answer to the accusation of abuse of trust, 'upon the indictment of the Sire de Rhynsault. That indictment was found to be justified by the fact upon which it was based. That fact was subsequently established by the confession of the accused himself. To charge me with having used this matter of a reprieve to pronounce a judgment counter to the wishes of your highness is by implication to accuse your highness of subverting the law of which you are the sacred custodian to private purposes of your own.'

Although his temerity in this last may have appalled the judges, upon the soundness of his main argument they were not to be shaken.

'We find,' said their dean and spokesman, the same who had urged Count Anthony's delay in the execution of Rhynsault, 'that the utmost complaint justly to be made against the Grand Master is of having acted with unnecessary precipitancy in the execution of the sentence. But that is not an offence at law, and it is not lawful to frame a law to meet an event subsequent to that event's occurrence.'

To which Count Anthony had ventured to reply that the senior judge had contradicted himself. Because, if a thing were not an offence at law, it could not justly be termed in a court of justice a ground for just complaint against any man.

Thus was the Duke baulked of his angry aims and compelled to pronounce the acquittal of the Count, the more incensed against him because the necessity was imposed upon him by the craftiness with which Count Anthony had gone to work in the matter of Rhynsault.

But though he acquitted him, see him again he would not. On his return to his apartments in the palace, an officer brought the Count a brief note in which he was requested to depart the Duke's dominions within twenty-four hours. Disobedience of this order of exile must, of course, be attended by very serious consequences. Because of the love that had existed between them, Count Anthony begged a last audience of Charles. This was refused him. Disgraced and banished, the Count set out for Guelders on the morrow.

CHAPTER XXXI

REALITIES

THE news of Count Anthony's disgrace preceded him to Nimeguen, where, indeed, little else had occupied the minds of the court since the hawk-faced Adolph had come back there with the tale of his brother's arrest and of the grounds of it. Adolph denounced Anthony's conduct as having ruined the credit of the House of Guelders at the Court of Burgundy, and presently brought the old Duke and the still handsome Duchess to the same view. From the court this view came to spread through the town of Nimeguen and thence to permeate the state itself.

It follows that the Count was given a cool reception on his arrival home.

The old Duke, bearded like a goat and bleating like one, bitterly upbraided his son, spoke of the shame which his conduct reflected upon his House and the grave consequences which the loss of Burgundy's friendship might bring upon the state. In short, like the Duke of Burgundy, notwithstanding the clear finding of the Burgundian judges and the Count's acquittal of the charge, the Duke of Guelders persisted in the view that Count Anthony had been guilty of a gross betrayal of trust and had dishonoured his office to serve certain dark ends of his own. In this the weak old man had been soundly educated by his enterprising and ambitious younger son.

'It is bitter to reflect,' he told Count Anthony, 'that the valuable services rendered the Duke of Burgundy by your brother Adolph, that his very alliance with the Duke's sister-in-law, should all have been wasted by your unpardonable and discreditable offences.'

Count Anthony roused himself from his listlessness and weary disgust with the world to defend this impugnment of his honour. He pointed out that he had been cleared of the charges by his acquittal; that independent and unbiased judges had refused to say that he had been guilty of violating his trust, but, on the contrary, had held that what he had done was no less than the duty imposed upon him by his office.

The fact that the good relations between Burgundy and Guelders had been jeopardized was, however, beyond dispute. It was even rumoured that a Chapter of the Golden Fleece was about to be summoned for the purpose of considering, upon the Duke's instigation, the expulsion of Count Anthony from the order. Count Anthony, however, anticipated it by the formal resignation of an honour, the insignia of which had already been torn from his neck by his passionate cousin. He did so in humble terms, studiously framed to avoid offence, so that the breach between the two duchies should not be widened. This, after all, in the Count's view was a grave matter, and one which his duty to the State of Guelders forbade him to neglect. After all, whatever the finding of the court, in his heart Count Anthony knew that Charles of Burgundy was justified of his anger. The Count had knowingly and deliberately proceeded in opposition to the Duke's wishes; he had tricked the judges and made himself secure by a sophistical and insincere interpretation of the law. And that he had abused the trust reposed in him by the Duke of Burgundy was beyond question. For the peace of his conscience it remained that in honour he was justified of that abuse.

Of the consequences to himself he troubled little. But of the consequences to Guelders he must think seriously. It was not beyond possibility that, if the present situation of severed relationship between the two courts were permitted to continue, there might be found in it, by the voracious ambition of Charles of Burgundy, a pretext for war, which could end only in the absorption of Guelders into the steadily spreading Burgundian dominions.

This was brought home to Count Anthony after he had

been a fortnight in Nimeguen at a council held by his father and composed of the six representatives of the noblest houses of Guelders, the Chancellor of the Duchy, and Adolph of Egmont, the Marshal.

The Chancellor voiced the general feeling when he put it to Count Anthony that it was his duty to the state to make some personal effort to conciliate the Duke of Burgundy, to seek to mollify his wrath by some act of self-abasement or reparation.

'I might wait upon him in my shirt, barefooted, and with a halter about my neck. That is the sort of self-abasement he loves to see, especially in cold weather. He has more than once imposed it upon the representatives of his Flemish subjects. Would that content you?'

His levity in such a matter shocked them. Adolph, feeling that the Council would support him, expressed himself strongly upon his brother's lack of grace. Anthony bowed to the rebuke, but his lips smiled.

'I have an alternative to offer,' he said. 'It is that I abdicate my rights of succession in the Duchy. That should give a full effect to the Duke of Burgundy's desire to see me suffer for what he accounts my misdeeds. It is a punishment that must entirely satisfy him and so restore the harmony between himself and the State of Guelders.'

Adolph's eyes gleamed. The old Duke, who was entirely under the sway of his younger son, sat very still with vacant glance and combed his goat's beard in silence. But the others, beginning with the Chancellor, dashed Adolph's hopes by the vehemence with which they repudiated any such suggestion.

After all, they were very far from reposing a full trust in Adolph; and his father, they knew, had ceased seriously to count. Anthony might have his eccentricities; he might be something of a dreamer and a poet, addicted to romantic notions; but at the same time they knew that they could build upon his honour as upon a rock, and they had received proofs of his considerable abilities, not only at home, but in the activities in Burgundy which in the past had so endeared him to Duke Charles.

Protest as they might, however, Count Anthony showed them that what he had put forward as a suggestion was already a deliberately weighed resolve.

'I was not born,' he told them quietly, 'to fill the office of ruler in a state. My endowments are not those for which the office calls, and, if I am to be frank with you, that is with me no matter for regret. I have seen little to admire in those same endowments. My brother Adolph possesses them in a high degree. Of this,' he continued more briskly, 'I have been long aware, and what I now propose to do, I should have done before but that I conceived it to be against the duty which my birth imposed upon me. From the moment that it becomes clear, as clear it has become, that, in consequence of the circumstances which have arisen, my abdication will actually benefit the state, my last qualm vanishes. My abdication becomes a duty, the highest service I can render Guelders.'

To this Count Anthony firmly adhered in spite of arguments which were protracted for some days. In the end, seeing him unshaken in his determination, and since no faintest opposition to it came from either his father or his brother, the Chancellor and the nobles bowed to his wishes, consoling themselves with the immediate advantages to Guelders in a reparation to the Duke of Burgundy beyond anything that he could have demanded or expected.

Indeed, when the news reached Charles that the abdication of his cousin Anthony's rights of succession to the Duchy of Guelders was the amend which Guelders offered for any displeasure the Count might have occasioned him, such a revulsion of feeling arose in him that he actually considered demanding the cancellation of that act, as unjustly excessive. That impulse subsiding, however, he determined to leave things as they were, and wrote a courteous and friendly letter to the Duke of Guelders in which he expressed his appreciation of this vindication.

Emboldened by the terms of this letter, which were communicated to him at his castle of Valburg, whither he had retired, Count Anthony wrote to Duke Charles, begging him for the sake of their ancient friendship to ease the decree of banishment at least to the extent of permitting him to pass freely through Burgundian dominions should he desire to do so.

The irascible and unforgiving Charles accorded him so much, but accorded it grudgingly. The Sire Anthony of Egmont — a ducal secretary wrote, deliberately omitting a title which had belonged, not to the man, but to the office of heir to the duchy — was permitted free passage through and sojourn in all the states under the dominion of his highness the Duke of Burgundy, upon the condition, however, that he should not come at any time within twenty miles of the ducal court, wherever it might happen to have its seat.

This befell early in March of the year 1469. At once Count Anthony made such preparations for departure that men must assume there was no intention of returning. He sold his castle and lands of Valburg, which belonged to him personally, went to take leave of the ducal family, and departed the duchy without any state and accompanied only by a body-servant, that same François who had been with him earlier upon his travels. Thus he passed out of Guelders and out of the history of nations, which, therefore, takes no account of him.

On a morning of early April he came to Flushing, and, leaving horse and servant at the inn, he repaired on foot to the big red house, in the courtyard of which the stork once again advanced to welcome him, on the wall of which the quail were fluttering in their osier cage, whilst beneath them in the beds the tulips reared again their white and yellow heads, those tulips which once he had borne for his device.

Old Jan gasped at sight of him, and breathless ushered him into the house, into that dining-room so full of memories, and there left him whilst he went in quest of his mistress. Not long was he kept waiting. The rustle of a gown heard through the door which Jan had left ajar soon heralded her coming. The sound seemed to draw the blood to his heart, to leave him pale, to quicken his breath, and turn his knees to water. Not in all his life had he known so overpowering an emotion.

Then as the door opened he span round, and they faced each other across that little space. She regarding him with startled incredulous eyes out of a face as pale as his own, her bosom rising and falling rapidly within its tapering corsage.

'My lord,' she said to him, 'why have you come?'

His answer went to the heart of things. 'Because I am no lord. All that is done. In Brussels, three months ago, you said to me that, had I been just the Anthony Egmont I called myself when first I stepped within this house, all might have been possible between us. To-day I am no longer a Prince of Guelders, no longer heir to a duchy. All that I have stripped off and cast from me, indeed, constrained to it by circumstances which leave me no regrets. I am just Anthony Egmont, a man of simple estate. Read the safe-conduct under which I travel, and convince yourself of that.' And he proffered her the letter in which the Duke of Burgundy sanctioned his sojourn in Burgundian lands. 'Read it, Johanna, and then, if your heart bids you, repeat to me what you said in Brussels three months since. The conditions are fulfilled.'

In her bewilderment, not knowing what else to do, perhaps because she needed a moment to consider, she took that scrap of parchment. When she had read it, she shook her head and looked at him almost piteously.

'I do not know what it means.'

'It means that I am here to seek work in your shipyards, to learn, if you will give me employment, the art of building ships, so that I may give my energies and such ability as I may possess to the safeguarding of your interests.'

'You will build ships? You?'

'If you will deign to employ me. A man must work to live, and I have little now of my own and am nobody. Just

Anthony Egmont, the man you said you would have welcomed.'

Suddenly and without warning she was sobbing upon his breast, this woman who had borne so much in such tearless fortitude.

And there the chronicle of La Marche, so far as concerns this story of the romantic Prince of Guelders, who threw away his honours and his state to grasp realities, comes abruptly to an end. But when generations later under the Austrian rule brought over these lands by the marriage of Mary of Burgundy with the Emperor Maximilian, we find abundant mention of the great shipyards of Egmont in the port of Flushing, the conclusion leaves no grounds for speculation.

THE END